MY PASTOR
DIDN'T DO IT

A Pastor Hook Mystery

EARL MIDDLETON

LOS ANGELES

Food for Faith Publications
P.O. Box 88445
Los Angeles, CA 90009
www.foodforfaith.org

Manufactured in the United States of America

ISBN 978-0-9770845-9-3

For my wife, Pascale—we finally did it, love!

ACKNOWLEDGMENTS

I acknowledge and thank the wonderful people of *First Baptist Church*, Milford, Connecticut and *First Baptist Church*, South Orange, New Jersey for the many invaluable lessons about the Black Church that I could not have learned in seminary. I also acknowledge and thank my phenomenal wife, Pascale, and our talented children, Johanna, Nailah and Omar, whose unconditional love gave me the time and courage to fail until I was ready to succeed; and my invisible agents, editors, and publicists, God the Father, God the Son, and God the Holy Spirit.

PRAISE FOR MY PASTOR

Having a pastor as a prime suspect in a murder is quite clever.
—Tracy Sherrod, former Senior Editor, *Simon & Schuster*

A quick, engaging read. Hook makes a terrific main character—as both a pastor and as an amateur detective.
—Diane Reverand, former Senior Vice President, *HarperCollins*

The writing itself is gratifyingly brisk.
—Lisa Erbach Vance, *Aaron Priest*

This is very good satire in the tradition of Chester Himes.
—Lawrence Jordan, Editor, *Cotton Comes to Harlem*

PROLOGUE

He knocks on the little pane of the door.

She loses the silk robe on the pull out bed and answers him in her birthday suit. She wants to please him, but it looks like it will be hard tonight.

They embrace.

She nuzzles up to kiss him. He takes her beautiful face in his hands, and with one quick movement swivels her head and snaps her neck.

He catches her before she falls and lays her at the foot of the bed. He pulls the gun from the front pouch of his jogging suit and fires one round into her temple. He laces her fingers around the handle, then the trigger, and heads for the door.

He stops, frozen by headlights stretching up the driveway. He waits. And waits. They don't move, so neither does he.

Finally, the light retreats. Safely under the cover of darkness again, he pulls the door behind him and returns to his cloaked life.

CHAPTER 1

Pastor Tony Hook unbuckles his belt, unzips his pants, opens his eyes, and looks down.

"Oh, no."

Someone taps on the window and light streams into the van. It's one of Belton's finest. His nameplate reads: MONSEES. Pastor scrambles to cover his still opened pants with the bottom part of his suit jacket and powers down the church van's window.

"Reverend? Are you alright?"

Pastor squints into the light. He's got the kind of good looks that make you want to smile, the kind of voice that makes you want to listen, and eyes that say he knows more than he's revealing. "I'm fine, Officer."

"Can I get you to pull all the way into the driveway please, sir? You're blocking half the street."

"I was actually leaving. Just needed to stop and pray a bit."

Monsees drops the beam to the bottom of the suit jacket. His face remains expressionless. "You'd be safer praying at the church. You have a good night."

Dude drives off in the black-and-white right past a man staggering out of the shadows up Fairview Avenue. It's Mowatt, the town drunk, and before the night's over BPD will probably pick him up again.

Pastor looks down once more at the lines on his inner thigh and the war between his flesh and spirit resumes. He really doesn't know if he wants to confront Anemone and tell her, this time in no uncertain terms, to cease and desist once and for all, or to surrender to her charms. His heart racing, his head pounding, he can't find the resolve to get out of the van. It feels like forever before he backs out of the driveway, floors it to the church, and flings himself onto the carpet of his darkened office.

"Daddy, help me! I'm feeling weak. I don't know how much longer I can do this. I'm so lonely. I need your help. Show me my strength."

Spent, he falls asleep right there on the floor. When he wakes there's no special delivery letter from God, but he does feel a little better, so he prays for Anemone, asking God—even though He's slow to answer sometimes—to take away her man-lust so she'll leave him alone. After all, how is he supposed to remain celibate and pure with attractive parishioners literally sticking their hands down his pants? He heads home, yawning and trying to air out the scratches etched onto his loins by Anemone's fingernails, hoping no one spots him walking this way.

It's late but it's still hot outside. He breaks another sweat pacing up the hill to the corner of Academy and Third. This is Belton's only modest neighborhood, home to domestics and their families back in the days when blacks couldn't afford to live here any other way.

Other pastors refer to this old side-hall colonial as 1313 Mockingbird Lane, because it's a three-bedroom-one-bath-living-room-dining-room-kitchen-unfinished-basement-and-attic house of horrors. The paint is peeling from its eaves and shutters, its facade looks like somebody just nailed up a bunch of tiles salvaged from the roofs of old outhouses, its floors lean so badly that nothing on wheels ever stays in one place, and its center beam is so buckled that Trustee Thorn had a hydraulic steel support installed just before Pastor moved in, to keep the house standing.

Not even Bob Vila could help this place. If Thorn ever tried to sell it out from under Pastor, as he's threatened to do in order to save money for the church, the city building inspector would have a hard time deciding whether to condemn it as a safety hazard or an eyesore. The church has even gotten a few calls from location scouts for grade-B gore-and-score flicks, and last Halloween Tamara Green from the local access cable program Eye on Belton Three asked to do a special on it.

Of course, Thorn says the church voted that for as long as this deathtrap is First Baptist's parsonage the pastor had to live in it. Something about preserving the tax exemption on the property. But, hey, Pastor likes to joke that maybe one morning he'll wake up in the basement surrounded by the rest of the second floor, or develop asbestosis. Then with the insurance money he'll be able to buy his own house, compliments of Thorn's stinginess. He'd be crippled or terminally ill, but he'd finally be a homeowner.

Pastor kicks the freshly laid arrangement of chicken bones and feathers off the stoop and into the company of the others in the shrubbery below and enters the gallery. The mail slot rattles as he closes the door, and sure enough, he's got mail. Waiting for him on the floor. Past due notices from Visa, Mobil, Belton Satellite Systems and New York State Higher Education Services Corporation.

Aside from the overdue bills there's one other letter. No return address. A Belton postmark. And inside? A three-by-five card saying the same thing the ones at the church do. Getting a little nastier lately, though. More violent.

He shoves the heavy front door behind him and bounds upstairs two at a time. It's still cool in the bedroom, almost frigid, since he left running the window units he put in last year. He shuffles over to the air conditioner to adjust it down and notices a black conversion van slowly turning the corner from Academy onto Third with its lights off. It stops for a couple of seconds in front of his backyard driveway, and then pulls off in a hurry up Third. Normally he would think *car thieves looking for the right model to fill an order*, but he's seen that same van do the same thing for the past seven nights and no one has tried to swipe his car yet.

He's got his weekly 8:00 appointment with Burro in the morning, a 9:00 at City Hall, and another long day of sermon wrestling after that. Pastor decides he doesn't have any spare energy to burn trying to figure out who's sending him the threatening letters, or who's driving that van.

His answering machine is blinking so he checks the message. His mom again, appealing to his sense of compassion this time to get him to call his father for Father's Day.

He's interested in nothing but the essentials of his bedtime ritual. Whisking into what has to be the most ill-conceived bathroom in architectural history he twists shut the mini-blinds guarding the big, street-facing tub-to-ceiling picture window in front of the tub-and-shower, and turns out the light. When Mrs. Brewington from across the street leaned up from her walker at her husband's funeral last year and whispered into Pastor's ear that she had been trying for 50 years to get

Leon to wash his privates regularly like Pastor did, he knew it was time to start showering in the dark.

After his shower in his darkened bathroom he slaps some Bay Rum on his loins and grits his teeth back to the bedroom, refusing to let the burning conquer him.

He digs out a pair of running shorts and an STU tee shirt from his athletic drawer and hangs them on the back of the chair, then hops onto the bed and points the clicker at the thirteen inch next to the alarm clock on the armoire.

The basketball game is over, so after checking with his favorite weather girl on NBC to see if it's going to be smoking hot again tomorrow, he snuggles up under the covers with Dr. Seuss for their nightly trip back to a time when his life made sense. He slips into sleep in the middle of *Oh, The Places You'll Go!*, wondering if he'll ever get a chance to live in a nice house of his own.

♪

The big red numbers on the armoire alarm clock flick to 2:25. The ringing wakens Pastor. He jumps out of bed, stumbles across to the armoire and bangs on the clock, but the ringing continues. He covers his ears and looks around, then grabs the phone from his side table. It's a Caribbean accent, crackling.

"Min ster, you ave to ome right away."

"Who is this?"

"Ike, Minister. Ik Allon."

"Who? You're breaking up, I can hardly understand you. Are you on a cell phone?"

"I'm in my basemen . I drop the ph ne just before I call you...it's Anemone. You have t come."

"Anemone? What's wrong with her?"

"She ot doing oo well, Minister."

"What?!"

"She not do ng too   ell. You have to come. Come through the basement d r. urry."

CHAPTER 2

After stalling out twice Pastor zips out of his backyard driveway, through the wide open sliding gate the trustees installed to deter those brazen car thieves, and races up Third. The old Saab's Automatic Climate Control system is blowing hard to offset the 88° outside temp displayed on the dash. He dials on his cell phone while negotiating the shifter with his free hand and the steering wheel with his knee. On the twelfth ring a very annoyed person barks into his ear.

"What!?"

"Dex, it's me, Pastor. Sorry to wake you, but I just got a call from Ike Allon of all people. Something's really wrong with Anemone and he needs us to come right over."

"Dexter is sleeping, Pastor."

"Oh, Malisa. I'm sorry. Would you put the chairman on the line, please? It's an emergency." Knowing he's talking to Malisa helps things to make sense again. Dexter isn't one to bark at people on the phone.

"I'm not waking him," she says. "He basically just got home. He's been cleaning out his office all day, he's exhausted, and he has more ahead of him tomorrow. Can't you call one of the others?"

"Deacon Walters, Deacon Lazaro, and Deacon Dials are at work. Deacon Gumbs is taking the bar again. Deacon Smith's in the nursing home and needs somebody to come pray for *him*. And Deacon Simms is Deacon Simms, everybody knows he unplugs his phone at night. That leaves Dex."

"What about your useless associates, Mall or Dawkins?"

"You know we don't ask them to do this."

"That is such a ridiculous rule. If you guys would practice some self-control and keep yourselves zipped up, dumb rules like this wouldn't be necessary. I'm not waking him up, Pastor. I'll come. I'm a deaconess, and I can't sleep right now any—."

The battery dies on the phone. Pastor winces and tosses it into the passenger seat as he flies up Irvington Ave. doing 90 mph.

The deacons decided early in Pastor Hook's ministry at the First Baptist Church of Belton that whenever he had to go visit a sick woman at her home, even if somebody else would be in the house, a deacon should be present. That would eliminate the possibility of rumors spreading about the pastor laying more than hands on the sick, which is tantamount to the career death sentence. Once a pastor gets the reputation of being a sexual predator, church membership tends to decline and it becomes harder to attract visitors.

After what happened earlier Pastor's still conflicted about seeing Anemone again. He wonders how she could have gotten so sick so fast. And he can't shake the feeling that he's headed into a set-up. All the more reason to have Dexter by his side. For a split second he reconsiders Malisa's offer and then decides to go alone and put a stop to this stuff once and for all. No time for any more ruses. His reputation, personal dignity, and spiritual power, his most valuable intangibles, are at stake and he's not about to let somebody like Anemone take that all away from him in a fleeting moment of pleasure, no matter how fine she is.

When he swerves onto Anemone's blacktop driveway it occurs to him how odd it was that Ike asked him to come through the basement door. He rolls through dark shadows to the back of the property and a set of floodlights on the front eave of the carriage house blink on. He deads the engine and eases down the back steps to the walkout basement door. An ADT sticker and white light show through the diamond-shaped glass pane in the door and Pastor figures if he's going to have a confrontation this is as good a time and place as any. Besides the cicadas and crickets whining their usual symphony, the three of them plus Malisa have to be the only creatures in Belton awake at this ungodly hour. Can't ask for any more privacy than that. His knock gets Ike's yell to come in. He opens the door and lets it swing in front of him before he steps in, just in case Ike's planning to surprise him with a right jab to the face. Then Pastor pauses for a minute and says the only thing that comes to mind at a time like this; something every Hook for four generations before him would've said. "Jeez on rice." The Caribbean way to say, "Jesus Christ" without technically taking the name of the Lord in vain.

Without the mass of people grinding and winding to Sly and Robbie's dub beats the basement looks like a giant chessboard. Jammed against the far wall under a framed poster of a luscious beach scene with white sand and aqua water and the word FLORIDA emblazoned in yellow across a clear blue sky is the sofa portion of a Balkanized four-piece black leather sectional, the only furniture in the room. It's flung open for sleeping, but the bed is still made.

Ike is sitting—no, reclining—in his brown jumpsuit with one leg crossed over the other on the wedge piece of the sectional in the far corner glaring right through Pastor with red puffy eyes that say he's been crying. Maybe they're lying. Maybe it's just his hay fever acting up again. The white cordless phone is still in his hand and Anemone is lying on the floor in front of the bed. But the way she's dressed, if you can call it that, gives Pastor pause. Why would Ike want him to see her like this?

The fluorescent lighting spilling out of the drop ceiling drapes a soft pall over her body. The way she's sprawled front-down in the middle of the black-and-white tiled floor in nothing but the soft cinnamon skin she came screaming into this world in, Pastor's thinking maybe she'd rolled off the bed during some acrobatic sex and lost consciousness. But her head lying on that pillow of drying blood, sporting a hole through the temple is giving it away. Big time.

"Me find her like that when me come home." Ike's sounding like a Jamaican Bela Lugosi in a trance as Pastor swings the door behind him and rushes over to the bed. He yanks the cover sheet off and drapes it over Anemone. "She wasn't in the bed and me search the whole house calling she name, but she never answer me. She never answer me."

Anemone has some perfect manicured nails, perfect long honey-brown salon-styled hair, perfect curves on a perfect body, and perfect pitch when she sings her stories to Ike. If there's one thing Pastor's Augustinian view of humanity has taught him to distrust, it's perfection. Pastor stoops over her and feels the inside of her wrist for a pulse. It's cold. And still. Nestled in her left hand is an unbroken egg, and the fingers of her right hand lace around the handle and trigger of a big black 9mm pistol with a silencer on its muzzle and the letters FCA etched on the barrel. The face that launched a thousand struggles for Pastor is drained of all life now and caricatures the face of the beautiful woman whose hand he pried out of his pants just five hours ago. That perfect body and perfect hair form still perfect, graceful, sensual lines even under the sheet. Still beautiful even in the end. Still perfect, even in death. Still unworthy of trust.

Pastor's looking for words, but they're playing hide-and-seek with him. Only memories show. And questions. How many dead bodies has he seen before during his five years of prison chaplaincy? Too many of them. Jailhouse shanks generally leave uglier wounds than bullets. But this is still one of the ugliest he's seen. His reflection in the big one-way window next to the door of Ike's deejay booth reminds Pastor that nothing ages a person like loss. And guilt. It seems like it was just yesterday that there were eight big accounting firms and he was 25 and on the primrose path to prosperity, fast-tracking to partner at Arthur Andersen and providing a life of luxury and leisure for his new family.

Ike said, "Is this the strangest thing you've ever seen or what, huh Minister?"

Pastor's feeling shame for having braced for a confrontation coming through the door. Ike is a fire hydrant of a man with no neck and a mane of graying dreads framing an unforgiving face. He's definitely built for fighting. But there's no fight in him tonight. This is new terrain for Pastor. Helping people deal with death is part of what he does, but rarely is he the first on the scene. He's usually called in to do the emotional mop-up.

"Ike, I'm so sorry," Pastor pitches, approaching him with his hand out. He wants to hug him, but Ike's not huggable, so Pastor reaches for his hand.

Ike's affect is disarming. Pastor had expected naked anger. He seems unsure whether to return the handshake or pull away. So he does both. Pastor usually lets them vent and then responds, but now he has to come up with something deep. And, indeed, what can be said at a time like this? According to his seminary training he's supposed to draw on his personal experience and tell Ike he knows how it feels to lose a wife, and getting through it will probably be the hardest thing he'll have to do in his life. He's supposed to tell him the only way to conquer this pain is to endure it one night at a time. He's supposed to put his arm around him and tell him some nights will be longer than others, but that God will give him sufficient strength to endure, even if the night lasts ten years. He's supposed to say to and do for him everything Dr. Noble said to and did for Pastor Hook as he looked down at Carla's embalmed face. But instead his anger bubbles up and messes with all his supposed to's as he remembers some of his counseling sessions with Anemone. He's beginning to feel not too pleased with Ike and not convinced that his affect is truly rooted in the shock of loss, of grief, of love for Anemone. He wants to ask him what *really* happened when he came home last night. But that's the police's turf, so Pastor drops the lid on his anger and does and says the pastoral thing. "Are the police on their way?"

Ike shakes his head and then he isn't looking through Pastor anymore but directly into him, into his eyes. "Me call here last night around 9:40, 9:50 and Anemone tell me you had just drop her home. So, you had to be the last one to see her alive. When me never find her in the house me grab the cordless from the kitchen and call Hazel, thinking she must be with her, but Hazel never home. Then me peep down here and find her like this. Me first thought was to call you."

"Me? Why not the police?"

"Me hear what she say about you. Me see how you watch her. Maybe there was more going on than what me could hear and see."

"What? What are you saying, Ike?"

"Sometimes a man get vexed when a beautiful woman tell him no."

Maybe Ike *is* in shock. People say and do all kinds of crazy things when in trauma. Despite his own emotions Pastor is determined to represent God and minister to Ike in this moment and leave the judging to heaven, so he doesn't even bother to respond to the not so thinly veiled suggestion that he might have killed Anemone. He grabs the phone from Ike to call 911, but can't get a sustained dial tone.

"There's another phone in the deejay booth," he says. "But when they come they'll want to know who was with her last. And they'll find out it was you."

"Ike, you're obviously traumatized. You're not thinking clearly right now. We *will* find out who killed Anemone. God is a God of justice."

"That's right, justice. I should shot you myself with that same gun right now. But spirit bring justice better than any man. When police get here they're gonna arrest *you*. The prime suspect."

"I'm sorry you feel that way, Ike. I'll be praying for you. And the police, that they find the killer."

The deejay booth is about the size of a walk-in closet. With the tiny video camera on the tripod and all the black audio components lined up in their cabinets and plastic crates with vinyl records stacked against the wall, it looks like the control room at WPST back when Pastor was in school. The phone is staring at him from the table next to the mixer and two turntables under the window and he has to move the tripod into the doorway get to it. This is his first time actually standing inside this room and he dismiss the pang of envy that flashes through him as he looks over at Ike still sitting in the corner staring in his direction, knowing that Ike couldn't see him. This room has it all and Pastor has to give Ike his props. Even though he stole the material from the church to make this room, he sure hooked it up the way any man would want it.

The 911 dispatcher advises him to wait there for the officers and to not touch or move anything. He bumps the tripod, catches it before it falls, puts it back in its original place, and closes the door behind him.

"Sorry I had to move your camera and tripod," he says. "I didn't want to knock it over getting to the phone. The police are on their way and they don't want us to touch or move anything, so why don't we go outside and wait for them."

"You go ahead, Minister. Me not moving from this spot. You still have time to run, get a head start before they get here and arrest you."

"That's okay, Ike. I'll wait here with you."

"I understand, Minister. Police will catch you eventually so you might as well stay and surrender. But you go ahead outside. At least get some fresh air. They going to take her from me when they get here. Give me just a few more minutes with her alone."

He's never seen Ike look so pitiful. Lashing out in pain. Incoherent. One of the hardest parts of pastoral ministry is knowing when to leave people alone. Pastor senses this is one of those times; when Ike needs a supernatural presence that only comes when someone is praying for you.

"Ike, I just want you to know, man, the church and I will be praying for you. We'll help you through this in any way you need us to," Pastor says before heading outside. Now's not the time to even attempt to discuss funeral arrangements. That'll have to wait until after the police interview them and wrap up their investigation, and the medical examiner rolls the body away.

After a couple of minutes of earnest prayer for Ike that God would wrap His arms around him at this time the first officer on the scene is Monsees, the same guy Pastor had seen earlier in the van after Anemone had scratched him. Pastor is explaining to him what happened when more flashing lights arrive. A few minutes later Monsees dips into the basement and the other officer stretches yellow crime scene tape around the perimeter of the property.

A lot more sitting around on the steps leading to the basement and bam! more flashing lights pull up. A crime scene van. Then the M.E. And then a couple of yawning detectives Pastor's seen around town on occasion, one a slim guy with bald head and red van dyke, the other a little overweight. Pastor keeps giving the same answers to the same questions to each round of new people on the scene.

The detectives huddle over the body, look at each other; then the heavier one, Royster, pulls out his cell phone over the objections of the baldheaded McManus, and calls in Chris Sears, who Pastor supposes is their boss. They tell Pastor to stay put and wait some more, then they march back to the street to wait for Sears. The cicadas and crickets they're oblivious to all of this and just keep singing their song.

Max Candy Jr's opened-top fluorescent-orange Jeep Wrangler screeches up to the yellow tape in front of the driveway and that's when it finally hits Pastor that he's in the middle of a really big deal and the bottom drops out of his belly. For more than a year Max Jr has been chasing that elusive story that would transport him from his father's afternoon daily to the front pages of a bigger paper in a bigger city. It's a lock that Anemone will be staring back at the whole town from this afternoon's front page of the *Mirror*.

It's like an ant colony in the back of the house before a burgundy sedan pulls up to the driveway and the detectives crowd the driver's side door. Then all three of them beeline for Pastor and his jaw drops to where the bottom of his belly used to be.

McManus says, "Rev, this is Sgt. Chris Sears."

"So, you're BPD?"

"So, you're the Reverend?"

"I was expecting a man."

"So was I."

Soft hands still. Stronger grip. Sharper tongue.

McManus trying to be helpful. "This is Reverend Tony H—"

"We've met," says Sears.

"I remember," says Pastor. "Some things you just don't forget."

The last time he'd seen Chris Sears was graduation day at Jadwin Gym when her announced name was Christine Higginbothom and she was headed to Columbia Law School. But it's Chris alright. Unkempt, short brown hair. Unlike Carla's. What Pastor's mother would call good hair. Cool sand eyes. Sharp features. Body still firm in those close-fitting jeans and that lumpy tee shirt. No man is she. In the two years they went together in college they managed to carnally connect in 47 of the 160 buildings on the 500 acre campus. Then she did the unthinkable and he met Carla and they seldom spoke again.

She displays those toothpaste-model teeth and then she's all business again and in spite of the smile and the beauty and the new name he's concerned she's the same old Chris so he doesn't want to be anywhere near her. He's convinced she'll find a way to bring trouble for him. He has that feeling in his gut that whatever it is will cost him plenty again and for the first time since he saw the Wiz with his parents and sister and the Gethsemane church family at the Lyceum Theatre on Broadway back when Stephanie Mills was Dorothy and his sister was still alive but still in the closet so not really alive he feels like he can identify with Evilene and understand how she felt when she burst out in song *Don't nobody bring me no bad news!* Because there was a time in his life when Christine Sears had a different last name and was the very definition of bad news.

◊

Sears assigns tasks to Royster and McManus, interviews Ike, and then tracks back to interview Pastor. She steers him into the now opened carriage house and rests her laptop on the roof of Ike's customized cherry red Corvette. They're alone except for the almost palpable odor of wood stain. Drying on a crude wooden table in the far corner is the memorial the missionary board hired Ike to create for their anniversary service this Sunday afternoon. Pastor is supposed to dedicate it at the morning service so they can stick it up among the others on the basement wall. It's as big and as thick as a library dictionary, and in the facial relief is the form of some kind of large animal.

Since the Benny Hinn Crusade his prayer life has been changing, intensifying, deepening. Standing across the Vette from Sears he's close to speaking in tongues, he's praying so fast under his breath. 'Cause she's now a powerful sister with a possible grudge, and after the last real conversation they had he's praying that she'll keep things real professional.

"When did you last see Mrs. Allon?"

"About 9:30. I dropped her off, watched her go inside, and then I left."

She's playing the keys on the laptop like a studio musician.

"Anyone else here? When you dropped her off?"

"No. She said Ike would be home at ten. The house was dark and she rushed inside because the phone was ringing."

"Where was Mr. Allon?"

"He said he was at an employee's house watching the game."

"Did Mrs. Allon ever talk about owning a gun?"

"No."

"Do you know if she had access to one?"

"I don't know."

"Was she in any kind of therapy? Pastoral counseling maybe? Come to you for...comfort?" Her face glued to the screen, waiting for Pastor to respond.

"...She tried to see me regularly," Pastor says, refusing the bait.

"Did she seem troubled when you dropped her off? Upset about anything? Depressed?"

"I know it looks like she committed suicide, but she didn't. Not Anemone. Somebody must have killed her."

"Gunshot deaths in Belton are almost always from self-inflicted wounds," she matter-of-facts. "The last murder here was five years ago, and that was by poisoning."

McManus pops in with an announcement. "No sign of forced entry."

"Thanks," she says, finally looking up to dismiss him with her eyes. But McManus sticks around.

"So what are you saying?" Pastor continues. "You don't think people can get shot to death in Belton?"

"Okay, then, suppose you tell me who would've wanted to kill Mrs. Allon?"

"I don't know that."

"Then suicide is still a possibility, isn't it? Maybe there were things going on in her life that no one knew about."

"She had problems, like every other 24 year old," Pastor says, "but I don't think she'd ever kill herself."

"We'll see."

"Wasn't burglary." McManus comes in like a scrambled station. "Nothing's missing except her keys, and the husband says she was always misplacing them."

"Thanks again, McManus," sings Sears. "Why don't you go see what Royster's got so far."

Just then Royster comes sidling up the driveway, leaving Max Jr scribbling on his Palm Pilot behind the yellow tape with a gangly officer looking over his shoulder. Royster motions to Sears. She drops the lid on the laptop and excuses herself, telling Pastor not to go anywhere because they're not done.

"What's this world coming to, huh Rev?" says McManus, shaking his head.

"Detective, you've seen these before, right? Doesn't this look like someone murdered her and then staged it to look like a suicide?"

"Of course. Any *man* can see that, Rev."

"The powder burns around the entry wound? The gun was fired at close range like it would be in a suicide, but that gun would produce a pretty nasty exit wound and some splatter. I saw the shell casing, but not the bullet."

"We haven't found the bullet yet. It's probably in the floor under the body."

"Which would mean that her head was already on the floor when she was shot."

"Makes sense to me."

"Not your typical way of shooting yourself."

"I agree," says McManus.

"And the egg in her hand. If she shot herself and then fell to the floor, how come it didn't break?"

"And why kill yourself with an egg in your hand? And why sleep naked in the basement on the pull-out when you have a king-size upstairs?"

Monsees bounces up the stairs from the basement and waves McManus over. "We've got a couple of things we need you to take a look at."

"What kinda things?"

"Um, electronic stuff," he says, glancing at Pastor.

"Don't go anywhere, Rev," says McManus, "or she might lock you up." He rolls his eyes and disappears into the basement with Monsees.

Pastor is leaning against the hatch of Ike's Vette, watching Chris Sears stepping back to him. She's re-dispatched Royster into the street and stares a hole into the toes of her Filas before setting her sight on Pastor again. She still has that provocative sway in her hips, but the nose isn't as high up in the air as it used to be and the eyes not as soft.

"I see some things never change," she says, cracking the lid on the laptop again.

"Meaning?"

"Meaning, is there anything more you want to tell me about when you dropped off Mrs. Allon?"

"Is there anything more you want to know?"

The hint of a smile creases her lips. "So far we've located one witness who says she saw two people wrestling in a van in this driveway around 9:30 last night. Another who says you were sitting in the church van with your pants zipped open? And one more who thinks you two had something going on."

Pastor's looking at Sears. Her eyes are locked on the screen. The whole truth is too complicated, would take too long to explain.

"We weren't wrestling. She was a little upset because she was going home to an empty house again. She and Ike had been having their problems, as young married couples often do. But theirs weren't exactly the garden variety type most people would understand."

"So you were trying to keep them out of divorce court."

"I was just trying to help her through her feelings."

She's playing the keyboard again, and Pastor at the same time, the smile becoming just a bit more evident. "Still helping all the ladies...are you sure you didn't go inside with her? To help her some more?"

"I know there's a lot that's been left unsaid between us. Do we need to get those things out in the open now? Is that what's going on here."

"What's going on here is a murder investigation. Everyone is a suspect until they're ruled out, and right now you're the last person to be seen with the victim, near the scene, alone, just before she was murdered."

"Have you changed your mind about this being a suicide because of me? Forgive me if I'm wrong, but this all feels like it's more about what happened 15 years ago than it is about what happened here last night."

Pastor had forgotten how her beach sand eyes turned to fire when she got angry. "Do you really think I've spent the last 15 years pining away over you? Antonio Hook, fellow PK and soul mate, the one that got away? Nigro, please. I'm so over you." The smile is now deeply etched into her mouth, but he's not fooled. "You were always more full of yourself than sense, but newsflash. This is not about you, okay? It's about a vicious killer whom we have to catch before he kills again and I'm not about to let personal relationships, past or present, get in the way of that."

"Chris, I was in so much agony when we broke up. But after a while I was able to let it go. I forgave you. It's okay. Let's move on."

"What?! *You* forgave *me*?! The next time you preach a sermon about judgment, Tony, take the log out of your own eye and preach it to yourself first. This conversation is over. I've got an investigation to conduct and a list of questions I need answers to yet. You can answer them here and now, or I can slap the cuffs on you and take you down to the station; it's up to you."

She turns back to the computer screen and waits.

Pastor consciously tries to slow his breathing and heart rate down before he says, "What else, Sergeant."

"Was Mrs. Allon afraid of her husband? Was he ever abusive?"

"I'm sorry, I really can't discuss the specifics of what a parishioner and I talk about in confidence. You know, the state Supreme Court, privileged information and all that?"

"She's dead, she won't sue you."

"I could still get in big trouble."

"You could get in big trouble if you don't."

"How about if I tell you what's common knowledge and then give you my professional opinion about it."

"How you choose to justify it is your business. I'm listening."

"Ike's known for a lot of things, but wife beating isn't one of them. Her uncle back in Jamaica sexually abused her for years until she finished school, so in my opinion her past convinced her that all she had to offer the world was her body. In her mind that's how she had to live: trading her body for what she really wanted—someone to love and protect her." Sears is pounding the keys. "That's why she married Ike. But she got more than she'd bargained for. He made her a virtual prisoner in her own home."

"Is that it?"

"No. Wednesday nights were the only nights he allowed her out of the house, and then only if the church van picked her up. He wouldn't let her work, or have a car, or any friends over, not even from the church. In my opinion, she wanted to leave, but didn't have the means."

"So he never hit her?"

"Who knows what really goes on behind closed doors? Like I said, that's not his reputation. And I seriously doubt she'd let it happen. I think she'd go to a shelter or turn tricks in Newark and risk getting murdered by that serial killer exterminating hookers before she'd let Ike beat her. Plus, I never saw any bruises on her."

"Was he mad at her about anything? A rumored affair maybe?"

"Ike is always mad about a rumored affair."

"Any friends outside of church that you know of?"

"Her best friend. Hazel Thompson. They used to work together here in Belton before Anemone got married."

"Address?"

"Somewhere in Newark. But she still works for the Vernons up on the Hill. She's their nanny. Probably easier to find her there."

She pounds the keys some more then says, still staring into the screen, "We're done for now. I'll find you later if I need more."

Pastor turns to scram and bumps into McManus. Sears calls him back and hands him her card and says to call if he remembers anything that might help with the investigation, even at her cell number because it's always on.

"This might be helpful. Last night during Prayer and Bible Anemone's pager went off in her handbag."

"Pager?" says McManus.

"Yeah. I didn't know she carried one. After service she went into the Walker Library and answered the page. She said it was Ike and that he'd be home at 10:00, but maybe it was somebody else. Maybe she lied."

"Or maybe she didn't," says Sears. "Why lie to you about who paged her?"

"You guys are the detectives. But what I know is she was expecting *somebody* at 10:00, and you say she died around 10:00. So somebody could have set her up and killed her."

"We did find a pager in her bag," said McManus. "But the memory's blank."

"If the killer paged her," I said, "he knew his number was in there, so he erased it. But the phone company should have a record of who she called from the Walker Library. Case solved. Right?"

CHAPTER 3

Something fell in the basement and Pastor's up before the sun again, wide awake and refusing to believe he's been back from Ike's and asleep for all of two hours. It felt like ten minutes. God must have been cracking a joke when He gave him these bionic ears at birth, because sleep is a precious commodity for him. He's one of those people who needs eight hours to function, and Walden Pond silence to get them.

Sometimes the mice knock things over down there, but no mouse could've caused the louder noise that followed. It was either a big rat, a dumb burglar, or Brother McArthur. Or Pastor's anonymous pen pal trying to keep a promise. Feeling the need to do something, he slips out of bed and peeks outside. No black conversion van anywhere on Third, nor on Academy.

No use trying to go back to sleep, so he slides his STU running gear on again, grabs his Louisville Slugger brand rat killer from the closet and creeps downstairs. The traps he buys never work, but his trusty Slugger has two rodents to its credit already.

There's light angling under the basement door. Must be Brother McArthur.

"Brother Mac? That you?"

"Yeah, Pastor. Just me. Good morning."

Thurman McArthur is the church sexton, looks like Mr. Clean on crack and sounds like Mike Tyson with marbles in his throat. He's lived on Academy Street all his life and was a boxer in the Army back when it was still segregated. Some say he's a little punch drunk now, but Pastor thinks it's just the years of wild living catching up with him. Every now and then he lets himself in through the storm cellar doors to attempt some maintenance work on the parsonage. In the summer he likes to work early before the sun rises too high.

"What you doing, Brother Mac? Rearranging the basement?"

The basement looks like the storage room in a junkyard. The only reason Pastor ever comes down here is to do his laundry once a month, when he absolutely has to.

"Naw, Pastor. Just looking for the screens for the doors upstairs. Summer's coming."

Pastor doesn't have the heart to tell him that summer's pretty much here. In two days it'll be official. He tramps back upstairs, gulps down a tall glass of OJ and throws himself into his morning run up the Hill, praying, and wondering what he would say to himself about all these recent events if he were Burro.

$$\mathcal{J}$$

Pastor Hook wrote GOD in the space marked CURRENT EMPLOYER on his malpractice insurance application two years ago, but in truth the pastor of a traditional black Baptist church doesn't work for God at all. Especially when he's as new at it as Pastor is. He's got as many bosses as members, and gets evaluated by almost two hundred of them every Sunday morning. That's why he bristled yesterday when Brian Mulady sent for him. He thought Pastor didn't know about the Showcase they've been trying to keep hush-hush, which is planned for Sunday. It would be another "surprise" assignment Pastor didn't want from another person he wouldn't be able to say no to. And Mulady's not even a member of First Baptist Church.

That's why Pastor's standing here on the corner trying to decide between O'Loughlin's and City Hall.

Anemone's murder is sure to have multiple repercussions that will affect him, including the likelihood that it'll require him to defend the black community against charges that blacks are bringing crime to town.

Yes, you heard right. Malpractice insurance. Pastor didn't have to worry about it during his five years as Protestant Chaplain at the New Jersey State Maximum Security Prison, but in these litigious times pastors need it. Intro to Church Administration I's stock horror story about violating the clergy-communicant privilege convinced him of that: A conscientious pastor hears a member's confession during a bereavement counseling session that he in fact murdered his wife and is seeking prayer from the pastor and forgiveness from God. The pastor prays for him, and then goes to the cops. The member is convicted, then later acquitted on appeal, after which he sues the pastor, the parish, and the denomination, and wins a multimillion-dollar judgment. The pastor, stripped of his property, his credibility, and eventually his job, commits suicide.

True story.

Pastor makes sure his policy stays current.

City Hall's sepia turrets and wide roof line and stone face remind Pastor of Alexander Hall at Princeton—the university, not the seminary—as he stands in the very center of town, at the corner of Valley Street and Belton Avenue, waiting to see which will change first, the light or his mind. Off in the already hazy distance behind him, where Belton Avenue begins its steep ascent through the Hill to the Reservation, the 9:01 to Penn Station--New York, not Newark--is pulling out over vast still-empty retail space that, according to Max, will one day become a tony department store and net Paul Vernon millions even if the Racial Balance Task Force is just marginally successful this year.

Many Beltonians dismiss this and all other Max Candy Jr stories as fanciful. Pastor has always given him the benefit of the doubt though, because he, too, traffics in the reputedly fanciful—tales of people who call down fire from heaven, and walk on water, and heal with their shadows. So, he feels like he has a rooting interest.

Flying past him from left to right and screeching around the corner virtually on two wheels is Sean Ellis, Chief of Police. An amiable bon vivant with a handlebar mustache, he's always speeding in his department-issued Expedition.

And pulling into the intersection in a burgundy Crown Victoria is Chris Sears. Even in the distant daylight, still the most striking woman he's seen in a long time. Their eyes lock and she smiles that smile he's seen a thousand times before. She really *does* smile like Carla and deep inside Pastor knows he'll be seeing her again today even though she may be going anywhere right now, because almost half of Essex County passes through this intersection on their way to the mall or the university or the County Courthouse or the jail. And he's sure he won't want to see her again because he's convinced she's going to find a reason to pollute the life he's building for himself in Belton. He looks back at the train pulling away in silence and the traffic flowing past him in slow motion and the surrealism confirms that she's just another impediment from his past assigned to keep him from getting ahead to his future.

He's still looking for some kind of sign to help him make up his mind when the light changes and a banged-up Mack truck carrying an illegally high mound of top soil shudders to a halt in front of him, spilling some of its payload over its cab into the pedestrian lane and onto his size 12 wing tips. Its unstable tailgate rattles a little also, spilling some more soil out of the back. Maybe not what you'd call a herald from heaven, but at this point it's good enough for him. Like most people, he really didn't want a direct answer from the Big Guy anyway, or he would've asked directly. He pretty much knew already what he really wanted to do.

ʃ

Musty offices are filling up around him as Pastor obediently climbs the creaky stairs to City Hall's second floor. Rachel Niagara waves back from Human Resources. And so does Dale Dawkins from the Office of Procurement.

Submission to authority, according to scripture, is clearly God's will. But is showing up for meetings rigged against your best interest also and always God's will? Or being a stepping stone for calculating people? Getting clear on what he really wants and what's in his best interest always helps Pastor to decide. Because true submission requires moving away from what we want to getting under what the authority wants. And he's still learning to train himself to do what he doesn't want to do, so he can be pleasing to God. And what he doesn't want to do right now is be used as the token black again.

At the end of the long wainscoted corridor hung with old daguerreotypes and some more modern photos of the Belton Green, in the anteroom of the Belton Administrator's office, a graying woman reaches into her black Coach shoulder bag and places a shiny orange-sized orb back on her desk blotter. She shatters every anatomical stereotype of the black woman: no hips, a flat bottom, even flatter chest. Maybe that's why rumors abound that she's a lesbian. She's Olive Oyl with a tan, a 'fro, and a trendy fashion eye. And she jumps when she hears Pastor's voice and sees his face sticking through the doorway.

"It starts with staples and paper clips, and before you know it, Padow!, you've graduated to spherical black marble paperweights. But since you're returning it, I won't leak a word to BPD."

"Obsidian. And it's an ellipse, not a sphere." Even her voice lacks feminine shape.

If looks could kill, Dexter would be dead by now because Malisa Hoard isn't much of a looker. And she'll never be mistaken for Miss Congeniality, either. In the two years Pastor's known her, she's smiled once. He has yet to figure out how Sister Niagara got her this job. Maybe it was the clothes.

"If you don't polish them every now and then they lose their luster," she says, stuffing the bag into her desk drawer.

"I could've sure used Dexter's help last night, Malisa."

She brushes past him with a harumph into a small adjacent restroom.

"Malisa, Joe in yet?"

It's Tubby Miglianacco emerging from Brian Mulady's office behind Pastor. Trailing Tubby, as Malisa abruptly closes the door without responding, is Lousy Farraday and Flo Ouderkirk, her brilliant red hair hanging evenly around her slight shoulders in a smart mop cut.

"The mayor just asked you a question. Answer him!"

"It's early, Lousy. Give her a break," says Tubby. Then he scrapes right past Pastor into the anteroom without saying a word. Didn't even look. Like a page out of Ellison's *Invisible Man*.

"Hey, Reverend, nice haircut. Looks good on you."

"Thanks, Flo. That green dress is working, girl."

She smiles. "Welcome aboard."

"Thanks, I think."

Pastor doesn't know what he's been conscripted to do, but he's sure that's what he's here to find out. He reaches Mulady's office reminding himself to suck it up, smile, and be a good soldier of Jesus Christ.

When he opens the door Brian Mulady is not there.

♪

After a leisurely breakfast at O'Loughlin's on Belton Avenue Pastor is back in his corner office in the lower level of the church trying to digest the plateful of raisin pancakes and side of Canadian bacon he just romanced. He's looking out through the slats of the sky blue mini blinds at the billboard of the print shop next door and the row of two-story wood frame office buildings lining Second Street down to the New Jersey Transit tracks, and retrieving messages from the voice mail system:

Thursday, eight-o-five a.m. -- A hang-up, no message. *Beeeeeeep.*

Thursday, eight-o-seven a.m. -- "Reverend, Trustee Thorn here. Where are you? I just called a couple minutes ago and you weren't there. I called your cell phone and you have it turned off." *Beeeeeeep.*

Thursday, eight-fifteen a.m. -- "Reverend, I called your cell phone twice and it's still turned off. I need to talk to you. Trustee Thorn here." *Beeeeeeep.*

Thursday, eight thirty-seven a.m. -- "Dr. Hook, this is Tamara Green at Eye on Belton Three? Just a friendly reminder that this week First Baptist *is* the featured congregation in the rotation and our crew will be there at nine o'clock Sunday morning to begin setting up for the eleven o'clock live local-access cable simulcast with WSTU. If you could fax or e-mail your sermon title to us by Friday night like you did last time it would really help out our pre-production guys. I'm looking forward to working with you again, Dr. Hook. We always have a great time at your church, and I can't wait to see what's going to unfold *this* Sunday. See you then. Byeeee." *Beeeeeeep.*

Thursday, eight forty-five a.m. -- "Reverend, Trustee Thorn again. Remember the church voted for you to keep that phone turned on for emergencies." *Beeeeeeep.*

Thursday, nine-o'clock a.m. -- "Dr. Hook, this is Harriett Jamison from Monumental Baptist Church in Newark. I'm delighted to inform you that you've been selected as the finalist for our Senior Pastor position. To complete the process before the church votes next week, the pulpit committee will attend services at First Baptist this Sunday to hear you and then take you to dinner immediately after to discuss the particulars of our offer. God bless you, Dr. Hook. See you Sunday." *Beeeeeeep.*

Thursday, nine-fifteen a.m. -- "Reverend, Trustee Thorn again. I'm gonna have to bring this up at the next church meeting. We have an emergency here and I, the chairman of the trustee board, can't reach the pastor." *Beeeeeeep.*

Thursday, nine twenty-five a.m. -- "Dr. Hook, this is Dr. Mulady at City Hall? We had a 9:00 meeting scheduled this morning. I offer my most sincere apology, Reverend. I was called away unexpectedly on an urgent town business matter. Would you give me a call as soon as you can to reschedule?" *Beeeeeeep.*

Thursday, nine thirty-one a.m. -- "Doc, I know you ain't still at the shrink, so turn your cell phone back on, bruh! I'm heading out to the office. I'll holler at you later when I get there. Peace and hair-grease." *Beeeeeeep.*

Thursday, nine forty-five a.m. -- "Reverend, we have a couple of emergency situations here. I hear Sister Bessom's in the hospital again and I need to know if you've been by to see her yet. And somebody just called and said Sister Allon died last night. Call me as soon as you get this message. Trustee Thorn." *Beeeeeeep.*

Thursday, nine forty-nine a.m. -- "Tony Hook, this is Mr. Cash at Finance One Visa. This regards the past due balance on your account. Please return my call as soon as you can, Sir. My direct number is **888-555-8888**, very easy to remember. I'll be expecting your call." *Beeeeeeep.*

After jumping around his office for several minutes like a high school point guard celebrating a state championship win, Pastor is just settling into his leather desk chair. His euphoria is tempered by his need to start putting Anemone's eulogy together when the bell rings.

"Yo, Doc." It's Cornel Brown, conservatively attired today in a lime-green five-button suit and absolutely nothing atop his shaved head. He's rocking the gold hoop earring today over the one-carat diamond stud, and it's matching his blond van dyke nicely. He could stand to miss a meal or two, but even with his bow legs they're the same height and somehow they wear the same size. As they say, he carries it well. "10:07, Thursday morning?" he says, plopping into the black leather couch under the window. "I figured you've got to be at your desk by now working on your message for Sunday morning. I know you made that *Ebony* top 20 preachers list because you work at your craft, but you need to be less predictable, Doc. Spoil your people that way."

Cornel considers himself a black activist, and claims to be a direct descendant of the John Brown of Harpers Ferry infamy. If Alan Alda can be a feminist then Cornel Brown can be a black activist. Pastor just wishes sometimes that he'd speak more like a regular white guy.

He adopted this 'style' eight years ago after finishing a dissertation-sized paper in their middler year on the differences between Bishop Daddy Grace and Father Divine. The prof wanted to send it to his publisher, but Cornel was even less interested in getting published than he was in attending any classes that didn't focus on some aspect of the black experience.

"What's up, Co. Just got your message. And I'm actually working on a home-going."

"Word? The Lord finally answer your prayer and kill that chairman of your trustee board?"

"You know I don't pray that way. He's still here. It was Anemone. Somebody shot her in the temple last night and tried to make it look like a suicide."

"Whaaaat?! Well, look at it this way—"

"Yeah, I know, I know. No more temptation."

He snorts. "You're looking kinda happy about it, though. I bet that's what you spent your 45 minutes with Burro talking about today, isn't it."

"That's because I just got some great news to balance out last night's bad news. Monumental called. I'm their finalist. They're coming to hear me Sunday!"

Cornel punches his fist in the air. "Yeah! I told you! I told you! You the man, Doc! You just be yourself Sunday and preach your heart out and you'll go from 200 members to 5,000 overnight. They'll have you driving a Rolls and living in a mansion by next month!"

Pastor can't contain his grin. "Thanks, Co. I don't need a Rolls Royce. I don't even need a mansion. But my own house would be nice."

"Well, that's not gonna be a problem, Bishop. Uh-oh, this means you're gonna be in one of those stand-up comedy moods again."

"So?"

"So why you always gotta be in one of those comic moods when I need a favor?"

"You need to stop being so predictable. Spoil your friends that way."

He laughs. "You're too quick for me today."

"What do you need, Co?"

"I've got a couple insisting they get married this weekend and I can't do it. Think you can pinch hit for me?"

Pastor wasn't able to convince Ike last night to have the funeral next week. He demanded it be on Friday, tomorrow, instead. So, Pastor could easily say yes. In fact it would be a welcome diversion. But he's talking to Cornelius Brown III, the only white preacher in the state of New Jersey to hold membership in the all-black Newark Ministers Conference by convincing the membership committee that he was indeed "black vis-à-vis the ontological definition of the term." Cornel sounds like he's selling something on the radio every time he opens his mouth, so Pastor figures there must be another angle to this. "I don't know, man," he says. "Why can't you do it?"

"See, I knew you'd ask a million questions. Can't just help a brother out, huh?"

"The last time I did a wedding for you the bride was four hours late and you were home sleeping the whole time. Now, do you *really* have something else to do?"

"Actually, I do. But that ain't the reason why I can't do this wedding...."

"Uh-oh. You're hesitating. This isn't good."

"You're gonna make me beg, aren't you. I knew it. I knew you'd make me beg. You know, you really need a woman in your life. Maybe she could make you treat your best friend better. Man, listen. They've been living together for a while and it might stir up some controversy for me if I do it."

"You mean they've been shacking?"

"Yup, they've been shackin'."

"Co, all 2,000 of your people recognize you as their leader. I don't have that here. For me to do this I'd either have to go through or around Thorn. And Monumental's coming this Sunday. You know what you're asking me to do, don't you?"

Of course he knows. He's the one that suggested two years at this tiny parish straight out of chaplaincy before candidating for four-figure churches. He's the one who said, "If you wanna do significant ministry, then Monumental is the place." He was the one that knew the secretary of their committee and arranged for Pastor to preach there on Sunday and impress them. He was the one that always reminded him he had two strikes against him: he's single, and he has only two years of pastoral experience. And he's the one who said, "Make sure everything's perfect with your reputation and you got a good chance."

"Doc, please. I'll owe you big time, man. I can't say no to these two, and I can't say yes, either. You're my only hope."

Pastor loves helping people. It's one of the reasons he embraced his call quickly; but he always ends up regretting doing Cornel favors. He's been there for Pastor when he needed him, though. They both know Pastor will eventually say yes.

"Will I have to counsel them?"

"They've been together for twelve years. They could probably counsel us."

"Does it have to be this weekend?"

"When's your funeral?"

"Tomorrow."

"Damn. That's early."

"And my plate's full on Sunday."

"So you could do them on Saturday."

"Rehearsals. Listen, Thorn's gone for two weeks beginning the following weekend. It would be a lot easier for me then."

"One was just diagnosed with cancer. She starts chemo on Monday. That's why they decided to do it now."

The bell rings again. "Hold on, I'll be right back."

"Paastah?" Mother Freddie is standing under a huge sombrero that hides the bald spots on her plaited gray head, holding a shoe box-sized package like an offering. "I was just on my way to ShopRite--they have their two-for-one coupon special today--and I saw this box on your porch. I was going to put it in the gallery, but the screen door was locked. So I thought, Let me bring this over here to you right now before somebody snatches it right off your stoop. You know they stole Sister Rose's Social Security check right out of her mailbox just the other day."

"I know, Mother. You told me. Several times. I'll take the package. Thanks a lot. God bless you." Pastor tries to close the door, but she wedges a new Air Jordan in between it and the jam.

"Is that Reverend Brown's Mercedes out there? Let me say hi to him. I won't be long, Paaastah."

With that Pastor kisses goodbye the hopes he had this morning for making progress on his sermon today and says through a warm smile, "Sure, Mother. Come on in."

She doesn't mention Anemone, so Pastor figures she probably hasn't gotten her call yet. She drags in her pink deluxe shopping cart with the foam rubber handlebar and extra-thick wheels.

"Can't leave this outside for the crooks to steal."

"New sneakers?"

"Just hit the stores yesterday, Paaastah. Gotta keep up."

Pastor leads her into the room. "Somebody wants to say hello, Reverend." Then drops the box on the table and begins to open it.

"Reverend Brown! How are you? I just wanted to shake your hand and tell you again how much I enjoyed that message you brought the last time you were here for Paaastah's anniversary. I still remember the title. A Bald-Headed Preacher, Two She-Bears, and Some Bad Children. That was *sooome* message. You keep preachin' like that and I *might* have to start putting you in that class just below my Paaastah."

"Thank you, Mother. Glad you remember it. It's easy to preach well when you're preaching for your best friend. Y'all make sure you treat him right now, or else I'ma come back and tell y'all about yourselves."

"I'm doing my best, Reverend," she chuckles. "Can't say the same for everybody else, but I'm doing *my* best. Paaastah's like a son to me. I make sure I take care of him. Can't let no other church come and steal him away from us. He's too great a preacher."

Cornel notices Pastor's expression eyeing what's in the opened box.

"What is it, Doc?"

"Just some foolishness from a practical joker."

"Lemme see."

"It's nothing."

"Come on, Prelate."

Pastor knows what's coming next once he grabs the box, because Rev. Cornel Brown takes this stuff *very* seriously.

CHAPTER 4

"What!? Doc, do you know what this is!?"

"I know what it's supposed to be. But it's no big deal."

Now Mother is peering into the box.

"My Lord," she says, and crosses herself three times.

"Mother, you've been Baptist all your life. Why'd you do that?"

"That's what my grandmother did whenever she saw any kind of hoodoo works. I don't claim to be an expert in these things, but I *do* know that's a mojo bag, and you don't play around with that. Somebody put a mojo bag on my uncle Jethro's front doorknob back in North Carolina? He was dead in six months."

"He was probably 95 and overdue."

"No, Paaastah. He was a young man at the time, in his 50s. They say he just didn't do anything to counteract the mojo. You're going to need a lot of prayer." She crosses herself three times again.

"There's a letter in here, too," says Cornel. He pulls a piece of paper from the envelope taped to the box cover. "Doc, what's going on here?"

"Lemme see, Reverend," says Mother, grabbing it from him. "Greek to me. I can't make out a thing."

"That's exactly what it is, Greek," says Cornel. "And Hebrew, too. Bad Hebrew at that. No vowel points, and it's even written…left to right! As a matter of fact, these aren't even real Greek and Hebrew words...they're plain English words transliterated into Greek and Hebrew. Rank amateur. Probably just copied the alphabet from a Strong's Concordance and roughed this together."

"Everybody's trying to learn Greek and Hebrew nowadays, Co."

"Whoever sent this probably never saw the inside of a seminary in his life. Probably couldn't even *spell* exegesis, much less do it."

Mother asks, "What does it say, Reverend?"

"Says, 'Get out or else I will blow you away.'"

"Why are you all looking at me?" asks Pastor.

"You get any of these before?"

Pastor leans back in his chair. "What, the bags or the letters?"

"Either."

Crossing his arms under his chest. "This is not a big deal. Just a silly prank."

"How long has this been going on? How many of these have you gotten?"

"A few."

"A few!?"

"What are you doing now, Co?"

He's got the telephone receiver in hand. "I'm calling the cops. What does it look like I'm doing?"

"To tell them what, that somebody's been leaving chicken bones at my door? This isn't 17th century Salem. I don't think they'll investigate. Besides, they're pretty busy right now."

"Oh, they'll investigate alright. That letter is a clear threat on your life."

"From somebody who leaves chicken bones on doorsteps."

He starts dialing. "*You* may not wanna to take this seriously, but *they* will."

Pastor hits the button on the cradle and squashes the call. "Okay, listen. I'll tell you guys everything, but no cops. They'll just make a mountain out of this molehill. And neither of you can ever say a word about this to anyone either, okay?"

"Okay, Paaastah."

So, Pastor tells them about the letters that have been coming for the last two months, one to the post office box and one to the parsonage. How he's gotten one every day this week. He tells them about all the nice little trinkets he's been finding on his front and back stoops. But he doesn't tell them about the black van. Nope.

"So, no cops, huh?"

"No cops."

"You sure?"

"I'm sure."

"Okay then, here. And I don't wanna hear no." Cornel reaches into the back of his waistband and comes out with a small pearl-handled pistol. "You won't have to worry about turning the other cheek with this."

"Co, come on. I don't do guns."

"Take it, Preacher. I keep a 9 in the car."

Mother reaches into her bag and comes out with a small black 9mm with a silencer on the muzzle. "That little twenty-two's not gonna stop anybody. You can borrow this, Paaastah. It's a Sig Sauer M11."

"Does *everybody* have a gun in this country?"

Cornel looks wide-eyed at Mother. "You got a permit for that?"

"Of course not. You know how long I'd have to wait and what I'd have to do to get one of these legally? I'd probably have to sleep with somebody for a license. I bought this on the street in Newark two months ago. And for a good price, too. The young man said it was government surplus, but I know it's probably hot."

Cornel shaking his head. "But why a gun, Mother?"

"My late husband may not have been good for much, but he sure taught me the virtues of protecting myself. Ever since that night he came home drunk and hit me for the last time in his natural life. I chopped his hand off with my meat clever and I've been packing something to protect myself ever since. It's a dangerous world out there for a young woman like me living all by herself."

"So what's the deal with the silencer?" asks Cornel.

"I wasn't going to buy a gun and not learn how to use it, so I made the young man throw in the silencer for free. I take quiet target practice in my basement every day without worrying about my nosy neighbors calling the cops."

"Please you two, put the guns away. The best way for me to let whoever's doing this know that this kind of stuff won't work on me is to ignore it. If I try to respond, or defend myself, they win. It's like getting harassing phone calls. Best thing to do is just hang up. Remember what Jesus said? Turn the other cheek? Remember that?"

"Naw, Doc. The best thing to do is trace the calls and find out where they're coming from. Folks are crazy these days."

"Listen, I'm too busy. I've got an obituary to file, a eulogy to write, a meeting at City Hall I'm not looking forward to and probably won't be able to wriggle out of, I haven't even finished the exegesis for Sunday's message, I've got to be here from 7 to 9 tonight for drop-in pastoral counseling, and pretty soon the phone's gonna start ringing off the hook. So, would you two let me get back to work, if that's okay?"

"Who died, Paaastah?"

Oh boy. "Anemone, Mother. And if you hurry home, you should be getting a call soon that will explain everything."

Her eyes are all aglow now. Mother loves funerals. "I better hurry to ShopRite. On two-for-one days the shelves empty out by noon." She grabs her cart, pulls the sombrero back on, and rushes through the door. "I'm praying for you, Paaastah."

"Thank you, Mother."

Before Pastor can close it she ducks her head back in. "Almost forgot to tell you, Paaastah. I'll be very late for church this Sunday. I have no idea why they decided to do this on Father's Day, but I'm being honored by the Historical Society at First Presbyterian Church of Belton. Their service is usually much shorter than ours, though, so I *will* be here."

"Alright, Mother," says Pastor. "And congratulations."

He closes the door behind her this time and gets back to his comfortable chair behind his desk. And Cornel is all over him.

"Doc, you can ignore this all you want, but I'm getting you some help."

"Suit yourself, Co."

"I'm serious, Doc. The only thing more dangerous than an educated preacher is an ignorant one. And if you ask me, some ignorant preacher is trying to chase you outta your church. A lotta those clowns at the conference wanted this house. And don't forget those two other candidates who ran against you."

Pastor did consider all that. "Could be."

"Now about that wedding."

He glances at his desk calendar and Cassie and says, "Alright, Co. Send them by tonight at 6. Maybe I can sneak this past Thorn on Friday night. On such short notice they can't be planning *too* big a ceremony."

Brian Mulady's appearance hardly matches his title. He's wearing a brown monogrammed dress shirt with silver-dollar cuff links, a lavender knit tie, a blond buzz cut that's almost fully integrated with gray, and wire-rimmed glasses that render him professorial in a self-made sort of way.

He springs like a jack-in-the-box from behind his tiny desk in what was essentially a supply closet only 7 months ago to shake Pastor's hand.

Brian Mulady is a big dude.

Newsday listed Pastor at 6'2" in high school, the Tiger media guide at 6'3", but he's actually just a shade over six feet without all his hair; and even with the extra ten pounds of muscle he's put on since his last game at Jadwin, Mulady still has him by at least 5 inches and maybe 70 pounds. And his hand is swallowing Pastor's even though Pastor can still palm a basketball.

"Sorry I'm late. I had a couple of surprise visitors."

"No, Reverend. I'm the one who's sorry. Thanks so much for agreeing to the reschedule."

Mulady's hand is like the rest of him, firm and meaty. This is their first daytime encounter, and the first time Pastor notices the number 14 tattoo on the back of his hand, between the thumb and the index finger. He files it in his mind's tiny suspicion folder.

Mulady quickly lets go.

Pastor files that, too.

"You play football in school?"

"At my size? How could I not?"

"Quarterback?"

"Lineman. I liked to hit too much to be a QB."

Pastor decides it's not a uniform number. *Maybe somebody's birthday?*

"So, what can I, or my congregation, do for you, Mr. Mulady?"

"Please, call me Brian. And I prefer to look at it as what we can do for each other and the City of Belton."

He shoots a thick manila packet across the desk to Pastor.

"I would've mailed it to you, but I felt it would be better if we met face to face. It addresses all of the major issues we're confronting as a community: the falling test scores at Belton Academy, the attempts at block busting, white flight, the growing threat to property values."

Pastor thumbs through the documents and looks up at Mulady. "Pardon the look on my face, Brian, but are you guys thinking there might be too many black people moving into Belton?"

"Reverend, this is what we're thinking." He taps the polished brass nameplate at the edge of his desk that reads, B. MULADY, INTEGRATION SPECIALIST. "This is what I'm about. This city established a Racial Balance Task Force and hired me to devise and implement a strategy to stave off re-segregation. We're interested in achieving balance."

"Alright. I think balance is a great ideal. How can I help?"

"You're a community leader. As minister of the only black church in perhaps the only suburban community in America where black per capita income exceeds white per capita income, you have the kind of influence that can be used to achieve quite a bit."

"You mean like a black activist or something?"

"Yes," he says, pumping his head. The degree on the otherwise bare wall behind him says Brian Mulady holds a doctorate in social psychology.

"Well, I'm no black activist, but again, what do you need me to do?"

"In the last twenty years the black population here has grown from 5% to just about 20% today. The school district's now 40% black. Many of our white empty nesters are selling to black families with school-age children. The most recent surveys we took are telling us that blacks and whites view integration very differently. Blacks define the ideal racial balance as 50-50, but whites see the ideal level as 20% black. Belton's dangerously approaching the racial comfort level of most whi—"

"Pardon the interruption, Brian, I'm so sorry, but I really have to get back to my office. What does this all have to do with me?"

"Well, the problem this is creating is that fewer whites are looking to Belton as a place to live when they're relocated or begin to have families and want to move out of the city. The packet outlines some of the steps we plan to take to reverse this trend."

"Okay, so you really do want me to help you stop more black people from moving to Belton."

"No, we want to attract more whites. We've been aggressively marketing the community in the metro area newspapers."

"Yeah, I've seen a couple of the ads in *The New York Times* recently. That's smart. They say diversity works."

"Thanks. The work we've been doing on the corporate level has begun to pay off as well. This Sunday we'll be inaugurating what we hope will become a monthly Belton Showcase. We're bringing in a busload of corporate relocation consultants and potential buyers from New York and taking them on a guided tour of the community. It'll culminate in a forum held here in the council auditorium at 1:00 pm."

"And you'd like me to address the campers right after church."

"Yes. If you wouldn't mind. There will be a representative on hand from the school board, the police department, the city council, and the ministerial alliance to answer any questions about the community from their unique perspectives and areas of expertise. It occurred to us that we have no one representing the black community and everyone felt you'd be ideal."

"I'm qualified to speak for all black people, but I *can* accurately represent my church. The problem is I have another engagement."

"Reverend, your presence for just a few minutes would mean so much. We finalize the programs today. Any chance you can just pop in?"

Actually, Pastor has become the proverbial thorn in City Hall's backside. They're really in a quandary about what to do with him. They know they can't exclude him without appearing suspect. But they can't fully include him and remain status quo ante either. So they often include him at the 11th and ¾ hour, and hope that he'll falter or arrive ill prepared.

"That doesn't give me much time. I'll do my best," says Pastor.

"I know this is a very delicate issue, but it all comes down to money. Both blacks and whites agree that when a neighborhood becomes mostly black, white demand and property values both fall. Maintaining the right balance in Belton makes life better for all of us."

Pastor is hearing Co in his head as he watches Mulady talk. "*White folks have been moving into and taking over neighborhoods inhabited by large numbers of blacks for almost five hundred years. Where was this phony eighty-twenty rule when van Riebeeck landed in South Africa? Or when all the waterfront land grabbing started in the Caribbean a few decades ago? Or when gentrification hit Harlem like a blizzard?"*

Mulady leans forward in his chair now and his cold blue eyes leave inquiry and go to meddling. "I heard what happened in the Mews last night."

"I'm pretty sure everybody has by now."

"This city hasn't had a murder in five years, and that one was by poisoning."

"So I've heard."

"She was one of yours, wasn't she?"

The suggestion in his tone is crystal: Anemone's murder supports his position that more blacks mean more crime, more problems, and more flight.

"Yeah, she was."

"You're taking it well. I'd probably be all broken up, unable to function."

"Yeah, well pastors don't have that luxury. We have to help others through it. Besides, at Jersey State it seemed like somebody was maimed or murdered or just died of old age almost every week. After a while it becomes part of the rhythm of life."

"This is just the kind of thing we can't have around here. Not if we're going to make this Showcase idea work. Nobody wants to live with crime."

Co is screaming into Pastor's mind now. *"Just the thought of actively recruiting white families to 'save' Belton from a supposed decline in property values should be making your blood boil, Doc! Later for your 'bosses.' You better make it your duty to figure out a way to blast this racist idea publicly on Sunday while still managing to meet with Monumental's pulpit committee!"*

"Yeah, murder doesn't do anybody any good," says Pastor.

"Just between you and me, Reverend, I'm disappointed with the way Chief Ellis has been handling the growing crime rate in this town. Riots at the Academy, cars being stolen right off driveways, home invasions and burglaries. If he can't make this murder investigation go away by

Saturday I'm going to recommend to the VC that they oust him and bring in Joe Curtin. There are a lot of people around here who think it's time that Belton hired its first black police chief. And if it should come to that, I hope I can count on your support."

Co is now jumping up and down on Pastor's head and stomping his feet. *"He's just trying to use a sellout darky to control the scary, dangerous darkies! He* must *be a neo-racist. And he definitely did his homework, because you and I both know Joe Curtin is a nice guy, but he'd make a horrible Belton Police Chief. Just look at his record as Deputy Chief of Police in Newark. He's* earned *that reputation for being overzealous fighting crime. Look at all those young kids, all of them black males, who died in police custody on his watch. And since he and most of his officers are black, brutality charges consistently fall on deaf ears. Hiring Curtin to police Belton would be like hiring Kevorkian to treat depression!"*

"I think it's in everyone's interest that this thing go away as soon as possible, Brian. I can support that."

Mulady looks at Pastor with those cold, hard eyes and says, "We're going to stabilize things around here, Reverend. And we're all counting on your support."

Pastor is too tired, too emotionally drained to respond with anything more than a smile and a head nod. And he has a long day ahead of him yet. He picks up his tired self and his packet and makes for the door.

Halfway down the hallway Pastor literally bumps into Dale Dawkins coming out of the Office of Procurement with a stack of purchase orders. Dawkins is a big, greasy dude with finger waved hair. Not tall, but wide like a squat building. Pastor's so tired he doesn't even remember the impact. Sitting there on the floor, looking up at Dawkins, Pastor sticks his hand out for Dawkins to help up.

He doesn't.

Dawkins just shows him the stack of purchase orders in his hands as Pastor collects himself and Mulady's packet off the floor. "How are you doing there, Reverend Dawkins. I see you've got your hands full."

"Yeah, Pastor. These folks are trying to work me to death up here. From what I'm hearing, you got your hands full, too."

"Want to trade hands?"

"Nah. *You* the pastor. That's why they pay you the *big* bucks. I'm just trying to support you when I can."

"Thanks, Reverend. You have a good day."

Pastor walks down the hall feeling Dawkins's stare on his back, and asking God to give him more wisdom. In two years he's still not been able to figure out how to get Dawkins on his side. Pastor's ready for their relationship to improve. He just never knows what to say to Dawkins.

On his way out of the building he stops in the lobby to give Max Jr another statement before he goes in to interview the mayor and anyone else he can find to talk about the murder. Pastor can tell he's been up since last night. He rumbles down the steps remembering the words of his Old Testament Prophets preaching professor, himself a modern day prophet. *"When you speak truth to power, three things will happen...four if God is with you: you'll be ostracized; you'll be persecuted; you'll be misunderstood; and if you're really blessed?...you might just change things."*

Pastor's pocket rings and he waits a beat before answering.

"Bishop, you remember Mary Welbourne from Contemporary Church History class?"

"Fine Mary? Most definitely. Whatever happened to her? Did she ever get a church? I lost track of her after she graduated."

"She's doing real well for herself, Doc. I just got you an appointment with her. I'll meet you at your office in fifteen minutes."

"But I don't have time to go looking up old flames with you, Co," Pastor says to the dial tone.

◊

Cornel's standing on the invisible passenger-side brakes with his eyes squinted. "Watch your speed, Doc."

"Then you should've driven. And you said 15 minutes. That was more like 50."

"Never know who's following you. I don't want *everybody* knowing my business."

"How's Mary Welbourne supposed to help me anyway? Is she an attorney now or something?"

"Why does everybody have to be credentialed for you?"

"Aren't you the same guy who was talking about the dangers of ignorance just a little while ago?"

"Hey, we don't all need multiple degrees or Mensa membership to be qualified to help people. Mr. Charlie's got you right where he wants you, thinking his university seals of approval are pre-reqs for prosperity. Me? All I need is my folk's approval on Sunday mornings."

Pastor shakes his head, but he's not as worried as he usually is when he follows Cornel blindly, because they're headed to Mary's offices in the swank Short Hills Mall. The whole place closes down at 6:00, guaranteeing that only people who don't have to work for a living can afford to shop there, so how bad could this be?

Mostly rich white women are milling around in the mall, some with strollers, some just strolling. Heads are turning everywhere as Pastor and Cornell make their way to a remote corner of the second floor.

New Insights looks like a cross between a psychiatrist's office and a hair salon. Lots of glass and black leather in a plush waiting room dotted with ficus and areca palms. There are three well-dressed women and one man in a business suit all sitting with their heads buried in magazines.

"Hey, Julie," says Cornel to the young receptionist sitting behind the semi-circled desk.

"Hello Mr. Brown, you're just in time. Is this him?"

"Yeah."

She shows off her braces, picks up the phone and then gets up, straightens out her mini-skirt, and shows them through a door that leads to a short corridor. She closes it behind them, smiling, and Cornel heads for the second door on the right, like he's done this before, and opens it.

A little money can make a big difference even for somebody like Mary. The charcoal pants suit looks designer, the hair and nails, salon. She looks even more elegant than she did in seminary, and back then they always commented that she seemed better suited for movies or modeling than ministry.

"Cornel! What's up!" They embrace, squeezing each other a little inappropriately before she breaks away. "I see you brought me some new business." She reaches up and pecks Pastor on the cheek.

"How you doing, Mary. You're still looking good."

"Thanks, Tone. I've still got some back for a white girl, don't I?" She turns to give them a better view.

Cornel laughs and Pastor tries not to, but she's right.

"You look pretty darn hot yourself, Tone. Have a seat guys."

There's a black leather couch, where Cornel and Pastor sit, and a black leather recliner, where Mary curls up with her shoes off. A ficus, a chair and an executive desk in the corner displaying an opened laptop complete the room's decor.

"So, Tone, let's catch up. Co told me a little bit about what's going on at your new church, but I don't know jack about anything else. Whatever happened with you and your advisor, that Christian ethics professor? You still see her now and then?"

Pastor winces.

"Awww, poor baby," she says, pouting. "Don't wanna talk about the past, huh?"

"I'm just not proud of it, that's all."

"He started hittin' it after you graduated. But then he got greedy and hooked up with the professor's daughter, too. She was a senior in high school at the time. The prof found out and threatened to flunk him unless he became her boy toy."

Mary's looking at Pastor the way she used to when the three of them hung out his junior year, calling themselves the original Salt-N-Pepa. She was actually down with Cornel, but always curious about Pastor.

"Then I started reading John of the Cross and Julian of Norwich and realized that scripture is right, there *is* a connection between sexual purity and mystical experience--"

"So he had a conversion experience and went to jail after graduation. Became chaplain at Jersey State. Next best thing to a monastery. Stayed there for five years playing inspector on the side and helping with investigations, until the warden forced him out because some guys ordered a hit on him."

"Monastery? No way. We used to spend more time in the Philly discos than in Miller Chapel. So what are you trying to tell me, that you're celibate now?"

"It's a lot better than the alternative." St. Origen, the ante-Nicene scholar who also wrestled with runaway sexual urges, convinced Pastor of that. He took the biblical injunction 'if thy right hand offend thee cut it off' literally and made himself a eunuch for the Kingdom of God's sake, only to discover that it didn't eliminate the urges. Pastor's theological education saved him on this one. At least a part of him. He chose therapy instead. Dr. Burro. Sho nuff. "So what's up with you? I don't see a wedding ring. Any kids?"

"Nah. I like my freedom too much. Besides, marriage as an institution is pretty much irrelevant now, and I'm not a farmer so I don't need any rugrats to help me till the soil, okay."

"So what is this place? And what kind of help do you have to offer to a man who doesn't need any?"

She giggles. "What, Co didn't tell you?"

"Tell me what?"

"Where did you think you were coming?"

"To see an attorney or something. I kept telling Co I didn't need one."

Now she's laughing out loud. "Sweetheart, New Insights is the leading house of spiritual mediation and intuitive learning for the well-heeled in the entire state. I get clients from as far away as Cape May."

"Whaaaat? You mean you're a psychic?"

"He always was a bright bulb, wasn't he, Co? Actually I prefer 'intuitive'."

She hands Pastor a card that reads: Mary Welbourne, M.Div., Spiritual Intuitive. They laugh again. The joke's on him. Instead of a super fine Marcia Clark he's staring at a pale Miss Cleo. And right then Pastor swears that if she pitches into a phony Caribbean accent and says anything even resembling, "Call me now!" he's going to excuse himself, go wait in the waiting room, and beg the Father for forgiveness. Preachers leading preachers to psychics? An absolute abomination. Nothing angers God more. It's right there in Deuteronomy 18. What is this world coming to? Pastor is ready to walk, but the same curiosity that overcomes him when he drives by a bad accident keeps him there.

"Hey, whada you want from me. I couldn't get a call after graduation because every session I interviewed with thought I was too sexy. This industry was booming at the time, I saw an opportunity to cross train into it, and I went for it. It's really not that big a stretch, and Tillich would support me on this so don't gimme a hard time, okay."

"Where's your crystal ball, etcetera?"

"Funny, Tone. It's a new millennium. We've gone high tech. I buy all my crystal balls from Dell."

"Doc, she knows the landscape. She's the best at what she does. I'm telling you. She can tell you, just by looking, who's been sending you those letters and that bag."

"And how are you gonna do that?"

"Research, baby, just like in school. I employ a staff of four other intuitives, so I really don't do too many readings anymore, only for friends. I've been spending a lot of time lately developing the multimedia dimension of our ministry."-- (*What!? A psychic referring to what they do as a Ministry?! What next, pedophiles calling themselves Child Maturity Instigators!?*) --"Our website is up, our hotline is always jammed, and we've got a cable show in the works. But, when Co called and told me you were having some problems I said, 'heck yeah, I'll do it.' I'm picking up some pretty strong signals right now. Good, you brought the box. Lemme have it."

Cornel tosses her the box. She looks inside, opens the bag and inspects it, reads the note, then covers it up again and closes her eyes.

"Two things," she says, eyes still closed, face contorted. "The person who left this is crazy with jealousy. He lives very near you. And you've met him before. The person who prescribed this to him is a low-level amateur conjurer operating in or around Newark. One of three people...Zeera, LeRoy, or Shaka-Babatunde." She opens her eyes and smiles.

"Thanks a lot, Mary," says Cornel, beaming.

"That's it?" Pastor's trying to keep his eyes in their sockets.

"That's it. You look...disappointed. Why?"

She appears genuinely hurt, like if she really wants Pastor to respect what she's doing.

"Look, Tone, this isn't an exact science. We can get you in the ballpark, the rest is up to you."

"I think the question Cornel wanted answered, and the reason he dragged me down here," Pastor says, glancing over at Cornel, "is whether or not this guy is really dangerous?"

"Who knows?"

Cornel reaches into his pocket and peels two Benjamins off his knot. He believes in walking around every day with a dollar for each one of his members. Pastor carries about a dime for each one of his, but in his mind that doesn't mean they're worth less.

"Co, put your money away. This one's on the house. Just glad to see Mr. Tony Hook again. You sure you're celibate now?"

"Yeah, Mary, I'm sure."

"You have my card. If you ever need me for anything, and I mean *anything*, gimme a call."

J

Pastor should've known better than to trust Cornel again. They're winding through the S-curves up South Mountain Reservation back to town and Cornel's standing on the brake again, but this time his eyes are open.

"Doc, didn't you hear what she said? It's *got* to be Oliphant. He lives near you, you've met him before, and he's crazy jealous."

"Come on, Co. That's true of about half the preachers who attend the conference."

"But Oliphant's the only one who was the front-runner for your church before you became a candidate."

He does have a point there. The other guy is now pastoring a monstrosity in Atlanta. "Okay, okay. We'll stop by his church real quick. But I don't have time for a wild goose chase today, I've got too much work to do."

"Wasn't that van behind us on the way to the mall, too?"

CHAPTER 5

Cornel's eyes are now squeezed shut as they slalom down the Hill. Pastor spins a left off Belton onto Ridgeway, then a right behind Belton Middle School and past the duck pond. Over the tracks he hangs another left onto Vose, another right onto Mountain, and a left onto Scotland. Conversion vans can't handle like Saabs. Even old ones.

"What van, Co?"

"Never mind, Doc. Just revive me when we get to Oliphant's."

Jervon Oliphant split an old church dying in a big building down on Broad Street in Newark a few years ago. He's been stuck in this storefront here on Scotland Road near Orange High School ever since, trying to raise enough money for a down payment on a building they could call home. The accordion gates are drawn, the big silver padlock is on, and a mangy dog is rooting around in the overturned garbage can by the curb.

"Looks like the entire administrative staff of The Way Truth & Life Holiness Baptist Church of the Fire Baptized is out to lunch. Probably at the Gateway Hilton."

"Don't make fun of him, Doc. I started out in a storefront."

"Who's making fun? He has a secretary, I don't. And it's time for me to get back to work."

"Hold up. He might be home. Let's swing by his house."

Pastor rolls his eyes, refuses to mutter the Lord's name in vain, makes a U-turn, and speeds back to Belton. Oliphant lives in a grand brick colonial overlooking Belton Park, just off Belton Avenue.

"His Jag's not in the driveway."

"Could be in the garage. Let's ring the bell."

"Be my guest."

"You're the one getting the threats and I gotta do all the work?"

"But this is all your idea. Remember?"

He smirks and opens the door. A curtain moves at an upstairs window, but no one answers the doorbell.

"Satisfied?" asks Pastor.

"He'll turn up sooner or later."

"And then what. Even if it *is* him, he won't admit it."

"Oh, I got my ways, Doc. I got my ways. Listen, I'm hungry. Let's head over to Shamblee's for some lunch."

"You go ahead, Co," Pastor says as he pulls up in the FBC parking lot next to his old Saab. "I've got to get back to work."

♪

Traffic is heavy up Valley Street. The eulogy will have to wait until later. Right now Pastor needs to get to the *Mirror* before their deadline. It's hot enough to bake bread on asphalt and the Automatic Climate Control is working overtime to keep the cabin cool. His heart sinks as he notices an old woman struggling up the sidewalk with two plastic ShopRite bags stretched tight with groceries.

Pastor pulls over and powers down the passenger window. It sticks twice before going all the way down. "Get in, Sister Walker. I'll give you a ride home."

Sweat collects in the creases of her smiling face. "Pastor, I'm sure glad to see you. Seems like the buses stopped running."

"Sister Walker, how many times do I have to tell you? If you *ever* need a ride, just call me, okay?"

"I did, Pastor, but you weren't in your office. And I can never remember the number to that little wireless phone."

Make a brother feel bad why don't you. As far as Pastor is concerned, unless some miracle happens and he gets married again, Sister Walker is still the first lady of First Baptist Church. But the way all of them treat her, her last name might as well be Dangerfield.

"Sister Walker, let me take you out on the town tonight." The window slides all the way up cleanly and Pastor pulls away from the curb. "I don't feel like eating alone again."

"Oh, Pastor, you don't have to do that."

"You turning me down again? Man! What does a brother have to do to get a date with a pretty woman these days?"

She laughs. "Alright, Pastor. I'll have dinner with you. But you'll have to do something for me."

"Name it, Sister Walker."

He asked for it. That familiar seriousness overpowers her smile and she dons the tone she must've used for 35 years as an elementary school teacher in the Belton school system. The same tone she privileges Pastor with at least once a week. "Now you listen to me." She wags her gnarled finger in his face. "You better pastor this church. You hear me? You pastor this church. You're the pastor. God put you here. Don't let those trustees tell you what to do. They don't run the church. You do. You're the pastor. You hear me?"

"I hear you, Sister Walker."

"You better pastor this church. They tried to do my husband the same way, but he wouldn't let them. He fought them until the day he died, and you better do the same thing. You pastor this church. Don't let them run you out of here. This is *your* church. God put you here. He's on your side. You're the pastor. Now you pastor this church, you hear me?"

It's rumored in some circles that Reverend Walker was hexed to death, but Sister Walker has never come out and actually said so to Pastor, and he's not about to ask.

♪

Silver Saab convertibles with blue ragtops, no matter what the model year, don't belong under shade trees. But it's too hot to be concerned about auto aesthetics or black conversion vans way back in traffic and Pastor is too hungry. It's well into the lunch hour and he really wants to be leaning over a plate of baby backs at the Parvenu Noir rather than pulling into this almost empty side lot of the *Belton Mirror* building, a flat circular structure of steel and mirrored glass that looks like the future. He grabs the black eel skin portfolio the youth choir got him as an installation gift and double-checks it before getting out. It's all there: an extra-slim Bible, a roman collar, a CLERGY: OFFICIAL BUSINESS dashboard sign, a cell phone battery, a twenty-dollar bill, the penlight from the case handed him a long time ago at his Saab Dedicated Delivery, and a sample-size flask of Eternity, because you never know.

A wickedly fly sister sporting a French twist hairstyle steps out of the building, strutting like she knows she's built, and knows how to please, and sho nuff could knock a strong man to his knees. She slithers into a brand new steel blue Jaguar sedan and darts into traffic. If not for the obvious uniform he would've pegged her for a blue movie star or an "exotic" dancer in high demand.

The mirrored glass-walled lobby is cool and empty.

"Obi Won Zenobi, what are you memorizing now, the names of all the companies on the NASDAQ?"

Zenobia is the nosy young front-desk girl with the Jerry Lucas mind and the Chaka Khan smile who's always good for a juicy piece of 411 whenever Pastor stops by.

"Hey, Rev." She looks up from her Saran-wrapped deli sandwich and a copy of the *Newark Star-Ledger*, her baby hair accentuated by a generous helping of Vaseline. "Why you cut your hair? Afros are back, you know."

"It wasn't an Afro, Nobi. And this is cooler."

"It's a'ight. My mother would love it. I'm telling you, you should call her. Y'all 'bout the same age."

Pastor laughs. Hard.

"Who was that maid driving off in the Jag?"

"Oh, her? I'on't know her name, but she be in here every Thursday around lunch time to renew her personal ad."

"Miss Brickhouse? She's the *last* person who needs to use the personals. She's got everything that a woman needs to get a man these days."

"She a'ight. But my mother look better."

"All she has to do is drive that car down any street in Newark and get out. They'll come running."

"You *know* that car ain't hers. Belton's rich, but y'all don't pay maids *that* good."

"Six to eight hundred a week plus health insurance is pretty tight."

"True dat. Still not enough for a Jag, though. She pro'bly work for one of them families up on the Hill who don't want people all up in their business."

"Probably? I thought that photographic memory of yours was more precise than that."

"John Doe? You know that ain't her name, Rev. She workin' for a married man cheatin' on his wife. She don't even know what she droppin' off. The envelope's always sealed."

"You're a psychic now, too?"

She smirks, peeling the plastic off her sandwich, and Pastor knows she's about to make a believer out of him.

"The address is a P.O. box, payment's always cash, and the ad never changes: very generous MWM seeking attractive black females for discreet fun. Now I don't know if sister girl married or not, but she *definitely* ain't white."

"And she's definitely not a man."

"Well, I wouldn't go that far. I was watchin' Jerry Springer the other day? Trus' me, Rev. You never know."

"Some kinky people up on that Hill, huh?"

"There's kinky people all over." She bites into the sandwich and Pastor realizes it's homemade—sardines on white—and 18 years of Saturday morning breakfasts flash through his mind and immediately his hunger leaves. Zenobia chomps on the sandwich and glances at his portfolio. "Don't tell me you need to make another change for Sunday."

"As a matter of fact," he unzips it and hands her the new sermon title and scripture verse to print in the Houses of Worship section of Saturday's paper, "I do."

"This is the fourth time since last week, Rev."

"I know. The others all seemed perfect when I started on them, but by the time I got half-way through the exegesis they just didn't feel right anymore. And this message has to be perfect."

"Daaaaag. Who you got coming, the President or somp'm?"

"Something like that."

"I hope they worth all this torture you puttin' yourself through."

"Oh, they're worth it. No doubt. Listen, I need to add something for tomorrow, too?"

She swigs her Fruitopia and before she can replace the cap the smell of alcohol wafts past his nostril and he realizes it's homemade, too.

"Now Rev, we talked about this already. You tryin' to get me fired?" She wipes her lips with her palm and covers up a small burp. "You remember what Max Sr said."

He pushes to her the manila envelope containing the small passport headshot of Anemone that Ike scavenged for him and the obituary they drafted together at Ike's kitchen table after they rolled the body out and they got their chance to talk again.

"This was a real tragedy, Nobi. Her husband's claiming to be a Falasha and wants her buried within 24 hours. I had to work hard just to convince him to have the funeral at the church tomorrow instead of at a funeral home later today, so please, do whatever you have to do to get Max Sr to run this for tomorrow. Even though you guys are an afternoon paper, it'll be better than nothing."

Her eyes light up. "When you gon' call my mother?"

"I'll call her. Just hook me up, okay?"

"Oh my Gawwwwd!"

"What?!"

Her eyebrows are practically bumping her hairline as she stares in disbelief at the headshot. "It's Tropical Breeze."

"No, her name's Anemone Allon. I'm sure it's in your paper today. You didn't read it yet?"

"Just 'cause I work here don't mean I gotta read this garbage. And that might be her name, but to me she Tropical Breeze. She be in here every week with her little accent. Pay cash, too."

She stabs under the counter, stretches open a copy of yesterday's *Mirror* on the counter top in front of Pastor, and points to an ad in the Classifieds. There are two others like it, advertising a blonde and a redhead much less imaginatively. But this one stands out:

TROPICAL BREEZE!

Want to be blown away by a beautiful Caribbean Queen? I'll be your Private Dancer. Page me: 555-BLOW for a discreet in call appointment.

First Baptist's subscription copy of the *Mirror* is waiting for Pastor near the back door rolled up in a red rubber band when he gets back to the office. The phone rings every few minutes as the news begins to spread along the congregational gripevine that Anemone took a bullet to the head last night and her funeral would be held at the church tomorrow morning. Pastor had instructed each deacon to call someone who in turn was to call someone else until every member of First Baptist had been notified--a system he's not too thrilled with because of its vulnerability to abuse by disgruntled members. Most of the people calling want more information than the deacons gave up or the *Mirror*'s front page story revealed under the screaming headline: SUICIDE IN THE MEWS!

So much for the murder angle. Pastor unrolls the paper and can't believe what he's reading. Max reporting that BPD ruled the death a suicide, but that a source close to the investigation revealed details about the crime scene that raised disturbing questions about the merits of a suicide ruling to close the case. Max found out about the raw egg and the bullet in the floor, but it's the part about the video camera that's mugging Pastor's attention. Max quotes Ike saying neither he nor Anemone ever owned a video camera. And the one found in his deejay booth was missing a tape.

Mayor Miglianacco, Chief Ellis, Sears, and Brian Mulady are all quoted in the story giving variants of the same predictable reaction: there hasn't been a murder in Belton in 5 years, and that was by poisoning; crime is not welcome and will never be tolerated in Belton; but suicide is a tragic fact of American life that we have little control over. And hidden between the lines is concern about the effect this could have on Sunday's Belton Showcase if it were ruled a murder.

To say that Pastor is still conflicted about his feelings for Anemone is a gross understatement. She was the only person on the planet who could instantly turn him into hot ice, making him so fiery with passion and so frozen with anger in the same minute. There were times he wanted her out of his life forever, never wanted to see her again. But not like this. Maybe it's guilt again, but it's rat-a-tat-tatting in his knower now that ruling her death a suicide means somebody's getting away with her murder; and that anointing to help starts surging and flowing again and he knows he's got to do something.

Pastor snatches the phone, calls BPD, and asks to speak with Chris Sears. And check out the secretary acting like she doesn't know who Sears is, trying to protect her from the flood of calls she must be getting now. Pastor considers it a pretty poor telephone acting job. As a consolation prize she lets him speak with McManus.

"McManus, what are you guys doing over there? This was no suicide. You said so yourself."

"What can I say, Rev." He doesn't sound like the same passionate McManus from the crime scene. He sounds like an android. Or maybe it's just sleep deprivation. "Sometimes we jump to conclusions in the heat of the moment, and then things come up that make us change our tune."

"Things come up? What things? She was murdered and then it was staged to look like a suicide. And I hate to say it, but the closest person to her looks guilty as sin."

"I thought so too, Rev, but Mr. Allon had no motive. Not even an insurance policy on the wife or nothing. And the M.E.'s sticking to the 10 p.m. time of death, so Mr. Allon's alibi pretty much checks out."

"*Pretty much* checks out?"

"He said he called his wife at home yesterday afternoon and told her he'd be at Donald Mason's house in Irvington last night watching the game, so he'd be home late and she didn't have to cook. I talked to Mason and two of Allon's other employees, and they all said the same thing. Everybody went straight from work to Mason's house to watch the game. They say Allon called home to check on her at the end of the 1st quarter. That was around 9:40. And you said yourself that the phone was ringing when she went inside. They also said nobody left until about 1 this morning."

"So it's three against one."

"And in court that would stand up. He has a decent alibi."

"Well why did it take him so long to call anyone? They say he left around 1, but he didn't call me until 2:30, and it only takes 5 minutes to get here from Irvington."

"Sometimes that happens, I guess. They say everybody handles shock differently. He said the first thing he did when he found the body was search the house, thinking it must've been a robber who could still be in the house. That musta used some time."

Man, Pastor wants to spill so badly what he knows about Anemone, that she was trickin'-n-treatin' through the classifieds. If Ike found out that his wife was sexing down anybody who had her number and a quarter that would be sufficient motivation for killing her. And Ike could have easily taken the pager out of Anemone's bag and erased its memory before he called Pastor. But, he knows he can't say anything. Zenobia would never admit that she gave out private information regarding a customer. She'd be fired. And not only would Pastor be responsible, but then he would *have to* date her mother.

"I don't think you're giving Ike enough credit. He's not only a smart guy, he's shrewd, too. It took both to build his business to where it is now. He could've told those guys to say he was there all night. He's their boss. If they need their jobs, they say he was there."

"Anything's possible, Rev. But they tell me we can only work with concrete evidence."

"Well what's this I read about a possible videotape of the murder? Did you guys look for one? Go through the tapes in the house? Anything?"

"There's no tape. They say that's just some more Max Candy makeup, trying to sensationalize the story and make a name for himself."

"Really? Are you the same McManus I met last night? It's not creation ex nihilo. I saw the camera on the tripod myself when I went into the deejay booth to call you guys. And I *know* you saw it, too."

"But there was no tape in it," said McManus.

"The killer's not going to leave it behind," Pastor says.

"Are you suggesting someone brought in a video camera to tape themselves committing murder, and then left the camera?"

"When you put it like that it does sound kinda far-fetched, but why not? Crazier things have happened. People like to video themselves doing everything these days. He steals a camera, videos the murder, takes the tape and leaves the camera to taunt you guys."

"Rev, all I can say is stick to preaching and leave the detective work to us."

"Ike said he'd never seen it before and that they never owned one. How do you know he's not lying? Did you guys check out the serial number to find out where it was purchased? That *could* tell you who it belongs to, or at least who bought it."

"Rev, I understand your frustration, but I'm sorry. There's nothing I can do about it. My hands are tied. As far as BPD is concerned, it's officially a suicide."

"Wow. Where's Sears? Shouldn't she be there? Let me talk to her."

"She's not here, Rev. Sorry. She gave you a cell phone number though, didn't she? Try her on that."

All Pastor gets is Sears's voice mail. He's so frustrated he doesn't even leave a message.

He stares at the blank page of MS Word on his computer screen. When Anemone married Ike she lost her money, her freedom, and her life. Literally. Now it looks like she'll be denied ultimate justice as well. And Pastor can't imagine what else he can do to get it for her now. He tries not to think about that anymore, and instead focuses on the effect the things he's just learned about Anemone from Zenobia will have on his eulogy.

Not much about Anemone surprises him because she was a walking enigma, a beautiful bundle of contradictions. He'd known since the day they met that there were two very different sides to her. In public she was sweet and demure and well-liked by all, but in private she was absolutely predatory. Still he's stunned by Zenobia's revelation and sits at his desk trying to wrap his mind around it.

Anemone Allon was turning tricks!

According to Zenobia, she'd been running the same ad for about a year. That explains why she was carrying a pager.

But how did she get away with it for a whole year? And where did she meet her clients for "discreet in call appointments" when she couldn't even leave the house to get groceries five blocks away at ShopRite without submitting to Ikean Inquisitions and to-the-minute phone checks? Unless, of course, she was meeting her clients at home while Ike was at work.... Maannn!, that would be scandalous, treacherous, sneaky....

Maannn!, that would be Anemone.

But why turn tricks? And in Belton? Just because she was angry with Ike for neglecting her and taking her for granted? Or maybe she really *was* planning her getaway? Pastor has to decide if he's going to rewrite the corny eulogy he started working on in his head last night at Ike's house, realizing that the more time he spends on it, the less time he has to invest in the sermon that will shape his future.

He's prepared to get very little work done again today. Without a secretary he's stuck answering the phone and regurgitating the same lines over and over, so it's a welcome reprieve when a call slips through from Cornel.

"Yo, Doc, I know you're busy, but you gotta come down here right away. You'll be gone 45 minutes tops. Tell 'em you took a late lunch."

"Why?"

"Oliphant's here. Walked in 5 minutes ago and ordered enough to feed my choir. But you know how fast this fool eats, so you better hurry up."

Maybe it's avoidance behavior. Maybe it's fear of failure. Maybe it's just simple anger. Whatever it is, it's got Pastor peeling out of the parking lot and heading over to Shamblee's. Weaving through traffic up South Orange Avenue he's replaying in his mind how he'll confront Oliphant. Neither threatening nor reprimanding him, he'll tell him he can *have* this church if he wants it that bad; and he'll find out if Oliphant's serious about blowing him away, because if he is, maybe he'll be doing them both a favor.

◊

Promised Land Baptist Church meets in an urban brick fortress over on Hunterdon Street, one block off Clinton in one of the roughest sections of Newark. The Baptist Ministers' Conference of Newark and Vicinity convenes there each Monday afternoon to "network", fellowship, and pilfer sermons. Shamblee is Promised Land's pastor and founder, but since Baptists can't name churches after themselves like Pentecostals, he has to settle for the soul food restaurant he established inside the church's main building to bear his name. They say he runs a hotel out of here, too. Shamblee means business. Heavy equipment is idling in the lot being cleared next door. Last Monday they all watched the complex that used to be there implode down to rubble amidst some talk about an ambitious expansion program.

Pastor parks next to the Promised Land bus in the fenced-in lot across the street. On Monday afternoons this place is a car thief's Shangri-La. In one place, left unattended for about three or four hours, is a collection of the most expensive late model cars in town, all shiny and with low mileage. Pastor yanks his Club onto his old Saab's steering wheel, takes a deep breath, and then sniffs his way across the scorched street hot on the scent of the best slow-cooked soul food in Newark.

A barrel-chested brother he's seen before in a hard hat and sopping wet tee-shirt brushes past him on his way out, almost spilling his steaming cup of black coffee on Pastor. "Take care of yourself, man," Pastor says to him. "It's crazy dangerous out here."

"You, too," he mumbles.

All eight booths are full. Oliphant's sitting by himself in the first booth with his broad back to the door leaning over a tableful of food. Shamblee grins at Pastor from behind the counter under his hi-top chef's hat. "Hey, what you say, Hook. Slummin' again?"

"They tell me that's where the best food is, Sham."

They laugh and Pastor joins Cornel at the booth near the counter. It's jammed with empty, greasy plates and two other preachers he barely knows who refuse to be interrupted. They nod at him without missing a beat. "So this nigro gets up after my message and preaches his own. He kept us there for almost another 15 minutes. The nigro had three points *and* some illustrations!"

Cornel Brown is now a bona fide star on the black preaching circuit because he's the most curious thing the black church has seen in a long time; a white boy who can really whoop. He gets revivals thrown at him from all over the world, so naturally the preachers in the conference all suck up to him.

"And you let him keep talking?" asks Cornel. "See, that's where you missed it, Rev'en. You got to talk them down or else they'll run your show for you every Sunday. If you gon' allow him to do that you might as well go ahead and ordain him, 'cause the people ain't gon' see him as just a trustee no more."

"Yeah, he right," says the other one. "If you don't talk him down in fronta all the people everybody gon' think they can jump up on you whenever they feel like it and say whatever they want. And you can't have that."

"That's right," says Cornel. "You got to maintain control. At New Life *nobody* says a word without looking to the pulpit and getting permission from me first."

Pastor orders a bowl of smothered chicken, a side of candied yams and some cream soda, then tiptoes over to Oliphant. He's made up his mind to handle this himself because Cornel would probably want to take Oliphant into the john and pull a gun on him. The fact that Cornel feels so strongly about this tells Pastor there's still a very good chance Oliphant isn't even the one.

"What's up, Preacher," he says to Oliphant.

Oliphant nods, sucking on a neck bone, his fingers dripping with grease, his wide face expressionless over the paper napkin-turned bib tucked in his shirt collar.

"Don't let me disturb you. I've got something to run by you, just between us." He nods again. "I've gotten a few anonymous letters of inquiry about the status of First Baptist's pulpit and somebody suggested they may have come from you."

Before Pastor finishes the sentence Oliphant's showing off his gold tooth and trying to stop himself from bursting out laughing. "So what you think, I want your church?"

"Do you?"

"Doc, lemme ease your mind some. When I was candidating for First Baptist I wanted it so bad because of the prestige and the location. But lately I been feeling like you gettin' that church over me was the best thing that could've ever happened to me. You see what I'm driving now, and where I'm living? My church may be small, Doc, but they take good care of me. So I sure don't wanna leave where I got control to go where some crazy nigro is gonna try to make me live in their outhouse and keep track of my every move, and *then* try to run me outta there if I speak up. Doc, it's your house now, and Gawwd bless ya wit' it." The dam bursts and he starts laughing so hard tears are pouring into his pigs' feet.

"Thanks for clearing that up, Preacher. Remember, this was just between me and you." And about fifty other preachers by Monday night if Oliphant is like most of the others.

Pastor bounces over to the counter and takes his order to go. He's already out the door before Cornel jumps up to give chase and grabs his elbow on the sidewalk out front.

"Where you going? What happened? Did he fess up?"

"Yeah."

"See, I told you Mary would help."

"It's not him."

"But you just said he confessed."

"Yeah, he confessed that it wasn't him."

"And you believe him over Mary?"

Pastor gives him that whada-*you*-think look.

"Doc, you one crazy preacher."

"Maybe, but Oliphant isn't." And he'd have to be to want Pastor's church over his.

Pastor leaves Cornel standing in the middle of the street with his hands on his hips and returns to a load of messages on his voice mail.

He spends the next two hours returning calls, answering the phone, and in between, writing Anemone's eulogy. With each paragraph the noise from the imp on his left shoulder intensifies in his ear: *Forget about it! There's nothing you can do! She's dead, and finding her killer won't bring her back!* But it's the Holy Ghost on his right shoulder who's really bugging him. He keeps whispering: *You know the right thing to do.*

And the truth is he does. He saves what he's written so far and shuts down the computer. Without betraying Zenobia, or slandering the defenseless dead, he's going to have to tell Sears about Anemone's alter ego.

CHAPTER 6

Pastor Hook cuts the classified out of his copy of the *Mirror*, crosses out *Tropical Breeze!* and writes *Anemone Allon* in its place. He slips it inside a plain white envelope with no return address and scrawls DETECTIVE SERGEANT CHRIS SEARS, BELTON POLICE DEPARTMENT, 100 BELTON AVENUE, BELTON, NJ, 07070 on the front with his left hand, sticks a self-adhesive stamp on it, grabs his keys and heads for the post office on Vose Avenue, just off Belton. Hopefully she'll get this tomorrow morning before the funeral, run the number, and put the pieces together. It certainly looks to Pastor like Ike is their man. Maybe with a motive established they'll reopen the investigation, build a circumstantial case and arrest Ike before the funeral, sparing the congregation and Pastor the spectacle of false grief at the grave.

Uh oh. Pastor stands in the hot parking lot, frozen.

Pastor doesn't consider the earth his mother and he's never given a dime to Greenpeace, but he does put his half-full recyclables bin out once a week so he can't in good conscience fire up the old Saab for a two block drive, because then he'll be just like his parents who still drive to their friend's house one block around the corner for their weekly Pokeno game. Instead he stuffs his keys back into his pocket and sets out on foot to do his part in the effort to replenish the ozone layer, and he tells himself that it can't be any worse than a midday hike along open trail with his teepee-mates back at Camp Orenda in upstate New York in the middle of July. By the time he crosses Second Street he's conceding that he's made a mistake, though; but only a wimp would turn back now, so he keeps going.

This New Jersey sun feels closer to his head than usual. The humid air is clinging to his white Nehru shirt. Every step sounds like eggs sizzling on a griddle under the soles of his brogues.

Outside the post office he spots Ike pulling off in his Vette from behind a new, gleaming white Range Rover parked in front of the building in a No Parking area, but Pastor's so desperate for that cool air-conditioned lobby that he doesn't even bother trying to flag Ike down.

He drops the envelope in the mail slot, and, since he's both pastor and secretary--for the price of one--makes for FBC's P.O. box with his eyes closed, savoring the cool, condensed air. And bumps into something soft and small. She was turning the corner from the corridor of newer P.O. boxes. And like Pastor, not looking where she was going. Probably sorting through her handful of mail. Mail that goes flying to the floor along with her. Pretty young thing, she's sprawled on the polished ceramic-tiled floor with envelopes covering the skirt of her expensive looking pink suit and white silk stockings.

"Are you okay? I'm sorry, I didn't see you coming." Pastor reaches down to help her up.

"Don't you dare put your filthy hands on me." She pulls the hem of her skirt over her clamped knees. "You should've been looking where you were going."

She's blonde and porcelain pale. Pastor has the feeling he's seen her before, and the good sense not to mention it. She's too pretty and too fragile for such ugly manners and harsh speech; or to be on her knees like she is, scraping up envelopes.

"I'll get those."

"Don't touch anything!"

"It's no problem, I'm already down here. It's the least I can do."

She snatches out of Pastor's hand the small stack he'd gathered and scrambles to her feet. Pastor is still stooping as she booms through the door under the mural depicting the Greek army storming through the opened gates of Troy. Stooping because he still can't believe what he's just seen.

All the envelopes were addressed to the First Free Church of Belton, which sounds like a part of the Free Church in America. The FCA. The same initials on the gun in Anemone's hand. The possible connection is one thing, but Pastor is more stunned by the very idea that there could be a Free Church in Belton.

He gets to the door in time to see her pull away in the white Range Rover, and even from this distance she still looks vaguely familiar.

Pastor cuts around the corner to pick up First Baptist's mail and finds another letter from his anonymous friend: "Last chance. Get out now or die." He pulls out Cassie, his Casio electronic organizer—he promises himself again that one day he'll get a Palm Pilot—and the closest thing he has to a secretary, punches up Gentry Charlesworth's direct number, and dials it on his cell phone as he stops at the window.

"Gentry, it's Antonio...yeah, well thanks for not hanging up on me. Listen, you have a few minutes? I'd like to stop by."

Rose is standing behind the wide counter beaming.

"Just got your hair done, huh? Looks good," Pastor says.

"Thanks, Rev. I do it just for you, you know. I see you get yours cut, too. It look good. When we going out?"

"How about Sunday morning, eleven a.m.?"

She puckers up and choopses, the way Pastor's mother and other West Indian women do, sucking air through the sides of her clenched back teeth.

"If I send something to a Belton address today," Pastor asks. "Will it get there by tomorrow morning?"

"Depends on what part of town it's going and when you drop it off today. Anything before one get delivered tomorrow for certain. After that I can't guarantee it."

"Thanks, Rose. You're still my favorite flower. You know that, right?"

"Still waiting to be plucked, Rev."

♪

Gentry Charlesworth recently celebrated his twentieth anniversary as pastor of the First Presbyterian Church of Belton. As president of the Belton Area Ministerial Alliance, Gentry makes it his business to know about any new congregations threatening to spring up in the city. He's also a member of the RBTF.

First Pres is located on the triangle where Belton and Irvington Avenues meet Academy Street, diagonally across from City Hall. The entire two block walk Pastor is thinking, *This must be what it's like to walk on hot coals*. By the time he gets there his face is like a waterfall, his shirt collar feels like it's just been papier-mâchéd to his neck, and the two deep scratches through his loins are beginning to burn and sting again.

"Antonio, how are you?" Gentry clasps Pastor's hand with his long pianist fingers. His slight frame belies his background, and his innocent good looks are deceiving.

"Hot and confused, Gentry." Pastor sits on the cool burgundy leather couch in the spacious office and mops the sweat from his face and neck with the hand towel Charlesworth hands him from his private bathroom. Pastor lets his eyes soak in the 200 year old stained-glass windows and the soft light they filter in from heaven. "I need your help."

"Sorry to hear about what happened last night. I just finished reading about it. There hasn't been a murder in Belton in 5 years, and that one was by poisoning."

Pastor smiles at the observation like he's just seen the photo of an old friend, then asks Charlesworth what he knows about a Free Church in Belton. As usual, Charlesworth comes off condescending in his attempt at reassurance.

"Do you know much about the Free Church, the organization?"

"Remember you're talking to a former prison chaplain," Pastor says. "I've dealt with some of their members, I've seen the tats, I've glimpsed the literature. They've been linked to Elohim City and the Christian Identity movement, the same folks who gave us Timothy McVeigh."

"That's never been proven. Merely alleged."

"Gentry, I think I know these guys. We all know what they believe, what they stand for. They espouse a racist theology that sounds like a more virulent strain of Armstrongism. According to them Anglo-Saxons and Celtics are God's chosen people. And their followers have a long history of racial violence."

"That may be a little strong. I haven't found them to be that way."

"Of course not, you're white. They see you as one of them. These guys believe all non-whites are descendants from the 'seed of Satan'."

"Not much different than Farrakhan and the Nation of Islam teaching that all whites are devils."

"Actually, the Five Percenters teach that. There's a difference between the two."

"Well, if the Five Centers—"

"Five *Per*centers, Gentry. The Five *Per*cent Nation."

"Whatever. If the Five Cents Nation wanted to set up a mosque or a temple or whatever they worship in, here in Belton, we would welcome them like anybody else. We believe in the free exercise of religion. That's what this country was founded on."

"Even if that religion involves murdering innocent people as part of its ritual?"

"Murder? Is that what this is about? You think the Free Church might be responsible for the death of that woman last night?"

"Given what I know about them, it was the first thought that entered my mind when I saw those letters addressed to the First Free Church of Belton. In fact, if I had to make up a suspect list, they'd be in the top two at this point. Besides, you said so yourself. There hasn't been a murder here in 5 years. They show up, and a black woman with no known enemies winds up murdered in her basement?"

"That's ridiculous. You're being extremely alarmist, not to mention racist. How is that different from whites immediately suspecting all black males whenever an unexplained crime is reported? And this wasn't a crime. It was ruled a suicide."

Pastor understands the comparison, but his suspicions are founded on the FCA's recent behavior, which they themselves publicly admit is representative of their collective purpose and methodology. Taken to its logical conclusion Charlesworth would have to admit the comparison is unbalanced. But Pastor doesn't have the time to pursue it to its logical conclusion right now, nor the desire to argue with another man of the cloth. The Apostle Paul advised Timothy and Titus to avoid these sorts of contentions because they're unprofitable and produce strife. So, Pastor lets it go.

"Doesn't the RBTF have a problem with this? A racist church in a community where we're talking about creating racial harmony and balance?"

"They're a small congregation, not even 10 members. They're not hurting anybody."

"Really? Are you sure about that? And what about Fellenbaum and Halpern? Are they laissez faire about this, too?"

"The rabbis are of the same opinion as the rest of us: if we oppose them or try to keep them out, the publicity it would generate would be counterproductive to the Task Force's aims."

"You do realize that's what the German churches said about Hitler."

"Antonio, I think you're making too big a deal about this. I've met some of them. They're not killers. Maybe if you'd been coming to the BAMA meetings and participating in the discussions we had about it you'd be less concerned, or at the very least you could have shared your views and maybe influenced some of the others earlier."

He went there. And Pastor is defenseless. He attended all the monthly BAMA meetings his first year as pastor of First Baptist. It was all he could do to stay awake during those endless sessions of rehashed minutiae about the last meeting, and constant requests to participate in poorly attended afternoon services recognizing causes contrived by people looking for something to keep themselves busy. So, instead he began attending the weekly fellowships with Cornel and the other Newark ministers exclusively. Charlesworth took it personally, as if Pastor's rejection of his organization was a rejection of him.

"Your congregation is what, about 15% black now?" Pastor asks.

"We're up to almost 25% African-American," he says, swelling. "So, actually, if there *was* a hit list, I'd probably qualify for it."

"Twenty-five percent? When did that happen? According to the RBTF you've crossed the comfort line. So, how do some of your black members feel about having a Free Church in their back yard?"

"To tell you the truth, none of them have ever approached me about it."

"So why bring it up to them, huh?"

"No. Why stir up trouble."

"So, where are they meeting?"

"What? Who?"

"The FCA. Where are they meeting? ...What, you don't want to tell me?"

"I just don't want you to go causing any trouble like you did last time. Especially not now, it'll ruin everything we've been working for."

"That teacher was clearly unjustified in what she did. She deserved to be removed. If the script had been flipped and we were dealing with a forty year-old black man having a sexual relationship with his 18 year-old white female student, he would've been lynched by the media, law enforcement, the PTA, and City Hall. But a white woman seduces her black student and everyone wants to blame the boy? And then you guys come out with a statement about parents inculcating a sense of morality and sexual restraint in their kids? That was definitely theatre of the absurd material."

"But did the education of all the kids in the district have to be interrupted just so you could make your point?"

"It was only one day. And that *was* a part of their education. Scripture teaches that all authorities are ordained by God, but Jesus also taught us that sometimes civil disobedience is necessary. When Jesus knew the authorities were looking for him he didn't just surrender to them right away, he avoided them because his time hadn't come yet. Hopefully those kids learned that along with doing good, we're also called to stand up against evil. So, will you tell me where they're meeting or not?"

"They're not dumb rednecks, Antonio. They're smart people."

Pastor looks at Charlesworth with a patient calmness that conceals his burning desire for the address.

After a short silence he says, "I can't. I know you too well. You'll just raise unnecessary hell."

"I understand. Thanks for your time and honesty."

From the lobby of First Pres Pastor calls Cornel, then Dexter. Neither of them knows about a Free Church in Belton. Dex called Malisa, but she says she doesn't know either, and she works in the Hall. Pastor would rather not ask Max Jr for a favor. He always collects on them, with interest. But Charlesworth was right. Pastor would find a way to raise the dead alright. He just doesn't agree that it would be unnecessary. He calls Max who promises to get back to him. Then he marches back to his office so focused he's not even feeling the heat anymore.

He's back behind his desk not even five minutes, head in hand, praying for more self-control and insight, when Max calls.

"They're renting a house on Fairview, just off Irvington."

"Are you serious? Last night's murder happened on that block."

"Tell me something I don't know. Got anything I can use?"

"Like what?" Pastor asks.

"Like a quote for tomorrow's piece on why Mrs. Allon's death was ruled a suicide."

Another thing Pastor prefers not to do: giving quotes off the top of his head; but at least he'll be paying this debt off before interest accrues.

"Sure. Ready? I was the first person on the scene and what I saw was clearly a murder victim. One of BPD's detectives said so, too. Perhaps police and city officials are more concerned about the success of the RBTF's Sunday Showcase than they are about justice for a murdered First Baptist member and the ultimate safety of the entire community. There's definitely a murderer out there. Are we going to let this person roam free to kill again? Are we genuflecting to the almighty dollar again? Did you get all that?"

"I had the tape rolling. Thanks, Reverend."

"One more question for you," Pastor says. "Who's their pastor?"

"They don't have one yet. They're still a mission. They're looking."

"So, who's the missionary?"

"I don't know."

"You planning to do a piece on them?"

"Nah. They're too small. Nobody'll care. When they get bigger, or when you give me something about them I can use, whichever comes first."

♩

Pastor turns onto Fairview and sees it pulling away from the driveway of the second house from the corner. The same steel blue Jaguar that the brickhouse maid drove out of the *Mirror* parking lot earlier. He can't see through the deep tint in the windows as it careens around the corner. He's less than surprised that the address Max gave him is also the second house from the corner.

There's no signage outside. Nothing to even hint that this modest colonial is a house of worship. Pastor thought these things only existed in the 'hood.

No one responds to the doorbell, but he hears activity inside. There's a tiny camera perched at an angle under the soffit. Maybe they're hoping he'll go away. He's sure their monitor has convinced them he's not a member dropping off his tithes.

Jesus was right, though. Keep knocking and doors open.

"May I help you?" It's the same blonde from the post office, and the venom is turning her pretty patrician face into a bitter lemon.

"Praise the Lord, my sister in Christ! It's so good to see you again. I was told this is a new place of worship in town. May I come in and learn more about your fellowship?"

He wonders if that was too far over the top and decides to tone it down just a bit because she seems to be charm proof.

Her attitude is still speaking for her. She hates the fact that she can't say no. Her neck is reddening just below the tightly coiled golden bun she pulled her hair back into this morning.

The last house church Pastor preached in was on 128th Street in Richmond Hill, Queens. Started by a convict who mended his ways through chapel inside. He used the skills he learned in the prison woodshop to build all the pulpit furniture and the pews. He'd knocked out all the walls on the first floor and was able to cram one hundred into that narrow colonial on a Sunday morning. That's kind of what Pastor's expecting here. That rough-hewn look. Ceilings dropped so low you can't raise your hands in the pulpit without bringing down a chalk and gypsum rain. Pews so close together they make legroom on a budget airline feel like the back seat of a limo.

But he's humbled, awed when he steps inside this place. The way he was the first time he walked into St. Patrick's Cathedral, but for a very different reason. There's no sense of the majesty of God in this place. In fact it's a monument to hate, and the power of the almighty...dollar.

The entire first floor looks like the offices of a hi-tech ad agency, only this is decorated in a postmodern white supremacist motif. It has to be the very nerve center of hate in Belton. Huge confederate flag along one wall, and above it a banner reading: HERITAGE NOT HATE. Swastikas. KKK emblems. A poster reading: STOP THE HATE, SEPARATE. On another wall, their logo: a white Celtic cross with the words FREE CHURCH OF AMERICA encircling it. Computers. Printers and faxes churning out hate posing as white pride. Copiers whirring, mass-producing seeds of intolerance. There are no people and just a few things in this world that Pastor allows himself to hate. That word—tolerance—and its antonym—intolerance—are two of them, because they're usually used like Rolaids to relieve closeted racists of their obligation to love.

But in this context he'd settle for a little tolerance.

One pamphlet-filled box is labeled: BELTON ACADEMY YOUNG REPUBLICANS CLUB. Below a large framed portrait of David Duke is a bookcase filled with scores of copies of *The Turner Diaries* and RaHoWa CDs. Racial Holy War. That's all he used to hear from boom boxes on G wing. That's where all the billies with shaved heads and Celtic crosses and number 14 tats were caged. And that's where he learned that among white supremacists the number 14 is shorthand for the fourteen words, *We must secure the existence of our people and a future for white children*, a shibboleth coined by David Shame, a former real estate broker who lost his license for refusing to commit "race treason" by selling homes in white neighborhoods to blacks because he believes the inevitable result of racial integration is death for whites by miscegenation. Shame became a member of The Silent Brotherhood, a terrorist organization linked to the Free Church. They believe in strictly separating the "political arm" of white resistance from the "armed party", and they wage a form of RaHoWa they term "mature, capable, ruthless, self-motivated, silent, deadly, and able to blend into the masses"; but like most people governed by hate, Shame shot himself in the foot by violating his own beliefs, for although he functions in the political arm of The Brotherhood, he also took up arms and was eventually convicted and jailed for his participation in the murder of a Jewish talk show host and now remains active in prison contributing to a column, "Focus Fourteen", published by his wife, Geneva's Fourteen Word Press.

The woman is back at her desk and picking up the phone, pretending to ignore Pastor as he walks around. Finally he asks, "Do we know each other from somewhere other than the post office?" She answers only with a cool stare. "May I have some literature about your church? I'm really interested in learning more about the Free Church."

She's not doing a very good job. Postmodern white supremacists are necessarily more subtle than those who ruled the Jim Crow south. She's decided she can't credibly ignore Pastor any longer and so looks up and hisses, "We don't have any available at this time."

"Well how about your pastor? May I see him? Talk about the requirements for membership? Just in case I want to join, or know somebody who does."

"We don't have a pastor."

"Oh. ...Is this the sanctuary down here, in the basement?" He opens the door.

"You can't go down there!" She jumps from her seat, and then, realizing she sounds like someone trying to hide or protect something, she sits down again and softens her tone. "Unless the pastor is here."

"The pastor you don't have."

"That's what I said."

"Well, how about upstairs?" He turns toward the staircase.

"Those are private bedrooms. Off limits."

"Let me ask you a question. Do you know where the pastor you don't have was last night around 10:00? Or any of your members for that matter, including yourself?"

Before she can give another evasive answer the front door opens with force behind it and three burly skinheads barrel in. They're wearing red suspenders and white-laced Doc Martens, the kind bootboys use for stomping parties. They look like they could be Mulady's younger brothers, and they don't say a word. Pastor's post office friend is smugging now as they close in on him. Pastor moves to his right, they move with him. He moves to his left; so do they. He steps back, they move against him.

He used to get triple-teamed a lot in high school—never in college, though, because Pete Carril just never employed that kind of offense—and he could almost hear Mr. Black's voice from the bench, "Let the pressure come to you! Stay under control!" But this is not high school basketball. He can't pass the ball and make these guys go away. So, he does the only thing a man of God should do when he's cornered by bad guys in what's supposed to be a house of worship.

He looks for a back door.

His father would probably let these punks beat him to a pulp in the name of turning the other cheek, but Pastor believes it's more like Jesus to avoid getting hit in the cheek in the first place. Everywhere he looks in scripture he finds Jesus escaping mobs intent on stoning him or pitching him headfirst over a cliff.

The path to the back of the house is blocked by boxes and desks. The only way out is through the still opened front door behind the three bootboys. Jesus escaped his angry mobs by passing right through them. Pastor prays for strength to do what Jesus did.

What a violent world.

They're holding their positions, waiting Pastor out, their glassy eyes fixed on him. So he fakes one step back, then puts his head down and rushes forward like Eric Dickerson trying to break through the line of scrimmage. That's the last thing he remembers. Maybe he should've just turned the other cheek.

He wakes up to an awful pain in his stomach, ribs, and groin; and mother Freddie on his mind. The sun is scorching his face even through the deep-blue tint of his window. There are boot prints on his shirt and pants, and a ringing pain in his left ear. He's slumped over the steering wheel of his car-turned-sauna drenched in sweat. In his mouth is a piece of card paper. It reads in bold type: THANKS FOR WORSHIPPING WITH US TODAY. PLEASE COME AGAIN. He turns it over and there's a personal message for him: ANY MORE QUESTIONS? The handwriting is so delicate. It has to be hers. And in between the waves of pain the thought keeps bobbing to the surface of Pastor's consciousness, *What are they trying to hide?*

He can still hear Coach Black growling from the sideline as he's curled up in a fetal position under the basket after a knee to the groin while taking a charge, "Come on! Suck it up! Only wimps need medical attention!"

Back in his office the phone is ringing. It's Top Brands. His video camera is finally ready. He'd brought it in for repair after dropping it at the church picnic up on the Reservation last week.

Pastor thinks about reporting his little experience to the police, but realizes it would be his word against four, and a half-hearted example of following Jesus. You can't follow his example into suffering and then abandon it once dealing with the suffering. He decides to man up and deal with his pain the way Jesus dealt with his on the cross.

"Father, forgive them. They didn't know what they were doing. They're blinded by hate. From my heart I forgive them. Give me the grace to walk in that forgiveness toward them."

Pastor leans back in his chair, begins mulling over the fact that he's still alive, and a fresh wave of gratitude comes over him. The steel toes on those boots they wore are designed to kill, or at least maim. But they exercised restraint. They must have. They didn't kick him in the head. Thank you, Jesus. They probably didn't want any bad pub. So, why would they leave a gun with their initials etched into its barrel at a murder scene? Evil needs anonymity to achieve its aims. But they *would* be an easy frame for somebody who wants to murder black people.

Pastor responds to persistent image in his mind with a call to Mother Freddie. When someone inexplicably surfaces on his mind and won't go away it's usually the Big Guy hinting for him to minister to them. But Mother Freddie isn't home, and now that he's exhausted all the Spirit gave him to intercede in prayer for her, he formulates his plans for the rest of the day.

His itinerary is simple: go to the Livingston Mall and pick up his camera, a new bottle of Eternity, and an extra cell phone battery to replace the one in his portfolio. And maybe get something else to eat there because getting his behind kicked has made him hungry again. And then if he's still feeling this way, even though he hates hospitals, stop by St. Barnabas on his way back and get something strong for this dizziness and the pain in his head and torso. All that before his 6:00 meeting tonight with Cornel's shackin' couple, dinner with Sister Walker, and his two hours of drop-in pastoral counseling.

❧

He snaps his Platinum Visa on the glass counter top at Macy's, next to the Calvin Klein bag with his two ounces of Eternity and gift samples of CK be. The clerk, an older black woman with short, permed hair, librarian-type reading glasses on a chain, and nails chewed down to the cuticle, is throwing him shade. He used to think wearing a suit was an automatic buffer against racism or prejudice. Not true, especially not against black prejudice. He's not wearing a tie, just his now-dried Nehru shirt under the now brushed-off bone Perry Ellis Mother made the

Pastor's Aide get him from Barney's for his birthday last year—along with a few others and a couple pairs of Alfani wingtips.

He's been in this situation enough times to know what she's thinking: young black man; no wedding band; apparently no job because it's still the latter part of a normal work day; nattily dressed; trendy timepiece; flashing a Platinum Card. Sophisticated credit card thief or one of the handful of young black men gainfully employed and in charge of their own schedules?

"Let me see your driver's license."

The contempt pours out over the lenses on the bridge of her nose. Pastor hands over the license. She draws it close to her face, comparing the signatures like an old treasury agent examining a suspect hundred. She slides his credit card through the authorization machine and it's like he can feel her hoping that a denial or theft code will pop up on the screen. He signs and she walks away without looking up. Tucking his card back into his wallet Pastor wonders if people like her sleep well at night, and if they have sons of their own. Then he whispers a prayer for her salvation (even though she probably goes to somebody's church), and for the next young brother she'll wait on.

He walks away thinking, for the thousandth time, about putting on all his credit cards the three letters in front of his name that can eliminate many of these experiences: Rev. And for the thousandth time he decides against it, because there are some places he still needs to go where those three letters are even more delimiting than the color of his skin.

Downstairs, he spies a couple of mall surveyors--a bespectacled man and a toothy woman wearing a rhinestone JESUS pin above her left breast. When their eyes meet as he nears them they turn the backs of their heads to him.

Until this moment he'd always assumed that one day he'd age into, marry into, or earn into the hallowed demographic that mall surveyors seem to be attracted to. But there's something complicitly sinister about the way they turned away from him that forces a repressed truth into his consciousness: only Eddie Murphy's cosmetician or Michael Jackson's plastic surgeon could ever get him into that demographic. For the first time it occurs to his conscious mind that he's never seen a black mall surveyor, nor a black responder.

♪

Pastor pays for his camera and the cell phone battery at Top Brands Electronics. Like most American men, he can never just walk in and out of an electronics store without sampling all the new gadgets. Before leaving he plays with the new generation Pentium computer on display that's so jack rabbit-fast it makes his P4 processor seem like a turtle. He tickles the keys on a keyboard, and taps on an electronic drum set. When he begins fidgeting with the new Viewcam video cameras, thinking about upgrading his, the clerk moves in.

CHAPTER 7

"Doc Hook?" He's squinting, his wavy black locks flecked with dandruff and hanging in his acned face.

"Do we know each other?" His nameplate reads Chuck and he looks like any of a handful of nondescript Belton Academy students Pastor may have talked to during black history month or MLK day or history department field trip tours through the church intended to enrich their understanding of black culture.

"Not really, Doc. I just finished up my freshman year at St. Thomas in the criminology department? You gave a righteous lecture on black liberation theology to my Intro to Religion class. I really dug that, man. It's the only lecture I remember from the whole course. You said a whole lot, but just Cone's concept about Jesus being black and the entire thing about reinterpreting the term black as a political construct rather than just phenotype was way cool, dude. Way cool."

"Glad it stayed with you. Doctor Fenelley's a good friend. He has me give that lecture every semester."

He notices the camera in Pastor's hand. "You know, the reason I came over's because I saw you looking at that camera."

"Thanks, but I don't need any help. Just browsing."

"No, it's cool. This is just a McJob anyway, man. I don't get commissions or anything. It's that camera. When I saw you and that camera it made me realize that I'd actually met the babe that got capped last night. I know the *official* word is suicide, but I believe the reporter. It was murder, dude. Whoa! Makes you feel like part of, like, history, ya know?"

"Oh, I've got to hear this one. How do you make a connection from me and a camera to Ms. Allon?"

"I know this is gonna sound off the hook, but it's the real deal like Holyfield, Doc. I pick up the paper on my way to work this afternoon, right? And read the stuff about them finding a camera at the scene? By the way, your quotes were real heavy, man. When I check out I hope somebody'll drop words like that about me. Anyway, I see you and remember what you had to say about the babe, and see the camera you're holding and remember that she bought one just like it from me last week. Straight up! I remember now because it was my first day on this McJob and the first camera I ever sold and she asked me a lotta questions about it, saying she was upgrading from a cheaper model. She was even kinda checkin' me out a little, ya know? I was about to start kickin' it to her, but she said she had to hurry up and catch the next bus back to Belton, 'cause her husband thought she was at ShopRite."

"Oh yeah? You remember all that."

"What can I say, I got a good memory."

"A good memory. Okay, put it to work some more. Was she buying for herself, or somebody else?"

"*That* I don't remember. But I do remember she was babetious. I knew right then I could be down with the swirl, ya know?"

"Down with the swirl?"

"You know, Doc." He elbows Pastor, grinning. "Chocolate and vanilla?"

"Ohhh! Okay. Learn something new every day."

He exits Top Brands with a lot on his mind. For once the glass mall elevator isn't crowded, so he rides to the second floor, surrendering to the inevitability of a St. Barnabas visit for some hard drugs.

Burger King is empty except for a vagrant trying to pass as a shopper. Pastor and his tender ribs wedge into a booth with some chicken tenders and a vanilla shake. Over the throbbing in his head he recalls the church picnic on Saturday, and Ike's face when he mentioned the camera to him last night. Why would Anemone buy an expensive video camera and not let anybody know she had one? Only one thing made sense. She must have been playing Candid Camera with her clients.

J

Okay, so Pastor wimps out. He submits to the battery of tests the doctor ordered and waits around for almost an hour to hear that his ribs are just bruised, not broken. She also says he has a slight concussion. She wants to keep him overnight for observation, to cover her butt as Carla used to say, but he refuses and signs himself out AMA because he just has too much to do. So much for the narcotics. All they give him is some Bacitracin for his private scratches. He'll have to make do with the extra strength Tylenol from his medicine cabinet when he gets home.

Since he's already here and in a particularly sympathetic condition, he trudges upstairs to see Sister Bessom.

He'll pray for his members in a heartbeat, but he hates hospitals.

A pastor who hates hospitals is like a surgeon who can't stand the sight of blood. He feels completely useless in hospitals, out of his element. And Thorn knows it. The sight of people clinging to life, oftentimes struggling to do so with very little dignity—although some might say there's dignity in the will to struggle alone—makes Pastor feel powerless, makes his prayers to God on their behalf feel like empty words, makes his office, his position as a spiritual leader seem like a weak joke. Like Chuck said, a McJob. He can no more help people die with dignity than he can keep them from it, yet he knows they're encouraged simply by his presence. Because the pastor has come to see them they feel they have a chance, that God somehow is now more attentive to their case, almost as if he's their spiritual attorney, their representative in the courtroom of heaven where God is a judge with a short attention span and many distractions. So many of them feel God is too busy to see about them, and think when Pastor prays God listens to him and gives their case some consideration. And that's why he pushes through his discomfort and goes to the hospitals anyway. There are times it seems like he can't even get God to come see about *him*, but He's seen God answer prayer too many times. He knows that even when He doesn't come when you call Him, He always manages to show up right on time.

Since the Benny Hinn crusade and his baptism in the Holy Ghost there's been a change in Pastor. Too many people got up out of wheelchairs, too many crutches were tossed aside. Healing's got to be for this age, too. And even though he doesn't feel like he is, scripture says he's just as valid a vessel as Benny in his white suit. So he figures if he keeps coming to the hospital, keeps showing up for duty, keeps doing what he doesn't feel equipped to do, eventually his faith is going to rise to the level where he can lay hands on the sick and see them healed instantly. The same way Jesus used to do it.

Sister Bessom's hand feels like a pack of straws with skin on it. Her IV tubes look like clear veins twined around a broom handle. Her teeth look horse-sized in her pale, gaunt face as she chomps the wafer and swallows the juice from the portable communion set Pastor keeps under the old Saab's passenger seat. His phone rings just after communion.

"What is it, Brother Thorn."

"Reverend, I'm calling a meeting. The constitution says I can do it under unusual circumstances like this if I get the signatures of a quorum of the church. Now I'm just letting you know that I have a few signatures already and I should have the rest by after the funeral, so I'm calling it for Sunday."

"What do you want to meet about *this* time, Brother Thorn?"

"With all these killings going on here we've got to do something about getting burglar bars and security lights and a full-time security guard at the church."

"There's been one murder, and it didn't happen on church property. Might you be over-reacting?"

"Look, I'm doing you a favor letting you know what I'm going to do. We'll see if the church thinks I'm over-reacting. I talk to the people. I know them. They listen to me. I've been a member of this church for over 50 years, and I know a lot of them will agree with me. Now I'll see you tomorrow after the funeral with those signatures."

"Okay. Whatever you say."

"And one more thing. I hear the cops are investigating you for Sister Allon's murder. Is that true?"

"Didn't you read the story?" I say. "They're calling it a suicide."

"All I can say is, if it's true then you've got big problems; because that would violate the character clause in the constitution. We can't have a pastor in trouble with the law. And you *were* the last one with her last night."

"No, actually there was one other person."

"And who was that?"

"The person who killed her. For all we know it could be anyone. Even one of our respected church officers."

"Now you listen to me. I don't have to take this from you, you sorry—"

Thorn slams the phone down so hard a loud 'pop!' jumps through the earpiece of Pastor's cell and jolts Sister Bessom's eyes wide open. David Henry Thorn has been behaving like a dangerously insane megalomaniac long before Pastor Hook arrived as pastor. But Pastor meant no specific disrespect when he mentioned that even a respected church officer could be the murderer. He doesn't believe Thorn's crazy enough to kill someone; not even just so he could frame Pastor. In fact Pastor is beginning to think one of Anemone's own clients must have killed her. But he knows David Henry hates him enough to turn this entire situation into a nightmare for him if God doesn't help him.

ᴊ

It's just after 6:00 when Pastor gets back to his office and finds Cornel's shackin' couple cuddling in the front seat of their Lincoln Navigator, in *his* clearly marked parking space. Not a good start at all. Things get exceedingly worse when they get out of the car and he realizes that he's been had by Cornel again. He neglected to mention one important aspect of this couple's relationship.

Burnette Adams is sitting in the black leather sofa across from Pastor looking like a player's worse nightmare. Not just fine, but *foine*. She could walk through St. Barnabas and heal the sick with just one look, or send them into cardiac arrest. The dimples give her mocha face a school girl innocence when she smiles. But the way she's draped in shape in that tight blue dress, and the way those salon braids sit on her shoulders say she'd put this look together with deadly forethought.

Biju Nnemdi-Obi is on the couch, too, holding Burnette's hand, rubbing its short unpainted manicured nails with her hammerhead thumb. She's blunt in every way: face, body, dress, manners, and speech. Back when Pastor's sister was alive he'd have definitely marked Biju as the Butch. The only time they ever talked about it directly, Mo told him she used to be a Femme before she went Butch. But he's since learned it's not so smart to make judgments about somebody's sexual orientation or behavior based on how they look or dress or talk.

They're caught in a time warp so he'll have to formulate his response to Cornel later. They've gotten past the logistics. A total of 15 people including the organist and photographer. No drama, just tastefully done. They want to jump the broom together, which they'll supply. They want a few pictures with Pastor afterwards, which make him cringe at the thought that there'll be evidence out there that could come back to haunt him in the future; and even as early as tonight in his sleep, before they're even taken. And they want to be in and out in under 30 minutes, which makes him sigh with relief. What pitches them into sudden silence and reflection, taking him back years to painful places, is the liturgy.

Deciding on the actual words to capture this occasion requires a decision about what the occasion really means, for him and them. Because although what they'll do tomorrow night at 7:00 won't be legally binding in this state, in both their views it *will* be spiritually binding. And once again he finds himself trapped in his principles. In God's principles.

"Dr. Hook, I don't know if Pastor Brown mentioned this to you, but Burnette went for a routine pap smear about a month ago and found out she has cervical cancer."

"He mentioned a cancer diagnosis, but no names or details. I'm sorry, Burnette."

She puts the dimples back on display. "I'll be fine."

"She starts chemo on Monday. We want to do this now while she's still herself. I want her to know that my commitment to her is for life, whether she's sick or well. I don't want her to ever think I'm hanging around just out of some sense of duty or obligation. This is the way this culture validates love. Committed love. Why should our sexual orientation deny us the same right? The same right to say 'I love you' in a way this culture recognizes as legitimate?"

"I agree that it shouldn't deny you that right. All I'm saying is that the words of the liturgy have a meaning that we can't arbitrarily change to suit our orientation, and that it would be fairer for all of us if we changed the words themselves. Even the Metropolitan Community Church uses a different liturgy."

"But changing the words doesn't allow us to participate with everyone else. It casts us as different. Not just different, deviant. It says we aren't capable of saying 'I love you' in the same way straight people do."

"But you *are* different. And I'm saying, Let's stop trying to redefine the difference away."

"All of this over one little word?" says Burnette.

"There *are* no *little* words, Burnie," says Biju.

"Biju, I don't care if the word 'blessed' or 'blessing' isn't mentioned in our commitment ceremony. The symbolism of the building and the presence of the pastor is enough for me."

"But words are the ultimate symbols. If we can't have the verbal symbol of blessing in our ceremony, all the physical symbology would ring hollow for me."

"Dr. Hook, I'm really grateful to you for agreeing to do this for us. You're a man of integrity and courage, but Biju's not gonna budge. She's as stubborn as a pit bull. Is there any way we can reach some kind of compromise?"

Pastor knows he's not going to find the answer to that question in their eyes, but he's looking anyway, nibbling on his bottom lip.

"Again I say, the word bless isn't just about God's approval, it's about imparting reproductive power, the ability to increase; marriages are blessed in order to produce children. So, okay, let me ask you this. Do you two ever plan to adopt?"

They look at each other as if they have a secret they don't want to let out of the bag yet.

"We've talked about it."

"Let's tell him like it is, Burnie. Dr. Hook, I'm pregnant as we speak."

Maybe they can tell that Pastor wants to ask, "How?", because they start volunteering all this information about when they decided to artificially inseminate and how difficult it was to decide what they wanted in a donor and how they will handle the questions at church. Much more info than Pastor wants at the moment.

"Was it hard to decide who would carry the baby?" he asks.

"That was the easiest part of the whole thing," says Burnette.

"She can stay beautiful," says Biju. "I'll do the grunt work. Rough as I am, I'm better equipped."

Just as blunt as she could be. Just like Mo.

Pastor struggles against his instinct to put principle before people again because the last time he was in this very situation he killed his sister. Eight years ago. Right after his ordination. She wanted him to "marry" her and her lover. He refused. They broke up soon after. She blamed him. Said she'd never speak to him again. Then a couple years later he heard she'd stopped going regularly to her job at the post office in Manhattan, and that she was hitting the pipe. Hard. She's been in and out of rehab ever since. He sees her maybe once a year. Still mad at him. Still Butch. Still hooked. She's not physically dead yet. But in every other way that counts she already is. And a part of him wishes he could have that moment back to say, "Yes, I'll do it," in spite of his theological convictions. He knows he's deep in countertransference here but Kierkegaard had a better term for what he's dealing with that doesn't come to mind at the moment.

"In light of this, and in the interest of compromise, I guess we can go ahead with the traditional vows. You've been blessed already I guess. Achieved unconventionally, but never the less, the union is technically fruitful...in a sense."

"Do you deny straight couples the traditional vows if they happen to tell you that they don't plan to have children?"

Biju ain't lettin' up and Pastor has to admit, she has him there. He's uncomfortable facing his own apparent hypocrisy and theological contradictions. "No," he says, unable to look her in the eye.

"You know, Doctor, homosexuality isn't about gender. It's about sexual orientation. No matter who I chose to sleep with, I'm still a woman."

"I hear you. The traditional language just might not accommodate present day realities. I'm still struggling with—"

"Biju, give it a rest and just thank the man, please? Dr. Hook, thank you so much."

They get up to leave and Burnette hugs Pastor at the door so hard it makes him wince; Biju gives him a cold handshake with a glare.

Once again Pastor is feeling stupid, ignorant, and insensitive in the presence of an angry lesbian. The same way he felt most of the time around his sister after she came out. Always saying the wrong things. After a while he just stopped saying anything at all. He thought he'd grown since then, but now he's thinking there's not much difference between him and those mall surveyors, or that Macy's clerk.

He's a heterosexual who believes that homosexuality is not God's original design. But aren't we all endowed with the same inalienable rights to life, liberty, and the pursuit of happiness? And who is he to define what happiness should look like for everyone? And doesn't God cause His sun to shine on the evil and the good, and send His rain on the just and the unjust? The Holy Ghost jumps up on his right shoulder again, and we all know what he's whispering in his spiritual ear. "Nigro, get a grip!"

Maannn. Pastor has a lot of growing to do. And five minutes to pick up his date for the evening.

◊

Sister Walker isn't a bad date…when she's not wagging her finger in Pastor's face. She felt like Mexican so they grabbed a booth under the big purple velvet sombrero at Que Pasa down the street from Belton Academy and gorged themselves on chimichangas. She insisted on sangria, too. He should've stopped the waitress after the first pitcher because Sister Walker's getting a little loud. He has to beg her to stop singing *This Little Light of Mine* as they leave because it's not mixing too well with the mariachi music streaming out of the overhead speakers or the people at the bar who are covering their ears and shaking their heads.

When he leaves Sister Walker at her front door his stomach and ears are full, and he's a little lighter on guilt. It's just after 7:00 so he figures he has a few minutes to kill and decides to swing by Ike's to see if he can get the truth out of him about the video camera. He only averages one-point-five drop-ins per Thursday night, and the ones who do come never show up until just before 9:00, and then usually keep him there until past 10:00.

Nobody answers at Ike's. The house is totally dark and yellow crime scene tape still hugs a couple of oaks, so he heads back to First Baptist to finish Anemone's eulogy while he waits for drop-ins and, if he's lucky, maybe make some more progress on Sunday's sermon. But all the cars in the parking lot immediately spike his Thursday night drop-in average, and his hopes of finishing the eulogy or Sunday's sermon nosedive.

Pastor pulls into his parking space and neutralizes the tortilla breath by popping a couple of Certs before getting out. The engine's still ticking on the big van parked in the handicapped spot near the walkway to the back door. He steps into the cool lower auditorium and the chatter immediately falls to silence. He counts 12 people sitting on folding chairs, but no couples. Burke Hill is in his wheelchair near the library with a pretty attendant in white by his side instead of his wife, Gloria.

He should've seen this coming. Not just because he's been praying for God to send more people for him to counsel and help on Thursday nights, but because small churches are really extended families, complete with dysfunctions and all. As popular as Anemone was, her death is bound to have a profound effect on the members. Pastor takes a deep breath, prays for God to use him, transfers the smile in his heart to his face, and prepares for a long evening of bereavement counseling. He says hello before unlocking his office door, but no one responds. He closes the door behind thinking he could really use a secretary right about now.

Pastor powers on his computer, keys in his password, and punches up the membership software he uses to track and document counseling sessions.

The first person in is the most unlikely of all his 200 members to ever show up for drop-in counseling. In fact Sadat Patterson has never actually been in his office before. At 5'7" in his bald head and Timbs, and wearing 210 pounds he doesn't look the part of a teenage drug dealer at Belton Academy—those guys are mostly white, button-down types. But that's what Sadat is. His parents are both musicians, on the road a lot, and often leave him to his own devices. He's super bright, but also a super blight on the community. He only shows up at First Baptist once in a while for Sunday School when his parents are in town.

Sadat plops into the couch. It sighs and hisses under his weight, and the spliff he has tucked behind his right ear falls to the blue pindot carpet Pastor had to buy himself because Thorn thought the dull tile under it was good enough. Pastor rolls his eyes and sticks his hand out. Sadat smirks, picks up the marijuana cigarette and tosses it onto Pastor's desk.

"Plenty more where that came from, Rev. I could hook you up if you want. Just lemme know."

"Son, it's only the grace of God that's keeping me from picking up this phone and dialing BPD," Pastor says, snatching up the spliff and tossing it into the garbage can. "How are your folks?"

"They in Vegas this week, gettin' paid. I'll tell 'em you asked about 'em when I see 'em next week."

"Rumor has it that you and Joy Gumbs have been spending a lot of time together lately," says Pastor. "I sure hope you're doing the right thing by her, because Deacon Gumbs still has that pro linebacker mentality." Joy is Willie Gumbs' oldest daughter and twice Pastor had to talk him out of crushing Sadat's face because he suspected they were having sex on his couch right after school.

"Yo, I'ma marry that girl one day, Rev," he says, slicing the air with his pudgy hand. "You watch. Deacon Gumbs ain't got nothing to worry about."

Pastor thinks about asking him what he deems worthy of worry, but decide that he's not ready for any more surprises. "So what brings you here tonight, Sadat? You want to talk about Sister Allon?"

He rubs his head and sits up in the couch. "Yo, Rev, I was checking out this magazine in the library at school last week? And one of your stories was in it, yo! I read the whole thing. It was *all* that. Reverend Snoop is a bad cat. He can find *anything*."

"Thanks," Pastor says, then quickly returns to the point. "So, how well did you know Sister Allon?"

"A lot better than you might think, Rev. A *lot* better."

"How do you feel about her death?"

"Do you think it was suicide, or murder, Rev? All the white kids are saying suicide, and all the brothers are saying murder."

"Would you feel different if it was murder?"

"Rev, you think there's really a tape out there somewhere?"

"Sadat, we're supposed to be talking about *your* feelings and there's a whole roomful of other people waiting to get in here."

"A'ight. I'ma be straight with you, Rev. Miss Allon was fine and she pushed up on me one day, so I hit it. I cut sixth period and we got freaky in her basement. Then the next week she shows me a tape of us doin' the nasty and hit me up for 5 gees. Now that she got capped I don't want that tape falling into the wrong hands, so I want you to do your Reverend Snoop thing and find it for me." He digs into the pocket of his baggy jeans and tosses a roll of bills in a rubber band onto Pastor's desk. "Here's one gee now, and you get one more when you deliver the tape."

Pastor rubs both eyes with his palms and stares at his desk calendar, searching for the most tactful way to ask him if he's crazy. "Um, Sadat...even if I were to believe this testosterone induced bragging fit on a defenseless woman, and I don't; and even if I were to believe that such a tape existed, and I don't; what in the world makes you think I have the time, ability, or desire to go find it? I'm a pastor, not a private eye."

"Aw, c'mon Rev. You can't write those preacher-detective stories without having some skills yourself. Like that old lady on *Murder, She Wrote*. I *know* you could find it, Rev. You got free access to more people and places than anybody else in this town, just like Reverend Snoop. I know you could find it. And *every*body knows you need the money."

Pastor is not just looking at the $1,000 in fresh fifties rolled up on his desk. He's fighting the urge to lust after it! Sadat is right, he *could* use the money. Maybe this is the Lord. And after talking to Zenobia, nothing Anemone's accused of would surprise him anymore. But Sadat's story just doesn't make sense. Five thousand dollars to keep it hushed that he had sex with the hottest black woman in town? When Pastor was 16 and not yet serious about the Lord he would've begged her to show it to the whole world. He wouldn't put blackmail past Anemone, but how do you blackmail a 16 year old boy with sex? Does he care about Joy that much? Does he fear Willie that much? Pastor has no clue what Sadat's trying to pull, but he knows he wants no part of it. What he wants is to help the roomful of people outside his door as much as he can and then get back to his eulogy and sermon. He picks up the knot of 50s and hits the B with it on Sadat's FUBU tee shirt. "I'm sorry, Sadat,

I'm not your man," Pastor says. "Please send in the next person on your way out."

He sits staring at Pastor for a couple of seconds before saying, "Well can I have my joint back then?"

Pastor just says, "Please send in the next person on your way out."

Sadat sticks the knot back in his pocket and gets up with a frown. "I thought you was the man, Rev," he says at the door. "I shoulda figured, somebody probably writes those stories for you."

He has a couple of minutes to write, pray, and recollect his thoughts before a yellow bow-tied Marcus Turner closes the door behind him spewing a nervous stream of promises not to keep him too long. Whenever they say that Pastor knows it's going to be a while.

Marcus is a new convert and has already become one of the most faithful members of First Baptist. He was just named the new principal of Maplewood Christian School and has a beautiful white wife who attends services occasionally with their three adorable children, but has never joined.

Marcus sits on the edge of the couch, cleaning his wire-rimmed glasses with the butter cream pocket hankie from his brown plaid suit, and refocuses his attention on the carpet.

"Pastor," he begins. "I've prayed about this a long time and you're my last possible solution. I was raised among whites and attended white institutions all my life. I married Judy because I loved her very much and when making the decision never considered race. But the combination of life in Belton and your preaching have led me to rethink my position on race. I still love my wife, but I've been feeling for some time now like I'm missing a part of myself. And then Sister Allon began paying me compliments and lavishing me with attention. One thing led to another and we ended up in bed in her basement one afternoon. It was my first time with a black woman, and it was so great it ruined my life. I was so confused. I knew it was wrong, that I sinned against God, my wife, Mr. Allon, my children. But it felt so right. I didn't want to lose my family, my life, but I didn't want to ignore a whole new part of myself I felt like I was just getting to know, either. I knew it was wrong, but I wanted to continue seeing her. And then Anemone showed me a tape she'd made of our intimate time and threatened to send a copy to my wife if I didn't pay her. I was devastated. I knew it was God punishing me for my sin. I should have confessed it right then to Judy, but I was afraid. Judy's not a believer yet and I knew she'd want nothing more to do with God or this church if I told her. I didn't want to lose my kids or my job, so I dipped into the kids' college fund and paid Anemone what she wanted. She never bothered me again after that, but I've lived the last few months in fear. Now she's dead and that tape is out there somewhere." He finally looks up at me. "Pastor Hook, if that tape gets into the wrong hands, I'm ruined. I've fasted and prayed and flogged myself enough. I've paid a huge price already and I know that God has forgiven me. But my wife, my children, my students, the people who hired me. It would hurt them too much."

Sadat Patterson claiming Anemone blackmailed him with sex is one thing. Marcus Turner making the same claim is a whole 'nother camel.

"Brother Turner, I'm sorry to hear this. I'd like to help you, but I'm not sure what you're asking of me."

"Pastor, I don't believe that Anemone committed suicide. If she blackmailed me, chances are she did the same to others. One of her marks may have killed her rather than meet her demands. I believe she must have hidden the tape she showed me somewhere in her house. If her husband finds it, things could get very ugly. I guess what I'm asking is for you to somehow get Mr. Allon to look for any tapes belonging to his wife and turn them over to you. I can't go to anyone else about this, and you have access to Mr. Allon. He'd listen to you. I'm willing to make a very generous love offering to you, or to the church if you'd like, for your help."

Marcus Turner is a decent family man who succumbed to Anemone's charms when he was most vulnerable. Decent people are capable of doing bizarre things when they're in a pinch, though, and Pastor wonders how far Marcus would be willing to go to protect his lifestyle.

"Brother Turner, you've been direct with me, so I'll be the same with you in return. Where were you on Wednesday night around 10:00?"

Their eyes meet and he says, "It's a fair question, but I didn't kill her. I was home with Judy and the kids playing one-hour Monopoly."

He dispatches Marcus Turner with a prayer and a promise that he'll talk to Ike. Then he leans back in his chair thinking about what Marcus had just said: if Anemone blackmailed him, chances are she'd blackmailed others, too. That would've been one way for her to finance her getaway from Ike.

When Annette Jenkins sashays in showing too much cleavage in her short-sleeved button-down and khaki shorts, and says that she, too, had sex with Anemone and then was blackmailed, Pastor knows he's just landed in the twilight zone. Annette is a fairly attractive, bored housewife. Her husband, Godfrey, is a rising star in the litigation division of Boyd, Winthrop & Fuchs, a venerable downtown firm with a global client list. Their prenup essentially tosses her out on her ample buns and grants custody of their school-age children to Godfrey in the event of proven infidelity. She can't afford to lose her children or her lifestyle and wants Pastor to help her locate the tape of her and Anemone. She, too, promises to make it worth his while.

The sessions move much faster than he'd expected, and by the time Burke Hill rolls into his office every single person before him has said the same thing about Anemone: she had sex with them one time in her basement—the most exciting sex they'd ever had—and then blackmailed them. They all have credible alibis, and they all asked the same thing of Pastor: to help them get their tape. This leaves him wondering about his pastoral image. Do his members see him as an idle preacher with nothing better to do? Or is Rev. Snoop making them think he can actually find their tapes?

Burke is a mess as he sits across from Pastor. He's crying and Pastor hands him a tissue to wipe the snot running from his nose. A city bus jumped the curb on Broad Street and made him a paraplegic 15 years ago, but other than that his story is the same old thing. Anemone seduced him, then blackmailed him out of a chunk of his settlement with the city. Burke can't afford to lose his wife, Gloria, because the accident wiped out all his confidence and he doesn't believe that in a wheelchair he can get another woman.

Pastor knows Anemone was deceptive and outrageous, but he didn't think she could be so cold-hearted. Blackmailing a crippled man out of part of his settlement is beyond low. When Burke wheels his broken body out of the office Pastor looks to heaven, breathes a sigh of relief, and utters a praise of gratitude. "There but for the grace of God go I. Thank you, Lord." If it hadn't been for God empowering him to consistently resist Anemone's overtures he would have probably ended up on one of those tapes himself. He'd be a lot poorer right now, too; and living in fear every day that someone would get a hold of that tape and his ministry would be over.

Just the thought of what could have been if he had fallen helps him to sympathize with Anemone's victims. He finds himself wanting justice for them more than justice for Anemone. He decides to find every single tape she'd ever secretly made in her basement with that video camera.

He shakes the Knicks screen saver from the monitor, closes the membership software, opens up Word, and tries to do more work on the eulogy, but finds he can't concentrate. So he saves the one additional paragraph he's managed to write, backs up the file onto a rewritable CD, shuts down the computer, and slips the CD into his portfolio. It's not until he's in his car that the thought floating around in the back of his mind during all those Anemone stories finally surfaces to conscious level: With so much riding on the recovery of all those tapes, somebody else is liable to die.

CHAPTER 8

Pastor snaps the Club into place, locks the door and listens for the chirps that tell him the old Saab's security system has armed. He walks around to the front of the parsonage and collects the latest letter from his anonymous pen pal, clears off the front and back stoops, and climbs the stairs to get ready for bed. After a long cool shower in the dark he grabs the CD from his portfolio, sits down at the computer in his home office, and spends the rest of the evening alternately thinking about videotapes and the next line in Anemone's eulogy. It's not long before imagined scenes of Anemone and Burke in his wheelchair start crowding out all thoughts about the eulogy. He gives up and flops into bed with a book.

It's midnight when he cracks open *Horton Hears a Who!* The Wickersham monkeys remind him of Thorn, and he drifts into sleep and dreams he's in a wheelchair and his arms are the rope in a tug-of-war between the Wickersham Brothers and the black-bottomed eagle Vlad Vlad-i-koff.

The scratching at the window near the closet, the one without the air conditioner, wakes him out of an unsettled sleep. Too heavy and sustained to be squirrels. The clock reads 5:35. He rolls out of bed and picks his way around the creaky floorboards to the window. He presses his face up against the cool glass and looks to his left. A head pops up in front of him.

"Whoa!"

"Ahhh!"

It's Brother Mac and he's so startled he almost falls backward off the ladder.

"Brother Mac, don't scare me like that!" Pastor yells through the glass. "You alright?"

He's clutching his chest and nodding his head. "Just scraping the windows and shutters, Pastor. I gotta paint before it rots away."

Pastor jumps into his workout gear, jogs downstairs and stares into the refrigerator like a person who's got choices. There's still only a full gallon of Deer Park water, an almost empty gallon of OJ, a few slices of Pathmark wheat, two eggs, and a foil covered plate of macaroni and cheese from Mother. He drains the rest of the OJ straight from the plastic jug and toss it into the recyclables bin, stretches for his run up the Hill, prays, and as he runs, rehearse to the birds what he's completed so far of Anemone's eulogy.

♪

She was a sneaky, calculating phony. And if he could've found the courage to get out of that van and confront her like he wanted to, like he should've, maybe she'd still be alive today. He says all of that. To himself. Then Pastor steps to the pulpit as the makeshift choir that includes all three Thorns settles back into the choir loft behind him after the last strains of *Precious Memories*, and begins the eulogy of Anemone Allon that he spent the last two hours locked in his office finishing.

The cheap wooden casket is nailed shut, draped in flowers, and crowned with a flattering photo of Anemone's pretty oval face and alluring almond eyes. One that disguises the deceit in her soul, and the matching pair of nine-millimeter holes in her head.

There are floral arrangements everywhere, the most lavish ones arriving this morning with no record of their senders.

A savory aroma wafts up from the kitchen. This is, after all, a celebration in the true black church tradition.

Sister Mary Pettaway, the missionary board president who looks like that fine-as-wine Nancy Wilson, and Malisa Hoard, designer down as usual, fill up the front pews to Pastor's left with the rest of the missionary board. They're all arrayed in black, paying their respects to the memory of their vice-president.

Ike sits alone in the front pew to Pastor's right, across from the casket, still wearing a grease-stained brown jumpsuit with his name stitched into the breast and untied work boots, sneezing frequently. Anemone doesn't have any living family in the country, and Ike's family disowned him when he married her. Ike's gaze is intently fixed in front of him.

Pastor notices that Sears is nowhere around so assumes she must not have gotten his letter in time. But from the look on Ike's face, Pastor doesn't think they'll be seeing any tears today anyway, crocodile or otherwise.

Deacon Smith is another story.

He's wiping his eyes with a big plaid handkerchief. The years have weather-beaten his body. His face is dotted with warts and liver spots, and he's so wrinkled that if you stretched his skin out you could probably fit another endoskeleton under it. But he *never* misses a funeral. They're more meaningful to him now than Bible studies and prayer meetings. He's sitting at the base of the platform with the other deacons, their backs to Pastor and wearing their communion uniforms of black suits and white ties, facing the packed sanctuary of 225 mourners. That's the building's limit as per the Fire Marshall.

Paul Vernon, Anemone's distinguished looking former employer, is in the pew behind Ike with his new half-his-age trophy wife, Lila. And then Pastor remembers where he's seen his blonde FCA friend from the post office before. On the society page of the *Mirror* last year, announcing her wedding to Paul Vernon. Paul's first wife, Mary, died 18 months ago. It was ruled an accident, but Max Jr privately swore that Vernon murdered her to avoid paying out a huge divorce settlement after she told him she was taking the kids and leaving because of his "extra-marital activities." Six months later he marries his physician's secretary. Pastor wonders if he knew then that she was a racist.

The Vernons are the only peaches here among this bushel of plums other than Rachel Niagara, who's been a member of First Baptist for so long that most of the younger members think she's just high yellow. Everybody else in the pews heard the news on the congregational grapevine and altered their schedules on this official last Friday of spring.

Dale Dawkins is looking more official than Pastor in the black robe with unearned chevrons on the sleeves he always wears in the pulpit and the Roman collar he wore to prayer meeting & bible study Wednesday night. He tells people he's a former Army chaplain when he was actually just a combat engineer who prayed for his platoon members and sometimes led them in bible studies.

He steps to the mic to sing a solo. All he needs is an academic hood to finish off the ensemble and he'll be a complete fake. The pomposity is comical as he tells the congregation, while the pianist softly plays the melody to *Because He Lives*, that he is on his lunch break and will soon have to return to work because he learned too late about the funeral and couldn't take the rest of the day off. Then he belts out the song in such a convincing falsetto that it makes Pastor wonder whether his normal phlegmy baritone is actually real, and shouts of "sing, Chap, sing!" echo throughout the congregation.

When it's time for the eulogy Dawkins walks out of the pulpit, drawing attention to himself as Pastor begins reading his text. Black Baptists compete for pulpits. One reason Pastor beat out Dawkins, besides the fact that Dawkins got all his degrees--B.D., D.D., S.T.D., and Th.D.—on discount from the same South Carolina degree mill, is that Pastor *can* bring in the train, a skill he acquired out of respect for the American Black pulpit tradition by studying and imitating one of the best whoopers in the country, the Rev. Dr. Ivanhoe Mañuel Noble. Of course his own father thinks it's foolishness, so he never heard whooping at Gethsemane. Little did Pastor know then that it could make him a more marketable pulpit candidate. He was just drawn to it as an art form with historical importance. But First Baptist Belton hadn't had a whooper in a long time, and according to Cornel they were yearning for the mountaintops again after a long season of dry sermons from doctrinaire old-timers with rich preaching pedigrees but no fire. That's why when he told Cornel he was resigning his prison chaplaincy and looking for a pastoral challenge Cornel called Dexter right away and recommended him for this pulpit.

He titled the eulogy "The Hallmark of a Meaningful Life". Paul's letter to the Corinthians. The love chapter. He tells them that Anemone's legacy was love. That she loved many people, and many people loved her. That few realize how quick she was to open herself to people she hardly even knew. And that this kind of love carried a price.

He says all the right things while meaning the truth in his heart, and notices Malisa Hoard slipping out the creaky front double door, probably going to the kitchen to help the Willing Workers with the food. He also questions the decisions of BPD and City Hall to declare Anemone's death a suicide. He says she was murdered, and that God will have the final word about it. Then some of the people start shifting nervously in their seats, so he moves on.

Because of what he now knows, he's struggling to give Anemone a "good send-off". He's been preaching for about 20 minutes and starts shifting gears for the climax. Dr. Gaye, the albino minister of music who claims to be a distant cousin of the late Marvin Gaye, scurries to the organ as Pastor begins to "tune up."

Some in the congregation are rocking side to side now. Two or three are standing and clapping. Out of the corner of his eye Pastor spies the Reverend Dr. Belove Mall, the oldest of his associate ministers and First Baptist's official Dirty Old Man—because he likes to pinch the fruit and squeeze the Charmin—jumping out of his seat. He walks over as Pastor shifts into overdrive, and with an unsteady hand starts slapping him on the back, encouraging him. "You go 'head, Doc! Help yo'self!" And the historically incorrect Jesus holding those two little white lambs in the stained glass window in the back looks baffled.

Pastor planned to give Anemone no more than 3 minutes of his best whoop because when it's done right it's so physically taxing and he wants to save something for Sunday, but when he scrapes his hankie across his brow and steps back from the pulpit the entire congregation combusts into a spontaneous expression of ecstasy.

So he keeps going. He can't resist. He feels like a robed rapper in front of a rowdy Standing Room Only crowd begging for more.

They want to shout, something First Baptists generally don't do. They want to release their reined in emotions, so it's his job to help them do it with some verbal direction.

The organ is answering his every phrase. The ushers are circling the wide bodies bucking and stomping in the aisles and pews, as if playing ring-around-the-rosies, keeping them from hurting themselves or others. A wig flies out of place. Somebody falls out into the aisle, supposedly slain in the Spirit, exposing some racy panties and thick flesh. And Ike, handsome in a roughneck sorta way, and looking almost demonic with red puffy hay fever eyes, remains stoic, catatonic even, as if steeling himself against this world, his gaze still fixed in front of him.

Pastor looks back at the choir, then at Dr. Gaye, and shifts into full song, a signal to the congregation that it's time to start coming down from this mountain. The last time they dragged in to this cemetery late they had to wait another hour for the workers to return from their lunch break.

Trouble in my way, he sings.

Trouble in my way, the choir responds.

I got to cry sometime.

Got to cry sometime.

Trouble in my way.

Trouble in my way.

IIIII got to cry some time.

Got to cry sometime.

I lay awake at night.

Lay awake at night.

But that's alright.

Thaaaat's alriiiight.

Because I know that Jesus—

Jesus, He will fix it.

After a while.

Aaaafter a while.

It's a while before they come down from the mountain.

The elegant funeral director with the gray wire-brush mustache rushes through his announcements about the procession to the cemetery. He readies the casket and begins rolling Anemone out of First Baptist for the last time as Pastor leads the procession down the center aisle reading scripture passages from *The Minister's Service Book.* He still can't believe he'll never see Anemone in these pews again.

Outside, sweat is stinging the cut he gave himself this morning while shaving his upper lip. The funeral director and a big assistant hurry the casket into the back of the hearse. The startling sound of skin meeting skin snaps Pastor's head around just in time to see a red-faced, cursing Lila Vernon being shuttled away by her husband from Reverend Mall, who's massaging his cheek. She's demanding that they go straight home and those around them are shaking their heads at Mall and snickering. He never could resist fresh meat.

Pastor closes the book, wades through the crowd, and rounds the corner to the Second Street entrance to dump his robe and grab some extra hankies for the committal. Dexter catches him at the door in his neat afro.

"Pastor, you want me to have Reverend Mall do the committal so you can stay here and get some rest?"

"Nah, I won't be long," Pastor says. "Tell the driver to wait for me."

He opens the door to his office. Cool air sweeps across his face, and Malisa comes rushing in through the back door from the parking lot toward the women's restroom, presumably overcome by the heat, or a hot flash, or both. Her face looks flushed and damp. Only the sanctuary and Pastor's office are air-conditioned. Another cost-cutting measure by David Henry Thorn.

"You okay, Malisa?"

She flashes him a grimacing smile and bores through the door. Pastor wonders if she's still mad at him about yesterday. He doesn't know how she and Dexter have stayed together this long. They share the same body profile but not the same temperament. Malisa's the type to hold a grudge and misinterpret a joke. And she's convinced herself she doesn't need anyone else in this whole wide world.

That's why Pastor persists.

"If I can help in any way, just let me know."

She slams the restroom door.

Pastor hangs his robe in the closet and turns on a small dehumidifier in there. He hears Dexter outside his door telling Mowatt to scram, that the pastor is busy and doesn't have time for foolishness right now. And Mowatt slurring slurs back at him as he ambles out the back door.

Dexter meets Pastor on Second Street and says he'll be late getting to the cemetery because he just noticed he has a flat tire and the church van is already full.

◊

Pastor's trapped in the passenger seat of the hearse trying to decide what to do about the driver. It's usually a quiet ride, a welcome chance to reflect on what lay ahead. But not today. The radio's going, 1010

WINS reporting about the still ongoing FBI investigation into another cache of weapons and explosives stolen from Ft. Dix and selling out of car trunks on Newark streets like crack. And the dumpy, milktoast-complected driver with the sparse mustache who helped load the casket into the hearse refuses to shut up for even a minute.

"Bet ya it's them white supremacists." He sounds like a bullfrog. "They always stealin' from the military. A lot of 'em *in* the military."

Pastor's mind runs immediately to the FCA as he listens to the report, but now he's thinking, *Why would white supremacists want to arm black people on the streets of Newark?*

The driver must've heard his thoughts. "Best way to get ridda nigros. Give 'em guns and turn 'em loose on each other. Divide and conquer. White man ain't changed a bit in fo' hun'ed years."

Maybe if Pastor stares long enough into the flashing blue lights of Mugsy Stallings's cruiser he'll slip into a trance and not be able to hear this guy's voice anymore. But then he realizes that Mugsy is escorting them the wrong way down Belton Avenue. They've just completed the traditional last drive past the Allon residence, but instead of turning left onto Belton Avenue to make another left onto Valley and toward interstate 87, they've turned right, past St. Thomas University and toward interstate 280.

"Why are we going this way?" Pastor asks when he's finally able to get a word in edgewise. "Eighty-seven's much quicker to the turnpike."

"I dunno, Rev'en. Somebody from yo' church said Mr. Allon wanted to go this way, and I just go the way they tell me."

Pastor nods in agreement, not wanting to give him reason to talk even more. But the news shifts to a report on the 17th prostitute murdered in Newark in the last year, and the special investigator brought in a few months ago to catch the killer, and that's all he needs to get going again.

"Now you know that gots to be a white man," he says. "'Cause there ain't no such thing as a black serial killer. We'll shoot up a street corner to control some drug traffic, but we ain't the type to plan it out for years and eat the people afterwards."

Wayne Williams and the Atlanta Child Murders pop into Pastor's mind, and again it's like his head is made of glass.

"I know you probably thinking about that boy in Atlanta a few years back, but he just the exception that cements the rule. I bet you it's one of them ex-army white boys who hates his mama. And I heard on the street that he done some freaky things to the bodies after they dead, too? Now you *know* that's gotta be a white boy."

Pastor feels for the door handle and for a millisecond considers bailing out, but the convoy of somber cars, its shining headlights competing with the blazing June sun, is rolling past the Cavalry Baptist Church of Orange at a pretty good clip now and he decides instant relief ain't worth a protracted hospital stay. Because he hates hospitals. Besides, he's scheduled to preach at Cavalry next week and could use the love offering to pay his satellite bill. He's still trying to figure out if they're a congregation of people who can't spell, or smart folks making a statement about radical, militaristic urban Christianity determined to "take the land." Brother Stallings has been little help with this. He used to be a member there and is still mad at the pastor, so Pastor really can't trust anything he says about them.

They turn onto Harrison Street and head toward 280. Their official escort abandons them at the entrance ramp. Behind them, the only other funeral home car is the black limo carrying Ike all by himself. The convoy snakes along the interstate to the New Jersey Turnpike. The cemetery is in Linden, just off exit 13, but as they approach exit 14, traffic slows to an eventual standstill.

The old driver croaks, "It never fails. Every time I go to this cemetery, there's always a jam. Like God tryin' to tell me somethin'."

Pastor refuses to dwell on the thought that if they would've gone the other way they would've missed this construction bottleneck.

"Maybe He's trying to tell you to get your spiritual house in order." He's not feeling very pastoral, but opts for the pastoral response anyway. "You know, giving you a sign that you're not ready yet?"

The driver scrapes a laugh along the back of his meaty throat. "You tell me, Rev. You the one on speakin' terms with the Man."

It's understandable why people make that kind of assumption, but the truth is some preachers aren't on any better speaking terms with God than the rest of the world's sinners. Pastor realizes this and takes seriously his promise to himself not to be one of them.

"I think God's probably saying to you what He's saying to everybody, 'Come to me as you are, I love you and accept you.'"

He laughs again. "Been a long time since I heard it that simple, Rev. Lonnngg time."

Pastor glances out the window at a jumbo jet making its approach to Newark Airport, its tail wagging like a dog's in the wind currents. Even with the air blasting his nose is burning from the smell of the fresh flowers in the back. Too much longer and he'll need to use his Proventil inhaler. He turns forward again to check the traffic ahead and is startled by a doughboy-looking hand in his face gripping a silver flask.

"See that accident up ahead? We ain't movin' any time soon," the drive says. "So cain't nobody say we drinkin' and drivin'."

"No thanks, man. I need to do something more physical to relax myself."

"Oh, I hear you, Rev. You got a little honey waitin' for you back at the parsonage?"

"Naw. I'm a single preacher. You know we've got to be celibate."

"Yeah, I'll let you tell it, Rev."

"I'll probably go to the Hole. I've got a game tonight before my wedding and ball always helps me get it together in times like this."

"Ain't that just like life. Single man, look the way you do, got all them fine women up in yo' church, and the only hole you thinkin' about hittin' is the basketball court." He laughs that scratchy laugh again and shakes his head. "Those who can don't wanna, and those who wanna, cain't." He chugs another load from the flask and wipes his mouth with the sleeve of his snug-fitting black polyester suit jacket.

In the silent pocket that follows Pastor assumes a very visible prayer posture with bowed head and clasped hands, interceding for the people in the accident. Partly because he's always convicted to pray for people in car accidents, and partly because he knows his driver friend will respect his effort with even more silence. He prays longer than usual. All the way to the cemetery.

Now that the ride is over Pastor has changed his mind about the chatterbox hearse driver. He isn't dumpy after all. He's what unkind people would call just plain fat. And heavy. Because when he gets out of the hearse the suspension sighs and straightens out, and Pastor realizes they've been riding at a slight tilt all along.

The air is still heavy from the humidity, the ground still soft. The dirt piled to the side of the grave looks like refried beans. All around them are towering monuments to the ancient hope that beyond this world is another, better life. Stone crosses ten feet high. A giant obelisk with the Ten Commandments etched into its face. An euro-centric image of what an angel supposedly looks like, blowing a trumpet to the sky, signaling the arrival in heaven of another weary immigrant with a permanent visa. And trees, lots of thick, shady, wrinkled trees; maples, elms, oaks, boasting graceful boughs and millions of rich, well fed leaves.

The cheap coffin is dangling above the cement vault on two winched straps. Pastor stands at its head on the green Astroturf covering the makeshift platform of wooden planks surrounding the grave, admiring the array of wreaths and bows the funeral director, the old frog, and the limo driver lay at the foot of the coffin, and drawing a blank again as he tries to figure out how best to approach Ike about Anemone's cache of hidden tapes. He's standing in the shade of this well-placed oak only about two minutes now, but the sweat is already beaded on Pastor's forehead and running down the side of his face. His summer-weight black wool suit feels like an electric blanket and his white cotton shirt is beginning to stick to his stomach and back from the moisture. In his discomfort he watches the mourners trail from the line of cars left idling with their air conditioners on through the path marked out by the pallbearers minutes before, stepping gingerly, trying to keep the mud off their expensive footwear. Mother Freddie is visibly upset because her Air Jordans are getting mud all over them. Ike is sitting near the huge oak to Pastor's right in the lone chair by the grave for the family of the deceased, staring blankly at the coffin.

The two drivers and the funeral director hand out red carnations to each person as they arrive at the grave. Soon a semi-circle of people in black forms behind the mound of dirt across from Ike and the flowers across from Pastor. And David Henry, Verma and Smiley stand directly across from him wearing such foul expressions that Pastor has to look twice to make sure they're not holding skunk cabbage instead of flowers.

Committals are generally very brief, no more than 5 minutes. It's always the pre- and post-committal stuff that stretches the ordeal into sometimes more than an hour. Sometimes it takes that long just to get a grieving family from the limo to the grave side chairs, or to retrieve a heartbroken mother who's leapt into the grave. And sometimes, as soon as one family member gets calm enough to walk to the grave, another would launch into a fit of convulsions and wailing. That's why Pastor wears the same old black suit to funerals. And he's seriously considering wearing shin guards and an athletic cup as well.

But things are going relatively well here. Even the scowls on the faces of the unholy trinity have begun melting away in the heat. The two drivers take up positions on the platform in front of the dirt mound, ready to escort mourners along as they lay their carnations on the casket and say their final goodbyes. The funeral director gives Pastor the nod, and he begins the service.

"We brought nothing into this world, and it is certain we can carry nothing out. The Lord gave, and the Lord has taken away; bles—"

He's interrupted by the almost simultaneous outbursts of a violent sneeze and a throaty, "Arrgh!" Ike lurches forward in his chair, and the chatterbox driver clutches his chest and collapses onto the coffin.

CHAPTER 9

Everyone is stunned, like on Pastor's first dunk in a game, over Chucky the Giant; frozen in a still, silent moment. Everyone but Ike, who's ducking behind the oak and peeking at the jumble of trees and monuments across the road, pointing and screaming, "Somebody shooting! The bullet gone right past me head!"

Pastor turns to the monuments, wondering if there really are shots being fired because he didn't hear any. And if there are, why? And the thought flashes through his mind like blue lightning that this might finally be his hot chance to get back to Carla and Carlton. A voice behind him calls out, "Get down! Get down!" and he's sucker-tripped and body-slammed onto his stomach by what feels like a lightweight. Wood is splintering all around him, off the big oak shielding Ike and the cheap casket shielding them and the turf-covered platform. And what must be bullets are whistling overhead, making heavy thuds in the dirt mound.

The effect on the gathering is like yelling "fire!" in a crowded theatre. Pastor looks to his left. Everybody is screaming and running. The flock scatters like a rumbling herd back toward the line of idling cars. Mud and sod clumps are flying everywhere. David Henry looks like a kick-returner breaking through the wedge, shedding bodies as he runs. Deacon Gumbs helps Verma up out of the mud after she's been trampled and now they're both dragging Smiley along, who is jumping up and down and clapping his hands, thinking it's playtime.

And whispers of gunfire are erupting above Pastor, too. The silenced muzzle of a black 9mm is spitting fire, a wrinkled hand holding the butt. It's Mother Freddie, pushing down on his head with her free hand, squeezing off rounds, yelling something indelicate.

Gunfights on TV and in the movies are always loud and smoky. If this is a gunfight it has to be the quietest, eeriest ever. Like a tornado churning up everything in its path, silently.

Several seconds later Mother is out of ammo and maybe the sniper's reloading, too. In the stillness Pastor pushes her off himself and crawls over to the old frog. He's thinking *Maybe he just had a heart attack from too much drinking.* He doesn't even know if too much alcohol can really lead to a heart attack, but the driver *was* drinking in the hearse and since Easter of '88 Pastor's always reaching for a way to reconcile the present with the past.

Pastor tries to turn him over to see if there's a bullet hole in his chest, but by doing so he unwittingly shifts the weight on the straps suspending the coffin above the cement vault 6 feet down. He hears the winch groaning and knows what's about to happen. He jumps back, falling on the seat of his pants into the dirt mound just as the straps give way and the coffin, along with the old frog, disappears into the hole. The loud crash startles the funeral director and the limo driver on the other side of the dirt and now they're spewing a stream of profanities mingled with pleas to God for their lives.

But Ike isn't startled at all. He's still focusing on the necropolis across the street from the more modest neighborhood of two and three foot tombstones that Anemone's remains will call home until that Great Gettin' Up Mornin'. And then he bolts from behind his ancient shield and charges toward that city, heading straight for the giant obelisk that stands at its center like the Empire State Building in the Manhattan skyline.

And Pastor takes off after him.

If Easter '88 hadn't happened it could be said that the Holy Ghost told him to do it, or that loving concern constrained him, but the fact is Pastor took off after Ike because if there's someone out there with a gun, it would be a great way to go, a heroic way to silence the voices from his past. PASTOR FELLED PURSUING SNIPER IN CEMETERY.

"Paaastah! Wait for me!"

Pastor's ribs are barking when he finally catches Ike just before he slows down near the obelisk. The pain makes him think twice about playing basketball later.

"What did you see, Ike?" Pastor's drenched in sweat and pain and Ike's ignoring him, looking off into the distance through the jagged cityscape of monuments and trees like a predator hunting on an entirely different frequency. He sniffs the air and cocks his head to the side. And then they both hear it, the faint sound of an engine turning over and tires squealing.

Mother Freddie finally catches up to them, puffing heavy under her huge sombrero, gun in hand, and throws herself against a merciful elm. Pastor looks over at Ike but he refuses to acknowledge him. Ike stoops down and stares at the soft dirt. It doesn't take a tracker to see the footprints there, or the empty shell casings, or the Beretta M9 with a silencer on its muzzle and FCA etched into the barrel, just like the one that killed Anemone, lying near the obelisk, or the two emptied clips next to it, or the wide patch of flattened grass and dirt with fresh indentations that look to be shoulder width apart.

Pastor tries again. "What did you see, Ike?"

"Maybe the bogeyman," he says, finally.

He charges back toward the gravesite. Mother and Pastor linger in the shade of the elm.

"Paaastah? You trying to leave us?"

"What do you mean, Mother?"

"If I didn't do my old schoolyard trick on you, you could've gotten hit."

If she hadn't pounced on him maybe he'd be with Carla and Carlton now. Man. He could probably jump off the Verrazano bridge right now and not even get wet.

"I just wanted to see who it was."

"Is that why you ran across this open field with no cover?"

"Yeah."

"Well curiosity killed the cat. Don't you scare me like that again."

Ike is already in the limo when they get back, and all the other cars are gone. The funeral director and limo driver are in the hearse talking on the phone, probably to the Linden police. Mother gets into the limo and Pastor steps to the edge of the platform. He has to find out if the old frog was shot. One look down answers the question.

It doesn't take long for the Linden PD squad cars to arrive all loud and disrespectful, nor for those remaining to give their statements. Pastor suspected it after talking to Chuck at Top Brands, but now he's convinced that Ike knows more about everything that had happened the last 3 days than he's letting on.

The hearse ride back is pretty unsettling. The funeral director's face is ashen, almost the color of his mustache, and he's mumbling all the way to Belton, "I can't believe it. I can't believe it."

Even though the funeral director makes his living presiding over and presenting dead bodies, this is probably the closest he's ever come to death itself. Walking up to a casket and staring at the corpse is not the same as looking at death. What's in the casket is not death, only its handiwork. Death is anything but still. It's dynamic. As dynamic as life, only moving in the opposite direction. Unlife. Pastor knows because he's been near it. Stared into its face. Been near its vortex. He felt its energy as it sucked Carlton away from him, then Carla. And he tried to jump into it, to ride its force to where they were going, because he so desperately wanted to be with them. He didn't want to be left alone.

Burro says that's why Pastor went to divinity school. To look for a way to confront God. To give Him a piece of his mind, and to try to convince Him to let him ride the death force to them now. Burro is okay, but Pastor thinks that half the time Burro doesn't know what he's talking about, because he also says meeting the right woman will be the turning point in Pastor's life and cause him to abandon his search. Burro's not saved, so he just doesn't realize that God draws people to himself in His sovereign time and will, and often uses crazy circumstances to do it. Maybe Pastor did go to div school to confront God, but when he did he ended up falling in love with Him. John Calvin's doctrine of irresistible grace. Go figure.

Pastor is glad they pull into the parking lot ahead of the limo. He says nothing to the director. There's nothing to say. The day's events have established what will be a tacit understanding between them for the rest of their professional association. The balance of power has forever shifted. They both know now that death, real death, is Pastor's province, not his. Pastor lays his hand on the director's shoulder, prays God's peace over his life, smiles at him warmly, and walks away.

Mother disappears inside as the hearse and limo pull off, leaving Ike and Pastor standing in the middle of the full parking lot staring each other down.

"You okay?" Pastor asks.

"Yeah, I'll live."

"Why didn't you tell the police the sniper was aiming for you?"

"Oh, so you're detective now, Minister? Is this for another magazine story?"

He unlocks his Vette.

"One bullet whizzed right over your head and would've killed you if you didn't sneeze when you did, and most of the rest hit the tree you were hiding behind. I'd say those bullets had your name on them."

"Just a random act of violence. We living in dangerous times, you know. Or they coulda been meant for you, who knows?"

Pastor had actually considered that during the ride back. There *is* his anonymous pen pal out there somewhere with all his promises. But if that's who it was then why kill Anemone, frame the FCA, and target Ike?

"Nah. If they were meant for me at least one would've found me, Ike."

"Me could say the same."

"Some people will kill to acquire or suppress certain kinds of information. Why don't you go down to the police station and tell the detectives what you know." Pastor knows he's wasting his breath as soon as he speaks it, because Ike Allon is the kind of guy who'd sooner take the law into his own hands than ask for help.

Ike slams the door and peels off. Pretty cavalier for a guy just ducking gunfire. He *had* to be the target, otherwise there's only one other explanation. Lila Vernon. Maybe she was so mad about Mall squeezing her bottom that she sent one of her skinhead goons over to shoot up the place. But why would the skinhead leave the weapon behind with FCA initials on it? And after the first shot, Mall was nowhere near them. Even from that distance blacks don't all look alike.

Heading into the cool basement of the building Pastor notices Dexter's car parked in his reserved space next to Pastor's empty space.

There's a puddle under it, and it occurs to him that he didn't see him at the cemetery.

Suddenly, the back door opens with a loud bang and Mowatt comes rocketing out with arms and legs flailing. He loses his balance, falls to the cement, and an angry voice flies behind him. "And stay out!" Then the door slams shut.

He looks up at Pastor. Pastor is speechless. This is the first time he's ever seen Mowatt with anger in his eyes. "Those cats are hypocrites, Hook. All of 'em goin' to hell."

Pastor's been in the church virtually all his life, but he's never before seen anyone literally thrown out of what's supposed to be God's house. He helps him to his feet. "What happened, Mowatt?"

"All I wanted was a taste, and they come throwing me out like I'm garbage. You can't tell me there ain't no liquor in that place. It's a funeral. Everybody knows you have liquor after a funeral. Hypocrites!"

Pastor digs into his pocket, pulls out his leather business card holder, looks around to make sure no one is looking, and sticks one of his cards into the breast pocket of Mowatt's smelly camouflage shirt. "Here, go get a hot meal and some coffee, man. Then go home and get some sleep. If I didn't know you I'd think you look homeless. And take a shower."

If you give a drunk a dollar to go buy a cup of coffee he'll figure out a way to turn it into liquor faster than Jesus at the Wedding at Cana, so Pastor brokered a special arrangement with Markie O, the owner of O'Loughlin's, for situations just like this one. Whenever Mowatt walks in there and presents one of Pastor's cards, Markie feeds him, signs off on the back of the card, and sends Pastor the bill.

"A'ight, Hook. It's cooler at O'Loughlin's anyway. And they gimme a little table all to myself in the back. But listen, I gotta rap to you about something."

"Can we talk another time, Mowatt? I really have to get inside. Just go to O'Loughlin's, man."

Pastor turns and heads for the door. Mowatt keeps calling his name, but Pastor just looks back and smiles. Handing him that card made Pastor realize how hungry he is. All he had for breakfast was a slice of toast and a forkful of macaroni and cheese he had to spit back into the plate and dump in the trash when he noticed the dead roach on the bottom shelf of the refrigerator. He's hungry enough to eat two platefuls of anything. Except macaroni and cheese.

The lower auditorium is still full of people eating the food the Willing Workers—the seven deaconesses and a few members of the Seasoned Citizens ministry—prepared for after the interment: fried chicken, candied yams with marshmallows, string beans...and macaroni and cheese. The buzz in the room drowns out the growls in his stomach. They're telling stories of individual heroism. How they stood face-to-face with death at the cemetery and won. What they told the police when questioned at the scene.

Church folk make the best liars.

Over in the near corner Mother Freddie looks like a bandito holding court. It's standing room only around her table. All men. Examining her pistol up close and passing it around, like show-and-tell time in school.

Pastor tries sneaking by them into his office, but he's intercepted by Cameron McNair, a tall, slim brother with slanted eyes. He slips something into Pastor's jacket's breast pocket and it jingles.

"What's this?"

"All the information is on the tag," he says, practically running for the exit. "Pick it up whenever you want and let me know after a week."

Pastor pulls out a pair of Ford keys. The tag has "Yel. Mustang Conv." written on two lines, and an ID number. "Cameron, I told you I'm very happy with my Saab," he protests as the door closes behind him. He owns McNair Ford and has been trying to convert Pastor ever since he donated the brand new fifteen passenger Econoline they use for the Transportation Ministry in exchange for ad space in FBC's weekly church bulletin. He moved into the old Mercedes truck plant a few blocks down on Valley less than two years ago and approached Pastor one Sunday after service about making the donation as a way of carving inroads to the African American car-buying market in Belton. He's one of few members who views as a positive the statistics Brian Mulady groused about yesterday. And his strategy seems to be working. McNair Ford bought out the rest of the businesses on their block and construction is underway on a state-of-the-art addition to the plant. So they have Cameron to blame for the cement mixers and dump trucks overrunning Valley Street the last few weeks.

Pastor opens his office door and sighs under the cool air. He plops into his chair and lets it hold him tenderly behind his desk. He leans back in the chair thinking about Ike. If he didn't kill Anemone, he certainly knows who did. Maybe he hired someone to cap her after finding out about her blackmail campaign. After all it's pretty hard to have sex with half the congregation in your basement while your husband is at work and keep it a secret for too long, no matter how inattentive that husband may be. Isn't it? Pastor puts his growling stomach on hold and picks up the phone to call Chris Sears and tell her what he suspects about Ike. Surely she'll have to reopen the inquiry into Anemone's death now, and it could give him the leverage he'd need to get those tapes back from Ike. But before he finishes dialing the number someone knocks at the door.

It's Sister Perot, the statuesque, acne-faced president of the Willing Workers, carrying herself like she's still a showgirl at the Cotton Club. She's offering Pastor's salvation in her upturned palms: a tray holding a plate of food, a slice of pound cake, and two cups of punch. Pastor puts down the phone and breaks into a wide grin. "Bless you, Sister Perot," he says, reaching for the tray.

"Pastor, what took you all so long? Everybody's been back for at least a half hour."

"We had to wait for the police."

She shakes her head. "They can't stop talking about it. I saved this for you. Now you go ahead and eat, and don't let me disturb your phone call."

She tip-toes across the carpet. "Thanks, Sister Perot. Before you go, do you know where Deacon Hoard is?"

She throws him a quizzical look. "Wasn't he with you, Pastor?"

Did Dexter say he was with me? "I just lost track of him, that's all."

"He's upstairs now. I just took a plate of food to him. It's like a sauna up there in that Deacon's Room. Makes this kitchen feel frigid." She closes the door gently behind her, careful not to let the hammer click into the casing. Sister Perot has always treated Pastor's office like holy ground.

Pastor stuffs a forkful of string beans and yams into his mouth and starts dialing Scars's number again. More banging interrupts him and the door bursts open before he can say, "Come in."

"Reverend, I have to talk to you!"

"Sure. Have a seat."

"Don't need one. This will be quick."

It's David Henry, looking like weary in his suit with his long torso and distended belly and short, spindly legs.

"So, you have those signatures?" Pastor asks, polishing off the yams.

"Not yet, but I'm working on it. Now I'm going to say this to you one more time, then I'm taking it to the church. With all this killing going on around here we need to do something to protect ourselves and this church!"

"Do you want to call a prayer meeting?"

"Hell no! We need to get some burglar bars, an alarm system, and hire a full-time security guard!"

Pastor sticks the last string bean in his mouth and before he starts on the chicken says, "I think we also really need a secretary."

Thorn's white hair rises up on his head like a mad dog's.

"Like I said, I'm taking this to the church."

"Bless him, Lord," Pastor says to his back. "Take away his anger." Thorn slams the door so hard that it rattles the rustic church scene print on its hook.

Sears isn't around, but maybe it's for the best. There could be another angle to this, so Pastor scarfs down what's left of the chicken on his plate, sneaks into the kitchen for seconds on pound cake and punch, and slips out in search of Dexter.

The Deacon's Room is a Spartan little loft perched high above the choir stand where the deacons gather to pray and discuss the business of the church. Dexter is sitting at the old conference table. It's the lone piece of furniture in the room besides the cabinet and copier machine desk. He's looking tortured, his head in a tattered Bible, the old Catholic in him constantly crossing himself. He hasn't touched his food.

"I didn't see you at the cemetery. Did you really have a flat?" He's not wearing his jacket, either, and his pants are a little soiled. Tire dirt?

Dexter shakes his head. "Two combat tours in 'Nam...and I've still never dealt with anything this heavy. I just couldn't handle it, Tony. She was good people. She didn't deserve to go like that. I wonder if she even got a chance to make her last confession of sins before she met her Maker."

Pastor figures this is how Job's friends must have felt. They sit in silence for a while. He wants to ask Dexter where he was, but all of a sudden it seems insignificant. He's Pastor's friend, and he's in pain. Grief is hanging in the loft as thick as the humidity and as visibly as the Shekinah that hovered over the tabernacle whenever Moses went in to meet with God. After a while Pastor can't take it anymore. He gives him a big hug, helps himself to Dexter's pound cake and punch since he said he isn't going to eat it, and leaves him alone with his sorrow.

Pastor's not surprised that Dexter is so broken up about Anemone's death. He's finally accepted the fact that she didn't commit suicide, that she was murdered. We all grieve in unique ways, and with things so stressful in his personal life, it's understandable how all this could just bring his emotional house of cards down.

♪

Back in his office Pastor notices Sister Perot has cleared away his tray. He whispers a prayer for Ike and goes hunting for more cake and punch, but there's none left in the kitchen.

Before heading home he stops and chats with the handful of seniors left at the long tables covered with paper tablecloths dampened by the humidity. Man, he'll miss them if he ever gets to Monumental.

"Pastor," says Sister Perot. She pushes a foil-wrapped plate towards him that's so packed with food it looks like a pan of Jiffy Pop popcorn. "I saved this one for you to take home. And I noticed you didn't eat your macaroni and cheese."

"And we know you love macaroni and cheese," adds Mother.

"Ohhhh. Well, you know I like to save the best for last. I ran upstairs to talk to Dexter, and when I got back my tray was gone."

"Don't worry, Pastor," says Sister Perot with a grin like if she's telling a big, delicious secret. "I gave you all the rest of the macaroni and cheese. You enjoy it."

"Oh, Sister Perot, you don't know what that means to me."

Sister Perot adjusts her hearing aid and says, "Pastor, you know we're going to have to do this over. It wasn't right how we left Anemone like that without laying her to rest properly."

"You're right. Maybe tomorrow. I'll talk to Dexter about it."

"And we'll be sure to bring the muscle with us again," she says, looking at Mother. A nervous giggle fills the room.

"That reminds me," says Mother Freddie. "I've got to hurry up and catch that downtown bus. I'm running low on ammo."

"Bye, Mother," says the table.

"Pray my strength," she says, and scoots off.

"And this time that husband of hers should just keep himself home." Sister Niagara pushes her saucer-sized glasses closer to her pale, wrinkled face.

"Why?" Pastor asks.

"Every time I see that young man he's so angry. I know all that shooting out there today was meant for him. You can't be that angry all the time and not have *some*body wanting to put you out of your misery. He passed by my office yesterday and when I tried to offer my condolences the young man just snarled at me."

Ahhh, that winning fender-side manner. "Ike does have a way with people."

"I said to myself, 'There'll be *trouble* at that funeral tomorrow.' I knew it. I could feel it in my spirit."

"What was Ike doing at City Hall?"

"I don't know. He was walking out when I saw him, and he was sure in a big hurry."

♪

Pastor has his handkerchief clamped against his nose, protecting his lungs against the exhaust fumes from the endless procession of buses and cement mixers and dump trucks on Valley Street as images of the old frog's blood-soaked torso and Anemone's opened head flicker through his mind. He's startled back to reality by a piece of construction debris that flies off a dump truck after it hits a pothole. Again, piled illegally high. *BPD needs to enforce that ordinance before somebody gets hurt.*

The parsonage feels like a dark and dreary refuge, the perfect haunt for an Anne Rice character. And that's how Pastor is feeling, as old as a vampire. He picks up another letter from his anonymous pen pal. This one reads: 'Bang, you're dead!' He marches straight into the kitchen, dumps the plate of macaroni and cheese into the trash on top of the dead roach from this morning, ties up the bag, and drops it in the big garbage can outside the back door.

The master bedroom feels a little warm even though he'd left the air on full blast. The light is blinking so furiously on the answering machine he's afraid it might blow up. News travels fast in Belton and he stares at the machine for a while before deciding to pick up the messages. The first is another plea from his mom to send his father a Father's Day gift if he can't make it home. This one includes a bribe of his favorite dish: coconut rice, stewed kidney beans, fried plantains, and red snapper with lots of gravy and onions on his own dining room table next Sunday after church. The next two are from Mayor Tubby and Chief Ellis chewing him out about the quote attributed to him they'd just read in today's *Mirror*. They both say he's stirring up trouble again and Tubby even accuses him of being anti-Catholic by pointing out his "pejorative use of the word 'genuflecting.'" Pastor doesn't want to hear anymore, so he hits the STOP button and peels off his clothes. He's stepping into his favorite pair of baggy Tigers shorts when the phone rings. It's line two, his unlisted number. Only three people have that number: Cornel Brown, Dexter Hoard, and Mom, but he screens the call anyway.

"Yo, Bishop, I heard what happened, man. You a'ight?" He's glad it's Cornel but he still doesn't feel like talking, just banging bodies, pain or no pain, to clear his mind for tonight. And if he's fortunate he'll have an overtime game or something and drop 50 points. Anyway, he knows Cornell will find him eventually, because he always does; so he grabs his car keys and ball and doesn't bother to listen to the rest of the message.

They converted this tiny backyard years ago into a blacktop driveway big enough for the new Cadillacs Dr. Walker had written into the by-laws as part of the pastor's annual compensation. They tell Pastor Thorn fought to get that clause expunged before they called their next pastor. The old Saab stalls three times before Pastor backs the car out onto the street and winces through a few practice shots on the portable hoop he'd bought at Hermann's. Basketball always helps him organize his thoughts. Usually, when he's stuck on a sermon point he shoots some free throws and it soon comes together. He's been shooting a lot of free throws the past two weeks, but he's still not done with Sunday's message. He'll just have to keep shooting. After he makes ten in a row he eases into the Saab and points it toward Newark and a time in his life when he was ruler of his world.

The Hole is a fenceless, sunken court on South Orange Avenue in Newark surrounded by benches and swings and jungle gyms and kids with nothing to do and no one to miss. The sun has just begun to dip below the line of tenements across the avenue and a shade is enveloping the court, drawing shirtless ballplayers from all directions like lemmings to a cliff. It isn't a big deal, really. Just a poorly organized 6'-and-under Friday evening league. But hey it fits his schedule, isn't too demanding, and allows him to taste competition against some young blood on a regular basis while staying in touch with what's happening on the street.

He's the tallest on his team, so he's forced to play center, screaming in pain from his bruised ribs the whole time, banging and being banged underneath. His preference is still the high-wire all-City PSAL finesse game he brought to Jadwin but seldom got a chance to display in Pete Carril's backdoor-cutting slowdown system, but on this day the banging and the pain proves cathartic. And 5 years of prison weight training is helping him give more than he receives. He completes his game-ending dunk with a chin-up.

"Get that boy an agent! The Nets could use him!"

It's Cornel, digging the scene in a gangster-lean against his white Benzaroni with the sunroof top and smoked-black tinted windows. His usual accessories are at his sides, one caressing his small paunch. His bald head is shining like a halo above his canary yellow pinstriped suit, and instead of the hoop there's now a gold cross hanging from his right ear.

"Sup, Cornel! You should be out here. You could use it."

Pastor climbs the steps to street-level dripping sweat. His towel can't soak it up fast enough but Cornel still gives him a hug. "You a'ight, Tony? I heard about what happened at the cemetery."

"Now that I just cleared my head I'm fine."

"You gotta stay outta the way of them bullets. Remember, you're supposed to do *my* funeral. I'm holding you to that."

"I never promised that."

"Listen, Prelate, I was thinking about your problem after you left Shamblee's yesterday? And it occurred to me, those letters never actually said get out of First Baptist. What if they mean get out of running for Monumental?"

"Who would know I'm a candidate besides us?"

"You never know what these committee members are saying to people. You know how word spreads. You think something's a secret and everybody already knows."

"Look, it doesn't matter. It's not going to change what I do."

"Listen to this."

"What."

"I talked to my friend, the secretary of the committee? She faxed me a list of all the preachers who sent in résumés. And Doc, there's a crazy brotha on the list! Shabazz McCoy. I heard the man keeps poisonous snakes in his house. Wife couldn't take it anymore so she grabbed the kids and moved out on him last month. He comes to the conference sometimes. I know you've seen him before. He doesn't have a church, he works for one of those demolitions and site clearance companies. The same one that did the building next door to Shamblee's. In fact, he was there in Shamblee's yesterday just before you came in. You probably walked right past him as he was leaving."

"I keep telling you, I don't care who it is. Let him do what he has to do, and I'll do what I have to do."

"Listen, Doc. I called Dexter and he said Shabazz applied for First Baptist, but they rejected him because he didn't have any training. When Shabazz got the letter he went crazy on them. They had to get a restraining order on the man. It's got to be him." He dangles an index card in Pastor's face. "I got his address right here. He's in Mapelwood, right off Springfield. Let's go pay him a visit."

"I don't have time, Co. I've got *your* wedding to do, which we *will* talk about as soon as we get some alone time, and I'm still not done for Sunday."

"Doc, there were bullets flying over your head just a few hours ago. And BPD doesn't have jurisdiction on this. By the time they get all the red tape outta the way you could be the *late* Rev. Dr. Antonio Hook."

"Co, I don't think those bullets were meant for me. If Shabazz or anybody else really wanted to shoot me, they could've done it already."

"At least let's go find out."

"...Alright, let's get it over with so we can finally put this to rest."

"Cool. Let's take my car."

He turns to his accessories, remembers his manners and introduces them. "Oh, Tony Hook, this is Virginia and her sister, Georgia. I'm taking them to the citywide revival in Philly tonight."

Georgia extends her hand and says, "Doctor Hook, pleased to meet you."

"Nice meeting you, too."

They slide into the back. Pastor drapes his towel over the front seat of Cornel's Eighth Pastor's Anniversary gift and eases in. Like her sister, Georgia is put together: perfect make-up, legs for days, curves in all the right places, designer accessories and a weave that must've set her back a grand. Ever since Pastor mentioned Burro's prediction Cornel has been trying to set him up with his idea of the perfect woman for him. All the wrong types. This smells like another set up.

"Is that your car in front of us?" asks Georgia. A couple of kids have their hands cupped around their heads pressed up against the old Saab's passenger window.

"How'd you guess," Pastor says as Cornel bullies his way into traffic bobbing his head to Mase booming through the speakers.

"Reverend Brown mentioned you drove a convertible," she says over the beat. "He didn't say it was a Saab, though. I just *love* Saabs."

"Yeah, I can't get it out of my system."

"You look even better in person than I imagined you on the radio," she went on.

"Oh, you listen to the broadcast?"

"Every Sunday on NJU."

"Dag, Georgia," whispers Virginia, who is sitting right behind Pastor. "Give the man some room."

"Georgia," says Cornel. "Did I mention that First Baptist is the only black church in Belton? The pulpit there reeks of prestige."

They giggle in the back. Pastor gives Cornel the eye. He gives Pastor the grin.

Traffic is heavy both ways on South Orange Avenue, but the lights have been with them until now. They're sitting in first place at the intersection, horns are blasting them from behind, and Cornel is staring into the rearview mirror.

"Co, the light's green."

He waits until it turns yellow before he screeches off and hangs a series of rights that bring us right back to South Orange Avenue, several cars behind a black conversion van. "That's the same van that was following us yesterday," he says, throwing the transmission into park and jumping out. "You drive!"

CHAPTER 10

The light changes to green and Cornel is racing up the double yellow line. Traffic's just beginning to accelerate and he's gaining on the van when he stops abruptly and doubles over, his hands on his knees, his tongue almost lapping the pavement. Pastor stops for him and he stumbles past the hood of car, tosses the towel on the floor and flings himself back in, heaving. Georgia and Virginia are stunned into silence.

"South Mountain YMCA is looking for new members," says Pastor.

"And BET's looking for comics," he manages between gasps. "Haven't you heard that bodily exercise profits just a little?"

"It would sure profit your breathing a whole lot right now, though. So what were you planning do, invite him to New Life or carjack him?"

He picks up his cell phone and punches in some numbers. "I always wanted to sit high above traffic."

"The bus is easy to get to. And no one will arrest you for riding it."

He shows Pastor his palm. "Hello, Deacon Wilkins? It's Pastor. ...Yeah, I was just exercising. Listen, I need a favor. Would you run a plate for me?" He reads the letters and numbers off and waits. They're about to cross the border into Maplewood when he says, "Okay. ...Why? ...Are you sure? ...A'ight, Deac. Thanks."

"Well?"

"That was my deacon that works at DMV. The guy's name is Joe Forte, but the address is a P.O. box in Bloomfield and there's no phone number." He scratches his bald head. "That usually means it's a celebrity or somebody in law enforcement."

Virginia and Georgia are reapplying their makeup in the car. Shabazz McCoy's house is at the end of a dead-end street bordering Maplewood Park. It's a narrow colonial with white vinyl siding that stands out among the terraced two-families dominating this section of Maplewood, a stone's throw from Irvington.

"What are you going to do, Co? Ask him if he was at the cemetery taking target practice this afternoon?"

"Why you gotta have everything planned out, Doc?" He opens the gate to the rusty chain-link fence. "Just let the Lord lead." And out of nowhere an auburn pit bull tears past a broken-down swing set, charging us. "Got-*damn*!" Cornel quickly steps back, slams the gate shut, and pulls out his gun.

"Is the Lord leading you to shoot that dog?"

The pit bull slams up against the fence barking, spraying saliva through the links.

"He's leading me to defend myself. This dog don't have to preach on Sunday."

Pastor dips into his old bag of Things To Do When Confronted By A Ravenous Canine. One of the few things bequeathed him by his mom. According to her all her relatives could do it.

"Yo! Put the gun away!" It's a shirtless Shabazz at his screen door, looking even more cut than he did yesterday.

"Call your dog off," yells Cornel.

"Put the gun away first!"

"Call him off first!"

"He can't jump the fence!" says Shabazz, still behind the screen. "Now either you put the gun away or leave, or I'm calling the cops!"

There are neighbors on their porches now. Cornel looks around, steps back from the fence and puts the gun away. Shabazz pushes through the screen door, but doesn't call off the dog. He meets them at the fence and grabs the barking dog by the collar. Sweat stipples the top of Shabazz's bald head.

"What y'all want?"

The dog starts calming down.

"Where were you this afternoon, Rev'en?"

"At work," he says, then he looks at Pastor. "Hey, what you doing, Hook? Trying to stare my dog down?"

"Never mind him, Rev'en, look at me. I got two pieces of news for you. One, I know you're looking for a church, but Monumental ain't for you. I know the chairman at a church in Philly, about a hundred members. I could recommend you, but you need more work on your Greek and Hebrew. The second thing, take this as a warning or whatever you like: stay away from Academy and Third, and don't send anymore letters. God don't like ugly and bad things happen to people who mess with preachers. So don't mess with God's anointed, and if you know what's good for you, don't do his prophets no harm."

The dog's tail is between its legs now, its hair standing up on its back, and it's trying to pull away. Cornel backs off the sidewalk, they get into the car and Cornel drives off, leaving Shabazz at the fence looking confused.

"You should try being more direct, Co."

"Hey, my style works for me. What'd you do to that dog?"

"Found its eyes, that's all. The man probably has *no* idea what just happened. I don't think it's him."

Cornel and his playmates-of-the-month are gone and Pastor is showered and dressed. He's already had another slice of toast and about half of the gallon of Deer Park water. He's in his bedroom tightening the knot in his blue-and-gold striped tie and praying for his sister when the doorbell rings, draining power from the air conditioners and briefly dimming the lights. He grabs his blue blazer and keys, bounces down the stairs and opens the dungeon door to a Talbot's model in a yellow dress who looks just like Chris Sears.

"Don't tell me," Pastor says. "You've finally seen the light and now you need my help cracking the case."

She doesn't return his smile so he knows he doesn't want to hear what she has to say, but she says it anyway.

"Reverend, would you come with me, please?"

She doesn't say another word during the entire ride.

"I really don't have the time for this," he says as they walk into the station house. "I've got a wedding in twenty minutes." And the last thing he needs is for Biju and her crew to be standing out in the parking lot, or even worse, on the steps waiting for him, attracting unwanted attention.

Sears instructs the desk sergeant to send McManus in, and then she leads Pastor down a long corridor to the back of the building.

Sears's office doesn't even have her name on the door. It's smaller than Pastor's and looks like it's been dashed together in a hurry for a low-level audit manager. Bare walls, dull carpet, bright lighting, sleek undersized furniture. No framed pictures anywhere, no clues to life away from the job.

She looks down into Pastor's face from across her organized desk. It contains only a telephone, a manila folder with his name inked on the tab, a stack of envelopes next to it, and her laptop. The chair she told him to sit in is much lower than hers, and is bolted to the floor. He feels like a freshman in Principal Meehan's office after his little gang of athletes was busted with stolen athletic department stuff in their lockers. Stuff they didn't even need because they all had better at home.

McManus walks in without knocking, towing a video camera on a wheeled tripod. He nods at Pastor with a look as serious as the sound of his voice the last time they spoke on the phone, then sets up the camera in the corner to Pastor's right. "It's on," he says to Sears, then steps out of Pastor's field of vision. Pastor glances over his shoulder and catches him leaning against the wall behind him, picking his nose.

During the silent treatment on the way over here he figured Sears was tripping over his comments in today's *Mirror*, just like Tubby and Ellis, and was escorting him to a hastily called meeting with BPD and city brass. He figured they'd try to solicit his cooperation and silence with assurances that they were still working on Anemone's case but told the press it was a suicide to preserve Belton's rep as a safe community and give the RBTF's Showcase on Sunday a chance to succeed. Pastor figured that because that's how they've operated in the past. But this is starting to look like an interrogation, and Sears is starting to look like a bully.

She powers on her laptop, bangs on the keys a little, then flips open the folder on her desk.

"Reverend, we'll be needing some hair and blood samples from you to do some DNA testing," she matter-of-facts him.

"DNA?" says Pastor, trying to hide his surprise. "Why?"

"Chief Ellis is under tremendous pressure from City Hall. The whole town now thinks it was murder, so they need to see some movement on this right away."

Ah. So this is punishment, and he has no choice but to play the game by their rules.

"That's all well and good," he says. "But why do you need DNA from me?"

"Because you were the last person seen with her before she was murdered. The M.E.'s preliminary report shows that Mrs. Allon put up a struggle. She had hair clippings all over her arms and face, two split nails on her right hand with a couple of short hairs caught in them, and some skin underneath two other nails on the same hand. More than enough for a decent DNA profile. Mr. Allon gave us samples here Thursday morning. We should get the results back pretty soon, but I'm not expecting a match."

"Why not?"

"He had no scratches on him, and forensics says they don't think the hairs are his either. It's only a matter of time before we find who they belong to, though. Whoever killed her must be walking around with some pretty embarrassing scratches. You have any recent scratches anywhere on your body, Reverend?"

Pastor refuses to let her see him sweat, but his armpits aren't cooperating, they're like a swamp now, and he's getting that queasy feeling in the pit of his stomach.

"But why do the skin and hair have to belong to her killer? She could've accidentally scratched someone earlier and then gotten killed by someone completely different later."

"Not likely, but it *is* possible. If that's what happened, though, we'd need a statement telling us when it happened, where, how, if there were any witnesses, and some kind of credible alibi for 10:00 Wednesday night."

"And if that person can't come up with any of that?"

"The physical evidence from the body is all we have to go on right now. If there's a match, we'll have to hold that person."

The scratches on his loins are beginning to heal, but his spirit is still raw. What a time to realize that part of him, skin and hair, was with Anemone when she died. Not enough for him to prevent her death. But just enough to put him in the mini cell at Trenton State, killing time until it's his turn for the Big Jab if the real murderer isn't caught. Sears is toying with him. She has that investigator's hunch, or perhaps righteous hope, that the skin and hair are Pastor's.

"Now let's look at the time line. You said you dropped Mrs. Allon off at about nine-thirty Wednesday night."

"That's right."

"Officer Monsees says he spoke to you that night at about 9:45. He says you were parked on Fairview, halfway in Mrs. Allon's driveway."

"I suppose so."

"What were you doing there?"

"Praying. Sometimes the urge hits me and I just have to stop wherever I am. It's probably the most important part of what I do."

"He says he left you there in the van. What time did you drive off?"

"A few minutes afterwards? I don't know."

"A few meaning ten or fifteen? Or—"

"A few meaning like maybe two or three. I don't know. I wasn't exactly timing my prayer."

"Where'd you go from there?"

"I drove back to the church, went inside, and stayed there in my office on the floor praying some more until about 12:00. Then I went home."

"What time was it when you got to the church?"

"I don't know. I didn't even turn the light on when I came in. But I know I left around 12:00 because when I got home the game was over and the news had just started. It's just a three minute walk from there to the parsonage."

"Anybody around who may have seen you pull into the church parking lot?"

"There's nothing but commercial property between there and the train station. That time of night the whole place is like a cemetery."

She looks at him with those cool sand eyes.

"So, basically, you don't have an alibi."

"Sergeant, what are you suggesting? I'm sure you investigated and found out what number Anemone called from the Walker Library Wednesday night. That's your killer."

"The call was placed to a J. Dough. D-O-U-G-H. Fictitious address."

"How's that possible?"

"It was a cellular number. Lots of places sell them now. You buy 50 bucks worth of pre-paid airtime and they set you up with a cheap phone and a phone number, and you don't even have to show ID."

"So you're saying she could've been calling anywhere."

"Anywhere," she says.

"And that puts everyone back in play and gives you a reason to interrogate me."

With her elbows on the table she laces her fingers together and rests her chin on them.

"Reverend, I'm sorry to have to ask you this question so directly, but were you and Mrs. Allon ever lovers?"

She had to go there, didn't she. Now he's feeling like Clinton even though the answer is no.

"What kind of question is that?" Pastor is proud of the way he's been capping his emotions so far, but his facade cracked a little on that one. Satan is the accuser of the brethren, and he knows how to lodge an accusation that will be damaging at just the right moment. God knows it's true, Pastor has been tempted by Anemone many times, but God's grace has been sufficient for him so far and His keeping power is real. But the truth won't do any good now. Sears has obviously made up her mind. Pastor guesses that's why Jesus never defended himself against his final accusers.

"We got a call from one of your members today who suggested you might have killed Mrs. Allon to keep her from exposing an affair you two were having. He said he could tell by the way she looked at you, but to me you seem too principled to sleep with one of your members."

He can tell by the way she's looking at him that she's enjoying all this.

"Some people will say anything, won't they?"

"So, basically," she says. "It looks like you had a motive."

"Looks can be really deceiving."

"Do we need to continue this, or can we go ahead and get it over with? I'm sure you'd like to be done with this, too."

"Am I under arrest?"

"No. We're just talking. You're here of your own volition."

"I am?"

"Sure. I asked you to come with me and you agreed."

"I didn't know I had a choice."

"You didn't ask, so I assumed you knew. You're not in custody. I never cuffed you. You don't have to give me the samples if you don't want to, but I'm assuming you want to put this case to bed just as badly as I do, so I know I can count on your cooperation, right?"

Pastor is cornered. With these red scabs running through his loins, surrendering the samples will mean an arrest for him eventually. But what choice does he have?

"I think I better speak to my lawyer. Can you give me some time to contact him?"

"Actually, that would just complicate things. If you were in your study, like you say, then you have nothing to worry about. Only guilty people need lawyers," she says.

"We both know that's not true. And only fools waive their rights."

She shifts some papers in the manila folder. Pastor notices on top of the pile of envelopes the letter he mailed to her. He can't tell if she's opened it yet.

"Did you have a fight with some gentlemen yesterday?"

"Gentlemen?"

"Mrs. Lila Vernon and three men came in here today and filed a complaint against you. They want you kept away from their property."

Pastor smiles and shakes his head, not knowing what else to do.

"I know, it doesn't sound like something you'd do. Walk into somebody's house and pick a fight with them."

"It's hardly a house, it's a church. A hate church. The FCA. And I didn't pick a fight with anybody. They assaulted me."

"We know all about them. When we saw FCA on the murder weapon we had to question them. All ten of them have solid alibis."

"They're hiding *something* in there, though. That's why they reacted the way they did when I stopped by to ask some questions."

"We've got some latitude when it comes to complaints like this. I'm willing to forget it in exchange for your cooperation."

"You already have it. The powers that be are ordained by God. That's why I'm here. But it feels like you're asking for more than just my cooperation."

"Reverend, let's face it. You were the last person seen with Mrs. Allon before her murder. Based on what we've gotten...let's just say the circumstances aren't stacking up in your favor."

He's trying to blow the sick feeling out of his stomach by exhaling. Trying to wake up from this nightmare by shaking his head. Nothing's working. This is spiritual warfare for real.

He feels like a sheep in wolf's clothing. The more he bahs and bleats, the more he looks like a wolf trying to get over.

"If I give you these samples, how long before you get the results?"

"Once we get the samples to the lab we could get results back, oh, within a couple of days."

"That fast? I've worked with inmates on paternity cases and it always took at least a month to get their results back."

"It depends on the kind of DNA test you do. There's an RFLP; that takes a few weeks. Then there's a PCR, that takes a few hours. That's the one we use in cases like this to rule certain people out."

"So, I'll know by what, Monday?"

"Probably. Could be later, or maybe even sooner. We use a private lab right here in Essex County. One of the best in the country."

She's right. Things aren't stacking up in Pastor's favor at all.

"So, what do you say?"

The subtext is clear. If he balks and calls His attorney she'll arrest him on suspicion of murder. By the time the media and the Thorns are finished with him he'll be the 22nd ex-pastor of First Baptist Church and an ex-candidate for the pulpit at Monumental Baptist Church. He breathes a prayer and checks his spirit for a green light.

"Alright. But please, I can't be late for the wedding."

"Great. You're doing the right thing by cooperating." She picks up the phone, keys in a four-digit number, and says, "Okay," then gets up and tells Pastor to follow. "The Chief's really on my back about this. It'll only take a few minutes, then I'll have Dt. McManus run you right over to the church."

Pastor glances down at his envelope again.

"I guess now you're getting a lot of information on Anemone from people who knew her," he says as they go through the doorway.

She harrumphs. "Dozens of letters and phone calls. If you believe them, she was everything from a hooker to an angel from heaven who gave up her immortality for love. We even had a psychic call in saying she was killed by a four year old who rode his bicycle from Newark to carry out a drug hit. People will say just about anything for some attention."

∫

McManus can't drop Pastor off after all. He has to run out on a car theft emergency, so Pastor is shown the backseat of a black-and-white. Valley Street is still under assault from the parade of cement mixers and dump trucks. They're on a 24/7 schedule trying to finish by their July 1st target date. The thoughts keep knocking around in Pastor's head like a pair of sneakers in a dryer: there've been cases prosecuted on thinner evidence with weaker motivation. He knows he can't get a lawyer involved. It would get out and then Monumental would immediately drop him as a candidate. And he refuses to go out like a sucker.

The black-and-white drops him off at the front steps of the church. Burnette and Biju are waiting with their entourage. And standing with them are three people who definitely don't fit in. Verma, Smiley, and David Henry Thorn with a camcorder slung over his shoulder.

The short ceremony is seamless, with Thorn grinning through the whole thing behind his camera, and by the time they jump the broom and surround Pastor for group pictures he's sick to his stomach. He'd let his emotions regarding his relationship with his sister get the better of him and he hadn't thought things through carefully enough, because he was unprepared for how he felt after he said, "You may salute each other." He doesn't know which nauseated him more, the sight of them burying their tongues in each other's mouth right in front of him, or Thorn zooming in close on their slobfest and proclaiming this his lucky day.

Biju sticks an envelope containing two crisp hundreds in Pastor's blazer pocket and Burnette gives him a kiss on the cheek before they leave. Thorn gladly offers to close up and Pastor walks to his car at the parsonage knowing two things for certain: Thorn will be on the phone before he even pulls out of the backyard; and Pastor will never do another same-sex union again. The issue is forever settled in his heart and mind. Women were made for men, not for other women pretending to be men.

Pastor feels like Judas carrying his 30 pieces of silver, but stops at the ATM and deposits the money anyway. Payday is a whole 12 days away and the coffers are empty. At least now he'll be able to get some credit cards current.

ᓂ

It's only about a half-mile from Third Street down Academy to Hixon, but after presiding over a wedding that could prove to be the second greatest fiasco of his life Pastor needs some speed to take his mind of his troubles. Some teenagers are playing touch football on the street, lamppost to lamppost, so he downshifts, negotiates the right gracefully and parks on the flattened grass at the edge of the rusted chain-link fence surrounding Belton Academy's field.

This is Academy Heights, a small neighborhood of distinctive Victorian homes ringing Belton Academy.

The Queen Anne Victorian across the street with the perky geraniums in its flower boxes is wide awake: lights are already burning on the porch, throughout the first floor, in a couple second-floor rooms, and in one of the turrets; and the central air unit is humming. The power meter is probably spinning like a CD in a 56X drive and Pastor figures PSE&G must be almost as happy with them as they are with him.

The large weeping willow tree in the middle of the front yard is doing the hula in the sticky breeze, and the tall poplars bordering the huge property are rocking and swaying in the dusk like one of Dr. Gaye's choirs.

Dexter and Malisa drive matching his and hers Volvos and both sport the same GOP, NRA, and Pro-Life bumper stickers, but Pastor knows Dexter is home because the car sitting in the driveway near the front of the house is missing the Icthus, the silver fish outline next to the Volvo nameplate, and the license plate border that reads:

I Want To Be Like Barbie Because
THE BROAD HAS EVERYTHING!

Dexter's rangy physique is lost in his bathrobe. He's wearing a forced smile that's hard to distinguish from a grimace, and a fresh bruise under his left eye. If Pastor is going to do a decent Reverend Snoop impression he'll need Dexter to buy him some time with the church while he um, snoops around.

Dexter shows Pastor into the family room and they sit down on the green leather sectional. Framed 8x10 photos of their three children at various ages, including their first communions when they were members of St. Joseph's Catholic, and family poses dominate the huge mantle across from them. So do pennants from Dartmouth, Howard, and Wheaton, and photo finishes of Malisa winning at the Colgate Women's Games, and Dexter at the Milrose. There's an old poster-sized color photo of a young Dexter and Malisa running with the bulls in the narrow streets of Pamplona, memorabilia from their Army ROTC days including two 8x10s of them in their dress greens, and a couple of shiny microphone statuettes, awards for their voice-over work at WSTU.

"What happened, Malisa upset with you again?" He knows Pastor is only half-kidding.

"I'll be fine."

Mmm-hmm, sure. The bruise under his eye is proof that Malisa has found another use for their frying pan, but it would pain an old jock like Dexter to admit he couldn't get out of the way in time, so Pastor doesn't press him. Malisa's the jealous type and has always accused him of fooling around with every pretty girl on the track team. And it's not hard to see why. Dexter's handsome in a healthy, black Ule Gibbons kind of way. Intense eyes. Not a gray hair on his head. Well preserved for 50, the result of running two miles every day at five in the morning. A black man with power. It's not hard to imagine a coed or two falling for him.

"I'd get that looked at in the morning. Concussions can be sneaky. I don't want to have to come see you in the hospital anytime soon."

"I'll be alright. Nothing a little rest and prayer can't cure."

"How's Malisa?"

"Mad, as usual. She just left again. Ever since she quit her Hormone Replacement Therapy she's been running every night to help her sleep. Add that to the two miles she does every morning and she might as well be in training for the sixteen hundred again."

"Why'd she quit? I thought it was helping."

"The progesterone was driving her crazy half the month, and she was scared to death of getting uterine cancer if she remained on the estrogen alone. So now she's taking St. John's Wort and exercising as much as she can."

"Still tough on the both of you, huh?"

"What can I say." He shakes his head as Pastor crushes a mosquito on the back of his left hand. "Gail Sheehy and the web can help me understand the science of the mood swings and the hot flashes and the diminished libido, but they can't make them go away. Anyway, she's been like this for a long time, so I don't think we can blame just menopause."

"Getting her old job back would help a lot, though. Any news yet?"

"It's not going to happen. Those schools they closed down were horrible, even for Newark standards. They're not re-opening any of them. And, the new chancellor's only filling positions in the other schools with young teachers. Malisa thought that year she spent volunteer teaching at the Essex County Jail would help her cause, be she can't even get a substitute gig."

"Sorry to hear that," Pastor says.

"Oh, I wouldn't worry about Malisa too much. She was always good at saving her money, and she got a real nice pension when she left. Then she invested in the stock market with me and made a killing. She's just working now to have something to do."

Pastor throws him the head nod, then smacks another mosquito on the back of his neck.

"Dex, I think you left the door open again."

He rises, apologizing, to close it. One of Dexter's idiosyncrasies. He almost never closes a door fully.

"So, are you all moved out now?"

"Yeah."

"The entire office?"

"The entire office. Never had to do it before. It took a lot longer than I thought it would. Almost everything I touched held a memory that made me sit back and reminisce."

"I can't believe you've had all that exercise equipment and extra running gear in a *first floor* office and no one ever broke in and stole anything."

"Security's always been great at St. Thomas. They don't even let *me* in or out without signing my name for the guard."

"How'd the sale go?"

"Made over a thousand dollars."

"Really?"

"If Nike would have known I was going to sell almost half the promotional stuff they gave me, they probably would've terminated their contract with me *before* I retired."

"Who bought all that stuff? Students? Professors?"

"All kinds of people came by. That ad we ran in the *Mirror* last week really helped."

"Oh. So you finally converted to the local paper."

"Never. We'll always be a *Star-Ledger* house. I just broke down and advertised in the *Mirror* because Malisa suggested I target only local people who would have a sense of connection with the stuff. If she hadn't gone down there with me I probably still wouldn't have done it."

"Anyway, Dex. I didn't stop by just to chat. Two things. First, we need to redo Anemone's committal service. The sooner the better, like tomorrow at the gravesite."

"Okay."

"Second, I need you to cover for me the next few days. I probably won't be able to make it to the cemetery. I have too much to do here."

"What's wrong, Tony?"

Pastor really doesn't want to tell him any more than he has to, but he can't keep him totally in the dark, either. Not if he wants his help.

"So far, I'm the last person to have seen Anemone alive. I got a haircut Wednesday morning and it turns out that they found hair shavings on Anemone's body; and whoever killed her was smart and covered his tracks well because they didn't find anything else on the body or at the scene, not even prints. Add that up with the fact that I have no one who can vouch that they saw me in my office at 10:00 that night and I have a pretty ticklish problem here. So, basically I need some time to prove to BPD that it couldn't have been me."

"...Don't feel bad," he says. "They're just being thorough."

"Yeah, well that's what worries me. And Thorn is trying to tighten the screws on me again. I can sure use some help with him right now."

"Don't worry, I've got your back. Take whatever time you need."

Before Pastor can say another word Dexter says, "I'll be right back," and jogs upstairs. He's back in a hurry but detours into the kitchen, then returns with an envelope sticking out of his robe pocket and two cold bottles of Naya in his hands.

"Thanks," Pastor says as Dexter tosses him one of the bottles.

"Tony, I'm really glad you stopped by. I have something to tell you, too. I've been meaning to tell you this for a while, but I could never find the right time or words."

"Sounds like you're about to make a confession or something."

He guzzles half the bottle and wipes his brow; and Pastor takes a gulp from his and gets that sharp pain in his head from drinking something too cold too fast.

"Sunday after service I'm handing you my resignation as Chairman of the Deacon Board."

Pastor laughs. Nervously.

Dexter doesn't.

"Retirement's made you funnier."

"I'm not joking."

"Steven Wright humor *and* impressions. Can I be your agent?"

Silence for a while. He drinks more water. It's the intensity in his eyes that finally convinces Pastor that he's serious.

"Why, Dex?"

He bows his head. "I've spent half my marriage away from home at track meets or on recruiting trips. I promised Malisa that after I retired we'd do more things together. Travel, you know. I'm trying to keep my word."

He opens the envelope and holds out two Continental Airlines tickets to Southwest Regional Airport in Fort Myers, Florida.

"Taking a vacation?"

"I picked these up from the travel agent this afternoon while you all were at the cemetery. I'm going to surprise Malisa. I bought a little place on the beach in Florida about two months ago. I'm taking her down there for a couple of weeks. We're leaving right after service on Sunday."

"I'm stunned. I don't know what to say."

"She doesn't know about this yet, so don't tell her, okay?"

"You know me. I can keep a secret. But what about her job?"

"It's a government job; she can call in sick. ...What're you thinking, Tony?"

The last time Pastor felt like this was at Magic Johnson's first retirement speech. Now he's thinking about how this will affect his standing at the church even if he can manage to avoid arrest. Dexter has been his first line of defense against the Thorns since day one. With David Henry reloading fresh ammunition after their encounter tonight Dexter is doing this all at the wrong time. He can't do this now, not until Pastor can get better control of things. He told Pastor at the beginning of the academic year about his retirement from both positions as phys ed professor and track coach. But he never mentioned anything about resigning as chairman. Pastor's feeling hypocritical because he hasn't told Dexter about Monumental. He doesn't know how to be anything but pastoral at this moment. His thoughts default to the people of FBC.

"Dex, I think this is going to turn this church upside down. Without you around to balance him out Thorn is likely to get out of hand."

"Willie Gumbs is a good man. He can handle Thorn."

"We both know he has no time. He can barely handle the vice-chairman duties as it is with law school and all. I know it's a lot to ask, but any chance you can put this off for a week? Especially since Malisa doesn't even know about it yet?"

"I'm sorry, Tony, but I've got to do this now, or we may not *last* until next week. Besides, the tickets are non-refundable."

They're about the same height, so Pastor is looking right into his eyes as they shake hands again. He's feeling shame now for asking Dexter to delay his chance at his own happiness just so Pastor could have a shot at his. Dexter has never been anything but good to him. He wishes him well as he reaches for the door and opens it to the frightening by surprise face of Dale Dawkins.

"Chap!" exclaims Dexter.

"I was just about to ring the doorbell, Deac."

"Reverend Dawkins, what's up?! I was just leaving."

When Pastor closes the door behind him he notices, for the first time, why their geraniums remain so spry in this wilting heat. They're all silk.

\J

The moon looks like a yellow button on the collar of a blue velvet sky. It's almost 9:00, heat is still squatting in the streets, and the two black-and-whites in Ike Allon's driveway are making Brian Mulady look like a prophet. Well-crafted FOR SALE signs are peeking on in curiosity all along the block. Deja vu all over again? Hopefully the cemetery sniper didn't come to Belton and finish the job before Pastor could make Ike confess that he knew who killed Anemone, or dig up the other tapes she'd made in their basement.

The house is looking tired under its gambrel roof, as if it's too old for all this activity, this commotion. Ike bought it five years ago, before prices began to rise again, in order to live the American dream. He started his body shop on Springfield Avenue in Newark on a shoestring. It became such a success that he was able to put a large down payment on this house. This was one of the last blocks in the Mews to integrate, and also one of the few now with only one black family. The expressions on the faces of the two neighbors talking under the street lamp tell their pain. All their worst fears are being realized. They've been saying all along that if too many blacks from Newark and vicinity moved into Belton they'd bring crime with them. The house seems to agree.

Pastor notices the ADT sign on the front door, shakes his head and knocks on the leaded glass before opening it. A young uniformed officer stops him from entering.

"I'm sorry, Reverend." Neat baby dreads peek out from under her cap. "You can't come in yet."

"Is Ike okay?"

"He's fine." She puts her hand on Pastor's shoulder and gently pushes him back through the door. He catches a glimpse inside. It looks like the aftermath of a cell tossing by a goon squad looking for contraband at Jersey State. He's about to allow himself to be pushed away when he hears Ike's voice from upstairs.

"Rass clot'! It's not here."

He repeats it several times with new vigor, as if he's found new things to refresh his disgust. Pastor stiffens under the officer's hands.

"Officer, let me go talk to him. I think he needs me right now."

Their eyes lock briefly and he sees she is a compassionate person trying to play it tough. Pastor's seen that look many times in the stone faces of younger inmates. No matter what side of the law you operate on, displaying compassion these days can be a death knell, because the world is getting colder. But it's only godly compassion that can heal the world, and it wins out this time. She looks over her shoulder at a grizzled older cop who's wearing a bushy mustache and two stripes on his sleeves. He's pecking away with his index fingers on a laptop.

"His minister's here."

The grizzled one doesn't even look up. "So? What are you telling me for? It's your scene."

She turns back to Pastor, pauses for a moment and then exhales. "Go ahead up," she says. "Just don't touch anything."

Whoever did this was either in a hurry, a bad mood, or both.

Ike is in the master bedroom on the second floor, a huge room that stretches back almost the entire length of the house on one side. Ike doesn't believe in air conditioners. "Didn't have them in Jamaica, so why here?" he always says. Two windows are open, but because they don't cross-ventilate it's still hot enough to draw beads of sweat onto his forehead. When he sees Pastor he says, "Bumba clot'! See what they do to me house, Minister?"

Going for his throat is probably the most efficient way to get the truth out of somebody like Ike, but with Jesus in him, the Holy Ghost on him, and a couple of cops still downstairs, it could never be an option for somebody like Pastor. He'll have to coax it out through love and prayer.

"I'm sorry, Ike. When did this happen?"

He's glad Ike's back to the in-your-face demeanor he'd become accustomed to. In that familiar rage he's incapable of erecting anymore barriers, because when a man's feeling the purity of his anger he's usually at his most truthful as well.

"Me gone visit me mother after the funeral to ask why she didn't come. No matter how much you dislike someone, you still pay you respects when they gone. They're human just like you. When me get home this how me find the place. Haul-and-pull-up."

"How did they get past the alarm?"

"Me no have no alarm, Minister. Not for me house *or* me car. Me just put the signs up, but me not throwing me money away on that foolishness."

"Why not? Didn't you read that article in the *Mirror* about the burglaries?"

He choopses. "Me no read that rubbish, and me no believe in alarms. All they do is tell you when something happen already, they no stop anything from happening. Me protect me property me own way."

Obviously, Ike needs to reevaluate his way. Pastor says, "Man, it looks like a Tropical Breeze just blew through here." Either Ike's an undiscovered stage talent or he's never heard the name before. He looks at Pastor through those perpetually red eyes more perplexed than Dr. Roberts did when Pastor showed up for the first day of Akkadian because it fit into his schedule and he was determined to learn it; when he told him he couldn't stay because it was a Ph.D. level language course not open to M.Div. students. "Anybody see anything?" Pastor asks.

"No witnesses. Everybody at work or school during the day here."

Or inside under the air conditioner like normal Americans.

"Anything missing?"

"Nothing so far."

"You know who did it, don't you?"

"How me supposed to know who do this?"

"Whoever did it must've been looking for something."

"You damn right," Ike says.

"And you know what they're looking for, don't you?"

"Minister, what you talking about?"

"Ike, at the cemetery today, you *had* to be the target. You know something that somebody doesn't want to get out."

"Listen, I taking care of this. Me one. Somebody do me something, I doing it right back to them. Like the Bible say, *An eye for an eye.*"

"It says a lot more than that, Ike. And I think you know who killed her."

He stares a hole through Pastor, the anger sizzling in his eyes.

Yeah, he knew. Pastor could see it in his face.

"Why haven't you told the police?"

"Revenge is the sweetest medicine. Me not getting mad, me getting even; and no police could help me do that."

"Candy was right, wasn't he? There *is* a tape. You saw the whole thing. You didn't know there was a camera in that deejay booth until I moved it into the doorway. When I went outside to wait for BPD you went into the deejay booth and turned the camera on, and you watched the whole thing on tape."

CHAPTER 11

"So what if there is a tape. It no change anything."

"Yes it does, Ike. You were shot at. Your life's in jeopardy. Not to mention that you tampered with crime scene evidence and they could arrest you for obstructing justice. You need to turn that tape over to the police and let them handle it from here."

"Me don't need to do anything, Minister. And nobody getting arrested, either. And since you're my minister you can't tell anybody what I tell you, or else I coming after you and your church."

Church Administration class and the major points of the New Jersey Clergy-Communicant law are making Pastor grit his teeth. "I'm not telling anybody anything. Even if I wanted to, I can't. But I don't understand why you're letting your wife's killer go free. New Jersey has the death penalty now. Go to the cops and the killer gets the death penalty. What better way could there be to avenge her murder?"

"Cho! O.J. kill his wife and everybody know it, but because he have money he buy his freedom. Me no trust the white man's justice. Not even a tape can guarantee a conviction. Remember Rodney King and Simi Valley? And even if we get a conviction, by the time we go through all the appeals it could be ten years before we get to the execution. Cho!, me using me own law and getting me own justice."

"Come on, Ike. They'll give a vigilante the death penalty, too. And what sense would that make. Tell Detective Sears what's going on, before any more people get hurt."

"And before they start suspect you, eh? Me hear what they saying 'bout you."

Ike's a pretty smart dude. So, he thinks he's read Pastor's motives, because he thinks he knows how to read men. Unfortunately, he never really learned how to read people. That's why Anemone's been able to fool him for so long. He looks at Pastor in the fullness of his anger. A drop of sweat falls from his chin. Pastor loosens his tie even more.

"Why would they suspect me? Since you saw the tape you know that I didn't kill her."

"They so blind. They think they see, but they no see. They think they know, but they no know."

"Do you still have the tape, or did the killer find it?"

"Me get rid of the tape yesterday."

"What? You destroyed it?"

"No," he said. "Me send it to you for safe keeping."

Again he looks at Pastor hard and long. Pastor wipes his brow with his handkerchief.

"Well since you know who killed Anemone, and we both know I'm not going to say anything to anyone, why don't you tell me who it was. Just to satisfy my curiosity, and so I could pray for them."

Pastor can almost hear heaven groaning as the words leave his mouth and he immediately disowns them. Unfortunately, each of them has a homing device attached. Desperation sometimes leads the best of us astray, in this case down to the level of the spiritual con man using his position as a cloak for his own agenda. Didn't the serpent pull the same stunt? But Ike's more cynical than Eve ever was, and refuses to bite.

"You'll find out soon enough, Minister. And when you do, you'll want to do more than just pray."

"What about the egg, Ike. Did you put that egg in her hand?"

He doesn't answer, he just keeps staring Pastor down and he knows that he did.

"Why? Why an egg? What was that all about?"

"Just my way." He nods.

The heat that's suffocating Pastor seems to be affecting Ike more now. He says, sharply, "Minister, think 'bout this. Anemone never own no video camera, so why the killer decide to tape the murder and leave it for me to find?"

Foolish Ike still doesn't realize that Anemone bought that camera behind his back with money she earned *on* her back. Man, hookers in upscale suburbia secretly recording sessions with their clients shows up on the news so much these days it's a cliché now. Whoever she met at 10:00 that night must've thought he'd gotten away with murder until he read yesterday's paper and got spooked, realizing Ike probably swiped the tape after discovering the body. Pastor doesn't have the heart to tell him now. He just shakes his head as Ike quickly answers his own question.

"A challenge. And Ike Allon no back down from challenges."

Pastor wipes his brow again and leaves Ike pretty sure of two things: he really *is* still in the dark about what Anemone was doing; and the murderer is probably one of Anemone's clients, who is now running scared trying to cover his tracks. It can't be one of the blackmail victims, because they all knew about the camera in the deejay room.

It's much cooler downstairs and Pastor asks the officers how the burglar got in. Grumpy says, "Either we're dealing with Alexander Monday here or the guy had a key, because there's not even a scratch on any of the doors or windows."

ᕲ

Choops. No packages in today's mail at home, and all Pastor finds in the church's post office box is another letter from his anonymous pen pal. He figures Ike was just yanking his chain about sending the tape to him for safekeeping, but he owes it to himself to make sure. Then it smacks him in the noggin that maybe there's someone else who knows something about Ike's hiding places.

Pastor races a few blocks away from the gaslights of cloistered suburbia to another world where glass glitters like fools gold in neon lights looming over abandoned playgrounds and graffiti laces up brick walls like silver metallic ivy and the smell of late dinners wafts through windows barricaded with child safety grating.

The last time Pastor was here at the Ivy Hill Houses, tucked into a forsaken patch of asphalt veldt on the edge of Ivy Hill Park in the Vailsburg section of Newark, just across the Belton border, he was practically assaulted getting out of his car by two Jehovah's Witnesses pushing a very expensive copy of *The Watchtower*. This is Mormon turf weekday mornings, and the Nation of Islam runs things at night. Pastor has wondered just what would happen if the three of them converged on a potential proselyte and debated each other for her eternal soul.

He parks right in front of Hazel Thompson's building, slaps the Club on, shuns a *Final Call* from the brother in the skull cap with the walkie-talkie who sounds like he's supervising the patrol tonight, presses the buzzer, and waits for Hazel to buzz him in.

The elevator has that public housing smell, like Dinty Williams's cell on two wing before they finally fixed his toilet, and it makes Pastor feel like he's back inside helping out on a case. It also makes him reflect on his own problems, which have ballooned so quickly he's sure he must be in the modern land of Uz. But good friends sometimes share secrets with each other, so he's not ready just yet to go sit in the ashes like Job, scrape himself with potsherds, and curse the day he was born.

"Come on in, Rev'en." Hazel Thompson shows him into her spare one bedroom with freshly polished floors. It's cool in here and the air conditioner has almost eliminated the smell of the fried fish she must've had for dinner, but not enough to keep his stomach from growling again.

"Can I offer you something to eat? I made a mean fried cat, some corn bread, and some macaroni and cheese."

"Oh, macaroni and cheese? No thanks. It smells great but my appetite's left me," Pastor says, taking a seat on the plastic-encased green sofa with the gold embroidered floral design in the fabric. "They don't let you eat at work?"

She chuckles, two protruding, widely spaced teeth marring a face otherwise so attractive that it makes her full lips look sensuous, not like forty pounds of liver—which is how Pastor's mother would describe them. "What they like to eat is a *whole* lot different than what I like."

"I *will* have some cold water if you don't mind."

Hazel Thompson is a "healthy" woman by community standards with something to hold onto in all the right places. She returns with a pink and green striped tumbler of cold water, no ice, serves it with hands accustomed to it, and sits down in the matching green love seat, flipping her long ponytail over her shoulder.

"Thanks much. I'm glad you were home tonight. I need to talk to you about Anemone."

She shifts her weight and a sadness moves in on her swiftly like a summer squall on the Sea of Galilee. That's Pastor's cue to draw on his pastoral anointing. For a millisecond he hesitates because grief counseling demands dipping into a pastor's Holy Ghost reservoir and he doesn't know what he has left after pouring out so much during this morning's eulogy. For five years he'd been giving lifers behind bars the hard truth, and if prison is anything it's consistent. Now he's still adjusting to the ministry pace of congregational life. Here surprise rules the day and it's easier to find yourself running on empty. He breathes a prayer for the Holy Ghost to overflow him once again so that he can offer a word in season to Hazel and be a blessing. He's also aware that he's taught and preached the Law of Reciprocity for over ten years now—*Give and it shall be given unto you; with what measure you mete it shall be meted back to you*—so he knows it's true. And according to that law, if he wants her to tell him what he needs to hear, then he'll have to first tell her what she needs to hear. He plucks his good hankie out of his blazer's breast pocket and hands it to her.

"It's alright, Hazel. Tears are good. That's one way God helps us to cleanse our wounds and wash away our pain."

"I just feel so bad, Rev'en," she says, clawing at her eyes with the hankie. "I let her down. She ain't had nobody else."

"...When a loved one dies like this, it's easy to feel responsible, like there's something we could have done to prevent it. You were her best friend. You loved her. That's all God asks of us."

"Aw, Rev'en. I just feel so bad. I couldn't even make the funeral. I had to work."

"What's most important is how you treated her in life, Hazel. And you can honor her in death by helping us catch her murderer."

"I already told the detective everything she asked."

"I'm sure you did, but they're still in the dark about some things. Let me ask you this. And you think real hard before you answer. Have you ever heard the name Tropical Breeze?"

Hazel drops her eyes into her lap for a while and fiddles with the mascara stained hankie before she buries her face in her hands and begins to sob.

Bingo!

Pastor slides over to the love seat, slips his arm around her shoulder and tells her everything's gonna be alright. She blows her nose with his good handkerchief, checks it, and gathers herself.

"I tried to get her to stop, but she'd made up her mind she was gon' make her own money and get away from Ike. She said she learned the hard way that a woman gotta have her own money, no matter how much her man got. And that she'd never let herself be financially dependent on no man ever again."

"God bless the child who's got her own," Pastor says, "but I wish she could have found another way to get it."

"Rev'en, I couldn't approve of the way she was doing it, but at least she was doing *something* to change her life. I *told* her not to marry Ike. I was seein' the same things in him that was in my late husband, and I *told* 'Nemone. But she wouldn't listen. She just wanted to leave that job so bad, and thought Ike was gon' take care of her. All she did was jump outta the frying pan, and into the fire."

"Hazel, did she ever mention anything about her clients, who they were? If she was having trouble with any of them?"

"No, Rev'en. She never talked about that. The only reason I fount out what she was doing was 'cause of that key she gave me."

"What key?"

She dips into her bedroom and returns. "'Nemone gave this to me about six months ago. It's for a safe deposit box at that bank on the corner of Irvington and Prospect, across from the Presbyterian church? She said I was like family to her and if anything ever happened to her she wanted me to have what was in the box. She wanted me to sign a card and everything, and I told her I wasn't signin' nothin' until she told me what was in it."

"...So? What'd she say?"

She dabs the corners of her eyes again and Pastor checks to see if he has an extra hankie because this is shaping up to be a two-hankie visit.

"She said she had to have a place to put her money and stuff, and I asked her where she was gettin' money from, 'cause I knew Ike would never let her work, and so she told me."

"Why didn't you give this to the detective?"

"I been black long enough to know you can't always trust the po-leece. She already was asking me where I was at 10:00 Wednesday night, even though Mr. Vernon had told her I was working that night while they went to their awards dinner. Wisdom told me to hold my peace. You don't have to tell folks everything you know."

"So why are you telling me?"

"'Cause you a man of God. I know I can trust you. And I know you cared about 'Nemone. I heard you gave a beautiful service for her this morning."

"Is there anything else in the box besides money?"

"I don't know. I ain't looked. But knowing 'Nemone, there could be anything in there."

"You've never looked in the box before?"

"Never, Rev'en. 'Nemone knew she could trust me. That's why we was so close."

"Hazel, Anemone bought a video camera last year. She was making videotapes of people and then blackmailing them with the tapes. That safe deposit box would be the logical place to keep them. It had to be somebody she knew and was expecting that killed her, and if we can get into that box we might find out who it was."

"You welcome to take the key and look, Rev'en."

"I wish I could, but only signees are authorized to use the keys, and they'd require ID. I'd have to go in with you."

"Well I'm off tomorrow morning, I could let you in then."

"Bless you, Hazel. I'll meet you at the bank at 9:00."

Pastor's jetting back from Hazel's with a snotty silk handkerchief in his pocket, feeling like he's just scored a major coup over Sears and will finally be able to show the whole town the truth. It's just after 10:00 and if he were in better physical condition he'd go out and celebrate, but instead he drags himself out of the car and through the back door without even bothering to close the gate, plops into the couch to watch the game, and lets sleep sneak up on him.

Kobe's already giving his post-game interview when Pastor jumps up thinking he heard something out back. Must've just been the television. Fans are celebrating another 30 point outburst by the brother who made afros cool again. He can't have anything new to say so Pastor wipes the drool and turns to the World Beat station on the DSS he put in four months ago after Cablevision raised its rates again for inferior product. Better access to the global village has meant less contact with the local community, though. He can't get Eye on Belton Three anymore, or any of the other local shows, and he's still having trouble paying the bill on time, but for now the trade-off is worth it.

There's a war going on in Pastor's stomach so he picks up the cordless phone and dials Peppie's Pizza. They're having a special on two one-topping mediums, so he orders one pepperoni and onion and one plain, then eyes the stairs. He decides against going upstairs to work on Sunday's sermon since he'll just be interrupted again in about 30 minutes, so he shuffles into the kitchen, grabs the large can of Raid from under the sink and opens the basement door to do some midnight roach hunting.

Whenever Brother Mac starts messing around downstairs he ends up seeing the little critters. Half a can in all the creepy nooks and crannies downstairs and around the kitchen baseboards usually does the trick. Then he spends the next two weeks sweeping up roach carcasses.

He's done by 12:15 and decides to kill the next 15 minutes watching the rest of the postgame show on NBA TV, but Bill Walton and Marv Albert are wrapping up the show so he switches back to World Beat and wrestles with the order of his points for Sunday's sermon.

By 12:45 the doorbell has rung twice, but no Peppie's. Just Mowatt for the second time today, and a little emaciated boy who looks like a poster child for Feed the Children selling cookies for his school. At the end of the school year? At night? Some people think the correct spelling for reverend is s-u-c-k-e-r.

He flops on the couch and decides to crash there for the night when the doorbell rings. He doesn't feel like chasing away any more people and is disappointed with Peppie's, so he just turns over and spoons with his throw pillow. But whoever's at the door is persistent. When he finally opens up it's Cornel, and Pastor's mood changes.

"Yo, Preacher. This is a bad year to be black in this town. We just peeped one of Belton's finest putting a Peppie's delivery boy through a sobriety test. The young brother was just doing his job delivering a pizza and they still got him for DWB."

"Ooo, I like that," says Virginia, wiggling to the World Beat. "It sounds different. He's got some culture."

"Virginia, be quiet. This man ain't got no culture. He bought a couple King Sunny Ade CDs and thinks that makes him a musical eclectic."

Virginia's wearing a bright smile, but Georgia looks like she just showed up at a Sister, I'm Sorry seminar with a lot to share.

"Don't listen to him. I actually do like all kinds of music." Pastor shows them into the living room. "So, the revival's over already?"

Georgia skins up her nose and pinches her nostrils on her way to the couch.

"They put the preacher up at 9:00. We left right afterwards. I had to find out about this wedding, man. I didn't even wait for a tape, and you know how important those are to me."

"You don't want to know about that wedding. Thanks to you I may have to start a new ministry in the jail again."

The three of them sit on what was going to be Pastor's bed for the night. He leans back in the easy chair trying to get his feet up on the ottoman without looking like an invalid.

"Get outta here, Doc. What happened? Did they show up?"

"Oh, they showed up, alright. I just wish they were the only ones who did. And it would've been nice to know the whole story on them before I agreed to do it. But we'll talk shop later." Pastor glances at Georgia. She looks much more respectable in this white linen dress and pumps than in the hot pants and halter outfit she wore at the Hole, but she's definitely dripping with some major Oprah Show attitude now. She looks around with upturned nose at the carpeting, and the ugly, bulging wood paneling hiding water-damaged walls, and the spots on the ceiling from the last time the bathroom pipes leaked, and Pastor's offended in a sympathetic sort of way. It's raggedy, yes, but it's still his home and she could at least wait until she leaves before revealing what she really thinks of this dump.

"A'ight, Bishop. We'll talk later. I was just telling the young ladies about Reverend Goolesby."

Oh no! Not another "preacher story." Pastor knows if Cornel starts telling preacher jokes he'll keep them up all night laughing and Pastor can't afford that because he's too tired and needs a good night's sleep.

This one's about a pastor of a Newark church who was having problems with his deacon board. At a church meeting his incensed chairman stood up in the middle of the meeting, called him a liar, pulled out a pistol, and squeezed one off at him. The punch line is that Goolesby ducked the bullet, ran out of the church, and must have kept running because he was never seen or heard from again.

"Man, they still don't know where Goolesby's at." He slaps his knee, showing teeth and gums. "One time a few months back somebody said he was at a little country church somewhere in Florida, but when they called down there it was just an old man with the same last name."

Pastor smiles at Georgia and Virginia. "That's what happens when you don't have a good relationship with your chairman."

"What you talkin' about, Doc. There ain't no such thing as a good relationship between a pastor and a chairman. Deacons *or* trustees. Both of 'em are always gonna be after that same limited, indivisible commodity. Power. That's why I ain't never had a chairman and never will. There's only one person with power at New Life, and that's the bruh who started it and signs all the checks: yours truly."

There goes Cornel showing off again. Next he'll brag about how they don't vote.

"That's right, I'll never have a chairman. I'm even thinking about getting rid of my deacon and trustee boards altogether. And I can do it, too, 'cause in my church we don't vote. We've never voted on anything in our eight year history. At New Life, I'm the law. And that's how it should be at every church. The pastor's gotta run it."

"Maybe I should turn up the air conditioner," Pastor says. "It seems like there's a lot of hot air blowing in this place right now."

"Yes, please do," says Georgia, squinting.

"I keep telling you, Bishop. You think you're chairman walks on water, but just like the other one, soon enough he's gonna show his true colors and stab you in the back." He demonstrates. "To the hilt. Boo-yah!"

"And I keep telling you he's nothing like Thorn. He's a really humble, caring, good brother. Anyway, he's resigning Sunday, so I'll need another one pretty soon."

"Word? Why?"

"He wants to spend more time with his wife."

"Dr. Hook," says Georgia, pulling on her nose. "What *is* that smell? Is that roach spray?"

"Georgia's got a real sensitive nose," offers Virginia.

"How many members do you have?" asks Georgia.

"About 200."

"Ohhh." She looks ready to leave. "Sounds like a lot more on the radio."

Guess she thought Pastor was rolling in dough like Cornel.

"So, how was Philly?" Pastor asks.

"It was alright," they say. "He stood everybody up at the end."

"Yeah? What did he preach about?"

"I don't know," says Virginia. "But he sure did preach!"

"He had good craft, but myself? I was underwhelmed by his theology," says Cornel.

That means it wasn't something he could recycle.

"Preacher, I'm starving." Cornel rubs his paunch. "You eat yet?"

"No time. Had something after the funeral, that was it."

"Well let's take this over to the spot. I'm buying."

"It's late, Co, and I need some sleep. Big day tomorrow."

Cornel won't take no for an answer, insisting Pastor come along. So Pastor gives in again, planning to ditch them after about 15 minutes and crawl back to his pillow.

♪

The sidewalk is pink herringboned brick where City Plaza meets Valley Street, in front of the Parvenu Noir. *The* place to spot Belton's newest black residents turning their glasses up and letting their hair down.

Pastor is always ambivalent about walking through these smoked glass doors because his love for the food is as strong as his knowledge of the true heart of the owner. The Parvenu Noir is the illegitimate child of black myopia and old white money and opportunism. It's owned by Richard Blake, who insists it be pronounced BLACK. He's a blond man who favors tight black turtlenecks even in the summer, has won several self-organized Fabio look-alike contests, and owns another successful restaurant in Newark, the Pauvre Noir, which specializes in soul food and attracts a very different clientele. When he inherited the modest Blake department store chain he quickly diversified and launched his own signature line of Noir restaurants, at which only black entertainers perform and only black maitre d's and managers are hired to oversee an all-black staff.

Blake is here. He greets and schmoozes Cornel's party himself, and leads them to a table in the rear solarium where the moonlight pouring onto the immaculately coifed hair of the talented tenth and the jazz ensemble playing on the small stage create the perfect setting for a Romare Bearden painting. Some people at nearby tables recognize Cornel and Pastor and are whispering behind their hands and table candles and smiling in their direction.

Loudmouthed Sylvia's working tonight and issues her usual caveat about Cornel to the ladies. They all laugh together before she leaves to get their drinks. All except Georgia.

"Charming, isn't she?" she says.

"Loudmouthed's alright," says Cornel. "Just don't get her mad, or she *will* go off on you."

"You guys must come here a lot," says Virginia.

"This is Co's world," Pastor says. "I'm just hanging in his shadow."

People still expect preachers to be home on Friday nights reading the Bible. And it's like Cornel's on a mission to explode that image every chance he gets. He grabs Virginia's hand, pulls her into the aisle near their table, and locks hips with her to the ensemble's velvety rendition of Grover Washington's *Mister Magic*, his hands moving rhythmically on every curve of her body-hugging black cotton dress.

"Won't that tarnish his reputation?" asks Georgia.

"Co's? Hardly. He's just adding to his legend."

"What about you?" she asks.

"There's only one Co, and I'm not *even* trying to be like him. Unlike Co," Pastor quips, "I *do* know Jesus."

Pastor recognizes the look she throws him. He used to see brothers who didn't measure up on blind dates get that same look when he was managing sports team audits at Price Waterhouse and turning up his glass, whenever he was in town, at B. Smith's before heading home to the Island.

He tells himself he'll be out of here right after the drinks. Georgia's watching Cornel and Virginia grind away on each other. And as soon as the drinks arrive she excuses herself to the ladies' room in a huff and a puff. Virginia goes after her, opening the door for Pastor's getaway.

"Where do you get these women?" is the first thing Pastor says to Cornel once they're alone.

"She's just a trick I picked up in Trenton last week when I did that revival for Willie J. When I met her sister I knew I had to hook y'all up."

"They drove all the way up from Trenton this afternoon to see you?"

"Ewing, actually. That's where they live. They work in Trenton, but since today's Juneteenth they took the day off. To come see *us*, not just me. Virginia works for the state and Georgia's a bank manager."

"A bank manager?" I say.

"Why? You like her? I knew you would. She look good, don't she? And just your type, too. Stuck-up."

"Man, I am so sorry I ever told you what Burro said."

"You looking for a deep relationship, right?"

"I'm not *looking* for a relationship, Co. You *know* that."

In ancient cultures men couldn't marry until they provided a home for their bride and future family. That was Pastor's gripe with his father's church for a long time: it emasculated him...it made him dependent on a woman, the "bride of Christ," someone else's woman at that, to provide a dwelling for his family. Many churches make their preachers kept men and Pastor never wanted to be like his father, a kept man raising his family in someone else's house. He has to have his own, just like the Apostle Paul. But in spite of these convictions the real deal is his paternal drive is in high gear and he's having a hard time honoring the promise he made to himself ten years ago not to get seriously involved with a woman again until he has his own house. He misses having someone to come home to at night. He wants a family again. And Cornel knows him well enough to see it.

"So, there you go," he says. "Neither's she. She's just like you. Your inner twin. Your soul mate."

"She's nothing like me."

"I must've wasted my time referring you to Burro if you don't see that she's a Xerox of you. A perfectionist. Same little extra holy attitude.

Secretly think she's just a little smarter than everybody else. This girl is you, man. You better push up on it, before she lose interest. You know that's how y'all are."

Pastor gulps the rest of his cranberry juice. "I'm happy to say I think she's already lost interest."

Cornel laughs to himself. "A'ight, man. Lemme leave that alone for now. Tell me about the wedding."

"Tell you about the wedding? How about this. Why don't you tell *me* why I didn't know I was marrying lesbians until they showed up in my office?"

He smiles. "Took you long enough. Listen, Doc, I was trying to help *you* out. You're Mister Always Evolving. I was just trying to offer you a shot at redemption so you could get past that thing with your sister."

"I think you didn't want the controversy, just like you said."

"That, too. I ain't gon' lie. They don't sanction that mess in the motherland, so neither do I. And, if I would've done it and it had gotten out? I woulda had faggots of every stripe beating my door down within a fortnight. So I was doing us *both* a favor. Keeping faggots outta my life, and exercising demons outta yours."

There you have it. Cornel Brown's version of a win-win. He could spit on the Dalai Lama and make him think it's because he's on fire. "Co, let me decide when it's time to exercise demons out of my life, okay?"

"A'ight, Doc," he says, raising his hands in surrender. "Peace."

"And the next time you ask me to do a wedding for you I'm going to demand pictures and dossiers first."

"Okay, okay, Prelate. Ease up. You still didn't tell me about the wedding."

"Really not much to tell. Your people showed up. They had a handful of folks with them. They even brought an organist and a videographer. I did the ceremony. They went home happy. That was it."

"So what was all that about starting your own ministry in jail?"

"The Thorns showed up, too."

"Word?"

"They stayed and watched the whole thing, so now he's trying to call a meeting to get me put out."

He starts laughing again.

"I'm glad *somebody* thinks it's funny."

"Sorry, Elder. Every time I think about that little man's wife I just have to laugh. She looks like somebody's been spiking her morning coffee with Rogaine."

Pastor tries to keep a straight face, but that's always hard with Cornel so he finally quits and starts laughing, too.

"But how did Thorn find out?" he asks.

"They'd stayed in town visiting after the funeral and were just passing by on their way home when they saw Biju and Burnette and the whole crew waiting on the front steps." Pastor dumps the rest of the crushed ice left in his glass into his mouth and slurps. "I probably would've been fine if I'd shown up on time."

"Late? You're never late. Why were you late?"

He realizes he's going to have to sooner or later, so he tells him everything and by the time he finishes they're both leaning in over the table and he's the most serious Pastor has seen him since his car was stolen out of his driveway last year.

"So lemme get this straight," says Cornel. "You're gonna try to find the killer by yourself?"

"You got it."

"By Sunday?"

"Have to."

"You *are* insane. This ain't some mystery story, Doc. This is real. Reverend Snoop may be able to crack a case in 24 hours, but it don't work that way in real life. It takes time to catch a killer, and if the real cops haven't been able to do it yet, what makes you think you can? And by Sunday no less."

"Because if I don't Sears will arrest me for murder and I'll lose my shot at Monumental. I don't have a choice." It's clear to Pastor that Georgia's gone for good, so he reaches for her cranberry juice with a lemon twist and takes a swig. "Anyway, it's not like I'm starting out completely in the dark. I do have some strong leads."

Cornel throws back what's left of his Pinch and sits still for a while with his arms crossed under his chest, his thinking posture.

"We can't have you getting arrested, Preacher, or Monumental will drop you like a poisoned apple. You need a lawyer. I'll call K.C."

K.C. Benton is the attorney Cornel keeps on retainer to deal with all the messy affairs at his church. They were drinking buds in college and Pastor thinks Cornel must've been drunk when he made a deal with this devil. K.C.'s an excellent attorney, and a nice guy to boot, but his client list reads like the closing credits to an episode of *The Sopranos* and he knows a little too much about the finer points of defending RICO cases for Pastor's taste.

"I don't need K.C. now. Monumental would definitely find out then. What I need is Anemone's client list. And I think I'm going to find it in that P.O. box tomorrow morning."

"Hate to tell you this, Bishop, but I think you're on the wrong track."

"And why is that?" I say.

"White supremacists move onto her block and then all of a sudden she's dead, their house is ransacked, somebody may have been shooting at him—"

"And they leave the murder weapon behind with their initials etched into it? Not even the FCA could be that stupid. Most murder victims knew their killer, so the odds say it was the client she knew and not the organization she didn't."

"You're underestimating the power of racist hate, Preacher."

"You're underestimating the power of perverted love, Co. Hell hath no fury."

"As a *woman* scorned, and as far as you know she didn't swing that way."

"The first part of that verse says *Heaven has no rage like love to hatred turned.* And that applies to erotic love too, but nobody ever quotes that part."

"Word? Who said that, anyway? I might could use that."

"William Congreve, *The Mourning Bride.* It's from like 1690 something."

He pulls a Mont Blanc from his jacket pocket and scribbles on a napkin. "Good lookin' out, Doc. But I still think you're off track. And you're such an either-or, black-or-white absolutist you ain't even considered the other possibility."

"And what might that other possibility be?"

"Maybe the client was hooked up with the FCA."

"Stick to macking, Co," says Pastor, laughing. "That's one of the most ridiculous thing I've ever heard you say."

"Excuse me. Can I sit here for a while? There's a guy at the bar who doesn't understand the word no and I don't want to have to shoot him."

Pastor looks up. His heart throttles. And all he can find to say is, "Speak of the Devil."

"Oh, no-no-no, Preacher." Cornel jumps out of his seat and pulls out the chair Georgia vacated. "You mean angel. And a fine one, too. Your face must be on *all* the milk cartons up in heaven. Point this offensive dude at the bar out and let me go punch him in the head for you."

"Awww, you'd do that for me? And they say chivalry is dead."

"Let's not have any punches thrown tonight," Pastor says. "Cornel Brown, meet Detective Sergeant Chris Sears."

CHAPTER 12

What does she want now? She'd obviously gone home to change after grilling Pastor at the station house. She's looking fly in a black cotton outfit that shows off her lines.

"The pastor of New Life Baptist in Newark, right? I've read about you." She even sounds...happy. Pastor suddenly wants to puke.

Cornel's eyes widen. He reaches for her hand. "Daaamn, Bishop. You didn't tell me she was the most beautiful flower in the garden state." He kisses her hand. She coos, and for a minute Pastor loses himself. He can't believe that he wants to grab her hand away from him and wipe it off with his table napkin and tell her to stop smiling if she doesn't want to get used up and discarded like yesterday's dessert. "You can slap the cuffs on me anytime, Sarge," Cornel continues. "I'll do whatever you say...for as long as you say."

"I'll bet you say that to all the lady detectives. By the way, how's Dr. Dana Faye Brown and the boys these days? Did she have that baby yet? And is she ever going back to work?"

Wow. It's hard to take the wind out of Cornel's sails, but she just managed to do it.

Pastor's thinking he's stayed too long and starts eyeing the exit. As if on cue, Virginia returns by herself with one of those looks like when a blind date's not working out and the self-absorbed girl wants to ditch the dweeb so she sends her friend to do the dirty work. Cornel is all cool about it and knows what's about to happen.

"Well it's about time," he says in mock relief. "I was about to send out the search party."

She whispers something into his ear and he excuses himself and they leave Sears and Pastor measuring each other from across the table through a candle flame so tall and so still it looks like a baby carrot.

"Got the results back already?"

She smiles all compassionate. Almost apologetic. "No, I told you not for a couple of days maybe. Although the chief did have me put a rush on it. Costs twice as much, but they're sparing no expense on this case. Enough about work, though. This is a social visit."

"Really?" The lipstick, the styled hair, the cleavage say she has a specific target in mind.

"A girl has to take *some* time for herself. You know how it is. Our jobs can consume us if we let them."

"No departmental policy against socializing with murder suspects?"

"I can handle myself."

"But what if the suspect were to get you drunk and coax sensitive information out of you that might jeopardize the case. Chief's not worried about that?"

"Look, my marriage broke up over this job. I *always* put work first. Besides, I don't drink alcohol."

"That's new. What made you stop?"

"Like Janet said, I wanna be the one in control."

"So what are you doing here, really? I've never seen you in here before."

"Drinking cranberry juice and watching people."

Pastor's like a moth caught in the flame. She just threatened him in her office a few hours ago and now she's acting like they're a couple of college crushes meeting over burgers in the rathskellar? She must be reading his thoughts because she says, "Look, I'm just trying to show you that it's not personal. You're still not too good at accepting olive branches, are you?"

The ensemble is doing a bang-up job with George Benson's *Masquerade* and the lyrics are getting all down inside Pastor's head and his heart and the fact that she's drinking cranberry juice just like him is starting to work on his soul. He tells himself that maybe he's behaving too stank, and this will probably all be over tomorrow anyway, once he gets into that safe deposit box. So he creases his lips with a smile and does what he knows in his heart is the right thing.

"You're right. I'm sorry. You're just doing your job and I'm acting like a complete idiot."

"A man who can say, 'Sister, I'm sorry'. Either you've been watching Oprah or you had good home training. Apology accepted."

They smile together.

"So why're you wasting your time at bars? There are better ways to meet guys you know."

If Helen of Troy's face could launch 1000 ships then Christine Sears's must be good for at least 950. She brushes his question off with a smile and asks one of her own.

"So why're you wasting your time in the church? Do you *like* the ministry now? I remember you always used to say you'd *never* follow your dad into the ministry."

"Good question. What about you? Did you go to Columbia Law to become a cop?"

"Good question, but I asked you first."

Pastor reaches for Georgia's abandoned cranberry juice with the lemon twist and takes another swig while he thinks about whether he should tell Sears the whole truth.

"I was taking Carla and Carlton up to a cabin in Maine I'd rented for the Easter weekend, and God sucker-punched me. Knocked me off my horse and made me an offer I couldn't refuse. So if you have to do something, might as well do it with excellence. I've always respected what could be accomplished through ministry, I just never liked how my father went about it. So now I'm trying to do it differently. I sure don't feel like God is accomplishing much through me at this church, though. I love the folks, but it's like we've got two different destinations."

"That's how I feel about my own job, so I understand." She shakes her head, a wistfulness settles into her face. "I have good memories of my dad. I couldn't appreciate preachers when he was alive, but now, I like the way the educated ones talk, the way they think, what they represent. I've got a tremendous amount of respect for the truth, and the people who tell it. That's what my dad always said a preacher was, somebody who tells the truth, no matter what, in season or out, and regardless of the cost. That kind of moral strength appeals to me more these days than it ever has, because nowadays it's hard to find people who are willing to stand up for something."

She's still reducing a relationship with Jesus into a moral obligation, but he agrees with the part about standing up for something. "I need more members like you."

She smiles, shaking her head. "You know I could never join your church, Tony. I know too much about you. And you remind me too much of Batman."

"That's a new one."

"I'm talking about the themes of burial and resurrection in the *Batman* movies?"

"You lost me there."

She looks surprised.

"Bruce Wayne descends into the Bat Cave a mere man, emerges from the cave a bat-man with heightened abilities? The Bat Cave a type of the grave and Batman a type of resurrected humanity?" She has her palms out in front of her shoulders, her neck stretched forward and her eyes bulged in that "um, hello? don't you get it yet?" pose. "You're Bruce Wayne and your office is the Bat Cave and by the time you get up into that pulpit you're transformed into a spiritual hero. That's how your members see you. Their spiritual hero. Their Batman. And that's what preachers mean to me now. You guys are heroes. If I become a member of your church you'll become Bruce Wayne and I don't want to give up my Batman."

He can't tell if she's yanking his chain or not, but it seems like she's saying more than he's hearing and it'll probably come to him one day when he's folding laundry or loading the dishwasher. She looks into his eyes and starts blushing.

"Preachers see biblical themes in everything," Pastor says. "But I have to confess, I never thought of that."

"Really? I'm surprised. *Batman* is rich in that stuff. Look at some of the villains. The Joker, Two-Face, to some extent Poison Ivy, they all fall into some liquid, or some liquid falls on them, and when they emerge, they're different."

"Yeah. ...Okay, I see it. Almost like an evil baptism using different doctrinal positions, some by immersion, some by sprinkling."

"There you go. Right now there's a Batman, a Batboy, and a Batgirl. Now all we need is a Batbro and a Bataplegic and the Bat franchise will be completely PC."

It's kinda funny. Pastor laughs. "I think you've been spending too much time in bars drinking cranberry juice and watching people."

Loudmouthed Sylvia bounces back. She looks at Sears, smiles and says, shaking her head, "You preachers are something else. You ready to order?"

"Don't confuse me with Co, Sylvia. And no, I'm not having anything else. I stayed longer than I was supposed to as it is. What about you, Chris?"

"No, I'm fine. Can't eat this late. I need to get home to bed. Long day tomorrow."

"Yeah. Me, too."

Sylvia drops the check on the table in front of me. "Okay, Rev. Y'all have a pleasant night." Pastor ignores the wink at the end and turns toward the front of the restaurant. He didn't bring his wallet with him because Cornel rushed him out of the house saying he was buying.

"Sylvia, where's Co?"

"Oh, sorry, Rev. He said to tell you that he had to take his friends back to their hotel right away, and that he'd call you later."

Maannn, Co. Pastor's eyes meet Sears's for a second as he contemplates Loudmouthed's probable reaction when he tells her he has to run home to get his wallet. They call her Loudmouthed for a reason. Without a word Sears produces an Amex Platinum Card, places it on the check, hands them to Sylvia, and says to Pastor, "You get the next one."

◊

Pastor watches Sears pull away before opening the door to the gallery. There's a box of Peppie's pizza at the front door with a note attached. It's an apology from the driver saying he had car trouble and that the pizza is free. Pastor sticks the note in his wallet to remind himself to give him the cost of the pizza as a tip the next time he sees him. It's too late to eat it now, so he sticks the pizza in the fridge and makes it upstairs after all. He's about to step into the dark shower when the doorbell rings, and rings again.

"Paaastah? Come on down, just for a second."

He throws his robe back on, sighs inside himself all the way downstairs, and lets her and her pink cart into the gallery.

"Mother, I was just about to take a shower. What are you doing out this late?"

"I was about to ask you the same thing, Paaastah. I saw the young lady drive off. She's cute."

"She's a detective. They reopened the case and she's working on Anemone's murder."

"You should bring her around more often. This place needs a woman's touch."

This place needs a whole lot more than that. "Your touch has been good enough for me, Mother."

She laughs. "You're still a young man, Paaastah. I think you need another kind of touch I can't help you with. But listen, I got you something from downtown while I was picking up my ammo."

She pushes the sombrero onto her back, reaches into her cart, and pulls out a handful of giant, plastic-encased fruit-shaped air fresheners. Just what he's always wanted.

"Oh, Mother, you shouldn't have," he says with a pasted on smile.

"Oh, that's alright, Paaastah. Like Reverend Brown said, we need to take good care of you. Now you just give me your keys and go take your shower, I'll put these in your car for you."

"You don't have to do thaaaat. I'll just take these from you and put them in later."

"Paaastah, I insist. I'll put them in now so your car will smell nice and fresh by tomorrow."

"No, Mother. *Really*, it's okay. I'd have to go upstairs, come back down, go up again. I'll just take these from you now. Thanks for thinking of me. Good night."

He practically pushes her out of the gallery, and she puts up a big fuss, but finally leaves. He's showered and in bed inside of 15 minutes. *The Cat in the Hat Comes Back* sends him into la-la land wishing he had some Voom to clean out all the bad stuff in *his* life.

◊

The big boom rattles Pastor out of a sound sleep. The clock's showing 1:57, so it can't be Brother Mac. But wait a minute. There's smoke pluming out of the backyard, the next-door neighbor's car alarm is squealing, and what sounds like chunks of metal rain is pelting the blacktop. He rushes to the window near the closet and peers into the backyard.

His car! What's left of it is on fire.

Something looking like a white Honda squeals away from the opened gate and screams up Third Street. And there's a body crumpled at the bottom of the far fence. Pastor jumps double step downstairs. A series of additional explosions send more metal flying everywhere. He waits a few seconds before covering his nose with his robe's lapel and running around the burning car to the body.

Not many distinguishing features are left to identify this guy, but it's definitely not Shabazz. An old Shaq Reebok's near his head. There's still a pager clipped to what's left of his baggy jeans. This was a skinny kid, with either long braids or dreads. Pastor whispers a prayer for his family and waits for the inevitable flock of sirened vehicles to swoop in.

◊

"What are you, the point man for the Grim Reaper?" says Sears. "This is your third dead body in as many days."

They're slouched at the kitchen table along with McManus. The back door is open and all the flashing lights have turned the kitchen into a kaleidoscope. She's wearing a Yankees baseball cap, black jeans, a white tee shirt, and fatigue in her eyes.

"I have no idea who this one is, though," Pastor says, almost shouting over all the hubbub outside.

"We're pretty sure he's part of the team that's been working the city for the past month or so," says McManus. "We had several reports earlier of two black males in a white Honda cruising restaurant parking lots trying to steal cars. What's left of this kid fits the description of one of them."

"If you ask me," says Sears, "I think you might've overdone it on the theft-deterrent system."

"Somebody rigged it," says Pastor.

"Obviously, Tony."

"Is this how you are when you're tired? I don't remember."

McManus gets up to leave. "I'm gonna see what they're doing out there, leave you two love birds alone."

Sears shakes her head at his back and smirks, then turns back to Pastor. "Any idea who wants to send you to heaven early?"

"Sure, you can have the whole list. It'll take a few hours to print it out, though."

"I'd hate to see it if you ever become unpopular."

It looks like Cornel was right this time. Shabazz McCoy works for a demolitions company. He blows things up for a living. And after the way Cornel talked to him this afternoon? It had to be Shabazz. Pastor refuses to let some crazy preacher derail his bid for Monumental. He refuses to let any of this stuff distract him. He'll let the police concern themselves with Shabazz. He has to finish his sermon. And get Anemone's client list. He gives Sears all the letters, the chicken bones, the mojo bag, which she places in separate plastic Baggies, and Shabazz's address. And he tells her about Shabazz's job, and the noise he heard in the back around 11:30.

Sighing she says, "These cases are generally pretty tough to make. We'll try to get a warrant in the morning and pray he's dumb enough to leave evidence lying around the house. But even if we get lucky, since he does this for a living we may not be able to make anything stick."

"Paaastah? You alright?"

Mother pops in wearing brown cotton pajamas, and Royster hobbles in through the screen door after her, apologizing to Sears for letting her get past him. "She kicked me in the shin with her Air Jordans. Those things hurt."

"I'm fine, Mother. Just need another car." Pastor pauses, looking wistfully into the parking lot, realizing his relationship with his old Saab is over, and remembering all the things they've been through together. He turns back slowly to Mother, shaking his head. "This is the detective I was telling you about. Sergeant Chris Sears, this is Mother Freddie Pearl. She lives down the street and looks out for me."

She pushes the sombrero onto her back, gives Pastor a hug, and turns to Sears. "This is my baby, right here, Miss Detective. You make sure nothing happens to him, you hear?"

"Yes, ma'am. Roy, it's okay, go back outside."

Before he can leave Brother Mac shows up at the screen door. "Pastor, you alright?"

"I'm fine, Brother Mac."

"Who gon' clean this mess up?" he asks, clearly annoyed. "This ain't in my job description."

Limestone and stained-glass from the St. Joseph's Catholic Church and School complex block Pastor's view of the horizon from his Staples-supplied home study like Jersey State's back wall at dawn. The white painter's cap on Brother Mac's bald head is bobbing under the window. Even though the windows are closed and the air conditioners are whining, headache-inducing paint fumes and the carillon pealing *Nearer My God To Thee* are drawing Pastor's attention away from his sermon.

The Fire Marshall didn't leave until 4:30 this morning. The dead kid took precedence over Pastor's toasted car, so he had to wait for the M.E. to clear out. He's been sitting here in a pair of old Tiger shorts ever since, trying to transform the four pages of handwritten exegetical notes he's compiled on the story of Cain and Abel into Sunday morning's message, "Murder One". Even though he'll be auditioning for Monumental he's still divinely obligated to speak to the *sitz im leben* of First Baptist, to where they will be in heart and mind as they grapple with what's been happening lately. In light of recent events this passage of Scripture is an inspired no-brainer. But the sermon is still refusing to come together. Who can think after all that happened last night?

The phone rings unanswered every ten minutes or so, and every ten minutes or so he reflects on how important this message is and what will be at stake when he preaches it. Talk about pressure. Game ending free throws don't prepare you for this.

Someone starts banging on the front door. And ringing the doorbell. Every ring slows the air conditioner down and makes the battery back-up on his PC buzz on. With so many bells tolling at the same time, he breathes a prayer.

This early it could only be one person, and if Pastor doesn't answer he'll continue indefinitely until either he passes out or the entire network of ancient electrical wiring in the house ignites.

"Hey, Hook! Hook! Come here. Lemme rap to you, blood."

Pastor smells the alcohol through the gallery screen and sees the familiar bloodshot eyes and unkempt hair, salt-and-pepper with an old red-black-and-green pick sticking up from the back of it like a feather. He's been up all night again and is just making his way home.

"Mowatt, I gotta go, man, I ain't got time." Pastor catches myself. Sometimes when he talks with Mowatt he slips back into speech patterns of old, back when he was a New York teenager trying to leave his mark on every court on the Island and in the City. "If you want to talk stop by my office after church tomorrow, or better yet, give me a call and we'll set up a time."

"Aw, come on, Hook, baby. You the man. I gotta rap to you. Who else gon' look out for you?"

The gray stubble on his reddened face makes his harelip look even more grotesque. He staggers backward, almost tumbling down the stoop, then steadies himself and brandishes a soiled, bent envelope from the back pocket of his army fatigues.

"See. This tell you right here. I was wounded in 'Nam. I'm a got-damn hero. And they finally gon' gimme my *got*-damn bread."

Pastor unleashes a hopeful smile. Maybe this will be the impetus for Mowatt to finally get his life together quit wandering the streets at strange hours.

"Mowatt." Pastor closes the door behind him and walks him down the steps with an arm around his shoulders. "I have things to do right now."

"But I gotta rap to you. I got somethin' heavy to lay on you, blood." He belches. "You know I be seein' things."

Brushing away the fumes Pastor says, "This is not a good time." He says it firmly, like he would to a willful child.

Pastor always feels bad at this moment. Mowatt's eyes sadden. He looks down, turns like a wounded puppy, and staggers up the street singing to the scattered clouds and low-hanging cable wires and stately trees and dormant houses, a black GI Joe with a Kung Fu grip sticking out of the other back pocket of his fatigues, "No-bo-dy knows the trouble I seen. No-bo-dy knows the sorrow."

Pastor's growling stomach reminds him that writing is hard work and it's time for breakfast, so he detours into the kitchen and stares into the refrigerator. He has two choices, eggs or pizza. There's no butter in the door, and he doesn't like the taste of eggs made in oil, so he decides pizza for breakfast is a great idea. But when he opens the box there's a roach stuck in the cheese and two more on the crust. He grabs a garbage bag from under the sink, sweeps the box of pizza and everything else from the fridge into it, and drops it in the can outside. He forgot that it usually takes the insecticide a couple of days to do its thing.

He forces himself back upstairs and into the chair at his desk, but no flow comes today, no stream of metaphors and illustrations, no losing track of time. English feels like a foreign language by the time Brother Mac cranks up the old Craftsman push mower to attack the little patch of crab grass they insist on calling a lawn. St. Joe's carillon peals *Onward Christian Soldiers* and Pastor bails for another bathroom break. The doorbell rings again and he opens the door this time to the drone of the mower circling the dogwood tree ahead of a waving Brother Mac, and Mother Freddie standing on the top step under her sombrero with a bucket in one hand and a plastic ShopRite bag in the other, the gleam in her dentured smile brighter than the sunlight reflecting off her wire-rimmed glasses.

"Paaastah, you've had a hard couple of days and we need you to keep your strength up, so I brought you some food."

His stomach's shouting "Amen!" and his tongue is hanging like a Pavlovian dog's. He's spared from saltines and water for breakfast, but even around Mother he doesn't want to appear too needy. "Mother, why the bucket?" he says, reaching for the bag as she steps across the threshold. "I'm not a kid. I can clean up after myself."

"Paaastah, I don't want to hear it this morning. I've been seeing chicken bones on your doorsteps and in these bushes for too long now, and we can't have our pastor living like that. Now you eat your breakfast and go on about your business today. I'm going to spend the whole day cleaning this parsonage from top to bottom."

♪

Pastor runs through the shower, steps into a light gray summer wool suit, and then enjoys the bacon, eggs and biscuits Mother stashed in the bag for him. He gives her a hug around her neck while she rubs the grime out of the dining room window, and pulls the back door behind him. He takes a moment to look at the burned out shell of his old Saab again and pays his last respects, touching the driver's side door one final time. He turns decisively and walks briskly down the littered blacktop driveway to First Baptist. He doesn't like the idea of using the church's van to run errands, but he has no idea when the insurance guy will show, and if he picks up the Mustang now it'll just give Cameron another excuse to put more pressure on him when this is all over.

"Hook." He answers his cell phone behind the wheel of the van.

"You a'ight, Doc?"

"Co?"

"Dana just called telling me what happened. It's all over town already."

"Yeah, I'm fine."

"You don't have to sound so disappointed."

"I thought it was the insurance guy calling me back. That's the only reason I'm leaving this phone on today."

"It was Shabazz. I know it."

"He works with explosives on the job, so you're probably right about this one. But they haven't been able to question him yet and the lab's just getting started on the evidence they gathered last night, so we don't know for sure."

"I told you we'd have to handle it ourselves."

"You're crazy, Co."

"Where you headed now?"

"To the bank."

"Bet. I'm waiting on the cops myself. Soon as I'm done here I'ma swing by you and we'll go get that space cadet ourselves."

"What happened this time, Co?"

"Brothas broke in again. You can have Walter Rauschenbusch and his weak social gospel. Gimme Sweet Daddy any day. He was right, it's all about the Benjamins."

Pastor chuckles. "Daddy Grace said that? All this time I thought it was Puff Daddy before he became P. Diddy."

"I don't know how they do it, Doc. They got the speakers this time."

"Wasn't the last one an inside job?"

He sighs. "Try to give brothas a break and they just stab you in the back. Boo-yah! But...what can you do. They're still our people. After the cops finally get here I still gotta stay a while. My sexton's out picking up some new speakers and I have to sound test them. By the way, I found your killer last night while fooling around on the internet, so you're gonna have to find some room for me in your next story. Did you check your e-mail this morning?"

"Get out of here. Really?"

"Seriously. ...Go ahead and laugh, it's a'ight. But I know I'm right."

"Okay, so what's the name."

"Check your e-mail when you get back. I sent you all the documentation so you'll see it's not just a guess. Peace and chicken grease. I'm out."

Pastor pulls into the bank's parking lot and spots Hazel's red Neon. It's already 89° and so humid that his sun glasses fog up and his Nehru collar collects sweat during the short walk through the parking lot to the lobby. Hazel's wearing a frumpy floral number that makes her look old. She glances at her watch and rises to greet him, her rabbit teeth peeking through her nervousness. Still a head-turner, though, in her own "healthy" way.

"You look good in light gray, Rev'en. I was just about to call you."

"Sorry I'm a little late. Something unexpected came up last night; blew my whole day off schedule."

"I explained everything to the lady. She was real nice."

They sign in and the branch officer leads them into a phone booth-sized room, places a metal box about the dimensions of an accountant's big briefcase down on the table, and locks the door as she leaves.

"Here, Rev'en. You open it. I don't even wanna look. I'ma just pray."

Wow. Stacks of hundreds in red rubber bands. Over fifty of them. Pastor guesses there's about $250,000 in all. There's also a video cassette, eight millimeter; and an expensive new pocketbook, burgundy leather with the Macy's price tag still attached. Inside: a Chevy key, probably for Ike's Vette, and two house keys on a new leather key chain that match the pocketbook; a matching leather wallet containing Anemone's driver license, social security card, Blue Cross-Blue Shield card and $1,000 in hundreds; and a small make-up bag with a variety of cosmetics still in their original wrapping complete with Macy's price tag. Everything a girl needs to make a quick getaway.

It all confirms the B word and makes Pastor's racing heart sink under the weight of his disappointment. Anemone weaseled about a quarter of a million out of church members and clients with that camera. But there's no list anywhere in the box of who any of those clients were. Pastor begins praying that the videotape will provide some answers.

Hazel's still praying in tongues so he nudges her.

"Welp, what we have here is a videotape, and a lot of money. I suppose this stuff all legally belongs to you right now. What do you want to do with it?"

"Jee-zos!" Her eyes bulge at the stack of bills. She waves her palms in the air like Miss America and clenches her eyes shut again. "Rev'en, before I got saved all I wanted was to be rich. But now? I can't take any of that dirty money. I know how she earned it. What does it profit a man to gain the whole world and lose his own soul? Just like I told you before, I want you to give all of it to Ike."

"Hazel, this money would change your life, and Anemone obviously meant for you to have it if anything happened to her. Are you sure about this?"

"I'm sure, Rev'en. This life only lasts a short while, the next life's forever. I got to stay holy and touch not the unclean thing."

Pastor slips the tape into his portfolio for future viewing, dumps everything else into a plastic bag he bummed off a teller, gives Hazel a peck on the forehead, and heads for Ike's before the money has a chance to corrupt him.

Fairview Avenue might as well have been barricaded when Pastor turns onto it. It's 9:30 and black-and-whites are all over the place. He parks as close as he can to the house and leaves everything in the van. The scene is eerily reminiscent of early Thursday morning. He starts praying under his breath.

Max Candy Jr's Jeep is parked in virtually the same spot, his scanner hissing in the passenger seat. Yellow tape skirts the Allon house again. The few residents milling around out front look extremely ticked off. And Pastor's friends from the Free Church are standing in front of their place. Grinning.

The M.E.'s van pulls away as Pastor ducks under the tape and through the front door, shaking his head. Ike's stubbornness cost him his life. What a waste. Pastor takes a minute to re-center himself and accept that Ike is now gone, too, when he's interrupted.

"Reverend," calls Sears, bouncing down the staircase in cut-off jeans and a tee shirt, holding a cell phone to her ear. "Just the person I needed to see. Okay, Roy, he's here. Find her and let me know. Fellas, let me talk to the Reverend alone. McManus, get going on that report please. And you, get some people out front to disperse that crowd." She snaps the phone shut.

"This one has nothing to do with me," says Pastor, quitely. "And after last night I thought we were past this reverend and sergeant stuff."

She smirks. She's wearing no make-up, her hair is damp but combed, and she's still fly.

She leads him into the kitchen. The back door is open and a tired-looking German Shepherd is leashed to the railing, licking a dog biscuit.

"Rin Tin Tin looks like he's ready for retirement," Pastor deadpans.

"Sparky is mine," she says, matter-of-factly, devoid of last night's warmth. "I was walking him when I got the call."

"Where do you live anyway?"

"The hi-rise at the top of the Hill, on Belton."

"Nice. BPD's paying well."

"They pay alright."

"You guys need a chaplain?"

"I got it in the settlement."

They squat around the dinette. Two large paper bags are rolled shut in the middle of the table. Pastor passes on the glass of orange juice she offers because he's still full from Mother's cooking.

"By the way, how'd you know I didn't have my wallet?"

"I'm a detective. You didn't have your jacket. And when you stood I didn't notice anything bulging in your pockets."

"Oh."

"I didn't mean it *that* way."

"Didn't *take* it that way."

"Of course, you know you owe me dinner now."

He nods. She looks at him with those steady beach sand eyes and says, "So why are you here?"

"Just stopping by to see Ike."

"I'm sure you know he's usually working on Saturdays?"

"I figured if I missed him I'd stop by his shop. No need now."

He's expecting her to ask what he wanted to see Ike about, but she just looks him in the eye, so he quickly adds, "When did this happen?"

"Late last night. Looks like it happened in his sleep. One bullet through the temple just like his wife. Same kind of gun left in his hand, too. Wiped clean, of course. I got the call at 7:45 this morning."

"Probably, whoever did his wife finished him off, too."

"My thoughts exactly, which is why I wanted to talk to you."

"But I told you, I didn't kill Anemone, and I certainly didn't kill Ike."

"I believe you know more than you've told me. As a matter of procedure we check out all the silly calls and letters that come into the station, just in case. So we went down to the *Mirror*. It turns out that Mrs. Allon was running a personal ad for about a year. She was basically a hooker. I'm thinking it was you who sent us that anonymous clip, because her clients wouldn't. You knew what she was doing all along, didn't you."

"...I found out Thursday. At the time I thought Ike might've killed her and I sent the clip hoping it would establish motive."

"Mr. Allon was murdered because he knew who killed his wife. Right? ...Tony, they're both dead now. You don't have to maintain confidentiality anymore. All I want to know is, did he tell you who he thought killed his wife."

"He didn't say. He just kept saying he was going to take care of it himself. How'd you find out?"

"We tracked down the serial number on that camera. It was sold out of Top Brands Electronics in the Livingston Mall. One of the clerks there said he remembered selling it to Mrs. Allon. So the only explanation is that she was making secret videotapes of her meetings with her clients. The night she was killed she must have been expecting a client. Her husband came home, saw the tape running, backed it up and watched his wife's murder. Then he took the tape out and wiped the camera down. He knew who the killer was, and he has the tape. That's why he was killed, and that's why the house was ransacked yesterday."

"So what do you need me for? Sounds like you've got it all figured out."

"Guess what else we found." She opens the bag labeled 'A. Allon' and pulls out a plastic Baggie containing a set of keys.

Yikes! "So?"

"These are Mrs. Allon's. They must've fallen behind her side table Wednesday night and we missed them."

"So?"

"You see this key right here?"

"Yeah."

"It opens a safe deposit box. Detective Royster tracked down the bank. And guess who they say *just* left there."

"Alan Greenspan?"

"This is no time for jokes. Tell me what was in the box. We need more to work with here. Did Mr. Allon hide the tape of his wife's murder in her safe deposit box?"

"I'd love to, Sergeant, but that darn clergy-communicant law keeps getting in the way."

"I thought we were past this reverend and sergeant stuff, Tony." She takes a sip of orange juice. "So you'd rather go to death row for someone else's crime."

"What happened to the appeal of moral strength and the willingness to stand up for something and all that stuff from last night?"

"...I sure hope you're not trying to play preacher-detective here. This isn't a plot line in some hokey mystery short story. And withholding evidence in an investigation is a crime, too."

"Unless, of course, that evidence was delivered by someone who confided in me in my professional capacity. ...Sergeant, if there was anything I could tell you that would help you catch Anemone's killer, believe me I would." Right after he checks it out himself first. No matter how nice she's suddenly become he's still not ready to trust Chris Sears again with his future on the line.

"I hope so, because if your results come back before we find that tape we're going to have to hold you. That *Mirror* article with the comments by a certain preacher has really stirred up the natives, City Hall's reeling, and the Chief's playing right along trying to keep his job, so it's really out of my hands. And getting arrested for murder won't look too good to Monumental's pulpit committee, either."

"How'd *you* find out about Monumental?"

"Word gets around. You know how church folks are."

"I'm guessing you haven't heard from the lab yet."

"Not yet," she says. "But don't worry, whenever it comes in, we'll find you."

Royster pokes his head around the refrigerator and calls Sears away from the table. She returns with a look Pastor's never seen in her eyes before.

"That was dispatch," she says. "You need to follow us."

CHAPTER 13

It finally happened. Pastor is standing in the middle of what looks like a war zone, trying to find the top floor of Munster Hall. It has collapsed into the basement and a cloud of asbestos is still settling over the rubble and the rusty burnt out shell of the old Saab on the driveway. Every car alarm for two blocks in every direction is howling, sirens and flashing lights are closing in from everywhere, and uniforms are ringing the leveled plot to keep all the confused neighbors away.

"Jesus Christ!" says the sweaty Fire Marshall as he jumps out of his Bronco. "We were just here last night."

"Pastor, I heard a couple of loud booms from the basement, like explosions," says Brother Mac, "and then the whole parsonage just fell in on itself. It's a good thing I'd just come down off the ladder, or I'd be in there, too."

"Where's Mother Freddie?" Pastor asks, already fighting that bad feeling and working his sphincter muscles trying to keep his insides from falling out.

Brother Mac shakes his head. "She must've still been in there."

"Mother! Mother!" Pastor tries to pull away from them to get to the pile of wood, brick and plaster. "Send Sparky in there! You gotta find her!" He yells at Sears.

The Fire Chief chimes in. "We have to wait until we know it's safe before we send *anybody* in there."

Pastor's palms are on his head. "Shabazz! This had to be Shabazz!"

"We don't know that yet," says Sears.

The fire chief butts in again. "It could've been a gas leak, or some kind of structural failure."

"Nooooo, you heard the man. It was a bomb. He's a crazy bomber. Somehow he got into the basement this morning." Pastor looks at Sears. "If you'd picked him up this morning this wouldn't have happened."

"Tony, I wasn't expecting to wake up this morning to another homicide investigation. Anyway, we can't just pick somebody up and accuse him of blowing up your car because you think it was him. We need evidence."

"I *gave* you evidence!"

"That could've been sent by anybody. The lab has to examine it first and link it to him."

"You had probable cause. You could've questioned him at least. Now Mother Freddie's dead and you could've prevented it."

"Look, we've got three murder investigations going and a bombing investigation. We're stretched thin. But we did send someone over there to talk to him this morning."

"And he wasn't there, right?" She nods. "Because he was here blowing up my home."

"Tony, I can understand your being upset and angry, and I'm sorry about all your losses, but I'm not your enemy here. Now I'll put a black-and-white at your church 24-7 until we can make an arrest, but that's the best I can do. You'll just have to be patient and trust me when I tell you that we're doing everything we can to get this guy."

"Trust you? Trust you?!"

Few have seen Pastor like this before. He's descended into anger and blame to keep from falling apart. He knows they're false supports, a fool's strength, but the alternative is prayer, and after investing his life in prayer for others he just can't go there for himself at the moment without getting all up in God's face and blasting Him with stuff he'd want to take back later. Stuff that can get you killed. Stuff like: *Why do you take away everything I care about?! You're a wuss! Why don't you face me like a man? I'll tell you why, because you can't explain your powerlessness!* You know, stuff like what Job must have been thinking in the midst of his calamity. Instead Pastor hops back into the van.

"Where are you going, Tony?" demands Sears.

"To do something I should've done sooner."

"Stay away from McCoy's house and let us handle it our way."

Fat chance. He's homeless, carless, and could soon be jobless, all losses he can handle and even rebound from. But now he's also Motherless, and that's just too much in one day to take sitting down.

$\downarrow$

If anger and blame are a fool's false strength then revenge is his false courage. There's a reason why God reserves it for Himself.

Cameron is grinning like the Cheshire cat and rubbing his smooth hands together as Pastor squeals off his lot at 10:15 in the wide-tired yellow Mustang convertible. Pastor just misses getting decapitated by a backhoe as he flies onto Valley Street, running two red lights while flooring it to Shabazz's house. He parks across the street and stomps through the gate. Bullies don't like to be bullied, pressing teams don't like to be pressed, and so it follows that a stalker like Shabazz McCoy who specializes in surprises won't like being surprised himself. As soon as he opens the door Pastor plans to burst in on him, grab him by the neck, choke him until he passes out, call the police, and make him confess. Then he'll come to his holy senses, find his flesh satisfied and his spirit embarrassed, fall on his face before God, and beg for mercy.

But the only answer to the doorbell comes from his pit bull, and with such force and racket that it rattles the door knocker. So he retreats across the street behind the Mustang's tinted windows and calls information to get Shabazz's number. Pastor almost detonates in frustration when the recording tells him that Shabazz's number is disconnected. After thirty minutes of waiting Pastor's feeling like he's gotta do something, so he grants Shabazz a short reprieve and decides to swing by the church and use Brother Yellowbear's 8mm camera to check out what's on the tape.

There's a black-and-white sitting outside the Second Street entrance when Pastor pulls up. He's about to turn into the parking lot when he notices McManus and Royster trooping from their blue Crown Victoria to the back door of the church. Brake check. Pastor's DNA test results and a signed arrest warrant must be in their pocket. Even genteel BPD wouldn't send a team to his door to tell him he's no longer a suspect so have a great life.

He bets the farm they don't recognize him in the Mustang and without an extra thought drives past them camouflaged in yellow-and-black and crosses the Rubicon from suspect to fugitive. A quick right and a short zip alongside the elevated tracks and he's at Belton Avenue.

Pastor can do without the hollow feeling in the pit of his stomach. It always makes it a struggle to think clearly, to remain focused, but he reminds himself that he can't help his cause or Anemone's, or her blackmail victims for that matter, while in police custody. Besides, the last time he read about an innocent man of God going to jail after rebuffing the advances of a married woman the story turned out the same way it always does: he spent 13 years in an Egyptian jail while God plugged His ears with holy cotton in order to bless him with character. Pastor adjusts for inflation and figures death row just seems too high a price to pay right now for the character of Joseph. After teaching for years at Trenton State and then at First Baptist that submission to the law is part of the character of a good Christian he absorbs the guilt pangs that this ostensibly selfish fugitive act brings. Decision made. He'll be like Jesus avoiding Jewry because the Jews sought to kill him. It's a left onto Belton and the beginnings of other arrangements to stay free, clear his name, preserve his bid for Monumental, and get some justice for the powerless while he's at it.

◊

It's getting close to the lunch hour and the Livingston Mall is teeming with people picking up prom stuff and last-minute Father's Day gifts. If he really wants to he still has time to get his Dad something and Fed Ex it to Gethsemane for tomorrow morning, but who is he kidding. Other than a new mindset there's nothing Bishop Hook really needs and Antonio was never much for token gifts. When he gives a gift it has to come from his heart and it's been a long time since he really wanted to give his father anything other than a piece of his mind. He'd mail that to him in a heartbeat if he thought he'd listen.

Pastor feels safe lost in the crowd at Top Brands. His new buddy, Chuck, is working again today. He catches on fast. Somebody Upstairs is honoring his decision to stay free. Chuck and Pastor shoot the breeze for a quick few and then Chuck gives Pastor his space.

He pops the tape into the video camera and presses PLAY. The Allon's empty checkerboard basement jumps onto the screen. The pulled out bed against the far wall centered in the frame under the Florida beach poster locates the camera behind the one-way glass in the deejay booth. There's Anemone, clad much the way she was when Ike found her the night she was murdered: skimpy undergarments that show off her cleavage, and stilettos.

She's looking directly into the camera and slithering into a strip club routine. Caressing and fondling herself to the music driving through the ceiling speakers Ike installed. Maannn, she's good at it. She'd make the Devil blush.

She lets somebody in. They talk for a short while. He tries to touch her but she backs away and shakes her finger at him. He gives her something, money. She sticks it in her thigh garter and leads him to the edge of the bed. It's Paul Vernon. Her former employer. She seats him and begins to dance. And *then* some. She's workin' him good, earning her dough.

Did I say she's good at it? Really good. And Pastor can't believe how he's responding. It's sick. She's dead and he's still getting worked up. Porn is porn. No matter how hardcore or soft, no matter if the subjects are living or dead, porn has an embedded power that can turn the most pious into perverts.

There's more of the same on the rest of the tape. Featuring different fetishes, positions, perversions. Sometimes she uses accessories. The dates in the lower right corner are all from last week. The times are all in the morning. There's even a segment with another woman at the end, and Anemone servicing *both* of them. Pastor can't wait to hear Paul Vernon explain this.

♪

Reservation Hill feels a lot steeper running it in the mornings than driving it in a new muscle car powered by a V8 with 250 horses. On a clear dawn up in the higher elevations the Statue of Liberty and the Manhattan skyline look close enough to touch.

Pastor turns onto Longview Road, on the Reservation's edge, and parks outside the gates of the massive yellow contemporary. It's surrounded by floral gardens and the noon sun is lighting up the breathtaking vistas. This very well could be the top of the world.

"May I help you?"

It's the brickhouse sister with the French pastry uniform whom Pastor saw Thursday driving away from the *Mirror* parking lot in the steel blue Jag. He takes in her big smile and realizes that Zenobia was right: kinky folks on the Hill who want their business kept private. So Paul Vernon must've been the very generous MWM seeking attractive black females for discreet fun; and also the person Pastor saw Thursday tearing away from the FCA building on Fairview. Maybe Cornel was in the ballpark after all.

"Hi. I'm Tony Hook. I'd like to speak with Paul Vernon, please. Is he in?"

"I'm sorry. Mr. Vernon is just about to step out. Was he expecting you?"

"No. But tell him it's urgent. Tell him Tropical Breeze sent me."

She looks Pastor up and down like a menu then says, "Wait here, please."

Mother and the bombing are temporarily locked in a crevice of his mind. He's trying to reconcile everything he's learned so far, but little makes sense. Anemone had to have had more than one client, so why was Vernon the only one on the tape for a whole week? Maybe she worked intensively, one at a time, and had others planned? But where were the tapes of the other victims? And did Anemone already blackmail Vernon, or was she canceled before she got the chance to show him the tape? If he'd already been scammed then he knew about the camera and wouldn't have killed her and left the tape behind, but if not was he capable of killing her? Or paying someone to kill her? And just what was his connection to the FCA? And who was the other woman on the tape? And who was Anemone planning to run away with? And where were they planning to go? She wasn't the type to launch out very far on her own. Pastor's not sure what tack to take with Vernon, so he decides he'll just drop some ideas and see how Vernon responds.

Ms. Brickhouse returns and says Vernon will see him. Of course he'll see him. He must've lost his tan when he heard the name Tropical Breeze.

She leads Pastor through spacious rooms tastefully decorated to a huge sitting area off a wide sun deck where Lila Vernon is sprawled face down on a chaise in the far corner with her bikini top undone, trying to get darker. Paul Vernon is watching three pre-adolescent kids through the triple sliders when Pastor enters the room—a boy and two girls swimming laps in white Speedo caps and goggles in the Olympic-sized pool under the supervision of an older black man wearing a whistle around his neck and clutching a stopwatch.

"Reverend, welcome to our home." Vernon jumps out of the giant leather sofa to shake his hand.

He's looking very chic in an off-white silk suit. What he lacks in looks he makes up for in cash appeal.

"Looks like you have some future Olympians in training there," Pastor observes.

"They started their summer schedule last week. Bradley works them so hard they're dead to the world by 9:00."

"No pain, no gain, right?"

"Would you have some iced coffee with me?"

"Sure."

"Greeta, we'll take it in the study."

Ms. Brickhouse gyrates out of the room with Paul's eyes kissing what she's twisting.

"You look like you're about to go out. Should I come back another time?"

"Nonsense. It's an omen that you stopped by now. I was just on my way out to have lunch with my priest. Anemone's death is having such a sobering effect on me. I felt I just had to talk to somebody who specializes in the mysteries of life."

"Well, don't let me keep you."

"No, it's fine. I just called Father Donnellan and rescheduled. Besides, it sounds like you qualify as a specialist in the mysteries of life as well. Right this way, Reverend."

His study is more like a huge antique-furnished library about the size of the First Baptist sanctuary. A giant picture window looks out over the deep rear grounds onto what must be the maid's cottage. He beelines for an ugly hardbacked chair behind a desk that looks like it could use a good varnishing.

Greeta wiggles in carrying a silver tray with tall tumblers and a sweating silver pitcher of iced coffee. She pours their glasses full, hands the glasses to them with a smile, and wiggles out. Paul sets his drink on the empty desktop without a coaster.

The narrow spindleback Pastor's offered in front of the desk feels as uncomfortable as Paul Vernon looks. No wonder the average life span was so short two centuries ago; a combination of bad health care and bad furniture. Lethal. Pastor sets his drink on the desktop as well.

"I ran into your wife Thursday at her favorite non-profit. Doing volunteer work. You were just leaving as I was arriving, but you were in a big hurry."

Vernon's mug is the picture of impatience. "Reverend, I don't approve of my wife's participation in that church. They're ignorant animals. When I learned about Anemone's death I rushed over there and demanded assurances that they weren't involved."

"Paul, may we just speak frankly?"

"Yes, let's. Why are you here, do you want money, too?"

So she *had* lightened his pockets already.

"No, not me. But I *have* seen the tape. If your wife gets her hands on it and finds out you've been running around behind her back with someone like Anemone, and the former help at that, then you're looking at a costly divorce settlement, even with a prenupt."

"...That greedy little whore. She said she was leaving town and that she'd mail me the tape and I'd never see or hear from her again. No one honors their agreements anymore."

"All I want is information, Paul. Do you know who she was planning to leave town with? Or where she was going?"

"How am I supposed to know that? Ours was a limited business relationship. I knew nothing of her personal life and preferred it that way. I'd been trying to get into her pants since the very first day she came to work for me, but she always resisted me. So imagine my surprise when I answer her ad and learn *she's* Tropical Breeze. I was a steady client for almost a year, and then she pulls this stunt."

"Who was that other woman with you guys last Friday?"

"Why?"

"Whoever killed Anemone didn't know about the hidden camera, and I'm guessing the mystery lady didn't get a blackmail note."

"She had nothing to do with Anemone's death. She was at the awards dinner with us that night, being honored as my best new agent for the month of May."

"I'd love to see her job description."

"How much do you want for the tape?"

"Hold on to your money, Paul." Pastor sips some iced coffee for the road. "When this is all over, I'll do the right thing."

Greeta slips Pastor a piece of paper as he leaves. Her name and number. If temptation was money he'd be a financial institution by now.

The Statue of Liberty is mocking him in the distance. His foot is off the gas and he's gathering speed down the Hill heading toward Prospect Street. Anemone's safe deposit box has led him right back to where he started. Whoever she was planning to skip town with might know who'd want to kill her, or why. He might be the killer himself. But how is Pastor going to find him? If it *was* a him. After seeing the end of the tape he can't even be sure. There's only one person he can think of who might know.

Pastor pulls his cell phone out of his pocket to call Hazel and it rings immediately. What was he thinking when he allowed Thorn and the trustees to get him this phone and publish its number in the church bulletin?

"Yes, Sister Walker, what can I do for you."

"What's this I hear about you leaving us to go over there to Monumental?"

Oh, just great. "Where'd you hear that?"

"It's all over the church. Sister Perot told me after Sister Niagara told her. Now you listen to me, you hear. You pastor this church. This is *your* church. *God* put you here. Don't let that old fool David Henry run you out of here. He tried to run my husband out, too. But he couldn't, because my husband was a man of God. And so are you. God is on your side. Don't let that fool David Henry run you out of here. This is *your* church. *God* put you here. That old fool called me just now, trying to turn me against you. But I told him *you're* the pastor. God speaks to *you*. And so whatever you do is between you and God. Now you pastor this church, you hear me?"

David Henry strikes again. "What exactly did Brother Thorn have to say?"

"He said you married two bull-daggers in the church last night. I told him, I said, 'Doctor Hook's the pastor. God speaks to *him*, not *you*. Whatever he does is between him and God.' Oh, he didn't want to hear that. Then he said he was by the church and the police came looking for you, because they think you killed Sister Allon.

"Now you listen to me. You pastor this church, you hear. This is *your* church. *God* put you here. David Henry's a fool. Don't let him run you out of here. He's organizing a meeting for tomorrow's service to vote you out. He wanted me to vote with them. I told him, I said, 'I'm voting for the pastor. This is *his* church, not *yours*. *God* put him here.' Oh, he didn't want to hear that.

"So don't you fret, Pastor. I'm praying for you, and I'm voting for you. *You're* my pastor now, and as far as David Henry goes, why he can just go to hell with the Devil."

Pastor finally manages to get her to hang up after a few more minutes, and he calls Hazel, but there's no answer.

He decides to try Excedrin next time because, since Mother's breakfast he's been snacking on Tylenol, but his head still feels like King Kong is playing the bongos on it. And his ribs are still hurting pretty bad.

It's 97°, the first day in a long time temperatures aren't expected to climb into triple digits, but the streets are still relatively empty. Nobody but the young and crazy is out. The buses are crowded, only air-conditioned cars are on the road, and there isn't a cloud in the sky to provide escape from the sun. Pastor keeps trying Hazel's number on the speed dial as he drives toward Newark, but there's still no answer so he parks on Manor Drive outside of Hazel's building and waits for her to come back. The dashboard clock reads 12:45 and he punches redial every five minutes just in case he misses her. At the end of the block, near the park, a mob of kids are splashing in an illegally opened hydrant and two boys who look no more than twelve were leaning in the shade of the entrance watching them. And there's a pushy Witness patrolling the complex in the heat who must be working overtime to be one of the 144,000. Pastor can't afford a scene so he buys a *Watchtower* from him just so he can continue in as much anonymity as the tinted windows of a new yellow drop top 'Stang will allow on these streets.

It's a good thing Cameron filled the tank before he drove off the lot because after an hour Hazel still hasn't shown up and the gas gauge has edged back to three-quarters of a tank. He's not about to turn the A/C off to save gas so he tells himself he'll wait no longer than one more hour before trying Shabazz again. The knuckleheads went back into the building a while ago and are back, still watching the kids playing in the sprinkler.

And there she is, coming from the parking lot with four ShopRite bags of groceries in her hands, hips swaying in that frock that must have been a summer curtain in the Vernon home at one time. The two knuckleheads in the entryway, with their pants riding under their skinny behinds, grab their little privates and say something to her then ogle her from behind and punch fists with each other as she ambles past them into the building without even turning her head, her long ponytail switching from side to side on her back like a long finger saying, "Nuh-uh."

Pastor gives her ten minutes to get upstairs before he grabs his portfolio and heads into the building after her. Her two pint-sized tormentors avoid Pastor's gaze when he says, "Sup, y'all," as he passes them. Not a good sign, Lo-Jack or no. They're not even teenagers yet but already they're hard. They're the type he needs to be working with instead of the kids in Belton who drive BMWs to the Academy. The type who need intervention before they end up in a place like Jersey State. And the type he'll be able to help influence and shape if he's named pastor of Monumental.

Hazel is surprised to see him. It's cool in her apartment and the glass of cold water she gives him hits the spot. And when he asks her about Anemone's love life she stammers.

"Why didn't you tell me she was seeing someone?"

"I don't know what you talkin' 'bout."

"Anemone's not the kind of person to just pick up and move to some strange place all by herself. She worked at Vernon's beachfront villa in Jamaica before she came here, so she knew him already. There's got to be somebody else in the picture. Who is it?"

"I don't know."

"Sure you do. You two were best friends. If she'd give you a key to her safe deposit box she'd definitely tell you who she was planning to run away with."

Pastor's counting on his clergy status to get the truth out of her. Hazel has too much respect for preachers to hold out for too long.

"You right, Rev'en," she says, sighing. "From the first day she came to work for the Vernons eight years ago we been close, but I wouldn't lie to you. I really don't know who it is. All I know she been messin' around with a married man for almost a year. They was supposed to leave last week, but 'Nemone said she had some more *business* to take care of first. So she was planning to leave Fourth of July weekend. She called it her independence day."

"A married man? How'd she pull it off? She couldn't go anywhere but church."

"'Nemone had her ways. He musta been the one gave her that pager 'bout a year ago. He'd page her whenever he could get away and they'd meet right there in her basement."

"While Ike was in the house?"

"She said it was like getting revenge on him for all the things he done to her. All I could do was hold her up in prayer."

"What's this guy's name?"

"She never wanted to tell me."

"You never met him?"

"No, and she wouldn't tell me nothing about him, except that he was married and unhappy just like her. I did hear his voice on the phone one time, though. Sounded like a white man to me."

"Did she at least tell you where they were going to live?"

"Rev'en, 'Nemone wouldn't even tell me the state. All she said was she had her ticket already, and that she'd call me after she got settled in to let me know how things were going."

So much for that. Pastor doesn't have time for hay stacks. At least he knows it's a guy. The only way left to find the killer is to find the tape.

"Hazel, Ike's dead."

When the words finally sink in she lifts her face to heaven and whispers, "Jee-zos."

"He was murdered last night, probably by the same person who murdered Anemone, because he had a videotape of Anemone's murder. Now we might never find out where he hid it. Did Anemone ever mention anything about Ike having hiding places?"

She excuses herself, disappears into the kitchen, and reappears with a tall glass of cherry Kool-Aid.

"It's probably still right there in that house," she says, shaking her head. "In his bedroom."

"It couldn't be. The cops would've found it already."

"'Nemone told me one time that—"

There's a loud banging at the door and a voice calling out from the hallway. "Ms. Thompson, it's detective Sears from the Prosecutor's Office. We just spoke on the phone. May I come in?"

After Pastor's brain takes a second to process what he's just heard he jumps at Hazel and covers her mouth with his hand. "Why didn't you tell me she was coming over here?" he whispers through gritted teeth. "I don't want to see her."

Hazel looks at him like he's crazy. "Why?"

"Never mind. Just don't let her know that I'm here. I'll wait in your bedroom until she leaves."

"No, not in my bedroom, Rev'en, use the bathroom."

He tiptoes into the bathroom wondering what she has in her bedroom that she doesn't want him to see. He can't help the cynical thought that no matter how pure we may appear to be, we all still have secrets.

Pastor listens at the bathroom door as Hazel invites Sears in. Hazel offers her something to drink and they pace through the superficial greeting ritual. Then Sears gets straight to business and tells her she knows about the safe deposit box and asks what was in it, explaining it could be evidence in an ongoing murder investigation.

Suddenly it's like two huge magnets on opposite sides of Pastor's brain coming together. The office with no name on the door, the police secretary sounding like she didn't even know who Sears was, the fact that she never did show him her badge at any time all add up to his being hoodwinked. Sears is no BPD detective. She's the special investigator assigned by the Essex County Prosecutor a couple of months ago to take over the Newark Serial Prostitute Murderer case. His head starts swirling. He was just beginning to accept the fact that Anemone was turning tricks in her basement. Is he now to believe that she was a Newark streetwalker, too? That would've been impossible without a body double and a time machine so he wonders what Sears is doing in Belton investigating Newark murders.

Hazel sounds scared. She tells Sears everything about the money and the tape, says she gave them to Rev'en Hook, and adds that she didn't know what he did with them after that. Their voices lower and they exchange whispers he can't make out. Then he hears the word bathroom and his ventricles blast an overdose of blood through his system and he almost faints.

CHAPTER 14

Thank God Hazel doesn't have one of those see-through shower curtains. These are more like drapes. Dark gray to match the tiny gray-and-white tiles and pink fixtures. There's nowhere else to go, so Pastor ducks into the bathtub and prays. He's not going to jail without exhausting every possible option. Sears will have to come get him and slap the cuffs on.

If he could just keep his heart from pounding in his ears so hard maybe he'll be able to tell if he's breathing too loudly. The door closes and he hears her zipper, and the brush of fabric against skin. Blood is pulsing everywhere in him. Her fragrance fills up the tiny room and her tinkling on the water sounds like rainfall and music. She goes to the sink and he thinks she might hear him. She's so close her aura is crowding his through the layers of vinyl and polyester. When the door finally opens and closes again Pastor lets it all go.

◊

"I'm sorry, Rev'en," says Hazel once Sears leaves and Pastor comes out of the bathroom. "She asked to use the bathroom. I couldn't say no."

"No problem. Could've been much worse. Thanks for not giving me up."

"Why didn't you want her to know you was here."

"She wants something I'm not ready to give up just yet."

"She was asking about that tape."

"I know. I heard some of it. You were about to tell me where Ike would hide something in the house?"

"Oh yeah. 'Nemone told me one time that she was scareda Ike because he kept a loaded pistol under a loose floorboard near his side of the bed. If he was trying to hide something, nobody would find it there."

He knew Hazel would come through. He gives her a big hug and a kiss. "Thanks, Hazel. One more thing."

"Anything, Rev'en."

"I've got about a quarter of a million dollars in my trunk downstairs. Ike's no longer around, so it's all yours if you want it."

She looks up at the ceiling, tears welling in her eyes, and looks back at Pastor. "...Rev'en, I told you, I don't want it. As long as I got Jesus I got everything."

Pastor closes his eyes. He knows he'll regret it, because he knows what she'll say, but he feels constrained by the Holy Ghost in him to ask anyway. "Well what would you like me to do with it?"

"Whatever the Lord leads you to do. I don't want it."

Pastor was afraid of that. A quarter of a million dollars would definitely change *his* life. He could pay off all his bills and even put a nice down payment on a decent house somewhere. Then he'd be free to start his life over again. Get married, settle down in his own house, raise a quiverful of kids, and maybe even retire from the pastorate and write for a living. But when she mentioned the Lord he knew he'd have to do the right thing and try to return it to the people who Anemone blackmailed. They never got their tapes, so the money is rightfully theirs.

On the elevator ride down he can't even hold his breath against the stale urine smell this time because the mental energy it requires is consumed by one thought. Hazel said Anemone told her she already had her ticket. The logical place for her to keep something like that would be her safe deposit box. She wouldn't leave her getaway ticket in the house and risk having Ike stumble onto it. But there was no ticket of any kind in that safe deposit box. Maybe it was in her pocketbook and he just searched through it too quickly, because women's pocketbooks are like ancient pyramids. He remembers sneaking into his mother's for the car keys as a kid and thinking she could hide a small army and its arsenal in there, it was so roomy and had so many hidden compartments. Pastor still has Anemone's pocketbook stashed in the trunk along with the money in the plastic bag the bank gave him. If there *is* a ticket in there he'll at least know where she was planning to go, and that could help him figure out who she was planning to go with.

⨖

The Witness Pastor bought the *Watchtower* from is standing in the spot where the Mustang used to be. And down toward the park at the end of the block the two knuckleheads are doing tire-screaming donuts with the top dropped beyond the spray of the fire hydrant in front of a cheering crowd. One is standing on the passenger seat with his peanut head bopping, pumping his fist to the beat blasting through the Bose.

"Yo, get outta my car!" Pastor can't afford to go hoarse before tomorrow, but he can worse afford to lose that car and what's in it. The words just keep flowing as he runs toward them.

All of a sudden the car spins to a stop, the crowd quiets as it looks in Pastor's direction, and the two joy riders bail out and take off through the park. How they could book so fast with their jeans practically around their ankles is a mystery. Pastor's close enough to hear the door chimes when a Newark PD squad car whizzes past him, barely missing the nose of the Mustang, jumps the sidewalk, and tears into the park after the two kids, its wheels spitting grass, its lights flashing and sirens blaring.

Pastor's about to grab the open driver's side door when another NPD cruiser screeches to a stop not five feet from him and out jumps two of Joe Curtin's thick-necks Pastor recognizes from a recent piece in the *Star-Ledger*. One of them has a long steel wrench in his hand.

Great. Now Pastor's convinced he'll have to show the papers on the car and they'll check the crime computer and talk to Cameron and find out it's on loan to a Belton preacher with an active code five for suspicion of murder. And then they'll search it and find the money and Anemone's pocketbook. Cell doors are already clanging in his ears over the beat booming on 97.1 fm when the Witness comes up behind him puffing.

"Officers, I saw the whole thing."

Maybe Sister Walker is right. God must be on Pastor's side because the thick-necks buy the Witness's story. They joke with Pastor about how those kids are so good at what they do that, aside from the Stanley screwdriver sticking out of the ignition, they didn't even cause that much damage, so there's no need to file a report. Then the one with the giant wrench closes down the hydrant and they rush off to join the chase. Pastor can only imagine what will happen if they catch those kids.

"Thanks," Pastor says to the Witness as he hops into the car.

"No, thank Jehovah."

Yeah. He walked right into that one.

He doesn't have time to debate Christology with a Jehovah's Witness. Scripture says he doesn't even have to bid the Witness Godspeed. So, he pulls the car into the parking lot of Hazel's building, pops the trunk, and fetches Anemone's pocketbook. He's damp with sweat from his brief chase so he pushes the A/C to full blast and unzips the pocketbook. He turns it upside down and dumps the contents like he did at the bank. But this time he squeezes the bag, and feels and hears something like paper crumpling. He feels around the inside and finds a zipper in the side panel under a flap. He pulls a crumpled Get-a-way Travel envelope out of the secret compartment. It contains a Continental Airlines one-way coach ticket to Southwest Florida International Airport in Fort Myers, Florida, $1,000 in new $50s and $20s, and a business card with an address written on the back in a very masculine print. Pastor digs his leather business card carrier out of his jacket and pulls the card on top. The addresses match. So do the names on the front of the cards. Dexter Hoard.

Pastor's been around church folks long enough and has lived long enough to know that we are all flawed, no matter how decent we are. But if he ever wanted to cry because of a human failing, it's now. He jams his forehead on the steering wheel and begs God. Let it not be true.

He's creeping back to the Mews hoping not to attract anymore cop attention. It's no secret that BPD uses profiling to make stops so his eyes are darting back and forth between the road and the rearview mirror.

He doesn't want to think about the possibility that Dexter might've killed Anemone, but thoughts keep trespassing anyway. Thoughts about Dexter begging off the night Anemone was murdered. Thoughts about Dexter not making it to the cemetery. Thoughts about Dexter and Malisa's relationship. Thoughts about Dexter being so broken up in the deacon's room. Thoughts about Dexter slipping out the window of his ground floor office on a murderous mission while his signature at the security guard's desk provided an airtight alibi. If it were anyone else's name he would've done something immediately. But Dexter is his friend, and a good man. If Dexter killed Anemone, Pastor wants to see it with his own two eyes before he believes it. The scene along Belton

Avenue becomes blurry in a hurry and Pastor turns the A/C vent toward his face to try and keep his eyes dry.

It's a lot quieter on Fairview than the last time he was here. At 2:30 on a Saturday afternoon there's usually lots of kids out riding their bikes and playing touch football, but it's too hot today for anyone to be out playing on the street. There's no breeze and even the FOR SALE signs are dangling perfectly still, sweating in the humidity.

The Allon home stands in the middle of the block like a shamed miscreant. Fresh yellow police tape clings to the hedges and the lawn is beginning to look a little brown and uneven.

Pastor slips into the backyard and down the steps that lead to the basement door. One of the two house keys on Anemone's ring fits perfectly and the lock clicks.

The basement is dark and musty with a hint of disinfectant in the air. The main odor reminds him of Ike's 30th birthday party back in January, though, when 50 sweaty bodies were packed in swaying to Aswad while Ike sequestered himself at the turntables behind the one-way glass in the deejay booth until it was time for Pastor to bless the cake. Pastor was afraid of places like this as a kid, but when he became a man he put away childish things.

The Florida beach poster shimmers under the dim beam of his Saab penlight. The shadows feel like people sitting in the three seats from the separated sectional set off against each other along the three walls.

He makes his way up the creaky stairs. Everything seems creaky in this house now. All kinds of little noises. Bishop Hook used to say it was just the house settling. With all the windows closed and the shades and curtains drawn the second floor feels like the inside of an oven set on bake. The bedroom looks restored. Everything is in its place. Except for the unmade bed with the huge dark spot on the pillows. And the smell.

It was Ike's predictable chauvinism that allowed Anemone to play him like an old tired song. He never invited her into his world: Eight Rivers, the deejay booth, his carriage house wood shop. And he never ventured too far into hers. Tragic irony that when he finally did stumble into her world it ended up killing him.

The loose board is exactly where Hazel said it would be, just under what must've been Ike's side of the bed, at the edge of the throw rug.

Hidden in plain sight. What better place to bury evidence than at the scene of the crime.

Pastor probably doesn't need to, but to be sure he won't miss anything he points the penlight like Alexander Monday anyway, the theme from *It Takes a Thief* rambling through his mind. There's some dried blood and brain matter nearby. And sure enough, there's a black 9mm stuffed in there, butt up. There's nothing under it, though.

Pastor knows the sounds an old house settling all around him makes, and a door closing downstairs isn't one of them. He's instantly looking like Lot's wife. Perfectly still. Its amazing how your hearing improves in situations like this. There are no French doors leading to terraces or balconies up here. The only way out is down those creaky stairs now bearing heavy footsteps, or a twenty-foot drop from a window.

Pastor skitters across the room into the walk-in closet and hides behind a rack of dresses and gowns. Many of them feel like they're still sporting the tags.

Who in the world could this be? They're splashing something on the floor. Maybe the same company Ike called to scrape Anemone's brains off the basement tile? These guys must make a killing cleaning up after dead folk. But who would've called them? And that smell. Why would they use something kerosene based?

It smells like the whole top floor has been splashed and the splasher is now downstairs. Pastor slides down on his haunches to get comfortable. At least he'll be sneaking out of a clean house. But the splasher must be either an idiot or an arson, because all of a sudden Pastor is smelling smoke.

He creeps to the closet door and cracks it open to three foot flames dancing in the middle of the room and spreading quickly. The doorway to the stairs is engulfed already, and he can't remember if he's heard the door close downstairs. *Maannn, Ike is already dead. Why torch the house?* There's only one thing to do and not much time to do it in if he doesn't want to be toast.

The windows face the house next door. All he needs is for someone to see him leaping for his life and BPD will soon be adding arson to the list of charges they intend to file. Thank goodness the ground is soft and the grass is high. Pastor tucks and rolls, and refuses to turn to see who's calling, "Hey you, what're you doing."

He jumps into the Mustang and roars off looking all around for any sign of Dexter. One way to get rid of evidence is to burn it. Whoever torched the house probably thought the tape was still in there. Dexter is nowhere to be seen, and Pastor scolds himself for convicting him in the back of his mind. Because he was planting in Anemone's private garden doesn't have to mean he killed her.

ᒐ

Jumping from Ike's bedroom window brings all the bile concerning Shabazz back to the pit of Pastor's stomach. When he gets back to the car he's careful to obey the speed limit through Belton into Maplewood. This time Shabazz is home. Pastor parks across the street from the white pick-up truck and storms through the gate the way he stormed onto the court at Madison Square Garden in high school for the City Championship game. Psyched. Focused. Ready to step up and get the job done.

Deferred revenge is even sweeter because it's had a chance to ripen. He's still gonna burst in on him as soon as he opens the door, but during the painfully slow ride to Shabazz's house Pastor decided to choke him even longer and harder before he calls the police. He doesn't need his windpipe to confess anyway. He can always write it down.

The growl behind Pastor changes his plans.

There's no time to make eye contact with the pit bull and he latches onto Pastor's right arm. He tries to stay cool so the dog won't rip his arm off, because he still needs it to choke Shabazz with all his strength. The pit bull's jaws send an indescribable pain shooting up Pastor's arm but before he can find its eyes the screen door opens behind him and the world turns upside down and dark and silent all at the same time.

One thing they don't tell you about revenge. It'll rob your true sight. It'll so impair your vision that you won't even realize you're not seeing straight. Guess that's why they say it belongs to God.

Pastor's eyes are burning. His head is throbbing. The floor is damp under him. He tries to sit up and rub his head, but it's like there's a sandbag on his chest, and a rubber band mooring his head to the floor, and glue between his lips. He obeys the urge to speak, to cry out, but only guttural gibberish thrashes around in his mouth.

Who is this person standing above me?

It's hard to think. The pain in Pastor's head is crowding out his memory. Or scrambling it. He can't decide which.

He springs erect, soaked. In a puddle. His head hurts even worse than before. Shabazz is standing over him with a bucket and a roll of duct tape. He puts his foot back on Pastor's chest and dashes the rest of the water into his face.

"End of the line, Hook. You'll steal from me no more."

There's duct tape circling Pastor's chest and hips, binding his arms and wrists to his sides. His ankles are bound, too. And there's duct tape over his mouth. Pastor decides they must be in Shabazz's basement. It's untiled. Cold cement. The rest of Pastor's synapses kick back in and the smell of urine and excrement reach his brain. And the noise of the pit bull barking, chained to a pipe in the corner next to a card table with an empty aquarium on it.

"You probably have *no* idea what's happening, huh? I tell you what, though, you scared the hell outta me. I was on my way to the cleaners to pick up my robe when you showed up? Man I thought I was looking at a ghost for sure, 'cause I just *knew* you were in hell by now. Guess that wasn't you I saw upstairs cleaning those windows."

Pastor thrashes about trying to break out of the tape to strangle Shabazz, and feels Shabazz's laughter through his foot on Pastor's chest.

"After what happened to your car you should've told your sexton to keep the storm cellar doors closed when he's up on the ladder. Y'all live in Belton, not heaven."

He's not laughing anymore. He kicks Pastor in the side, puts his foot back on Pastor's chest, and looks him in the eye.

"Now you know how it feels to lose something. Because of you I lost First Baptist, and my wife, and my kids. I'll be damned if I let you take Monumental from me, too."

This nigro *is* crazy. He has a better chance of becoming President of the United States than he does of getting called to Monumental. He takes his foot off Pastor's chest and saunters up the stairs with the duct tape. Pastor tries to get to his feet, but it's impossible without use of his wrists and elbows. So he rolls over to the stairs and tries to prop himself up before Shabazz gets back.

"Trying to get away, huh?" says Shabazz from the head of the stairs. "I don't blame you."

He rolls Pastor back to the middle of the basement, stoops over him, and pushes a bottle of hot sauce into his face.

"See this? Thanatos loves this stuff. Anything it's on, he devours. So I'll be sure not to put any on your face. I want the cops to be able to recognize who the burglar was that broke into my home and got mauled by my dog while I was away. And bitten by my snakes. You heard about my snakes, right? Without medical attention? You should be dead in about, oh, I'd say two days. Then I'll say, 'Officer, I didn't even know there was anyone down there until I noticed the smell.'"

He should've cackled like Vincent Price and launched into a soliloquy then, but instead he empties the bottle of hot sauce on Pastor's chest, stomach and legs, puts the empty bottle on the table next to the aquarium, and unchains Thanatos.

"Don't worry, I'm not taking him out for a walk," he says, pulling the barking dog by the collar up the steps as Pastor struggles through a sit-up into the upright position. "I'm just squeamish."

He opens the door and turns. Pastor wants to call on Jesus, but the duct tape has sealed in his voice. His only hope is to make eye contact with Thanatos.

"I'll let him go from up here and when I get back from the cleaners I'll call him upstairs again so I don't have to witness the carnage. You should be ready for the snakes by then."

He lets go and slams the door, and Thanatos bounds down the steps.

Thanatos is at the bottom of the steps barking and Pastor is stiff as a board, his eyes fixed on the dogs'. Thanatos' hair is standing up on his back and he's advancing cautiously. His bark is loud. He's all confused. He's close enough to smell the hot sauce, but also close enough to feel whatever is coming out of Pastor's eyes, Pastor's soul. Looks like Pastor really does have some Jesus juice after all. Some Holy Ghost power!

Thanatos nips at his heel then whimpers and backs off. He repeats this several times before the whimpers increase and eventually overtake the barking. Finally, he backs up all the way to the steps and lays down. Pastor feels like Daniel in the lion's den.

He shuffles backwards on his bottom to the table, inch by inch using alternating cheeks like a drunk caterpillar, all the while keeping his eyes on Thanatos. If he can jostle the table just right and knock the empty hot sauce bottle off it he could use a glass shard to free myself. But the empty aquarium is heavier than he thought it would be, so he gives the table a big shove with his shoulder. And the entire table and all of its contents come crashing down around him.

Glass shards are everywhere. And what a time to find out that the aquarium wasn't empty after all. From his vantage point Pastor just couldn't see the diamondback rattlers coiled on the bottom.

His first instinct is to go fetal, but he's always heard that when snakes bit humans it's usually out of self-defense, so he remains perfectly still hoping they won't consider him a threat. But their whole world has just been shattered, and Pastor's the next living thing they encounter. To them he must be the Uncaused Cause, so they lash out at him the way we humans do at God sometimes when things go terribly wrong.

Fire surges through Pastor's neck, his right cheek, and his right shoulder. He screams from somewhere deep inside of himself and bursts through the duct tape as if it were gossamer. He jumps to his feet and realizes he's in the living room, and a snake is dangling from his shoulder, still biting into his flesh. He grabs it with his left hand, throws it to the hardwood floor and stomps on its head with his heel.

The gospel of Mark says that true believers, the ones with real Jesus juice, can be bitten by serpents and suffer no harm. Some churches even make a liturgy out of it, which Pastor thinks is just bad hermeneutics. But, in any case he's about to find out what he's really made of pretty soon.

He looks around. There are light spaces on the walls where pictures and a wall unit or breakfront used to be. The floor is bare. Shabazz's wife must've taken everything when she left. Pastor looks down at his clothes. No hot sauce stains to be found anywhere. No duct tape either. There's blood running down his right hand though, and the sleeve of his jacket and shirt is ripped apart. A chunk of red flesh is poking through.

And the back of his head is throbbing, like if somebody just drove a railroad stake through it. He puts his hand to the back of his head and comes back with blood.

Pastor doesn't know what's real anymore. All he knows for certain is that he's been bitten by a pit bull, and a rattle snake. And that Shabazz McCoy blew up his car, his house and everything he owns in it, along with his adopted mother. And his sermon notes. And that Anemone Allon was planning to skip town with Dexter Hoard and live in his beach house on Captiva Island in Florida.

Pastor could just walk out of Shabazz's house, call the Maplewood police from the car, and press charges. ...*Not!* He squats right there next to the dead rattlesnake in Shabazz McCoy's no-longer-furnished living room and waits to hear his pick-up truck pull into the driveway.

Pastor's jolted when the doorbell rings. Why would Shabazz ring his own doorbell? Somebody starts banging on the door, and Thanatos starts barking behind the basement door, too, and Pastor realizes he hasn't thought things through far enough. He just assumed Shabazz had no friends.

"Open the door, Shabazz!"

Pastor peeks through the peephole, sees a bright red suit, and opens the door. "Co?! What are you doing here? Put the gun away. I don't know whether you look like Santa Claus or the Devil."

"Damn, Doc! What happened to *you*!? You've got blood all over your arm."

"Long story. I'm alright, though. You didn't bring anybody with you, did you?"

"Naw. I stopped by your crib to pick you up like I said I would, and the whole thing was, like, *gone*. You're not having a good week, are you? I didn't see you, so I just *knew* you'd come after this clown by yourself."

Suddenly Shabazz comes darting through the front door calling out Pastor's name, saying the ambulance is on its way, and Cornel reflexively coldcocks him in the temple from his blind side. He drops like a sack of rotten potatoes. Cornel jumps on Shabazz like a fly on you-know-what, raining blows on his swiveling head, disappointed that Shabazz isn't even putting up a mild struggle. He wants to hear Shabazz scream for Thanatos a couple of times while he pummels the living consciousness out of him.

Mother's face, Pastor's old Saab, and his sermon notes whizz through Pastor's mind. And then strangely an image of Jesus on the cross jumps into his head and his heart begins to betray him. Compassion slips back into his soul and he starts feeling sorry for Shabazz! Protective of him even.

"Co! Stop! Stop!" Pastor is pulling Cornel off Shabazz, but he's still swinging furiously. "Co! Stop! He's had enough. Enough!"

Cornel finally comes out of the pugilistic trance he was in and kisses his reddened knuckles as Shabazz lays still and bloodied on his own living room floor.

"Sorry, Doc. I didn't mean to kill him."

Pastor puts his ear to Shabazz's chest.

"He's not dead."

Pastor hops to his feet and pulls Cornel with him into the cluttered, appliance-free kitchen.

"Look at this. Wires, detonators, ...whatever these are. This guy was building bombs at his kitchen table," says Pastor.

"What you looking for?"

"Duct tape," Pastor says, going through the drawers. "...Here it is. Help me get this around him before he wakes up."

Pastor winds tape around Shabazz's torso and hips like he thought Shabazz had done to him. Cornel points his gun at the basement door. Thanatos, if that's his name, is barking up such a storm that Pastor has to yell over the noise. "What are you doing?"

"Shutting that damn dog up."

"No, you can't shoot the dog. Are you crazy?"

"It's vicious. It might get out and attack us."

"He won't get out. And it's Shabazz who made him vicious."

"Then lemme shoot *Shabazz*. He won't feel it, he's out."

"This is no time for jokes, man."

"*Now* what are you doing," says Cornel.

"Writing a note to the cops. Just put some duct tape around his ankles and mouth, please. And make it tight. Real tight."

"I hope you know what you're doing."

Pastor tapes the note to the front door. "Yeah. Me, too." Then he grabs his cell phone and dials 911. "Hello? My name is Shabazz McCoy and I'd like to confess to a couple of bombings in Belton. Would you send a squad car to pick me up? I'll give you my address...."

⌡

Reservation Hill seems steeper still. They turn right onto Wyoming Avenue and Pastor pulls behind Cornel into his long, winding stamped-brick driveway. Pastor always loved Tudors, but even in his homeless state he doesn't need six bedrooms and five baths. And if he ever did he'd have to get called to a church like Monumental because he sure wouldn't be able to afford one like this on what First Baptist pays him.

It's uncharacteristically quiet inside.

"When'd you get the new frame for American Beauty?" Pastor nods at the oil image of a skeleton in a coffin with two silicone gel sacks flanking its breastbone.

"Dana picked it up yesterday."

Pastor gave it to them at their house-warming five years ago. At the time *El Négro de Belize* was a poor man's Basquiat, now he's the bomb. And at the time Cornel promised he'd hang it in their bedroom, not over their gray-and-white striped living room couch.

"Where is everybody, in the pool?"

"Yup," Cornel says, walking to the back of the house.

Something is simmering on the center-island Jen-Air. Pastor sits at the table in the breakfast nook and flips through an old May-June issue of the *Utne Reader*, the tag line "Adultery: The Upside" teasing its cover.

The sliders whoosh open and twin four-year olds pour in with wet Looney Tunes trunks clinging to their little legs. Dana looks like she's hiding a beach ball under her maternity dress as she shuffles after them with their towels. She still looks fly despite the inflated nose and her chocolate brown skin has that pregnant glow to it.

"Uncle Tony! Uncle Tony!"

"Charles-Grace! Emmanuel-Grace!" Pastor rubs their bald heads. "Sup, partners!"

"My God, Tony. Cornelius said snakebite, he didn't mention a thing about lacerations."

"I keep slicing my arm shaving."

"That can't be blood." She waddles over to Pastor, grabs his wrist to check his pulse and gently pokes at his sleeve. "Tell me it's not blood."

"I forgot to tell you about the dog," says Cornel, drying the kids.

"A pit bull confused me with lunch," Pastor says to Dana. "We finally got it straightened out, though."

She rolls her eyes then glares at Cornel. "At least *some*body has a sense of humor around here."

"Don't start, okay Dana?"

Here we go again. This is why Pastor doesn't like coming over to Cornel's too often. Maybe it's guilt. But there's nothing he can tell Dana that she doesn't already know. Cornel's rascality masquerades as charm to women like Dana. That's what attracted her in the first place.

"Uncle Tony! Wanna know how to make a tissue dance?"

"How?"

They almost can't get it out for the giggles. "Put a boogie in it!"

"Hey, that was pretty funny." Pastor palms their heads.

"Alright guys, go in the pool bath and take off your trunks. I'll be right there. And no playing with the shower."

They run back outside, howling.

"Walk, please!"

"Yes, ma'am."

Cornel opens the refrigerator. Once again the kids save the day.

"Ever since Cornelius called they've been dying to tell you that one. I'm sorry about everything that's happened to you, Tony. You need to get out of that church."

"I'm trying."

"I know your running buddy over there has probably already said this, but I'll say it again just in case. You can stay with us for as long as you like. We have plenty of room."

"Actually, Co didn't offer," says Pastor, manufacturing his best pout. "I was going to check into a seedy motel."

Cornel groans, sticks an IBC Root Beer in Pastor's hand and sits at the table swigging his Heineken. Dana cuts him another look.

"Are you hungry, Tony?" She turns to Cornel. "Honey, why don't you take him upstairs and get him something to wear to the hospital while I fix him a sandwich."

"Hospital? I'm not going to any hospital. Like I told Co, I'm fine. I agreed to let *you* look at it. You know I hate hospitals. I don't have time to go to any hospital."

"The man is delirious already. Tony, you *have* to go to the hospital. You need to be treated with antivenin. And you probably need stitches for that arm. I still have privileges at Saint Barnabas and I've already called ahead. They're expecting you."

"I'm fine. The bites themselves hurt, but since then there's been no pain, no swelling. I'm fine."

"Sure, you're fine now, but depending on the kind of snakes that bit you and whether envenomation occurred or not, you may not see any effects for 12 to 16 hours, and then all of a sudden you can experience paralysis, parathesias—"

"Speak English!" chides Cornel. She rolls her eyes.

"—even tumble into respiratory distress or worse, respiratory failure. This is nothing to fool around with."

"I'm fine. ...How long would I have to stay?"

"They can stitch you up in minutes. The average stay for snakebite though is about five days. But the longer you wait to get treated, the longer you'll have to stay."

"Nope. No can do. If I start feeling any effects I'll go, but not until after service tomorrow. And you can just wrap my arm up with some gauze, can't you?"

"It might be too late by then. You could die."

"Maybe those snakes weren't even poisonous. Anyway, scripture says we're protected against snakebite."

"Cornelius? Aren't you going to do something?"

"He's a grown man. Whada you want me to do? If he doesn't wanna go, he doesn't wanna go. Faith can accomplish some things medical science can't."

She throws her hands up. "Fine. Well at least let me clean the wounds here to guard against bacterial infection. I just hope we won't be at the hospital in a couple of days praying for you to wake up from a coma." She turns toward the sounds of giggling in the pool bath and adds as she leaves, "You guys know I'm no Bible scholar, but I *do* remember Jesus saying something about not tempting God."

"I hope you know what you're doing, Doc," says Cornel.

"Yeah. Me, too. Listen, I need to run over to the mall and pick up something real quick to wear tomorrow."

"Good luck," calls Dana from the bathroom. "The boys and I just got back from there an hour ago and it was an absolute zoo. Between people buying graduation suits and Father's Day gifts those poor sales people didn't know which way to turn. And they're short-staffed as it is."

"She's got ears like the Bionic Woman. C'mon, Bishop, you don't have to go to the mall. I'll hook you up. It's not Barney's, but we'll find you something."

Dana comes back from the bathroom with a first aid kit and a bottle of peroxide. She pours the peroxide into Pastor's open wound, wraps it in gauze and tells him he still needs to go to the hospital to get antibiotics and a rabies test for the dog bite, and antivenin for the snake bite. Pastor thanks her for her concern and climbs upstairs with Cornel.

The second floor of the house is airy, with high ceilings. Their bedroom looks like an exhibit at Huffman Koos, and opening the door to Cornel's walk-in closet is like popping the top on a brand new box of Crayola crayons. Pastor's never seen so many colors in a man's closet before.

He tells Cornel what he found in the safe deposit box and what Hazel said about the loose floorboard under Ike's side of the bed. Ike said he hadn't destroyed the tape and Pastor has to believe him, because finding it is his only chance to prove who really killed Anemone. He sorts through the rainbow on the rack wondering aloud where the most likely place was for Ike to hide a tape he didn't want anybody else to ever find. And Cornel says the most useful thing he's said all week. "Usually, when I want to hide something, I stash it somewhere in my office."

CHAPTER 15

Eight Rivers Auto Body is housed in a brick flat with four bays on a dull stretch of Springfield Avenue just west of Bergen Street. There's a used tire shop across the street, a used car dealership next to it with faded red, white and blue pennants still strung above the lot, and various Mom & Pop establishments jammed in on either side with too much old inventory and not enough new customers. Ike named it in honor of his hometown, Ocho Rios, Jamaica. Since he spent so much of his time at work, maybe Ike hid the tape that cost him his life somewhere in his shop. Pastor figures it's worth a shot, since he's running out of ideas and time.

"C'mon, Doc, lemme come inside with you. We could be a team, like Watson and Holmes cracking cases, Crockett and Tubbs busting heads."

Or more like Wilder and Pryor trying to break out of stir if Pastor lets him get involved.

What Dana said spooked Cornel. He insisted on playing chauffeur in his car so that if Pastor suddenly stopped breathing he could rush him to the hospital. But, as usual with Cornel, there's another angle to his concern.

"No, Co. You might just go waving that gun around again if a dog pops up and the last thing I need is Newark PD looking for us. Just wait here, I'll be right back."

"Still don't know why you're here, you don't need a tape. I told you it's Lila Vernon who capped Anemone. Seven years in juvie for murdering a black couple? It had to be her."

"She was at a restaurant with 100 others who say she was there."

"Anybody can come up with an alibi. Why you putting on the collar?"

"Collar effect, remember?"

Pastor doesn't particularly like wearing a collar. It usually makes him feel like he's just put on human repellant cologne, a bulls-eye on his back, and a blinking sign on his chest that reads "Please disrespect me, treat me like a complete idiot, take nothing I say seriously, and do wonder why a reasonably intelligent guy like me would waste his time telling ancient stories instead of making money for a living." But there are times when it's the quickest way to establish his identity without having to say a word, something that comes in handy when he has few words to work with. This is one of those times. Plus, Cornel believes that when a black man sees a collar on another black man, archetypal images of slavery and the middle passage and capture in the motherland flood his subconscious, forcing a suspension of his sense of place in this country, and making him feel an unexplained kinship with the clergy at that time—though Cornel would never be caught dead in one himself. If there *is* any such "collar effect" Pastor will need to take advantage of it quickly, because he knows it'll wear off as soon as they notice the car they pulled up in and the cut of this loud purple suit he's wearing.

Hey, it was either this or a pink number.

From the looks of things Ike was nothing but a vapor—two people are arguing over an invoice in the small front office. Business as usual and he's not even in the ground yet. The shop floor is filled with late model foreign cars in all stages of repair or customization. Sparks are flying from a metal sander smoothing out the rough edges on the door of a Benzino with its top dropped.

Pastor is looking for the busiest of the five people at work. He doesn't want anybody with time on their hands and minimal distractions to think too much about why they should answer questions about their recently canceled boss from a badgeless, gunless, Barney-the-dinosaur looking preacher they don't know from a can of paint. He taps the busiest brother he can find on the shoulder and dodges the sparks from the sander grinding against the door of the blue Benz. He stands and turns with the sander still whirring in his hand. The name stitched into the breast of his brown jumpsuit leaps out at Pastor: Donald.

It looks like he's going to go right back to work on the Mercedes and ignore Pastor, but then he notices the collar and it seems to change his mind.

"Excuse me," Pastor yells over the whir of the sander. "I'm Tony Hook, pastor of the First Baptist Church in Belton. Can we talk for just a minute?"

His response surprises Pastor. "Sure, Rev, what can I do for you?" He turns off the sander. Pastor just assumed he'd be like Ike. Score one for Cornel and the 'collar effect?'

"It's about Ike Allon."

"Yeah, we found out this morning." He shakes his head. "First his wife, now him. They say it happens in threes, right Rev?"

"That's what they say."

"Well put in a good word for me or somp'm, 'cause I can't afford to be next. I got too much bills, man."

His eyes are smiling behind his safety goggles. In fact, his whole face is smiling. His teeth are so small they look like baby corn in his big gums and the two biggest ones up front are capped with gold. If the tape is here Pastor is confident Donald will lead him to it.

"If it does happen in threes, Donald, I don't think you have anything to worry about. Ike was number three. Number two happened at the funeral yesterday. Limo driver got shot."

"Word up? Ike didn't say nothin' about it."

"That's why I'm here. I'm hoping you can help me find out who killed his wife. It's probably the same person who capped him and the limo driver."

"Are you a preacher or a detective?"

"I knew them pretty well, so I'm trying to help the police out on this one."

"Well I don't know nothin' about who killed his wife."

"I know. I'm not saying you do. I'm just looking for a videotape Ike might have left here."

"You too, huh? Cops came by here searching the whole place for the same thing a couple days ago. And I'll tell you the same thing I told them. I don't know nothin' about no tape. They searched everywhere up in here and didn't find no tape, so trust me, there ain't no tape."

If Pastor didn't know it before he knows it now. Sears had been playing dumb at the crime scene. She knew all along it was murder and believed it was connected to the Newark Prostitute Murders, but for some reason wanted to keep it quiet. Now she's using Pastor as a pawn in her private chess game with someone or something and it just might cost him his best shot to date at turning his life around. Pastor bows his head for a second, exhales, and remembers to recite under his breath a verse of scripture he sometimes uses to stave of crippling anger: *The wrath of man worketh not the righteousness of God.* Sure would've been useful at Shabazz's.

"The last time I talked to Ike," Pastor says to Donald, "he gave me the impression he may have sent the tape out in the mail somewhere. It sounds crazy, I know, but maybe he sent it here. Any packages come in the mail recently?"

"I don't know, Rev. Ike was here yesterday afternoon when the mail came. Here today, gone tomorrow."

"How about today. If he did mail it, he probably put it in the mail on Thursday and it takes a couple of days to get to Newark from Belton. The mail come yet?"

"Yeah. It's in there on the desk now, but there wasn't any packages, just a buncha bills. Story of my life, Rev."

Maannn.

"Okay. Okay. How about if he wanted to send something to somebody for safekeeping, any idea who he might use?"

He laughs. "You talking about Isaac Jerome Allon? Man, Ike wouldn't trust *nobody* to keep *nothin'* safe for him, you-know'm-sayin? He didn't even trust his own employees with a key for this place. I had to call him up at home this morning when I came to work and didn't see him. That's when I found out what happened. A cop answered and said he got shot. I had to go down there and beg them to take the key off his ring just so I could open up, 'cause I got kids and bills, Rev. I'ma miss him, but life goes on, you-know'm-sayin?"

"How about on Thursday. He had to come in late that day, because he was in Belton that afternoon. Did he go anywhere else where he could have left it?"

"Naw, Rev. He wasn't late on Thursday. He was here before everybody else as usual. He left early, though. That's how I knew something was goin' on. The only time Ike left this place during business hours was for an emergency meeting. He was always first in, last out. I asked him what was up and he told me Anemone got shot the night before and he had to go to the funeral home. Then right after he left the cops came and questioned all of us."

"You know if he went anywhere else besides the funeral home?"

"He had to, 'cause he was gone almost the whole day and I know it don't take that long to do business with a funeral home. My little nephew just got capped last month and all it took us was a couple hours to work everything out."

"Where else could he have gone?"

"Brother LeRoy's."

"Who's that?"

"His spiritual advisor."

"What?"

"You know, Rev." Donald makes a motion with his fingers like he's sprinkling salt in a small circle in front of himself. "Hoodoo doctor?"

"Ike?"

"Most of your folks go see you once a week, right? Well Ike went to see his man once a week, too. Except he went every Saturday before he opened up here."

"So why would you think he went there on Thursday?"

"'Cause I know Ike. He's the most superstitious Coconut I ever met. Anytime anything went wrong, he'd run over to Brother LeRoy's. Come here."

Pastor follows him into the office. The invoice argument has moved to the just installed spoiler on a new black Lexus with gold rims. Donald lifts the soiled mat with the word WELCOME grimed out. There are seven shiny pennies taped to the floor in the shape of a cross. Pastor shakes his head and grimaces. The last time he'd seen something like it was in his senior year of high school when an obeah woman convinced one of his teammates' mother that her son was going to die in a car accident if she didn't do something to "protect" him.

"And look up there." He's pointing to the transom. A horseshoe, and what looks like a palm leaf shaped and tied into the form of a cross. "Ike swore this business was doing so good because of all the things Brother LeRoy was telling him to do. Come on. Look at this."

The little lavatory behind the cluttered desk is about the size of a closet. A large green votive candle is stuck on the back of the grimy sink where the soap is supposed to be. Taped against the wall above the dirty commode is a badly blurred copy of the 109th Psalm on yellowed paper.

"This is the first that candle wasn't lit before we opened for a business day since I been working here."

"Okay, so he went to Brother LeRoy's after the funeral home. Think he might've trusted *him* with that tape?"

He shakes his head and shows Pastor those big gums again.

"Thanks a lot, Donald." They shake hands and Pastor pulls out a business card and writes his cell phone number on the back. "You've been a big help, man. If you remember anything else, give me a call."

"A'ight, Rev. I answered all your questions, now here's one for you. My grandmother always said Ike was goin' to hell for dabbling in that hoodoo mess and not believin' in Jesus. My mother said he was goin' to heaven because he always tried to do the right thing and was always fair with his employees. What you say? Where Ike at now?"

Pastor can tell he's already made up his mind. He's just asking to get a better feel for who Pastor is, to locate him on Donald's personal religious map. It deflates Pastor a bit, because he knows the only answer he can give is going to sound like more religious tripe and he'll be perceived as just another jack-leg in a purple suit out here taking people's hard-earned money to spout off about things he really doesn't know.

"According to the Bible if he didn't know Jesus he's in hell. And only two people can answer that question for sure. One doesn't seem to be talking right now, and the other one can't anymore."

He nods, all gums. "Uh-huh. I figured you'd say something like that."

♪

The sign in the second floor window of the old office building at the corner of Harrison and Main in East Orange reads: Brother LeRoy,

Spiritualist. Maybe only white people get to call themselves psychics. To Pastor's mother he would just be a plain old obeah man. Donald Mason found his card in the top drawer of the office desk and Cornel went off into another 60 second plug for Mary Welbourne.

The second floor hallway is dingy but cool, and smells like floor wax. Brother LeRoy's nameplate juts out from the top of a door. The same door through which a well-dressed man exits. He's a preacher Pastor recognizes from the Ministers' Conference, but doesn't know by name. Pastor hopes the Barney suit will serve as a disguise for him. He notices fear in the preacher's eyes when they pass each other pretending not to know one another. Probably wondering if Pastor realizes where he's coming from. Pastor continues past Brother LeRoy's door toward the law office down the hall and waits for the preacher to disappear down the stairway before he doubles back. No use feeding unnecessary rumors.

It's several seconds after Pastor knocks before he hears a tinny voice say, "Read the sign." Sure enough, right in front of his face is an engraved sign plate that reads: If Open, Come Right In. Brother LeRoy is sitting at a white circular table in the middle of the room, leafing through a white Bible. He's gaunt with ashy skin, like someone who's lived in the desert all his life. His close-cropped hair is entirely white, and very thin on top. When Pastor approaches and shakes his hand, like his demeanor, it's cool to the touch.

The office doesn't look or smell like Pastor imagined such a place would. He was expecting to see candles and jars filled with herbs and feathers and rooster feet and salamander tails, and statues and trinkets lining dozens of rickety shelves along the walls in a dark, creepy place.

This space is anything but creepy, though.

The room is clean and spare. The red carpet smells like Potpourri Carpet Fresh. The white walls are bare except for a crude wooden cross hanging over a door.

"Sit down, Reverend." The Caribbean is still evident in his diction. "Anywhere you like."

Pastor sits opposite him and LeRoy nods his head without looking directly at Pastor Hook.

"How do you know I'm a Reverend? I took my collar off."

"I work for God, too." He shows Pastor a full set of neat, yellowed teeth, but still doesn't look directly at him. "So I can tell a man of God when I see one."

"Then you must know why I'm here."

"Of course. You're a man who's been searching for answers for a long time. You want information. You want to know things you think you don't know already."

Pastor smiles at the Barnum-like response.

"Then I've come to the right place. I need information about a man."

"You sure that's all?"

"That's all."

LeRoy pulls a slip of paper from the pocket of his white button-down and slides it across the table to Pastor. It's a fee schedule and includes a list of the credit cards he accepts.

"As you know, Reverend, even a man of God must eat. Man does not live by bread *alone*, but it *is* the staff of life."

Pastor knew he'd have to pay for the information, but he didn't think it would be this much.

"Pretty big staff there." He hands over almost all the money he withdrew from the ATM on the way over here.

"I'm the best at what I do in this area, as I am sure that you are the best at what you do in your area. I see that in you."

Pastor smiles again and shakes his head. "Last Thursday someone came to see you. Ike Allon. Do you remember him? He owned Eight Rivers Auto Body on Springfield in Newark."

"I remember all my clients."

"He didn't make his regular appointment this morning, did he?"

"No, he didn't."

"And of course, you know why."

"Because he's dead."

There's no way he could've heard this from anybody else so soon. Perhaps Pastor tipped it off in the way he described Ike. Anyway, he hides his surprise.

"Do you want to talk to him?"

"Um, let's not disturb him," Pastor says, remembering the Witch of Endor, and Saul's end. And even if he could speak to him now it would do Pastor no good anyway, because he's sure that wherever he is, Ike is playing it close to the vest; giving up nothing and trusting no one, like a scared fish in his first week on the tier at Jersey State.

"He died before time. He wandering the earth in timelessness until his proper time come, so it doesn't matter to him now."

"No, I'm here to talk to you. I'm looking for something I'm hoping you can help me find."

"No, he didn't leave the tape with me."

Pastor wants to ask him how he knows about the tape, but decides not to supe' his head up. Ike must've told him about it on Thursday.

"He gave me the impression he mailed it somewhere. Any idea where?"

"You know the answer to that already. He told you the last time you two spoke."

They stare each other down for a few seconds and Pastor doesn't know whether to ask for his money back, or slap his own self silly for throwing his hard-earned dollars away on a soothsayer; because so far he's learned nothing he didn't know already. He's determined to get some kind of bang for his buck, so he chooses another tack.

"Since you know about the tape, I guess you also know about his wife. That she was murdered Wednesday night?"

"That's why he came to see me Thursday. He wanted revenge. And revenge is very expensive."

"So which recipe for revenge did you sell him?"

It's like he's rattling off instructions for baking homemade bread. "Write the name of the killer on a piece of pure parchment paper nine times, dip it in vinegar, and put it together with a rusty nail, some Damnation powder that I give, and nine hot red peppers, and then put it all in a wooden box and leave it in the killer house for three days and three nights."

"And what's that supposed to do?" Pastor asks, thinking Mary Welbourne must've really found the proverbial pot of gold at the end of the rainbow when she "cross-trained" into a gig like this.

"The killer will go crazy and have trouble the rest of his life. But Isaac wanted more. He wanted the killer dead, dead, dead. And as soon as possible. That cost him $500 extra. And for that you write the killer name on nine black candles and burn them twelve hours every night and I do the rest."

His gaze is steady as a surgeon's knife and cuts through the young pastor. LeRoy no doubt believes what he's saying.

"Sounds serious."

"All spiritual things are serious. Read the 109 Psalms and tell me David wasn't serious."

"David was a man of war, but God is a God of love."

"You know very well that the God of love is also a God of justice. I provide the kind of justice for people that the church or government can't."

"*Vengeance is mine; I will repay, saith the Lord.* Romans 12:19 in that book," Pastor says, knowing in his heart he had surrendered his right at Shabazz's house to lecture anyone on the evils of seeking revenge; but the prophetic unction in him provokes him. "Ike ignored that, and now he's dead."

"As you know, it's hard sometimes to leave vengeance to God. *To everything there is a season, and a time to every purpose under the heaven.* Ecclesiastes 3:1, in this same book. Give it time and see what happen to the killer."

Pastor smiles again, but the truth is the guy is starting to get under his skin and Pastor is summoning help from the Holy Spirit to maintain self-control. "How can I? I don't know who it is...and neither do you. That's why I need the tape."

LeRoy smiles the way a father smiles at a child when he wants to say "you'll understand someday".

"You know already," LeRoy says. "You just don't know it yet but you will soon enough."

Pastor smiles again. *I can't believe I paid him for this.*

"Getting back to Wednesday night. Ike put an egg in his wife's hand after he found her dead. Why? You couldn't have told him to, he hadn't seen you yet."

"You want a lot." He stretches his palm to Pastor. "To whom much is given, much is required."

Pastor slaps another $20 into his hand and promises himself to preach a sermon about these guys one Sunday soon.

"When you put an egg in a murdered person's hand, the killer has to wander around the scene until caught. Isaac's been coming to me for a long time, he knew a lot."

"One more question. How was he supposed to get the box in the killer's house?"

"I just tell him what to do. It was up to him to figure out how."

When Pastor steps out of Brother LeRoy's office his face is hurting from all the smiling, and he succumbs to a guilt attack. He tries telling himself it's not like if he'd paid a psychic for spiritual information, he was just looking for a lead on Ike's tape; but his conscience is having none of it. Pastor's conscience keeps telling him he must preach an entire series of sermons on the occult, its devices, and its practitioners, because spiritually conning vulnerable people out of their money is more pernicious than anything Thorn has ever done. Pastor and his conscience quickly agree on it. They begin strategizing on the way back to the car.

It's a long ride back to Belton. Cornel's still going on about Lila Vernon and Mary Welbourne when they pull into Cornel's driveway.

There's a couple hours left until dark, and with all the extra attention Ike's house is now getting Pastor knows he'll need cover of night to slip into the carriage house unnoticed. He's now officially a fashion calamity, and hungry enough to apply for famine relief, but he doesn't feel like listening to bickering while he eats. So he declares his independence in the Brown kitchen, escapes to the Mustang, and makes a mad dash for the Livingston Mall to go deeper in debt to the tune of a new suit and a decent meal at the bistro across from Burger King.

Mistake.

Proms and graduation parties plus shiny fast presents and the invincibility of youth equal surprise DUI checkpoints. The sea of red-white-and-blue police lights at the bottom of the S curves spin him right around. He's never seen a DUI checkpoint in Newark though, so he pulls up to The Shack on South Orange Ave, grabs a barbecue rib sandwich and a grape Mistic, and heads downtown to eat it in Monumental's huge parking lot. Pastor has a lot on his mind. Maybe sitting in the presence of significant ministry dreaming about what could be will inspire him to finally finish tomorrow's sermon. His exegetical notes are crushed somewhere under a pile of rubble so he'll have to compose from memory in the little time he has left.

Monumental completed construction on their $5,000,000 complex about a year ago. Now they run a soup kitchen out of the new basement from 5:00 to 8:00 every night that draws the hungry from all over, not just Newark.

Pastor turns into their parking lot and spots Mowatt getting off the bus, heading straight for the church. The soup kitchen. In sober gait.

And why is Pastor surprised? They don't have soup kitchens in Belton. Low demand. Most Belton churches think it would attract the wrong crowd. Instead they fulfill Jesus' commission to feed the hungry and clothe the naked by writing checks. To his credit, at least Gentry Charlesworth got his folks at First Presbyterian to set up a satellite ministry in a storefront on Bergen Street.

Pastor parks next to a black conversion van near the building's basement entrance and watches the door close behind Mowatt as he ducks inside. It's a minute before it registers. This van is just like the one that's been following him. Same plate number. Same van. Joe Forte's. There was a time when Pastor suspected Joe Forte might be his anonymous pen pal, but Shabazz, and Cornel's DMV deacon got Forte off the hook with that. So why would an ex-cop be following him? And what, if anything, does he know about Anemone's murder? Pastor grabs his sandwich and decides to have dinner inside with Mowatt and see if he can meet this Joe Forte dude.

The basement of the massive structure is bustling with a hive of workers ministering to more than 200 people hunched over trays at cafeteria style tables and chairs. Some of both groups look like they've just come from work.

"Let's go, young man," says a plump woman in an apron behind the counter. "This line's closing soon. Get it while it's hot."

Pastor compares his sandwich in its greasy brown paper bag to the well-balanced meal she's holding on the plate and decides to do the right thing. He grabs a tray, the plate, and finds Mowatt.

"Ay, what you doin' here, Hook? Slummin'?"

"They tell me that's where the best food is," he says, taking the seat across from Mowatt at the otherwise empty table.

"You need to do something about that suit," says Mowatt with his nose squinched up. "You lookin' like one of us."

"You sound almost sober."

"Pigs made me sleep it off last night. They don't know who I am, man. They don't know."

"I've been brushing you off a lot lately, Mowatt. I'm sorry about that."

"That's a'ight. I was just trying to tell you about the Rev who's been hanging around your crib."

"What about him."

"I saw him leaving things on your stoop."

"Good looking out. I don't think you'll be seeing him around anymore, though. I took care of him this afternoon. Since you see so much, let me ask you. Ever see a black van lurking around the parsonage?"

"Last two weeks. He been hanging around, too."

"You know anything about him?"

"Yeah, baby. I see him here every day."

"Know his name?"

"Naw."

"You sure?"

"I'm sure."

"Is he here tonight?"

He looks around. "There he is, right there."

He motions to an older man with wavy salt-and-pepper hair wheeling a garbage bin through the aisles of tables, collecting empty plates and trays. "Thanks, Mowatt. I have to talk to him for a minute. I'll be right back."

CHAPTER 16

"Excuse me, sir. Joe Forte? Do you own a black van?"

He's shorter than Pastor, shabbily built, and the tic in his eyelid says he's as surprised to see Pastor as Pastor is to see him.

"Along with a few thousand other people in Essex county."

"That's why they make license plates in prison. Who are you working for, Shabazz? Sears?"

"I can't talk to you, Reverend."

"Did Thorn hire you to follow me around? Are you trying to find dirt on me?"

He wheels the cart away. Pastor can't afford to make a scene. One call to his police buddies and you might as well stick a fork in Pastor. Pastor watches him to see if he'll turn around, but he just keeps dumping Styrofoam cups and spaghetti sauce-stained Styrofoam plates into his rolling bin. Pastor weaves back to his seat to break bread with Mowatt.

Mowatt's a pretty interesting guy when he's sober. He has a million war stories. Before Pastor knows it, it's time to head back to the Mews.

He won't be able to explain to anyone with a badge why he's driving a brand new convertible sports car with a screwdriver in the ignition, or why his name comes up as wanted on their crime computer, so he obeys the speed limit all the way into Belton, enjoying the full length rendition of Dave Brubaker's *Take Five* on WGBO, Newark's jazz station. When he turns onto Fairview from Belton Avenue nothing seems out of place. Until he gets half-way down the block. The Allon house is a soggy mess of a shell in front of the scorched carriage house. Weird shapes and shadows command the darkened space. Pastor parks two houses down and prays that no one notices him stealing through the trees to the side entrance.

Ike's Vette is still here. So are all his woodworking tools. And the smell of wood stain, still noticeable even through the strong odor of burnt wood. Only the memorial is missing. Pastor pulls Sears's card out of his business card holder and flashes the penlight on it.

If this doesn't work out and he ends up before a judge at the Essex County Courthouse, he'll have K.C. plead temporary insanity for him. Say that he tripped into a moral loophole, Kierkegaard's teleological suspension of the ethical. Yeah, that's the term he was looking for earlier. He leans against the Vette's hatch and punches in the number.

"Chris, it's Tony. Please just listen to me for a minute. I know where the videotape is. Come to church tomorrow morning and I'll deliver it to you. In the sanctuary."

He might have just played matchmaker between Dexter and 50,000 volts in the state electric chair, but what choice does he have? Pastor's about to press the END button when Sears says, "Tony! Don't hang up!"

"I'm on my cell phone, so you can't trace it."

"I don't care where you are," she says, sounding annoyed. "I care what you did. Or didn't do, actually."

"I told you, I didn't kill her."

"You went to Shabazz McCoy's house, didn't you?"

Pastor keeps his mouth shut, waiting for her to make her point.

"After I told you not to. After I asked you to let us handle it, you went over there anyway. Didn't you? ...You still there or are you running away again?"

"I don't know why, but yeah, I'm still here."

"You know what your problem is? After all these years you still don't know how to trust. The only way to enjoy the people God puts in your life is to trust them."

"Are we going there again? Back to fifteen years ago? What's your point?"

"My point is," her voice is steadily rising in volume and intensity. "McCoy told Maplewood PD that the edge of his screen door caught the back of your head by accident and knocked you out cold. He went to a pay phone to call you an ambulance and when he got back you'd already killed his pet snake and then you attacked him and tied him up with the duct tape they found him in. He just pressed charges against you for assaulting him in his own house--the *second* such charge against you in the last three days?--and now there's a *real* warrant out for your arrest. *That's* the point. Don't you *get* it yet?"

"Um, first of all, it seems to me like Shabazz doesn't always tell the truth. And second of all, what do you mean by *real* warrant? Don't you mean *another* warrant?"

She tosses him a condescending chortle. "I mean Maplewood PD just courtesy-called BPD to say they're planning to pick you up tomorrow at your church."

"What, and you guys aren't?"

"God you're slow when it comes to detective work. If we wanted to pick you up, we would've pulled you out of that Mustang a long time ago." Through the sudden silence on the phone she must be hearing Pastor's heart pounding and the gears grinding in his confused mind. "What, you thought they wouldn't run the plates when they saw a suspicious looking yellow Mustang approach the parking lot and then suddenly take off? We could've picked you up anytime we wanted, at the mall, at Brown's, at Hazel Thompson's."

"What?!" Pastor is way past shock. He's almost comatose.

"I thought about saying hi to you in the bathroom, but your heart was beating so loudly I didn't want you to drop dead in the tub from a heart attack. Oh, and by the way, they have web sites on the net now that give you a much better view of women going to the john, if that's what you're into these days."

Pastor doesn't know if he's embarrassed or mad. "How did you know where I was?"

"You didn't even notice the tail, did you. See *professionals* know how to do that. I keep telling you, this isn't one of your mystery stories, this is real."

He's out of the carriage house and racing down the driveway to the street before she finishes the thought.

"I don't know *what's* real anymore," Pastor says, standing on the sidewalk under the gaslight, looking up and down the block. "What did McManus and Royster want then?" The only other cars parked on the street are a camper toward Irvington, near the FCA house, a maroon Mercedes M-Class with a pair of jet skis hitched to the top, and one of those new VW bugs, a lime-green one, up toward Belton Avenue. Pastor heads for the Mustang.

"You weren't answering your cell phone and tomorrow's your big day, so somebody had to let you know you were off the hook. Actually, you were never on it. I just needed to buy some more time without you interfering in the press."

"You've lost me," Pastor says, sticking the screwdriver back into the ignition.

"I'm sure you know by now that I sort of work for the Essex County Prosecutor."

"Sort of?" He makes a U-turn and rides slowly to Belton Avenue, checking all driveways as he goes.

"When I finished law school I was already disenchanted with the corporate thing. Seventy hours a week behind a desk is not for me, no matter how much they pay me, so I went to the FBI academy. I guess you can call me a special prosecutor/investigator now. The Bureau lends me out to other agencies with cases that require a *special* touch. Since the prosecutor here is a woman she wants to make a statement that crimes against women won't be tolerated on her watch, so here I am, catching a serial hooker murderer. Sure beats boring contract disputes."

"Thanks for the life story but I still don't understand what those Newark murders have to do with Anemone's murder, or with me being off the hook." Before he turns left onto Belton he notices a pair of headlights in the rearview mirror, but has no idea where they came from.

"We found all the Newark victims in identical conditions, so we sent a victim profile to every PD in the county and instructed them to call me for anything that matched. Mrs. Allon's body fit the profile."

"And you think the Newark Prostitute Serial Killer murdered Anemone, too."

"We know his name, his address, what he eats for breakfast, when he takes a crap, everything. We've been tailing him for two months now. In that time he's committed seven more murders, and each time he slipped our tail. He's very crafty and hasn't left much behind for us to work with. We've been locked in a dispute with another government agency for almost two months now over access to his DNA profile, because it's the one thing we need to make a hard physical case against this guy and we haven't been able to legally bring him in on anything else. We were on the verge of a ruling when you started spouting off in the press. We couldn't afford to have him go underground or take a long trip to a very foreign country thinking we were onto him. So, because of your mouth and idealism you became our sacrificial lamb until the ruling came in."

"And the ruling didn't go your way."

Her voice falls. "No, it didn't."

"Which means you need the tape." Pastor is driving slowly toward Reservation Hill. His palms are sweaty and he tries to ignore the light traffic behind him.

"After months of hard work, sometimes it just comes down to a lucky break. Are you positive you'll have the tape tomorrow?"

"Yeah, I'm positive. So why did you hang me out there when you knew all along that I didn't do it? Now I might lose a great opportunity."

"If you would've kept your mouth shut and trusted me none of this would've been necessary."

"You keep saying to trust you. Trust you about what?"

"Tony, when we were in college I loved you like I've never loved anyone before, or since. Remember, you're the one who ended it, not me. Did you really think that after what we had together I was capable of pinning a murder on you? Do you really think you could've been in love at one time with that kind of monster?"

Pastor remembers being so devastated by what happened between them that he stuffed all his feelings for her, bad and good, into a safe and shoved it into a corner of his soul in order to survive the ridicule and maintain his GPA; so he honestly doesn't have access to what he really thinks or feels about Chris Sears. He doesn't know what to make of her. But what she said sends the numbers to the safe's combination spinning back through his mind.

"Let me get this straight. You wanted me to trust that you were *lying* to me?"

"I wanted you to trust that it would all work out because it was me you were dealing with, not someone who's never cared about you."

She's talking about the present, but it sounds to Pastor like she's speaking to the past.

"Well, all I care about right now is showing up at my best tomorrow morning and winning over that pulpit committee." Actually he cares about one other thing. "So who is it? Who's the killer?" He doesn't want to wait until he reads it from the parchment paper tomorrow to have his suspicion confirmed, he wants to know now.

"What was it you cited with me, confidentiality? Hmph. I'm just giving you enough to clear my conscience."

"Well what does he do for a living then. And what kind of physical evidence did he leave behind, a hair? Some skin under a fingernail?"

"Why would I tell you any of that?"

"Because it could inspire an award winning Rev. Snoop story. And since you dangled me in the wind to save your case, it's a way to show it wasn't personal." Rev. Snoop is actually the last character on his mind. He's thinking about Dexter. He can't believe Dexter killed Anemone and all those Newark prostitutes. Pastor wants Sears to confirm that he's not a *complete* fool. He had not even a vague suspicion that Dexter was "comforting" Anemone for so long, and pastors are supposed to have suspicions about those kinds of things. They're supposed to see it long before anyone else does. Is he so self-absorbed and spiritually dull that he can't tell when his best friend in the church becomes a serial killer?

"Look, I'm not telling you anything about his identity," she says. "But I *will* tell you this. He's a *very* dangerous, sick man. According to the M.E., cause of death in all the Newark cases was coital asphyxia, so this guy is *really* sick. I mean beyond sick."

"Coital asphyxia? They were strangled to death during sex?"

"There were signs of post-mortem sodomy, too. The Allon case was different, though. Just asphyxia. No sex."

"But the news reports said he shot all the prostitutes in the temple with a nine millimeter."

"He did, *after* he strangled them. Then he took every stitch of clothing, shoes and all, and left them naked, holding the gun he shot them with. These guys all try to make a statement one way or another, and that was his commentary on their lifestyle. The old They Were Undone By Their Lifestyle bit."

"That *is* sick."

"Yeah, and he'll be there in church tomorrow, so I want you to be very discreet. If he knows that you have the tape, you'll be in serious danger. He's already killed two people going after that tape, I don't want you to be the third. Now I'll have a couple of my people outside, and I'll be in the pews myself, but this guy's full of surprises. The number one priority is safety."

"You mean he's a member of my church?"

"Like I said, I'm sure he'll be there tomorrow morning."

"I've had a serial killer in my church all this time and I didn't even know it?"

"Tony, you just be discreet and remember he's *my* problem not yours, and everything'll be fine. *Your* problem is Maplewood PD."

Pastor's lost all his worldly possessions in the last 24 hours. He's dressed like a pimp, a pit bull and a rattlesnake had a piece of him for lunch, and he's being reassured that if he plays his cards right he could avoid getting shot through the head and just get arrested for assault instead. This isn't what he had in mind when he went to divinity school. He creeps up Reservation Hill trying to figure out how his life got so screwed up, and promising God He can have all the parts of himself he's ever held back from Him as soon as all this is over.

∫

The twins are knocked out in their room upstairs when Pastor gets back from Ike's. Dana is in her study web-surfing and Cornel is in the family room laid out in his swivel-rocker recliner fine tuning his whoop under the 60 diagonal-inch tutelage of Bishop Huey Rogers on tape.

"Thanks for letting me stay, Co," Pastor says, flopping into the navy leather sectional.

"Doc, mi casa su casa." He uses his normal voice. "So don't even insult me with your thanks." He reaches down into the side pocket of the navy leather recliner, hits the pause button on the remote control and swivels back to Pastor. "Where's the suit? I thought you went to the mall."

"I had to change my plans."

"So where you been all this time?"

"What are we, married now? I was snooping around."

"Without me? You wrong, Doc. We supposed to be a team." He yanks the lever on the side of the recliner and restores it to its upright position. "Well? What'd you come up with?"

"What Ike did with the tape."

"And? What'd he do with it?"

"He hid it in a memorial I'm supposed to dedicate tomorrow."

"So, let's go get it. Where is it?"

"At the killer's house."

He laughs and rocks in the recliner. "You a trip, Doc. So how do you plan to get it?"

"When he brings it to church tomorrow."

He laughs and rocks even harder. "I told you I already know who your killer is."

"But until you can prove it in a way that'll satisfy a jury your guess doesn't matter to anyone but you."

"So you just gon' keep your fingers crossed that the killer brings the self-incriminating tape to church tomorrow?"

"Exactly. Because he doesn't know he has it."

"And what if he doesn't bring it?"

"Then somebody's going to get away with murder."

He sits motionless for a minute then swivels and clicks the remote at the screen again, and Huey Rogers comes back to life.

"Co, I need a solid."

"What."

"I love you like a brother, man, but I can't wear another suit like this tomorrow morning. Don't you have anything conservative in your closet, like basic black?"

"The man comes up in my house and insults my fashion sense." He's glued to the screen and everything he says now is flowing in the same flawless cadence as Huey's whoop.

"Oh snap. What happened to 'mi casa su casa'?"

"With all those degrees you have I thought you realized that by extension it also means 'my tastes are your tastes'."

"...It does not, man." He starts laughing and turns his head to Pastor, but his eyes are still on Huey.

"A'ight, Doc. I got something *real* conservative for you. And it's black, too. The only one I own."

"Thanks. One more thing."

"What now. My unborn child?"

"Naw, just your laptop. I'll probably be up all night with this sermon."

"You're not done yet?"

"What time did I have? And all my notes were in the house."

"Just let the Lord lead you, Doc. You know how the old folks say, 'Just open your mouth and He'll speak for you.'"

"I'm not like you, Co. I need to write mine down first."

Pastor spends the next few hours tucked away in the guest bedroom with his slumbering muse and one of the twins' many copies of Dr. Seuss. His muse is more stubborn than Seuss's Zax in the prairie of Prax, so he tries to jolt it awake by reading through to the abrupt ending of *The Sneetches*. He doesn't know when he falls asleep. The last number he remembers seeing on the clock is a 2.

When morning comes Pastor is running late. Tiny beads of water cling to the windowpanes and drip from the eaves as he rushes to the bathroom. He showers with the lights on for a change, in his mind and heart forgiving Cornel for not making sure Pastor was up before he left with Dana and the kids for church. Pastor makes up a few of his own when he realizes the only thing he has to shave with is Cornel's Norelco, or one of Dana's Lady Bics. Pastor needs the closest shave of his life so he slaps on a baby oil base, a wad of Edge, grabs the Lady Bic, and gouges a chunk of flesh from the right corner of his square chin when he finally looks at himself in the mirror.

He didn't even hear the rain last night, but it broke the will of the heat wave. Sunday has drifted into Belton on the back of a cool front that has brought with it 70° temperatures and dry sunshine under a blue marble sky. Cottonelle cloudbursts are dangling from the heavens like the Bellini crib mobile in Dana's already prepared nursery.

Oh. And his right eyelid is drooping.

He can't lift it into normal position. There's also a tingly, prickly feeling in his fingers and toes, and around his mouth. And his breathing is heavy, labored. All the signs of delayed systemic reaction to snake venom poisoning that Dana mentioned yesterday. Seems Pastor was right the first time; not enough Jesus juice in him?

He dresses, prints out the half-page sermon introduction he wrote last night—that's all he could coax out of his tired muse before succumbing to fatigue himself—slips the manuscript into his portfolio, adjusts his cummerbund, and heads for the kitchen. Yeah, you guessed it. The only black suit Cornel had in his closet was a tuxedo. Can it get any worse?

There's a place setting for him at the kitchen table and a Tupperware canister of Frosted Mini-Wheats left on the counter. Pastor reaches for the milk and OJ from the fridge, and the phone rings. It's Cornel making sure he's up and telling him to break a leg.

♪

Ma-ma-ko ma-ma-sa ma-ko-ma-kossa, ma-ma-ko ma-ma-sa ma-ko-ma-kossa.... Manu Dibango and his band's driving percussion and bass beats are thumping through the Bose. Pastor gave Cornel this CD in February for his 33rd birthday...but he never listens to it, so Pastor borrowed it. He needs something booming to get past the sluggishness and labored breathing, and Hal Jackson's Sunday Morning Classics or any other Sunday morning New York radio fare is not going to do it. When *Soul Makossa* was a fresh street anthem Pastor was living in Flatbush, Brooklyn doing the bump to it at block parties on East 26th Street, and Cornel was looking out over the East River from Sutton Place studying violin. Pastor still doesn't know what the lyrics mean exactly. Manu is more cryptic to him than James Brown on a bad speech day. Some say it's a Cameroonian love incantation, others a call to arms, and others still a plea for solidarity. Pastor's chosen the amalgamated meaning. Today it's *his* anthem.

He rounds the corner off Valley and there's a black-and-white still parked on Second. The officer is dozing at the wheel. Eye on Belton Three's production van is sitting in one corner of the parking lot with its antenna raised as Pastor pulls into his parking space. WSTU's van is parked next to the TV van. Pastor pulls the screwdriver out of the ignition, puts it into his portfolio and jumps out in full tongues.

Pastor figures Tamara Green must be going crazy. Her big eyes probably look like cue balls right now. He forgot to send her his sermon title on Friday. He's praying Maplewood doesn't have detectives lurking near the doors to grab him before he makes it inside. He'll have to beat Dawkins into the pulpit and keep David Henry away from the mic if he wants to avoid a public airing of the congregation's laundry on Channel 3 and WSTU. And if he wants to preserve his shot at Monumental.

In the lower auditorium he exhales. Not a Maplewood detective or uniform to be seen anywhere. Just Tamara standing at his office door holding a clipboard and checking her watch. She's splivy-down in a sharp teal pinstriped suit with new sun-bleached dreads dangling. Everybody's wearing dreads these days.

"Doctor Hook! A tux? And what happened to your face?" She grabs his hand and slaps it just above her left breast. "Feel that? My heart is *racing*. You scared the *crap* out of me—excuse my French, not to mention I don't have a title from you."

"I know, I'm sorry. It's been a busy few days."

"Well give it to me now real quick."

"Okay. It's Murder One."

She smiles and scribbles it down on her pad.

"Let me just grab my robe and I'll be right up."

"Oh no you don't," she grabs his elbow and starts walking fast toward the back stairs. "We don't have time. The voluntary's almost over and there's wall-to-wall people up there. I'm not letting you out of my sight again until we wrap."

Boy was she right. On Sundays First Baptist is usually filled to her 225 capacity, but today there must be 300 people crammed into the sanctuary. Folding chairs line the aisles and stretch three rows deep behind the last pew. And folks are tucked shoulder to shoulder behind them, spilling into the vestibule, crowding the two cameramen on their tiny platform in the back. The roamer with the portable on his shoulder barely has any room to move about. Brother Yellowbear is stuck in the corner with his hi-8 rolling, looking rather insignificant. And David Henry is crouched in his regular spot grinning like the Cheshire cat. The old rabble-rouser has summoned in his evil cavalry again to try and vote Pastor out.

But all Pastor's thinking about right now is locating the memorial. And the committee. The missionaries, all dressed in white, are in the front pews to his left. Sister Pettaway is sitting next to Malisa again. And there is the memorial Ike made in between them on the pew next to a white Coach bag.

Chris Sears is jammed into the middle of the fifth pew to Pastor's right, wearing a slamming black-and-white suit and a blank face.

First Baptist is staring at Pastor like he's crazy, but, aside from his being overdressed and looking like Quasimodo, this must all be very impressive to the folks from Monumental sitting in the far left back corner—two ordinary-looking men behind mustaches; two ordinary-looking women under wide-brimmed hats; and the ex-cop owner of a black conversion van, Joe Forte. Pastor does a double take to make sure the snake venom isn't impairing his vision as well.

He's heard of churches hiring PIs to follow their pastors for various reasons, but this is ridiculous. Apparently Monumental wants no surprises from whomever they call.

The service is coming as close to perfection as one can in this life. The youth choir is singing like they're ready for their own record deal, Doctor Gaye is playing like Billy Preston on the organ, even Dawkins is somewhat coherent offering the Prayer of Consolation. And when Reverend Belove Mall welcomes the visitors he doesn't utter even one sexual innuendo. And during the Welcome to Visitors Monumental's pulpit committee is all smiles and says they're enjoying the service thus far, that the turnout is proof that God is moving in the church and using the pastor, and that they're looking forward to the message.

And the sermon is a hit. As far as Pastor can tell.

Black preaching is an intuitive group exercise. The preacher can feel when his people are with him, and when they're not.

And today they're not just with him, they seem to be in me, and he in them.

From the moment he begins his incomplete sermon about Cain and Abel, "Murder One", it feels like the words are lightning bolts dancing out of his mouth. He has no idea what he's saying, or what he's going to say next, but the congregation is electrified, in a call-and-response frenzy from the start. As the words crackle out of his mouth he's not even aware of any shortness of breath. Yet it seems like the committee members from Monumental are spending the entire sermon looking down at their Bibles. Or even worse, maybe dozing. Either they don't want to tip their hand, or they don't like antiphonal preaching.

Pastor gives the invitation to discipleship and announces the hymn feeling like he did during the last minute of Princeton's upset of defending champs UCLA in the first round of the NCAA tourney in Indianapolis a few years ago. He just wants the end to come quickly before something spoils it: dedicate the memorial, give the benediction, expose the killer, and then scamper away to the Parvenu Noir with the committee to stake his claim on Monumental before the Maplewood PD shows up. Then if he has time he'll go over to City Hall.

Sister Pettaway is looking even better than Nancy Wilson today in her all white. She hands the Memorial up to Pastor. He shakes it and something rattles inside. There is a horse carved on the front. Sort of. Actually, a donkey. Under a rider being pummeled by light rays. Paul on the Damascus road. It looks heavier than it is, and the back is a thin beaverboard panel slid into a square u-shaped groove and secured at the top by three screws. Pastor steps back from the pulpit and holds it high above his head.

"We dedicate this plaque to the memory of the first missionaries, the blood of the martyrs, and their spiritual descendants who have toiled in obscurity all over the world, and yes even here in this vineyard; and to the memory of Anemone Allon, vice-president emeritus, posthumous, of the missionary board. May this be a constant reminder of the light that shines in darkness, and a perpetual witness to the truth that makes us free." He anoints it with a drop of oil and declares it done "in the name of the Father, and of the Son, and of the Holy Ghost. Amen."

He lays the memorial on top of his open Bible on the pulpit. Then he turns to Dexter and calls him to the pulpit microphone. Always respectful of old time protocol, Dexter rises from his seat on the front pew with the other deacons, refuses the pulpit mic and instead bows with his index finger in the air and takes his place behind the lectern on the floor level.

Dexter pulls an envelope from the pocket of his gray plaid suit, removes the letter from it, and reads his resignation to the congregation. Then he turns and looks up at Pastor. "Pastor, I regretfully and respectfully ask you to accept this resignation, effective immediately."

CHAPTER 17

Dexter looks so sincere and humble standing behind that lectern. Pastor's praying it isn't him when a loud voice shatters the solemnity of the moment.

"He can't do that! It has to come before the church. We have to vote on it."

Aww, Maannn! Overtime. David Henry found a way to be heard. Only this time he has a greater audience in the congregation than usual. The coup is on.

David Henry jumps to his feet and begins to squeeze his way down the crowded aisle toward the front. It's too late to stop him now, outside of physical force. There goes parliamentary procedure. Roberts' Rules has just been over-ruled and ruled out. The committee members are looking at each other puzzled. Dr. Gaye is hanging his head and praying. And Tamara Green is motioning to her camera people to keep rolling.

"Brother Thorn, take your seat," says Dexter, with as much force and authority as a wet paper bag, his heart no longer in this stuff.

"You've said all you had to say," says Thorn. "I have the floor now."

This is no time to fight with David Henry. Cornel says you need to talk people like him down when they rise up, but that only applies in churches like New Life, where he's the law. What Pastor needs to do is weather this storm. Show them how cool he can be under pressure. And get his breathing back under control, because the anointing has lifted and he's laboring again, almost hyperventilating. If he loses control of himself now he might as well kiss Monumental goodbye.

"Now, this constitutes an emergency meeting of the church," says Thorn. "Brother Moderator, call the church to order, there's some things we have to discuss right now that are going to affect the future of this body."

Dexter is the moderator and he doesn't move, so Thorn calls the church to order himself anyway, then goes off on a rambling discourse about the integrity of the pastorate and the need to protect the church from ill-repute.

"I happen to know that the police have been looking for Reverend Hook since yesterday because they think he murdered Sister Allon. That's why the lead detective is in the building."

Sears stands, shaking her head. "With all due respect, that's really not the case. Reverend Hook has been helping us with the investigation, providing valuable information. We just wanted to ask him for more help." She sits and puts on her blank face again.

"Well, anyway, I was here Friday night when he married two lesbians, right here in our sanctuary. And I got the whole thing on tape. And furthermore...." He digs into the waist pocket of his suit jacket, pulls out a plastic Baggie and holds it aloft. "I found this cigarette in his office yesterday when I went in there to drop off his mail. They tell me it's pot. Now I don't know about you, but I don't want a pot-smoking murderer who encourages homosexuality for a pastor. It looks bad on the church. So I make a motion that we get rid of Hook immediately. The constitution says we can vote him out if he brings ill-repute on the church. And with all these visitors here today, and this service going out live on radio and TV, I say he's done that."

The congregation starts buzzing.

"You can't do that. The constitution says the whole church has to be notified two weeks in advance of any vote. Besides that, it has to come through us. You know the process full well, David Henry. And you know you're wrong."

"Shut up, Dexter. You resigned, remember. This is my show now."

"According to you I haven't resigned yet. The church has to vote on that, remember?"

"Well, we'll take care of that now, too."

Someone shouts from the right side of the pews. "Sit down, Brother Thorn. You're not the pastor. You're not even a spiritual officer. You're a trus-tee. You oversee buildings and finances, that's it!" It's Sister Perot.

Someone responds from the other section. "You be quiet yourself and stop trying to shush people all the time. The man's just looking out for the welfare of the church."

Another voice. "Well I for one don't want my daughter attending Sunday School with a killer and rapist."

Rapist? Where'd that come from?

"And I don't want no drug dealer teaching my kids that it's okay to be gay. It's against the Bible."

Drug dealer?

Sister Walker joins the fray. "Oh, hush up! Listen to yourselves. God says we should love one another. This is not the way you show love. Now this man is the pastor. *God* put him here. And God speaks to *him*, not us. This is *his* church. *He's* supposed to run it. And we need to listen to *him*, not that old fool David Henry."

That does it. They're on the brink of uncivil war. The shouting is so animated not even David Henry's demands for their attention stops it. Pastor looks over at the committee. They still have their heads down. He's about to lose them and any chance at Monumental. He has to do something. He looks at Sears. She's still blank-faced. Then he throws his hands up and waits for calm.

"Look at him, he even disrespects the church by the way he comes into the pulpit without a robe. The two associate ministers are wearing their robes, and he's wearing a tuxedo. Is this what we want from a pastor?"

Pastor bellows into pulpit mic, "OKAY! OKAY!...ALRIGHT!...LET ME TALK! PLEASE!"

Concern creeps into Sears's face.

The heads of the pulpit committee in the back have snapped up now and their eyes are bulging again, trained on Pastor.

The church simmers down to silence.

"Everybody take your seat and let me explain."

Pastor tells them about what happened Wednesday night, and about Anemone's plans to flee town with a secret lover, and about her gig on the side to get away from Ike, and about Anemone thinking she was meeting a client the night she was killed, and even about the safe deposit box and the blackmail money. The more he says the lighter he feels, but the look on Sears's face is closer to horror now.

"I don't know who killed Sister Allon, but Ike did. Remember the missing videotape Max reported in the *Mirror* on Thursday? Ike grabbed it when I went outside to wait for the police. That's why he's dead. But before he was killed he told me he had hidden the tape, and now I know where it is."

Sister Walker, sitting behind the missionaries, nods in agreement and shouts, "Yes-suh!"

Tamara Green is still giving her camera people the signal to keep shooting, even though their two hours of broadcast time are up. And who knows what the radio folks have decided to do.

Getting up and leaving now would be tantamount to admitting some guilt, so not a soul moves.

Pastor tells them about Ike's take on justice and his misgivings about the legal system. He tells them about Brother LeRoy and his recipe for revenge, and his instructions to Ike to write the killer's name nine times on a piece of parchment paper and put it, along with some other things, in a package and leave it in the killer's house for three nights.

David Henry, standing next to a frozen Dexter, is rolling his eyes, shaking his head, repeating to everyone, "This is ridiculous."

The congregation is buzzing again.

"Now how did Ike get that package into the killer's house without raising suspicions?" Pastor lifts up the memorial. "Remember the Trojan Horse? The only way was to put it inside this wooden memorial."

And right then it hits Pastor. Ike sent him the tape after all. He knew this memorial would eventually end up in Pastor's hands for the dedication. Pastor steps back to his seat to retrieve the screwdriver from his portfolio then returns to the pulpit and asks, "Sister Pettaway, how did you get this, and when?"

She stands. "It was on the communion table when I came in this morning, Pastor. I don't know who left it there. Originally, Sister Allon was supposed to bring it with her to church this morning, but with all the confusion from recent events, I didn't know how I was supposed to get it. Deacon Hoard said he'd take care of it, so I just came on faith, believing it would be here somehow."

Pastor lays the memorial face down on the pulpit, unscrews the back of it with the Stanley and sure enough, there it is: the piece of folded parchment paper and the nail and the powder and everything that Brother LeRoy mentioned. And wedged underneath it all is an eight millimeter videotape.

Everyone is leaning forward as Pastor scoops out the paper and the tape and raises them up like a championship trophy after beating his school's crosstown rivals with two big jumpers at the end of the game. "It's right here! And so's the name of Anemone's killer."

"Read the name, Pastor!"

"Who is it?"

"It can't be anybody here."

Sergeant Sears stands and says, "Reverend, you don't have to read the name, just put everything back in the memorial and hand it to me." She sits down again, coolly, and reaches into her handbag.

Maybe he shouldn't have been raising his hands so much. The room is starting to spin, and it's so quiet he can hear himself wheezing. Dana may not be a Bible scholar, but she sure is a prophetess.

Pastor looks back at the committee and decides he has to read the name. If he doesn't, they'll leave with Thorn's accusation ringing in their ears and nothing concrete to refute it. To wash out a front-page accusation you need a front-page retraction and this is his best chance.

The name is written in angry block letters and before Pastor can spit it out of his tingling mouth a horrified look comes over the congregation, it lets out a collective gasp, and suddenly Pastor feels something cold and hard jammed against his right temple and heavy breathing on the back of his neck.

Sears springs up from her seat like a jack-in-the-box with a serious face. She has her gun pointed at them with one hand and her cell phone to her ear with the other hand. "Police!" she says. "Drop the gun, Dawkins! Now!"

Yeah. Dale Dawkins killed Anemone. He killed Ike and the hearse driver, too. And a whole bunch of prostitutes.

The guys on TV or in the movies always look so calm and cool in situations like this, but this is no movie. This is real, and Pastor's about to pee in his pants in God's holy pulpit. Funny what goes through your mind at a time like this. He didn't care anymore about showing Monumental how well he can handle pressure, or about finally buying his own house. More than anything else, he realizes that he loves life; that it's God's most precious gift and not to be taken lightly; and that he's not ready to go to heaven just yet, he wants to stay on the planet. In his heart he makes a deal with God, that if He'll get him out of this, he'll never attempt anything suicidal again. But the way Dawkins starts talking, it seems like God hasn't heard Pastor at all.

"You drop *your* gun," he says to Sears. "Or I'll blow his head off and take as many more with me as I can, because I ain't got nothin' to lose no more."

Everybody's heart must've stopped beating at once because it's become so still and silent Pastor can hear a dump truck rumbling by outside on its way to McNair Motors, and distant sirens closing in. He knows Sears won't drop her gun and completely turn the situation over to Dawkins. She's already dangled Pastor out there to preserve her case, she's not about to just let Dawkins walk out now. There's no tremble in the gun against Pastor's temple, and Sears is as still and emotionless as a bronze statue. Pastor doesn't like the way this high-stakes game of chicken is turning out at all. And the only thing he can think to do is indeed suicidal: to use his quickness advantage on the heavier Dawkins and try knocking the gun from his hand before he can pull the trigger.

Sears shifts into copspeak. "Drop the gun, Dawkins! The building is surrounded by police. You've got nowhere to go. For God's sake, don't kill any more innocent people."

"Innocent?! Ain't one of them innocent. They all deserved to die. They all killed themselves by the way they lived. Now drop *your* gun, or I swear I'll blow his brains out."

And inexplicably, Sears lowers her gun. Pastor's hopes sink with it momentarily.

"Good," he says. "Now take the clip out and toss it on the altar."

The clip hits the base of the pulpit with a thud then lands on the communion table, knocking the floral arrangement on it to the floor.

What?! Sears, what are you doing?! Okay. Pastor figures she must have a spare gun tucked in her bra or strapped to a garter holster or something. She's just waiting for the right moment to whip it out. That *must* be it.

"Now put the gun in your shoulder bag, zip it up, put it on your shoulder, make your way into the center aisle, slowly walk to the back of the church and stop at the double doors."

When Sears gets there he tells her to go outside and tell all the cops out there that if any of them comes in, he'll empty his clip starting with Pastor and save the last one for himself.

"Before I go," says Sears, "and since you're obviously going to take the coward's way out, I have one question. Why? Why kill the Allons, and blow up the pastor's car and home? Why?"

Pastor was already feeling faint from the combination of snake venom and fear in his system, but now he's thinking he must be losing his mind, too. Shabazz McCoy blew up his car and house. Why was she blaming Dawkins?

Dawkins starts laughing. Cackling, really. "I loved her," he says. "That's why. Like a fool I loved and trusted her, and she lied to me, just like all them sorry Newark streetwalkers that told me I was cute. Like the government that told me they would take care of me after the war. Like the God who told me He loved me and yet took all my friends and loved ones away from me. She said that when I became pastor she'd leave her husband and we could be together. So I tried to get the pastor to leave, but he wouldn't get out. Then one day at work I'm flipping through the *Mirror* and see her pager number in the classifieds in a sex ad. The pager *I* bought her. She admitted to everything that night. She didn't want me, she wanted the pastor, and was just using me to get information on people in the church. So I had to kill them all. All liars must take their place in the lake of fire. Pastor, too. I tried to end everything at the cemetery. I wouldn't have had to use the explosives if he woulda stayed standing. I ain't missing today, though. Not from this close."

Many people thought they loved Anemone. Too bad she couldn't love herself. She used Dawkins's knowledge of what was going on in the lives of the congregation's members to plan her blackmail campaign.

And all along it was Dawkins sending those letters, and blowing things up, not Shabazz. He must've torched the Allon house, too.

Sears still has the cell phone to her ear and says, "Thanks for the confession."

"You're welcome. Now, goodbye."

She drops the phone from her ear, snaps it shut and says to Dawkins, "Just one more thing before I go."

"What now?" Dawkins is clearly irritated. The gun shakes in his hand against Pastor's temple. "Say what you gotta say and then get outta here. I've got people to kill."

"You know, after a war the clergy are usually more messed up than the people they helped because they're often so conflicted about the God and war thing. The guys in your platoon nicknamed you Chap, didn't they?" Dawkins gives a "So what" grunt. "Because you were a boy preacher, ordained at ten in your uncle's church. So you told everyone that you were a chaplain in the army, but you weren't, were you? You were a munitions specialist. But you prayed for people who got shot up in your platoon, buried them, and even married some of them later because you were an ordained preacher and there weren't enough trained chaplains to go around in the field. And all the death you saw, all the inhumane things, you're still carrying the rage from all that with you now. What you've been doing to those women in Newark. The prostitutes? You saw your buddies do the same thing in Vietnam, didn't you? They'd rape the Vietcong women and girls, and then strangle them during the rape. In fact, five from your platoon were court-martialed after the war and did time in military prison for that, didn't they?"

Dawkins is shaking now and for a moment takes the gun from Pastor's temple and points it at Sears. "So what's the point, 'ho!?'"

She doesn't even flinch, and with a clear, calm voice says, "The point is, I understand. You don't have to do this. You don't have to end up like your buddies. You need help. And we can get it for you. Now give me the gun." She stretches her hand toward us. "And I'll personally see to it that you finally get the help the Army never gave you."

Dawkins is frozen for a couple seconds, the gun still aimed at Sears, perhaps considering the offer. Then he yells, "Skank, I already told you what to do!" He pulls the trigger and takes out Jesus and the little white lambs in the stained glass window above Sears's head, and everyone is frozen quiet in fear. "Now go deliver my message!"

Sears marches through the doors and images of Gethsemane and Pastor's family and his years in growing up in New York flash through his mind. He looks at Joe Forte and hopes he's packing today in the Lord's house, but Forte looks as helpless as everybody else.

Dawkins tells Pastor to get down on his knees. Pastor's feeling so weak that he would've probably ended up down there sooner or later anyway. He drops to his knees and promises himself he won't be going out like a sucker. As soon as the muzzle of the gun touches his head he's going to elbow Dawkins in the knee with all the strength he has left and see what happens from there. But before the gun touches me, Thorn speaks up.

"Chap, you're not really going to shoot the man, are you?"

"Once through the temple," says Dawkins. "Then you and your whole family is next, you trifling punk."

Pastor hadn't heard a peep out of the congregation again until David Henry said that. They let out a whimper and then go silent again.

"But Chap, this is me. I'm your friend, remember? What did I do?"

"You ain't nobody's friend, Thorn. You been holding this church back ever since I been here. Now maybe the next pastor can have a chance to get something done around here."

Dawkins puts the gun to Pastor's temple and Pastor slams his elbow back against his meaty knee cap.

Pastor remembers three things before leaving consciousness: seeing a huge straw sombrero and a pair of new Air Jordans; hearing sound-suppressed gunfire; and not being able to breathe under what felt like a million tons of dead weight crashing down on him.

CHAPTER 18

Was Betty Jean Eadie actually right all this time? The all-consuming light. It's everywhere. But Pastor doesn't see any loved ones. No Carla, no Carlton. He doesn't hear any music. No angels strumming on golden harps. And he's not moving toward the light, either. He's stuck. In outer brightness? In silence? Could this be an unreported vantage point of hell? A ring Danté omitted? What torture this will be. For the rest of eternity, looking, but not being able to touch.

But now a dark cloud eclipses the light. Maybe it's worse than he thought. Hot air goes down his throat. Burning in his chest. Softness on his dull lips. Moist. Tense. Purposeful. It feels like his first real kiss. Debbie Roach, a girl five years older than him and at the time a senior in high school, on the merry-go-round at Rye Playland. Reflexively, Pastor reaches with his tongue into the soft moistness.

He wakes up with Sears's lips locked around his. Their mouths are open and for a second he thinks they're back in the vestry of the chapel before their 8:00 English Lit class, so he slips his tongue onto hers. They're tongue wrestling for a few more seconds before shortness of breath and her fingers clamped over his nose blast two jolts of reality to his brain in rapid succession: they're on the floor of his church next to the pulpit in front of 300 people and three live television cameras; and she didn't resist his tongue, she welcomed it.

Sears is breathing almost as deeply as Pastor is when she breaks away. "Is that ambulance here yet?" she cries out. "He's breathing now. We've got a pulse again. Get them in here!"

Pastor takes a deep breath, and it doesn't register right away that the roaring in his ears is the congregation applauding the news that he's back in the land of the living.

He tries to sit up, but his body hurts everywhere, like if a small building has just fallen on him. Sears gently pushes down on his chest. "Stay, Tony," she says softly with a worried look. "You were gone for almost five minutes. Don't want to lose you again." Her eyes fill up. They're still like cool beach sand and her big pupils are directly on his. "You still owe me dinner, and I plan to collect."

Pastor can't deal with the intensity in her eyes, so he looks away and notices a pair of blood-stained Air Jordans, one of them on the neck of a mountain of greasy black flesh about five feet from him. Standing in them is Mother Freddie Pearl, her sombrero cocked to one side on her head, her gun in her hand. Pastor is sure he must be hallucinating, or he's still dead, so he closes his eyes and opens them again. She's still there. He checks his head and torso for bullet holes, and finds none.

"Poor thing," she says. "He must think he's seeing a ghost." She takes her foot off Dawkins's neck, kneels next to Sears and talks to Pastor as if he's hung over and she doesn't want to give him a headache. "I wasn't in the parsonage when it blew up, Pastor. I ran out of Windex, so I had to go pick some up at ShopRite. When I got back the parsonage was gone, and so were you. I called your cell phone but kept getting the voice mail. Then when I got back from the Presbyterian Church today I went to the ladies room and heard all this commotion going on up here through the speakers in the lower auditorium. I was going to stay down there until it was all over, but when I heard Dawkins tell the detective to drop her gun I knew I had to do something."

Pastor grabs her empty left hand, squeezes it, and gives her a smile. She gives Pastor a kiss on the cheek and then Sears clears everyone off the platform and the paramedics show up.

In less than a minute they stick an IV in Pastor and he's on a stretcher rolling down the center aisle. He sees smiling faces all the way down the aisle and thanks God he's not going out in a coffin like Anemone did, or in a body bag like Dawkins soon will be. And he catches a glimpse of the committee from Monumental, too. They still have their heads down and won't look at him. No way they could've been sleeping through all of this, so Pastor figures that's it for his candidacy.

When the paramedics get him to the back the cheers turn to boos and hisses and complaints and he can't believe how quickly the congregation has turned on him, like Jesus' crowds from Palm Sunday to Bad Friday. Then Pastor flips his head, glances down the aisle before the paramedics roll him out the door, and sees that they aren't booing him at all. They're booing the two uniformed BPD officers who are escorting Mother Freddie down the aisle in handcuffs. One of the officers is carrying a gallon-sized Baggie with Mother's unlicensed gun tucked inside. And Rev. Mall is standing behind the pulpit pleading for order.

Pastor can't believe they're arresting Mother for saving his life, and he hopes Sears isn't responsible. If she is then she's capable of arresting her own grandmother and who wants to go have dinner with someone like that? Besides, she's a PK, too, so she should know better. You can do many things to a black church, burn it down or even mess with its pastor, and probably get away with it. But you don't mess with the church Mother. Whoever's responsible has just awakened a sleeping giant with a history of getting its way, and is about to get a lesson in black church power politics.

The paramedics carry Pastor down the front steps, all of them awash in a shower of crisp, clean sunshine. The fresh light sends a searing thought through his mind: *with the parsonage gone and Monumental now out of the picture, I really don't have a place to live any more. I'm literally homeless.* And then a moment of clarity that sets him at ease: *a house is not a home. I'm surrounded by people who care about me; people I care about. That's the best kind of shelter a man can have.*

There's a Maplewood squad car parked right behind the ambulance. The paramedics open the back door to the ambulance and are about to shove the stretcher in when a hand stops them.

"Please, may I have just a minute with the pastor?"

It's Marcus Turner in a green bow tie and beige suit. They stop the stretcher at the door and Marcus bends down to Pastor's ear. "Pastor, I just want to thank you for everything you've tried to do for me, and all the others who Anemone blackmailed. I couldn't let you go without saying that I don't want any of the money back that you recovered. I want you to keep it. After all you've done and all you've been through, you deserve it. And I'm sure all the others feel the same way."

He squeezes Pastor's hand and promises to pray for him. Then the sunshine fills up the space where Marcus had been and something leaps inside of Pastor. Maybe he'll be buying his own home soon after all.

They shove the stretcher in and Pastor hears the Maplewood squad car's engine turn over. The ambulance door slams in the middle of Pastor's prayers that he survive the hospital stay, and that Mall be somehow able to keep his hands off the women and hold things together for the next few weeks. Because until Pastor returns, the First Baptist Church of Belton, which finally feels like *his* church now, his new family, dysfunctions and all, will be in Mall's hands; and there's no telling what David Henry Thorn will try next.

THE BENEDICTION.

ABOUT THE AUTHOR

 **Earl Middleton** earned a BBA in accounting from Adelphi University and an M.Div. from Princeton Theological Seminary, then went on to preach more than 2,000 sermons, create over 400 YouTube teaching videos, and write 10 books under the anointing of the Holy Spirit. A former pastor of congregations in NY, NJ, CT, and CA, he loves preaching and teaching the Word of God across multiple platforms despite his retirement from the pastorate after 22 years of service. He's a past member of the Professional Comedians' Association and the creator of the internet's first Christian dramedic series, *Fine Church Girls*. A longtime member of Mensa, he lives in Los Angeles with his family and gets up 500 shots a day at his local YMCA. He's currently at work navigating new, hilarious plot twists with Pastor Tony Hook and the rest of the zany characters of the First Baptist Church of Belton, NJ, but is still available for revivals, keynotes, preaching engagements, family healing seminars, writing workshops, and basketball jumpshot coaching. Connect with him at:

- ❖ earl@earlmiddleton.org (e-mail me)
- ❖ facebook.com/earl.middleton (friend me)
- ❖ @earlmiddleton (you should follow me)
- ❖ earlmiddleton.com (visit my site)

MY PASTOR CAUGHT SANTA

This Christmas when Santa breaks into First Baptist he grabs more than the cookies & milk!

Earl Middleton

Masked, armed robbers in Santa clothing break into First Baptist Church during the Christmas Morning service and stickup the entire congregation, making off with all their valuables, the Christmas offering, the pastor's Saab convertible containing a priceless heirloom, and a deacon's daughter to have their way with.

During the one hour siege they also force some of the people in attendance to perform unmentionable acts with each other, on the altar, in front of everyone. And they force Brother Yellowbear to continue rolling the tape.

They get a one hour head start in their escape by taking away every cell phone, forcing all two hundred people into the boiler room and locking them in like sardines, and then cutting every phone line outside of the church.

When the police decide that they're looking for delinquent boys from Newark who have probably fled the area, and call in the FBI to investigate the kidnapping, Pastor Hook gets involved. He has to start the New Year right, can't do so without the heirloom tucked in his glove box, is convinced that the authorities are heading down the wrong track, and doesn't have time to wait for them to hit their inevitable dead end.

Join some of your favorite Belton characters and fall in love with new ones as Pastor races against time to catch the thieves and recover his property before the ball drops in Times Square.

Conceived in Queens

What happens when a son kills his father…and then tries to raise him from the dead?

Earl Middleton

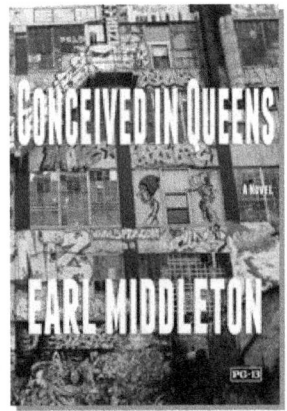

He's the product of an ancient, unholy union. She's a pawn in a high stakes, prophetic game of deception. When he accidentally kills his father an avalanche of unforeseen circumstances turns their worlds upside down and threatens the ultimate salvation of an entire species. Will a miracle resurrection be enough to restore order to his universe now spun out of control? And will *their* baby turn out to be the AntiChrist?

In a heart stopping romp through the streets of New York City, *Conceived in Queens* manages to carve out a new genre, the BUFF novel (biblical urban faith fantasy), while following the transformation of Rain Reynolds, a New York City public school legend with real angel's blood in his veins, and Lisa Vickers, a former D.C. anchorwoman turned pastor with a secret, from immortal basketball icon and crack investigator to enlightened spiritual emissaries and perhaps their kind's last real hope to find a place in heaven. And as usual the way to enlightenment goes straight through the dark.

"Finally a biblical faith novel your sons & husbands will read, too."

"An unforgettable story of one teen's struggle with parental rejection, on earth and in heaven, that will make you want to be the best parent, and best child, possible."

"A classic story of loss and redemption painted with masterful prose against a hardscrabble canvas."

www.ingramcontent.com/pod-product-compliance
Lightning Source LLC
Chambersburg PA
CBHW070815180626
46818CB00001B/269